"Lora Leigh delivers on all counts."
—*Romance Reviews Today*

Praise for Lora Leigh's Novels of the Breeds

Navarro's Promise

"A powerful and highly erotic saga."   —*Fresh Fiction*

"Not to be missed!"   —*The Romance Readers Connection*

Styx's Storm

"Delivers with Ms. Leigh's trademark fast-paced, high-adrenaline ride into the intriguing world of this series and leaves readers ready for more. And of course, it has that special brand of 'scorching sex' that only Ms. Leigh can deliver . . . I was hooked from page one."   —*Night Owl Reviews*

"Amazing . . . brilliant . . . everything you could want from a Lora Leigh Breed book!"   —*Smexy Books*

"Scorchingly intense."   —*RT Book Reviews*

Lion's Heat

"Powerful and sensual with enough fast-paced action to make your head spin. A Lora Leigh novel is always a must-read!"
—*Fresh Fiction*

"The incredible Lora Leigh continues to write about the Breeds while keeping the story fresh and new. Go, Lora Leigh, go!"   —*Night Owl Reviews*

"I couldn't put it down and I have since read it two more times. It is phenomenal."   —*Joyfully Reviewed*

continued . . .

Bengal's Heart

"Wickedly seductive with sizzling sex scenes that will leave you begging for more. I've read every book of this series and always find myself eagerly anticipating the next."

—*ParaNormal Romance*

Coyote's Mate

"A tantalizing read from start to finish . . . Lora Leigh will touch your heart with the kaleidoscope of emotions she weaves into this novel. Breathtaking . . . Ms. Leigh never fails to deliver the red-hot romances that I have been enjoying for many years, and this one will grace my keeper shelf right beside all of her other great novels. Grab your copy of *Coyote's Mate* and get ready for a rousingly fantastic read. Enjoy!"

—*Night Owl Reviews*

Mercury's War

"Erotic and suspenseful . . . Readers will laugh, readers will blush, and readers will cry."

—*Romance Junkies*

"With two great twists, fans of the Breeds saga will relish [*Mercury's War*]."

—*Midwest Book Review*

"Intriguingly powerful with plenty of action to keep the pages turning. I am completely addicted! A great read!"

—*Fresh Fiction*

Dawn's Awakening

"Held me captivated."

—*Romance Junkies*

"Heart-wrenching."

—*Fallen Angel Reviews*

"Erotic, fast paced, funny, and hard-hitting, this series delivers maximum entertainment to the reader."

—*Fresh Fiction*

TANNER'S SCHEME

"The incredible Leigh pushes the traditional envelope with her scorching sex scenes by including voyeurism. Intrigue and passion ignite! . . . Scorcher!"   —*RT Book Reviews* (★★★★✦)

"Sinfully sensual . . . [This series] is well worth checking out."   —*Fresh Fiction*

HARMONY'S WAY

"Leigh's engrossing alternate reality combines spicy sensuality, romantic passion, and deadly danger. Hot stuff indeed."
     —*RT Book Reviews*

"I stand in awe of Ms. Leigh's ability to bring to life these wonderful characters as they slowly weave their way into my mind and heart. When it comes to this genre, Lora Leigh is the queen."   —*Romance Junkies*

MEGAN'S MARK

"A riveting tale full of love, intrigue, and every woman's fantasy, *Megan's Mark* is a wonderful contribution to Lora Leigh's Breeds series . . . As always, Lora Leigh delivers on all counts; *Megan's Mark* will certainly not disappoint her many fans!"   —*Romance Reviews Today*

"Hot, hot, hot—the sex and the setting . . . You can practically see the steam rising off the pages."   —*Fresh Fiction*

"Leigh's action-packed Breeds series makes a refreshing change . . . Rapid-fire plot development and sex steamy enough to peel wallpaper."   —*Monsters and Critics*

"An exceedingly sexy and sizzling new series to enjoy. Hot sex, snappy dialogue, and kick-butt action add up to outstanding entertainment."   —*RT Book Reviews*

LAWE'S
JUSTICE

LORA LEIGH

BERKLEY BOOKS, NEW YORK

THE BERKLEY PUBLISHING GROUP
Published by the Penguin Group
Penguin Group (USA) Inc.
375 Hudson Street, New York, New York 10014, USA
Penguin Group (Canada), 90 Eglinton Avenue East, Suite 700, Toronto, Ontario M4P 2Y3, Canada
(a division of Pearson Penguin Canada Inc.)
Penguin Books Ltd., 80 Strand, London WC2R 0RL, England
Penguin Group Ireland, 25 St. Stephen's Green, Dublin 2, Ireland (a division of Penguin Books Ltd.)
Penguin Group (Australia), 250 Camberwell Road, Camberwell, Victoria 3124, Australia
(a division of Pearson Australia Group Pty. Ltd.)
Penguin Books India Pvt. Ltd., 11 Community Centre, Panchsheel Park, New Delhi—110 017, India
Penguin Group (NZ), 67 Apollo Drive, Rosedale, Auckland 0632, New Zealand
(a division of Pearson New Zealand Ltd.)
Penguin Books (South Africa) (Pty.) Ltd., 24 Sturdee Avenue, Rosebank, Johannesburg 2196,
South Africa

Penguin Books Ltd., Registered Offices: 80 Strand, London WC2R 0RL, England

This is a work of fiction. Names, characters, places, and incidents either are the product of the author's imagination or are used fictitiously, and any resemblance to actual persons, living or dead, business establishments, events, or locales is entirely coincidental. The publisher does not have any control over and does not assume any responsibility for author or third-party websites or their content.

LAWE'S JUSTICE

A Berkley Book / published by arrangement with the author

PRINTING HISTORY
Berkley mass-market edition / December 2011

Copyright © 2011 by Christina Simmons.
Cover art by S. Miroque.
Cover design by Rita Frangie.

ISBN: 978-0-425-24395-4

BERKLEY®
Berkley Books are published by The Berkley Publishing Group,
a division of Penguin Group (USA) Inc.,
375 Hudson Street, New York, New York 10014.
BERKLEY® is a registered trademark of Penguin Group (USA) Inc.
The "B" design is a trademark of Penguin Group (USA) Inc.

PRINTED IN THE UNITED STATES OF AMERICA

10 9 8 7 6 5 4 3 2 1

Dedicated most sincerely to the advance readers of
Lawe's Justice *who stuck it out to the end. Alexis, Gail,*
Lynn, Monique, Sabrina and Sandra.

Your help has been tremendous, and your perceptions
into the Breeds, as a series and as individual books and
characters, has given me a thought-provoking look into
the depth of love you have for them.

Thank you for that. For loving them, and for all the
hard work, hours of reading, and the wonderful insights
you've brought to Lawe's Justice.

To Sharon, for your advice and for all your help. There
are no words to describe or to express how much it's
meant to me. Just because I don't always listen ☺
doesn't mean I don't always hear you.

And to Bret. You make me think when I'd prefer not
to, and you make me laugh when I'd prefer to cry. You
make me stand strong when I want to lie down in defeat,
and you make me remember what it's like to be young.

Thank you, just for being my son, for being patient
as I find my feet, but even more, for being such an
independent, loving young man. Thank you for
being yourself.

Did you wish upon a star and take the time to try to make your wish come true?

Did you try to paint the sunrise and find the gift of life within?

Did you write a song just for the joy of it?

Or write a poem just to feel the pain?

Did you find a reason to ignore the petty injustices, the spoken barbs, or the envies, jealousies and greed that crossed your path?

Did you wake up this morning and whisper inside, "Today, I'll find every reason to smile, and ignore the excuses to frown."

Today will be the day I'll whisper nothing snide, I'll say nothing cruel. I'll be kind to my enemy, I'll embrace my friends, and for this one day, I'll forget the slights of the past.

Today will be the day I'll live for the joy of it, laugh for the fun of it, and today, I'll love whether it's returned, forsaken, or simply ignored.

And if you did, then your heart has joined the others who have as well, uniting, strengthening, and in a single heartbeat you've created a world of hope.

Screams echoed around the steel walls.

The sound bounced, splintering through the cavernous area and slicing through the senses of those forced to listen.

There was no place for the sound to go, no cracks, no ventilation to the outside. There was no way for it to dissipate easily. The sound ricocheted from wall to wall and from ceiling to floor before making the return trip to blend with the continued agonizing sounds.

Surrounding the theater-style examination/operation room were twelve eight-by-ten cells created from steel and iron bars. The cells ran the entire length of the steel wall at one side and were connected by frames of black iron bars at the front.

The barred doors were reinforced; the locks were digital as well as electronically keyed and almost impossible to crack unless total power, including that of the backup generators, was lost. Only then would the locks disengage and allow the animals held inside to be freed.

Or were they humans?

There were times when even they were uncertain of who or what they were, other than the fact that they had been created at the hands of the doctors and the scientists who were now inflicting a hellish death rather than creating a hellish life.

The screams echoed around the cavernous room again, filled with pain, fear and the knowledge that time had run out and there was no escape.

But she had been crying for days. Inconsolable wails that had left those locked behind the bars fighting the restless rage beginning to fill them. They had even seemed to affect the guards created to rule over them. Men, animals, whose eyes held no mercy but who now seemed to glance at one another in uncomfortable silence as the time of death grew closer. As the imprisoned creations watching them seemed to grow more still, more calm and silent than ever before.

They were her young, of a sort.

Conception had occurred in the artificial environment of a lab before the fertilized egg was transplanted into her womb and carried to term. As the time of birth neared, she was injected with the monstrous paralytic they had created that paralyzed all but the vocal cords, leaving their victims with only the ability to scream. Once she was restrained, then the child was cut from her body as she screamed in agony.

Unable to move.

Unable to fight.

Unable to control any part of her body except the vocal cords that the scientists refused to silence.

She would scream until her voice broke and then only silent animalistic growls would emerge from her throat.

But *she* wasn't an animal. She wasn't even a half animal as her young were. She was a young woman who had forgotten what gentleness and freedom were. She knew only the captivity, the pain, the endless pregnancies and forced births.

And now she would only know the agony and fear of a senseless, vicious death, which her young were forced to watch in uncaring silence.

Breed number 107 sat on his cot in the corner of the cell, his head laid back against the steel bars as his mother's terror-filled sobs echoed through the room once again.

He and the one he called brother, the one they called 108, were only a few of the young in the lab that were products of her genetics. Born not just of her body but also of her egg, which had been fertilized in vitro with the animal-tainted genetically altered sperm used to create the Breeds.

And they were forced to remain silent, outwardly unconcerned, as though her screams meant nothing. As though they weren't ripping through their souls and tearing their guts to ribbons each time she begged, each time she screamed in agony.

Each time she begged God for mercy.

Breed number 107 kept his eyes closed, his breathing regulated, and called upon fourteen years of training to maintain the control needed to restrain his rage and pain. If just one of her young broke, if just one of them showed a reaction or showed an emotion, then three of them would die.

As so many had already died. So many had already known the inhuman agony that waited when they were strapped down on the autopsy table in the center of the room.

The day before, the scientists had tortured one of their favored pets as well. As though they couldn't sate their hunger for the blood, screams and agony forced upon the

Breeds. Their victim, the Coyote lieutenant Elder, had been a surprising addition to the scientists' mercilessness. Because, strangely, in an act so out of character for a Coyote, Elder had attempted to slip the woman from the labs and to shut down the generators that kept the scientists' creations caged and under control.

Elder had failed, though. He'd been betrayed by one of the twelve who now sat silently in the cells as their dam's voice began to rise in horror.

Breed number 107 wondered if this would be the final horror that would break the only female in the group. The young Cheetah female also suspected to be the woman's natural child. The one who lay, as though sleeping, on the small cot in a far cell.

Morningstar wasn't just being punished, though, and they all knew it. They had all watched Elder's vivisection the day before and heard the scientists' muttered conversation about a mating. So it was no surprise to 107 when they dragged the gentle, weeping woman from the enclosed room where she'd been kept confined since Elder's failed attempt at removing her from the labs.

Her long, heavy black hair had flowed around her naked body, tangled and mussed from her battle with the soldiers who'd had to drag her away from Elder's unconscious body after they were captured.

Now she was insane with rage from Elder's death, and the pain from the soldiers' touch. She had fought them as he had never seen her fight.

She cursed, raged, screamed out obscenities and called down all manner of curses against them. Her normally dark brown eyes, strangely flecked with blue, were a pure ice blue now, like flames burning in her Native American features.

She kicked, fought to trip her guards' and swore vengeance.

To no avail.

"Bastards!" she shrieked. "They'll come for you. My father and his father and those who have gone before. They will visit you in the dead of night and your blood will flow." Her voice ragged and savage, 107 had never heard such a sound from any creature's throat, even those of the Breeds tortured on a regular basis.

His nostrils flared as her scent reach him.

From the corner of his eye he could glimpse her as they strapped her down to the autopsy table in the center of the operating room. Once they inserted the IV and the paralytic's slow drip reached her system, then she would be unable to move, unable to fight anything they did.

It didn't take long for the drug to take effect. Her body went slack, and as she wept in pain and horror, the lab techs slowly released the straps holding her to the table.

Breed number 107 couldn't see their eyes, but he caught a hint of human fear and compassion, of silent horror and desperation that didn't belong to Morningstar.

It was the first time she had been injected with the paralyzing drug that it wasn't to take a child from her body. The first time she had been placed on a table in the center of that room that she wasn't to be inseminated.

She was to die and she knew it.

Her children knew it.

Breed number 107 forced himself to close his eyes once again. To concentrate on the scents of the humans and the Coyotes who were a part of this demonic practice.

Because one day he would be free, he vowed. One day, he would find them, each of them, and he would ensure they paid for the hell they created within these labs.

Until then, he could do nothing but force back the emotions churning, burning, ripping through his soul. He could do nothing but lock them away, place them so deep inside his spirit that there was no chance they would ever surface again.

His chest was tight as he fought to contain them. His eyes were damp. Breeds didn't cry. They didn't feel sorrow.

Or so they were taught.

They weren't named; they weren't cuddled, cherished or loved.

They didn't go outside to play as young, nor were they allowed sleepovers as human children were.

Because they weren't human.

They were animals that walked on two legs and who dressed, spoke and acted like humans.

But they weren't human.

The knowledge that they weren't human, that they weren't born they were created, was one of their first memories. One of the first lessons they were taught.

"Nothing will change your deaths." His mother's wails were filled with tears. And fear. "Nothing can save you!"

And nothing could save his mother.

The scientists wouldn't be punished. There were no laws to protect the Breeds or the helpless women kidnapped to give birth to them. There would be no justice for the creations brought to life within these steel walls. Or those sent to their deaths on the table beyond.

Panic filled Morningstar's screams as the cold steel of the scalpel touched her flesh.

It was a sound of horror, of hysteria.

Her scent became stronger. He recognized the unique, fresh fragrance, mixed with the dark fear, and he knew he would always remember it as that of the only creature that had ever shown him kindness.

There was another smell mixing with it, though.

Elder's scent was there and a scent of something

deeper, stronger, one he had always associated with a deep, unnamed emotion. An emotion he had only scented when shared between two humans. Humans who carried a bond he had never understood.

It was a scent he had only caught a wisp of when taken out on missions in the past year. One he had come to associate with what the soldiers had sneeringly called love. A mix of lust and summer warmth, of comfort and contentment overlapped with a hint of adrenaline and excitement. And when mixed together, it was a fragrance that had called so strongly to him that it had been all he could do to maintain his composure.

And now it had regret welling inside him as he fought to hold back his rage.

Pushing it back, pushing it down took every ounce of strength he possessed. His brother, 108, was feeling the same rage, forcing back his own fury.

No reaction.

Those who existed within this lab had watched far too many littermates die from the inability to hold back their fury, their pain, the fact that they knew emotion and couldn't hide it. That they knew honor and refused to ignore it.

They weren't allowed to pretend to be human. Only humans had emotions and they were animals. Those with the arrogance to believe they could be human too were killed instantly.

Breeds weren't allowed emotion, honor, loyalty to anything or anyone outside their creators, and they sure as hell were not allowed to form any bonds with each other or their dams. Those bonds, any bonds, were the basis for instant death.

"Please, God, kill me now . . . !"

She was begging now.

His mother. Her name was Morningstar and she was the daughter of a Navajo medicine man.

On his last mission the week before, 107 had mailed her father pictures, a map, a letter requesting his help, asking that he come and save the woman he had known as his daughter.

No one had arrived.

And now Morningstar was dying.

He didn't flinch as the sound of her howls became sharper, filled with a horrendous agony, and the scent of her blood and horror began to fill the room.

His gaze slid to that of his brother, 108.

His twin.

They shared another bond as well that so far they had not revealed to the soldiers, scientists or other Breeds they shared the cells with. A bond and a knowledge of each other that they could be killed for, if it were ever discovered. They shared that bond with their mother as well, and he knew 108 was sharing her agony as well.

Breed number 107 knew his brother as he knew no other. A knowledge that allowed them to sense and glimpse into the emotions and into the heart of each other.

He had to inhale slowly, deeply as the scent of her blood became stronger and her screams sharper with agony, with the horrific knowledge of what was being done to her.

A vivisection. The dissection of a living body.

And he had to ignore it. He had to remain outwardly unaffected.

He had to pretend to be uncaring that his mother was being cruelly tortured for the scent Elder left on her. In her. The scent he recognized on a primal level as one that marked her as belonging to Elder. It was a scent he had never known, never smelled before.

The animal senses that were so much a part of him knew it on a primal level. That knowledge was transmitted to the man, and though it confused the man, he still knew it for what it was—a mark of belonging that pierced to the soul and refused to be denied. And in this place, in the horror of the life they were born into, it was a death sentence.

This was the pain of belonging to a Breed? The horrific nightmare of a vivisection because of a change within her body? A change that every Breed would know marked her as belonging to a Breed, if she had had the chance to live? A scent that marked her as belonging only to Elder.

This was how Elder had been caught. This was why he had been unable to rescue the woman he had bound himself to, because another Breed had detected the mark and reported it. Because one of Morningstar's 'get' had betrayed the strongest of them all.

The Elder.

107 could have understood if it had been another Coyote who had turned the Coyote commander and that scent in to his masters. He could have understood it if it had been a human.

But it hadn't been. It had been a Breed. It had been one of the Breed whelps who had been sheltered, nurtured and protected within her body until the scientists had cut it free.

It was a Breed that would die, 107 promised himself. He would kill the bastard and he would ensure that the Breed suffered.

That traitor would suffer to the very pits of hell, just as Morningstar Martinez now suffered. Just as her mate, the Coyote Elder, had suffered in his attempt to save her. Her and the Breeds she had given birth to.

The vow marked his soul as the screams became even more tortured, as they knifed into his soul and nearly broke his control.

His guts tightened as he pushed back all emotion. It was the only way to hide it. The only way to hide the rage.

The muscles of his thighs were steel hard, his back clenched and unclenched painfully. He couldn't let anyone know the agony tearing through him. An agony that couldn't compare to his mother's. His screams could never match hers in pain, agony and defeat.

And the only way to save his brother, to ensure 108 didn't suffer for his mistake of showing his rage, was to bury it. To bury it so deep inside his soul that it wouldn't exist, so that he could function amid it.

To wipe away that final vein of grief, loyalty and the need to call some emotion his own, a need to feel and to howl in rage.

All that remained now was the need to be free, a need to taste, touch and hold freedom. To know justice, to understand the laws he followed.

The need to have a name.

He sat still and silent, showing none of the rage, the agony or the slow burial of the hungers that had begun to ride him in the past year.

All that remained was that need for freedom, that hunger for justice and the overpowering, enraged hunger for vengeance.

He wanted rules, a law to follow, and in that moment he realized there was nothing, no one, he could follow but himself.

He needed justice, but if he didn't take it himself, then he would never know it, never taste or feel it.

He would become his own law.

He would become his own justice.

And in that moment, 107 found a name.

In that moment, he became his own law, his own justice.

Lawe Justice.

Jonas Wyatt stared at the files spread over the desk, photos, medical diagnosis and research reports glaring back at him in black and white as he wiped his hands over his face wearily.

The files that had finally been decoded from the information gathered over the past months were horrifying. Storme Montague, daughter of one of the lead scientists in the secluded Andes Omega lab for Breed genetic research had finally relinquished the information she'd carried for far too many years.

The death of Phillip Brandenmore, as well as the files his niece had uncovered, had given them information on the continuation of the projects that had begun in Omega lab.

Continuations that had the power to horrify even him. And he had believed that neither the Genetics Council nor Phillip Brandenmore and his research scientists could horrify him any further.

So many experiments on innocent men and women, both human and Breed, mated and unmated, some tested gently, others tortured endlessly, were more than he could take in at once.

The truth of the cruelty man could impose weighed heavily on his soul. The truth of the deceased Phillip Brandenmore's pure evil had a band of horror tightening around his chest.

He'd thought he'd seen the worst man could do to his fellow man, beast or the Breeds that existed in between. And perhaps he had, but what he saw in the files before him were just as horrific—perhaps in ways more so, because they weren't done in the name of research or in the name of creating or improving the perfect species the Genetics Council had envisioned.

The files here represented their evil in its worst form. Scientists who had done the worst they could do in the name of science, curiosity and then in the name of immortality.

Lowering his hands he stared at the files again before choosing one from the bottom of the pile.

Brandenmore had been detailed on this one regarding the sound of the victims' screams, inhuman and agonized. The sound of horror from a Breed medically paralyzed from a customized paralytic created by the Genetics Council that left only the ability to scream. For some reason, the scientists had rarely disabled their victims' ability to sound their horror, their pleas or their agony. And for this victim, it had been almost never ending.

A male Bengal whose animal DNA was strong enough that he was labeled "primal"—a Prime. For at least two years he had been given not just the serum Brandenmore had created to repress aging and cure the cancer he had tried to eliminate from his own body but also the mind-control drug he had created. A drug that had already been proven disastrous on another Breed, Dr. Elyiana Morrey, when it had been used to convince her that one of their Enforcers and code breakers, Mercury Warrant, was a danger to the Breeds.

"He was drugged with the paralytic the Council created and was vivisected to the point of death three times." Lawe Justice spoke from the chair across from him, his expression, his voice unemotional, icy in its complete lack of feeling.

The emotions were swirling beneath the surface, though; Jonas could sense them, like a volcano ready to explode.

"He escaped when the scientists and soldiers were preparing the lab, him and two other subjects for termination. He was recaptured again, ten years later. That was when the vivisections began. He escaped the last time just after Phillip Brandenmore's death," Jonas stated as he opened the file and stared into the face of the Breed that had endured two years of vicious, horrific testing.

Pale green eyes stared back from a hard, bronzed face bisected with a stripe. From his left eye, across his nose and right cheek, the flesh was a vibrant dark gold in the form of a Bengal's stripe.

His teeth were clenched, his lips pulled back in an enraged snarl. Sharp canines dropped from the sides of his teeth, glistening white and savagely sharp.

The picture beneath showed large, broad hands chained to a gurney as a soldier held one of the powerful fingers. The nail was slightly rounded and from the soldier's pressure against the pad of the finger the "claw" had been forced from the nail bed. Though it was filed to be less lethal, it was still harder than a normal human nail, its construction and almost bonelike hardness making it a formidable weapon.

"They named this one." Lawe remarked on the Council scientists' habit of giving the Breeds numbers rather than names.

"They've learned the power of a name." Jonas sighed. "But they gave this one the wrong name I believe. If they intended to reinforce his submission, then they should have chosen a far less powerful name than Gideon."

He watched as Lawe turned his attention back to the identical folder he held. Jonas could guess the thoughts, the torments going through his mind.

The memories.

Memories of the woman he had called mother and of forcing himself to remain still, with all apparent unconcern, as she died beneath a scalpel during a vivisection.

"Three times," Lawe stated. "They cut him open three times." His head shook briefly as he lifted the file once again. "And we're going to punish him for doing the same to the bastards he's hunting down?"

There was a vein of anger in Lawe's voice, disapproval that Jonas might agree with silently but didn't have the power to allow to continue.

"And once the news agencies catch wind that it's a Breed committing these crimes rather than a serial killer?" Jonas questioned Lawe's disapproval. "We've managed to cover this so far, Lawe, but we won't be able to much longer. Once the truth is out there, we'll be forced to terminate him or turn him over to the courts for their brand of justice versus ours. I'd much prefer to capture him, see if the damage to his mind can be reversed and save him. It seems no less than he deserves."

"And once again Breeds are forced to bow down to their makers," Lawe accused condemningly.

Despite the sneer in his tone, Jonas knew the intent behind it. It was the same intent he felt when he made similar comments. The injustice of being forced to turn the other cheek so many times was slowly building an aversion for the reality of their situation. And for humans in general.

Breeds had no choice but to garner the goodwill of society and of those untainted by the animal genetics Breeds carried. There were so many more of them, and so few Breeds, that if public opinion turned against them then they were screwed.

"Gideon's search for the Roberts girl is intensifying," Lawe said as he read further. "Three of the scientists involved in the testing she was a part of twenty years ago as well as two of the soldiers are dead. The single survivor, a female lab tech, reported that a man slipped into her bedroom, restrained her and questioned her extensively on the escape of the young male Bengal and the second human female as well as any friendship that may have developed between them and the Roberts girl while she was there." His gaze lifted once again. "She was terrified but left alive. She was the only one he left alive."

"And strangely enough, she didn't call the police or her employers," Jonas mused. "She contacted me instead."

"Did she say why?" Lawe's gaze narrowed as it lifted to Jonas's.

"Public knowledge that she was part of the experiments and tortures against not just Breeds but also humans could potentially lead to charges being filed against her and a conviction that could send her to prison for up to six to ten years." Jonas shrugged. "She was hoping I would be more lenient in exchange for the information concerning Gideon and what he's searching for.

She'd had an insurance policy of sorts and Jonas had been in the mood to bargain, as she'd guessed he would be. After all, the injection Phillip Brandenmore had given his daughter was now public knowledge thanks to files Brandenmore had hidden before Jonas had managed to kidnap him. Some of those files, the authorities had found before Jonas could get to them.

"Did she remember anything more than she stated in her initial report about his visit?" Lawe asked as he glanced to the next page and slowly stiffened.

Jonas nodded, his gaze knowing as he ignored the commander's reaction to what he had read while bringing it out into the open instead. "Diane Broen and her team are due back tonight with their report. They've questioned the female tech and completed an investigation into the Roberts girl's disappearance twelve years ago—just after the other two escaped termination. There's no doubt she ran away from her parents' home. We're simply uncertain why, where she would have gone, or how she disappeared so easily. From Brandenmore's files, and based on their friendship in the labs, Gideon suspects that the three were together somewhere. He simply doesn't know where. Diane's been investigating her possible whereabouts for the past three months. I believe she knows where the three are located and that she's withheld the information for some reason until she arrives here."

Lawe's head lifted slowly at Jonas's admission that he had sent Diane Broen and her team into the line of fire. For years, the Breeds and her enemies had only known the female mercenary as Diana. The huntress. It was a cover even her sister had perpetuated when needed. Commanding four human males and, one at a time, two Breeds, she had hunted rogue Coyote Breeds as well as Council soldiers, trainers, scientists and backers.

In truth, her name was Diane Broen, Lawe's mate. The woman Jonas had sent out in search of what was becoming one of the most dangerous rogue Breeds and the three research victims that could bring the full fury of the remaining Council down on Diane's head.

Jonas had expected a reaction from Lawe, but the

sight of the anger flaming in those normally icy, almost violet, blue eyes was surprising.

It was extremely rare to see Lawe pissed off. It was even rarer to see him pissed off over a woman.

Lawe was completely ignoring the fact that Jonas believed Diane may have the information they needed, of course. Nothing mattered at this moment; no one mattered but his mate. Whether he had completed that mating or not.

"Sending her was the wrong choice," Lawe stated, his voice rumbling with savage undercurrents.

The underlying challenge in that tone had Jonas's brows arching and he tensed at the deliberate questioning of his decision.

He refused to allow himself to react, at least for the moment. For Lawe. He forced himself to exercise restraint rather than immediate retaliation as he would have with any other Breed.

Lawe was being groomed to take the assistant director's chair, which allowed him to voice more of an opinion than most would have. It allowed him privileges Jonas would have never given another Enforcer or alpha leader, Breed or human.

Jonas had no need for a "yes" man, but he was damned if he'd be challenged much further over this particular decision. Or any decision regarding the search for the three research victims. Victims who could help find answers to the changes his tiny daughter was experiencing. Changes that made no sense and that so far couldn't be reversed or explained.

Especially considering the fact he was being challenged over the woman who had undertaken that search. The woman Lawe refused to claim. The mate he refused to mark, or to take. The mate he was attempting to cage and restrain as one would a pet. A decision

Jonas highly disagreed with and one he would block at every chance.

"And why is that?" Jonas asked as he closed the file, restraining the need to flex his claws in warning.

Lawe didn't hesitate to answer him either.

"The mission was too dangerous. Dealing with the various forces also searching for the girl has turned it into a bloodbath waiting to happen. I don't want her in the middle of it and neither should you, considering she's your mate's sister."

"Mate her, make it official, and get it over with, then you can deal with the situation yourself," Jonas growled as he felt the prick of the "claws" threatening to stretch free. "Otherwise, as long as she's making her men available to cover for the Enforcers we currently have out on assignments, I intend to use them."

And Lawe couldn't enforce any wish he had where Diane was concerned until he had fully mated her, marked her and ensured the mating bond between them.

More to the point, until she officially accepted the mating, Lawe had no rights where she or her safety was concerned. It was an amendment to Breed Law that had been unanimously voted in after a female mate had denied the Breed who marked her, because of her perception of his lack of honesty and his treatment of her.

Lawe stared back at Jonas for long moments, the animal genetics he carried burning inside him in the need to challenge the Bureau director.

There was also the damning knowledge that he had no right to that challenge.

He should have known Jonas was aware that mating heat was brewing between himself and Diane. The blood tests would have revealed the potential for it the moment they were conducted. But even more, Jonas would have detected that she carried Lawe's scent the moment Jonas met her.

A scent her body had refused to relinquish since the night he had aided in her rescue from a Syrian jail cell sixteen months before.

He had refused to take the final step that would initiate mating heat past the preliminary stage it was currently at. Any further and they would be burning for each other. At the moment, it was simply an irritant and a knowledge of what he was denying himself.

Enough of an irritation that he had been running in the opposite direction from the girl for far too long.

The glands beneath his tongue were only slightly swollen; the hormone within them hadn't yet begun seeping into his system. The hard-on that the need caused came and went with frustrating regularity, but the need for her wasn't yet a vicious bite in his balls.

He was simply uncomfortable.

It wasn't yet a biological imperative, but it would take very little to create an overwhelming hunger that would erode the restraint he had so far managed to keep in place.

Allowing his hunger to have its way was a step he had yet to take.

To kiss her or to touch her in any way would send the mating heat spiraling out of control. It was something he refused to do.

To lose a lover to the viciousness of the forces attempting to destroy the Breeds was one thing. To lose a mate, the one woman who would soothe his soul and heal the bitter, ragged wounds a Breed carried inside himself, was something else entirely.

For a second, the memory of his mother, so delicate and fragile beneath the scalpel that cut her open, flashed across his mind. He heard her screams, her pleas, the moment her voice broke and the scent of her horrifying death.

The chances of such a thing happening to a Breed and his mate were much higher than any Breed wanted to face, especially those who had mated.

Mates were protected, kept behind the walls of Sanctuary, the secured Wolf Breed compound of Haven or the newly named Coyote base overlooking Haven, aptly code-named the Citadel. Every unmated Breed made a pledge to protect the mated females and any children of a mating, with his very life. They were too important. They were vital to the survival of the Breed they were mated with and to the future survival of Breeds as a whole. No chance could be taken that they would be harmed.

There were those with mates who allowed their women to travel with them, to fight beside them, but they were few. And though those Breed males were forced to allow their women that freedom for the sake of their female's happiness, it was still a risk Lawe couldn't image allowing.

"You'll lose her," Jonas spoke softly into the silence, as though he were aware of the thoughts tormenting him. "Just as Dawn nearly lost Seth when she separated herself from him. Continue to ignore it, Lawe, and the mark of your scent will dissipate and leave you vulnerable to losing her."

Lawe stared back at him as a savage fury threatened to burn through his control.

"I never had her."

The director's lips quirked with an edge of knowing mockery as he sat back in his chair, relaxed and at ease despite the fact that Lawe couldn't control his tension and the need to confront the director over Diane's position within the Bureau.

She was an Enforcer, one of the well-trained, armed,

often covert operatives who fought to eradicate any threat to the survival of the Breeds.

"She's supposed to text her arrival when her plane lands tonight," Jonas stated, ignoring the challenge Lawe was silently directing toward him. "Have Rule meet her at the hotel we use and get the information she's acquired. I know she found something, but she seemed hesitant to discuss anything either electronically or via the sat-cell she was using. Rachel says something has her sister spooked, and I'm assuming that's the reason for with-holding the information."

Lawe stared back at Jonas thoughtfully, his gaze nar-rowing, nostrils flaring in sudden realization. He knew Diane. If she was spooked, then she felt she was being tracked or somehow watched.

Diane wasn't a paranoid individual. And she was too well trained to make such a vital mistake.

Lawe's fists clenched as he forced himself to ignore that sudden unnamed threat the animal inside him was raging to confront.

"And Gideon?" Lawe asked. "How close do you think he is to finding the Roberts girl or the others?"

Jonas sighed at the question, one brow lifted in a slow, mocking arch at Lawe's restraint. "He's closer than we are, I believe. I won't know for certain until Diane arrives and completes her report. Hopefully she has the informa-tion we need and she's willing to turn it over."

"And if he finds them before we do?" Lawe asked.

To that, Jonas's mouth thinned. "If he becomes a threat and we can't capture him, then we neutralize him. Call in Dog, Loki, Mutt and Mongrel, and have them ready to roll out in case Gideon's found. I don't want to take any chances."

Lawe stared back at him in surprise at the four names. Those Breeds were the most highly trained trackers and assassins to come out of the Genetics Council creations. To pull all of them in was a testament to the threat Jonas feared Gideon could become.

And to reveal the fact that they were Bureau operatives was a move Lawe hadn't expected Jonas to make. Especially Dog, whose cover was still that of a Council-controlled Coyote, though he was known to freelance on occasion where the Council's interests were concerned.

"Have Rule report back to me tonight after he meets with Diane as well," Jonas ordered.

Jonas was pushing for that confrontation. Lawe ground his back teeth together, hesitant to confront this issue, or Jonas, much further. The animal inside him was raging to settle the issue of any threat to this mating.

The human side, the icy logic that ruled him, realized the mistake that would be. Whether Jonas or the animal genetics wanted to admit it, Jonas would never deliberately endanger Diane. She was his mate's sister, he would protect her as much as possible. Still, the fact that she was facing any danger, period, had Lawe's guts tightening in reflex.

Lawe rose to his feet. "I'll meet with her." He couldn't help the growl in his response or the command in his voice.

He'd be damned if he would allow his brother, a Breed with genetics so similar to his own, around Diane at the moment. The silent fear that Rule could perhaps end up mating her was too great a risk. The fear could just be the possessiveness lashing out rather than any true risk of it. Still, it was a threat he couldn't ignore.

Should it happen, Lawe knew he'd never control the vicious fury that would erupt inside him against his brother. A brother who had risked his life countless times to save him.

Lawe moved for the door, the tension in his body

nearly impossible to control or to hide as he left Jonas's office and headed for his own.

The rogue Breed cutting a swath of blood through research scientists involved in Breed development was a problem. The young woman the Breed was searching for, and the danger he represented to her and the two research victims she was hiding with, was nothing short of horrifying.

But it wasn't his mate's place to handle it or to find either of the missing parties. It was her place to stay safe. He may not have mated her yet, but she was still his mate.

It would still destroy him if she were harmed, or perhaps even killed.

God help whoever so much as scratched her because he would lose his mind, as well as his perspective, and shed a swath of blood that may well destroy the Breeds forever.

She was as essential to him as the very air he breathed.

But as long as he didn't have her, as long as he maintained his distance, his control, then perhaps, just perhaps he would have a chance—

A chance of surviving, of maintaining control and his sanity if the worst did happen.

It was the only chance he had of holding back the pure, burning rage he could feel ready to ignite inside him. The rage of too many Breed lives lost, too many mates tortured, and far too many nightmares haunting him—

The knowledge that he now understood how a Coyote like Elder, a creature born to mercilessness and blood thirst, had given his life for one tiny, fragile, helpless breeder, sank inside his soul.

He would give his life—he would give his soul—for Diane.

· C H A P T E R 2 ·

ARLINGTON, VIRGINIA

Some would say he was insane, and some would be no less than completely accurate.

He was insane.

Staring down at the helpless, terrified research technician before him, Gideon acknowledged that fact with a sense of aching, bitter regret.

His sanity had been stripped from him with each day, with each injection, each slice of the scalpel against his flesh as Phillip Brandenmore's monsters conducted their experiments on him.

So many years. So many broken bones, so many demonic experiments.

So many times he had prayed for death and death hadn't come. Insanity had come instead. Insanity, and the overwhelming thirst for the blood of his enemies first, then for the blood of those who had betrayed him when they should have allowed him to die.

Crouching down to the floor where he had stretched his victim out spread-eagle, Gideon tilted his head and stared at the panic in the research tech's wide hazel eyes.

Gideon had injected him with the same drug that had been used to paralyze the victims in the Council and Brandenmore labs.

The same drug that had been used on him.

Scott Connelly had been a particularly sadistic bastard to the research subjects he had been assigned to. The evil that had existed inside him had gotten off on ensuring his charges felt as much pain as possible.

And they had felt pain. An agonizing, horrible pain that could never be forgotten.

All but one. Only one of those innocent victims had been spared his cruelty, his insanity. The one Gideon considered his ultimate prey.

Vengeance for the night death had been ready to receive him with gentle, comforting arms, only to be torn from them. To be given blood that had tainted his own, that had created a fever inside him he couldn't endure. A feral rage he couldn't exist within.

Gideon tensed at the memory, still so clear and vivid, the agony of so many years ripping through his senses and causing an involuntary growl to pass his lips.

His muscles bunched as if preparing to move in for the kill and he felt his mouth water for the taste of blood.

An enemy's blood.

A primal snarl rumbled in his chest, scraping his throat as he bared the sharpened canines at the sides of his mouth.

He was rewarded with a whimper of terror, and panic. The fear scented the air around him but did nothing to ease the primal violence swirling inside him.

Control was hard won. It was won only because it was now his turn to inflict the pain. His victim awaited him. The scent of his terror wafting through the room. Though it was an addictive aroma, it did little to appease the rage building inside him.

Gideon twirled the scalpel between his fingers as he rested his arms on his upper legs, his wrists lying over the edge of his knees as he watched the former research technician. He barely felt the rasp of his denim jeans against the underside of his arms where the sleeves of the white shirt he wore were folded back. Normally, the thin white scars that lay over that flesh didn't tolerate the rasp of clothing well. But this time, he barely felt it.

Blood would spray, he thought as he contemplated his victim. It would stain the shirt and jeans, but stealing more clothes wouldn't be a problem.

"Gideon, please," Scott wheezed from his position, flat on his back, naked to the chill of the air conditioning that Gideon had set at its lowest setting.

Any sensation that touched the flesh or the organs would be amplified because of the drug. Reactions to each sensation would be purer, stronger, allowing the scientists to better predict how each wound affected the body.

The bastard couldn't even shiver, though his teeth did chatter on occasion. That sound was another sign of success, of hard-won vengeance, and helped to restrain the animal prowling beneath the flesh.

"Please what?" Gideon rasped.

The sound of his own voice never failed to enrage him.

How many times had it been broken from his screams of pain?

How many times had he begged, pleaded, and cried for mercy?

He was a Prime, a primal male Breed. His pride was as intense as his natural strength and inborn animalistic abilities. To be driven by such agony, such horrific torture to beg, to shed tears and plead for death, had broken that pride to its core and all but destroyed it.

Even in the labs he had been created within there hadn't been such horrific pain that the Breeds were driven to beg unless the scientists intended death to be the final conclusion to that experiment.

The scientists that had created the Breeds in the Denali Labs in Alaska had prided themselves on the strength and power that filled their creations. They'd had no desire to bow the shoulders of their Breeds by damaging them to such an extent.

The scientists, research assistants and techs, the soldiers to the janitors in the lower depths of Brandenmore Research, had found great pleasure in doing just that. In turning their Breed victims into whimpering animals that begged for mercy.

And Scott had taken more pleasure than most in torturing the two Breeds held in what Gideon suspected was the pits of hell.

"Beg me," Gideon whispered to the research assistant. "Shed tears, Scott, and plead for mercy from the monster you helped to create."

The horror intensified in the man's eyes as his lips trembled with the knowledge of what was coming. His gaze centered on the scalpel and Gideon couldn't help but smile.

"Shall I tell you what it feels like?" he asked, lowering his voice until it sounded gentle, reassuring. It was nothing less than horrifying to his victim.

Because he remembered. Sweet God, he remembered the agony, every day, every second of his life.

His abdomen tightened with the scalding sensations

of the scalpel slicing into it as the remembrance tore through his senses.

He snarled in fury, causing Connelly to cry out in horror. His eyes widened, the certainty of death flashing in his gaze.

"Please, Gideon . . ." Scott choked on his own tears, gagging for a second as he fought for breath. "Please don't do this. Just kill me. Just kill me now."

Gideon knew what Scott felt in that moment. The way the stomach clenched and spasmed, recoiling in terror as he fought not to vomit. The struggle not to beg, because begging didn't help.

Yet the terror had a mind of its own after a certain point, and the words spilled from the lips anyway.

"It feels like hell has descended to your guts," Gideon told him with relish. "The agony begins with the first cut, and you believe it can get no worse." He leaned close, reaching out with the scalpel to draw the tip along the graying curls that covered his victim's chest. "But it can get worse, Scott. So much worse. And when the cold air meets the warmth of your insides, then you'll swear a hundred scalpels are biting into your organs, tearing them apart with jagged steel and ripping your mind out along with it."

"Please, Gideon!" Scott screamed hoarsely, the tears beginning to fall, the fear rising inside him with an acrid scent Gideon inhaled with heady satisfaction.

That scent was becoming addictive. Like a drug he couldn't resist. Now he knew, he knew why Coyotes thirsted for blood. For its coppery sweet scent and the feel of it gliding like wet silk over the hands.

"Please," Gideon repeated the plea. "Please, Scott. Scream for me in mindless pain. Please feel what I felt. Please beg as I begged. God, please, let me watch you die as you watched me each time you stopped my heart."

Then Gideon chuckled and glanced down at the stream of wetness flowing from the man's flaccid cock.

Scott was pissing himself.

The poor little coward.

It was something Gideon hadn't done during the experiments until the chill of the air actually hit his guts. Until the pain had been worse than hell on earth, and his body had fought to die amid it.

And there was nothing he wanted more than to slice into the monster at that moment and allow him to feel that same agony. To watch his blood seep from his flesh as it parted. To see it run in bloodred streams along his chest and abdomen to pool into the creamy carpet beneath him.

But first, first, he needed information. He needed information more than he needed to smell his victim's death.

At least, for the moment.

He could wait to kill him. He could wait until Scott gave the truths Gideon knew he held. The truths the man had so far hidden from his friends, coworkers and priest. The truth of the location of the one person Scott had shown any gentleness to in those labs. But he wouldn't be able to wait for long.

"Unlike you and your scientist masters, I can be merciful. I don't want to be, but I can be. If you cooperate."

Scott's lips quivered as he sobbed, snot dripping from his nose and running along the side of his cheek.

"Anything, Gideon," he begged desperately. "Anything you want. I swear it."

Gideon looked to the safe he had found earlier. Tucked into the wall across the room, and hidden, not very imaginatively, behind a framed print of Scott, his wife and two sons.

His sons didn't look as pathetic and weak as Scott. Surprisingly, they more resembled their mother with her strong Nordic features and direct blue eyes.

How had Scott Connelly managed to find a wife of such strength when he was such a weak, pitiful excuse of a male? How had he bred sons whose scent was mixed with the sweat of hard work and whose palms were calloused with it? Men whose reputations for honesty and a hard day's work were so well known in their small community that parents often held those sons up as examples to their own children?

Perhaps they weren't his sons, Gideon mused before turning his attention back to Scott. Unfortunately, Gideon couldn't be certain. Familial lines weren't scents to which he was particularly sensitive. His primal strengths ran to other areas.

"The combination to the safe," Gideon demanded, keeping his voice low. "I want it."

The combination spilled from Scott's lips as his teeth chattered in a cold Gideon had been created to ignore.

When he finished, Gideon nodded then smiled again. He knew the image he presented.

With the slash of the Bengal's strip across his face, the sharp strength of his incisors and the icy mercilessness of his cold pale green eyes he appeared every bit the animal he had been created to be. That image and the chill of ice in his eyes assured the researcher that Gideon had every intention of causing him to suffer however possible.

Strangely, the primal stripe across his face was new to him. It hadn't appeared until the first vivisection and transfusion of viral blood two years before. It had only grown darker with each horrific experiment he was forced to endure. With each transfusion of the only blood they had found that his system would accept after the feral fever had overtaken him twelve years before.

Her blood.

Only her blood was compatible. Only her blood could save his life and with each transfusion the insanity seemed to take a tighter grip on him.

Rising to his feet, Gideon moved to the safe, followed the directions and hummed in satisfaction as the steel door swung open.

Cash, jewels, bonds and several false identifications filled the interior, along with a laser-powered side arm.

It was the typical items anyone who worked with the Genetics Council kept on hand since the revelation of the Breeds and the horrific experimentations the Genetics Council had practiced.

No one who worked with the monsters responsible for the creation of the Breeds wanted anyone to learn they were aligned with them. At the moment, sentiment was with the Breeds, not with the Council.

Once such individuals were identified, it wasn't unheard of for Breeds to descend upon them with the full fury of years of torture, blood and death. Very discreetly, of course.

"Very good, Scott," Gideon murmured approvingly as he filled a bag with the very profitable find.

It was his best haul. Scott Connelly had been a bit more frugal than some with the proceeds he'd been given for his participating in the Breed research at Brandenmore Research.

Too bad. He was losing this little stash of it tonight. But then, dead men had no need for wealth, and if Gideon's research was correct, then the wife's family would protect her and her children from destitution.

Dropping the bag to a chair next to his victim, Gideon

crouched down beside him once more and picked the scalpel back up.

"You promised," Scott suddenly sobbed. "You promised not to hurt me."

"No, I said I would be merciful," Gideon reminded him patiently. "But we're not finished yet. There are a few other things I need before I can be on my way."

Scott would die, of that there was no doubt. There was no way Gideon's conscience would allow him to let the bastard live, to continue on with his life unpunished for the crimes he had committed against every law nature possessed.

"Honor Christine Roberts," he said the name slowly, clearly, watching Scott's eyes the entire time. "How can I find her?"

Scott had been her main caretaker while she had been at the research center. He had recorded the effects of the serum pumped into her. He had watched over her after her release to her father, a United States Army general aligned with the Council, and it had been Scott who had led the search for her after she had run away twelve years before.

She hadn't been his favorite, but she had been his most important subject. The only one he'd known the Council would never risk killing.

Scott's gaze flickered and the scent of fear thickened. There was more than fear there, though. Strangely, there was also the scent of—affection? Scott Connelly had felt something for somebody? Something he had evidently told no one else if the scent was anything to go by. But even more, he knew something. Gideon was certain of that now.

Gideon grinned at it. "What do you know, Scott? Tell me, my friend, so I can go away as silently as I arrived."

Gideon ran the scalpel along the other man's stomach, watching the thin trail of blood as it oozed from the deep scratch and heralded a pained cry from his victim. "Don't bother lying to me. I can smell it. And it would just piss me off worse to have to ask you again."

He let the tip of the scalpel press deeper into the vulnerable, soft flesh of the man's pelvis. A bead of blood welled then slowly eased down along the side his inner thigh.

"No one knows where she is," Scott blubbered pathetically, his voice high, terrified. "All the Coyotes working with Brandenmore could find out was that she may have been in contact with one of the other two children who were in the labs with her, just before she ran away."

Gideon almost cursed. *Fuck*, he hadn't expected that. Hadn't heard the rumors that the Council or Brandenmore had suspected the other two were alive. He had suspected Scott knew, but Scott was the only one, and he hadn't believed Scott would ever reveal that knowledge to any other living soul.

"The other two were terminated." Gideon stated the story his other victims had related to him. The story they had believed.

Gideon let himself appear a little less threatening by pretending he was ignorant of their survival—it would encourage the former researcher to talk. If Scott thought it would save his pitiful little life, he would turn over his own family, let alone one little research project—as long as it wasn't his favorite. As long as it wasn't the only creature on the face of the earth for whom Scott Connelly seemed to have any warmth. But, there was nothing as important to Scott as his own life.

"No, no. They weren't." Scott sobbed. "They were supposed to be." His voice hitched violently with fear. "They were being transported to the facility where they would have been. Then the Bengal kid managed to get free of his chains and attack the driver and the soldier transporting them. The van wrecked and the two kids escaped. No one knew where they went but they found evidence that there was someone else there."

There was. Gideon had been there. But no one should have known that. Even after he had been recaptured weeks later, far from the area, weak and all but dead, they had never thought to question him about them. And Gideon had never used the information. Even when it would have eased the pain they inflicted, at least once.

Deception still edged Scott's voice though. There was just a hint of it, and Gideon knew the researcher was hiding more.

Gideon allowed the scalpel to scrape along Scott's hip bone, peeling the skin from raw flesh as he screamed in pain.

"What do you know, Scott?" Gideon lowered his voice, the tone a warning, dangerous rasp.

Scott was sobbing. Gideon knew how it felt to have the thin layer of skin peeled back from living flesh to feel the agonizing caress of cold air meeting it.

"It can hurt more," he warned the research assistant. "Much, much more. I want everything Scott. Tell me everything you know."

His lips trembled a second before he wailed in pain and fear. And fury. Gideon knew that inner, agonizing fury when the will breaks and the instinct to survive kicks in. "They're with an old Indian. I didn't know his name or who he was and I fucking didn't care. He was looking for a girl kidnapped decades ago by the Council. Everyone knew he was searching for her. All I had was a contact e-mail. He was rabid about his identity. I e-mailed him their location and the approximate time they'd be there. But Brandenmore's men found someone who saw this old Indian bring them into a café three days after their escape. They ate, then headed west. They were in Missouri. The waitress remembered them clearly despite all the years because the little girl seemed ill, and the boy had a broken arm."

Headed west. And yes, the girl had been ill. With whatever illness she had infected Gideon with as well. That still infected him.

"And a team has been sent out?" Gideon asked.

"No. No." Scott swallowed tightly. "The team is still in Missouri trying to identify the Indian. It's been too many years. They have to find the Indian to find the kids now, because they're adults. Because they had no idea what they would look like now." He licked his lips nervously, hopefully. "I destroyed all the pictures of them. All the files because they were supposed to be terminated."

Only Gideon had been recaptured. Because they had left him. Left him in the cold and the emptiness of the night after infecting him with her illness. After saving him when death had been rocking him in her gentle embrace.

"You were supposed to have escaped." Scott sobbed again. "I gave you the means to do it. I helped you too." Rage filled his eyes. "She made me." Tears were pouring from his eyes, snot running in streams. "How else could you have slipped out so easily, Gideon, after so many years of failures? You and the boy. That was all she cared about, you that damned boy.

Gideon hadn't known that.

The boy wasn't exactly a boy, if Gideon remembered correctly. He would be in his midthirties. Like Gideon, he'd endured the research for years before the girls were added. The one who had been slated for termination had been a submissive little thing if Gideon remembered correctly, and he was certain he did.

Dark hair and big dark eyes. She had only been fourteen at the time of the escape, just as the Roberts girl had been. It was only weeks after the escape of the other two that she had run away from her home.

Honor Roberts had simply disappeared after leaving a short letter to her mother. That letter, as Gideon had read himself, was a good-bye, and the hope that she would understand. Although the mother had seemed as confused as anyone else that the girl had left.

Gideon wasn't confused.

Honor Roberts had been too intelligent, even in the labs. And she had always seemed to know, and to hear, more than was good for her well-being.

He was betting his own life on the hunch that she had learned, or suspected, that the research scientists were trying to convince General Roberts to allow them to do more testing on her.

And he was betting, once again, his life that the other two had contacted her. They had been close in the labs, so there was no way in hell they had completely lost contact after the other two were free.

He only knew he had to find the other girl. The one with those big dark eyes and vulnerable expressions. The one he had held despite the punishment to come, after a particularly brutal experimental session with the drugs she was being pumped full of.

"Very good." Gideon sighed at the useless memories. "What else did Wallace tell you?"

He had yet to catch up with Wallace, but he was on Gideon's list. His time would come.

"They had a list," Scott wheezed. "A list of names, of Indians who were known to be in the area at the time but didn't live there. But I know that the person they're looking for wasn't on that list. When I heard it was an Indian, I knew who it was and I didn't tell them. I figured it out over the years and I made certain his name never showed up."

Gideon tilted his head to the side curiously. "Really?"

He wasn't lying. Greedy little fucker. He'd thought he could capture them himself and gain the reward, no doubt.

"Who was it?" he asked.

"There was a girl the Council killed when they learned she mated one of their Coyote soldiers," Scott rasped. "It was over twenty years ago. Morningstar Martinez. She was taken from Window Rock, Arizona, because of the suspected psychic talents that ran in the family. I know her brother, Terran Martinez, was in the area at that time, but no one else knew. And I never told a soul." His gaze was tormented. "I let it lie, Gideon. I helped them escape." He sobbed. "Doesn't that count for something?"

"For something," Gideon agreed, lying as easily as the Council trainers had taught him to lie while he was under their less than tender care.

This information was interesting, though. Very, very interesting. The Genetics Council had always searched for breeders who had shown, or whose families had shown, a high rate of psychic or other paranormal talents.

Gideon considered the information for several long moments, wondering if he could satisfy his need for vengeance without spilling blood now. Without hearing Scott Connelly scream in inhuman agony.

Why was he bothering? he wondered. Why did he care if the son of a bitch believed Gideon had lied to him or not, once he began torturing him?

Because, Gideon admitted, he had made a promise.

He'd promised mercy.

Cutting into the man's guts as he lived wouldn't be considered merciful, he thought in resignation. And unfortunately, Gideon couldn't think of a worse death that he could use to assure Scott that the vivisection would be less painful.

And that sucked, he admitted to himself.

Scott had given him something no one else had, though—he tried to appease the animal that snarled restlessly inside. That counted for something, for mercy at the very least.

The researcher had tried to aid his escape, Gideon hadn't known that. But what he knew, he would tell anyone who tortured him. Gideon couldn't allow that.

Unfortunately for Scott, it didn't count for a reprieve.

Gideon finally nodded slowly. "No vivisection for you, Scott. You did what the others haven't managed. You gave me something useful."

Relief mixed with distrust filled Scott's eyes.

There was nothing Gideon could do about the distrust, because he couldn't explain that he would indeed die.

"I have to be going now." Gideon tossed the scalpel aside as he rose to his feet and glanced around the room.

The small pillow on the couch caught his eye. Moving to it, Gideon picked it up before returning to his victim.

"Here. I'll lift your head so you don't choke on your own snot." He snorted. "That wouldn't exactly be a comfortable way to die."

"Gideon."

He paused as he stared down at the helpless, vulnerable monster that had once filled his nightmares, but would no more.

"Yes, Scott?" Arching his brow mockingly he stared

down at the tearstained face as he remembered the sneers that had once covered it.

"You're after the girl, aren't you?" Scott's lips quivered as more tears fell. "You're after Fawn."

Gideon bared the sharp incisors in warning. "I'm after all of them, Scott. Every last one of them. And I'll have what's owed me. Never doubt that."

"I've done everything to keep them hidden." He swallowed tightly. "To help you. I didn't know they would use the vivisections on you. I wasn't there the day the decision was made. They didn't warn me in time."

"No one warned me either." Gideon shrugged as he moved once again to place the pillow beneath his head.

"Gideon, if they find her first . . ." Scott swallowed tightly. "They'll find out what I've hidden all these years."

"And that is?" He really didn't care.

"She's special," he whispered. "The last time I tested her blood there were additional hormones in it. Changes that didn't make sense. Changes the scientists would have killed her to understand—and still will."

"And why did you care?" Gideon lifted Scott's head to adjust the pillow beneath it.

Crouched behind him, he pushed the pillow in place.

"She's my daughter," Scott whispered.

"Liar!" Gideon snarled at the same moment he twisted Scott's head with brutal force.

The sound of Scott's spine cracking clashed with the scent of instant death as Gideon closed his eyes and fought back the shock, and the regret, he insisted on feeling.

He refused to even consider Scott's final words because they didn't matter. Nothing could make him more determined to exact his vengeance, not even the paternity of his prey.

He should be able to kill easily, he thought instead,

without remorse or guilt. He should have never felt the need to keep his promise for mercy when he himself had never been given mercy.

He settled Scott's head upon the pillow and stared down at the limp form. Gently, he closed the empty eyes that still reflected the abject relief he had been feeling at the moment of his death.

Gideon refused to acknowledge that glimmer of resignation he had heard in the other man's voice, though. As though he had known he would die in that second.

"I couldn't allow you to live," he said softly as he stared down at the lifeless face of the man that had tortured him for so many years. "Monsters can't be allowed to live past their usefulness, Scott. And your usefulness ran out."

Then his gaze was caught by that damned family photo.

Son of a bitch. He didn't want to see that. He didn't want to see nor consider the family that would return later.

Yet his conscience refused to allow him to do otherwise.

He re-dressed his victim before picking him up and carrying him to the couch where he laid him against the cushions as though the man were napping rather than entering hell. Then he cleaned the floor of the urine and excrement, disposed of the rags he used and carefully returned the room to its pristine condition.

Connelly's wife was considered a kind, compassionate woman. The week Gideon had spent watching the family and learning their habits, he'd found reason to believe it.

The two young men who were his sons were considered friendly and generous young men who laughed and enjoyed life with an apparent sense of humor and a love for people.

Even for Breeds.

They didn't deserve to find their father laid out naked and so obviously tortured. It would be a sight they would never forget. One Gideon would have regretted leaving for them.

Though where he'd found the ability to care, he wasn't quite certain.

Scott Connelly hadn't given a damn about anyone or anything in those labs, except the girl whose big, dark eyes watched the world with somber resignation. Gideon had shown the scientists he'd found over the past months the same lack of mercy they had shown him. But as he'd watched Connelly's family over the past week, he'd found himself feeling sorry for the wife and the sons who lived beneath the tyranny of the bastard who was rarely home and who cared little for their feelings.

They would be at peace now.

If only he could find a moment of that peace as well.

Stepping from the living room he shut off the lights, then slipped through the house as silently as he had entered it. Leaving through the back door, he left the security system disabled and didn't bother worrying about any fingerprints that could have been left.

He had none.

Those had been burned and peeled off long ago, leaving only calloused, roughened flesh in their place.

Moving through the shadows of the backyard, he made his way to the small park several blocks from the house and then to where he had parked the black pickup he'd stolen the week before.

Tossing the bag of cash and other items onto the passenger's seat, he started the vehicle and pulled from the darkened slot he'd parked in.

He would use his own fake ID and buy a vehicle

when morning came and ditch the stolen truck. It would make the trip ahead safer.

If he drove day and night, he would reach his destination quickly.

Window Rock, Arizona, the home of Terran Martinez and his family.

Gideon had heard of Morningstar Martinez and knew well the story of the Coyote Breed who had mated that lab's favored Breeder. The information found during their vivisections had been used in Brandenmore Research for the serum created there.

And apparently her girlhood home was also now the home of the girl that, for a while, he'd only known as subject number 4. The girl who would now pay the price for the last two years of agonizing experiments Gideon had suffered.

Once he found her, she too would find herself inflicted with the same pain, the same torment and the same overriding agony Gideon suffered because of her.

Her time was coming.

But first, first, there was one small problem he needed to deal with. The four-man, one-woman mercenary team searching for the girl as well.

He could kill them. Or, he could find a way to make contact with the commander, the only member of the team he trusted, and use her to ensure he got close enough to take possession once the girl was found.

There was no doubt his prey would never trust him. He remembered in his pain, in his fury, the threats he had made as she watched him with those dark, tortured eyes.

"I'll find you." The growl that left his throat was animalistic and enraged as her blood flowed into him, burning him, awakening the animal genetics his loss of blood had silenced. "You will both pay. I'll ensure it."

"You'll have to find us first, Gideon." Judd's voice had spoken softly from a point behind his head. A point Gideon couldn't see, because he couldn't turn his head. He couldn't strike out. He could only speak.

"I'll find you both," he had sworn to her as she sobbed.

"And I'll make certain you don't," Judd had promised. "We'll hide you before we leave, make certain you're safe. But you won't know where we are. And you'll never have a chance to harm either of us."

He would find them both. And he would keep the promise he made. They would both pay.

· CHAPTER 3 ·

There were few things Diane Broen hated worse than she hated late night landings and forcing her tired body to yet another hotel room.

One of these days, she promised herself as she entered the lobby of the exclusive, expensive hotel Jonas Wyatt sent them to, she was going to have her own bed, her own apartment, and her own clothes to fill it.

Rather than whatever she had in her suitcase, whether it was dirty or not.

"Boss, don't forget about that meeting we have with the accountant while we're in town," Thor, the big deep-voiced blond Swede reminded her as they stepped into the lobby of the D.C. hotel and headed for the elevators.

"Do we have an appointment?" she asked, all but dragging her bags behind her as she fought to stay on her feet long enough to get to her room.

Three months. She and the four men who had once

fought with her uncle and now followed her command, had been on the trail of one of the most elusive damned targets she'd ever been sent after.

They had gone after terrorists, extracted kidnap victims, provided security for heads of state, kings and even a few shady characters, but never in the history of her time with her uncle's men had they failed to complete a job. Until now.

It was as though she had disappeared off the face of the earth and the message she had received the night before returning to D.C. hadn't settled her mind.

An anonymous message left in her hotel room and a warning that there was a spy too close to her. A spy who didn't care to kill. And with that message was a reference to a possible location that she still couldn't believe.

Hell, she didn't need this.

"I'll get an appointment, boss," Thor promised. "But you have to keep it."

"Yeah, yeah, yeah," she said with a sigh as she punched the elevator button and watched the lit numbers descend as the elevator moved from the upper floors back to the lobby.

She was taking that warning to heart, as much as she hated to. There was too much at stake, and she wasn't risking her men without more information.

She leaned against the wall and stared back at the four men.

The Swede, Thor, was their moneyman. He kept them solvent and well supplied. He paid the bills and managed to keep their paychecks from bouncing. Next to him was Aaron, their logistics expert, emergency medical needs, and travel agent. Brick was their communications expert and supply tech while Malcolm took care of weapons and, before they'd joined the Bureau of Breed Affairs, he'd scheduled their missions.

They'd lost two of their men after joining the Bureau though. The two Breeds that had fought with them since the team had rescued them from a small lab several years before. They'd moved on to security in Sanctuary, the feline base in Virginia.

Now Diane and her remaining team were expert consultants to the Bureau, a glorified title for gophers she liked to think, but it kept her close to her sister, Rachel, and Rachel's daughter, Amber.

It kept her close enough that she could ensure she was never again unable to help her sister and niece when they needed her.

The elevator pinged its arrival.

"Hey, boss, want me to haul your gear?" Thor's voice was softer as she opened her eyes and stared back at him.

She was tired, and evidently she looked tired too.

She was aware of the other three men watching her curiously.

"I have my gear, Thor." She straightened as the doors slid open and a couple left the elevator. Their expressions were wary as their gazes moved over the less than reputable-looking group.

Diane snickered up at Thor as she stepped into the elevator and caught his disgruntled look. Readjusting her gear on her shoulders, she almost wished she had taken him up on his offer.

Yeah, she would have loved to have had Thor haul her gear for her. His shoulders were a hell of a lot stouter than hers, and he carried his own gear as though it weighed nothing. But her uncle had warned her that no matter how tired or wounded she was, she had to pull her own weight if she wanted them to respect her. The day she couldn't haul her own gear, and she wasn't wounded, was the day her men would start protecting her instead of following her. It would be the day she would lose her command.

She'd fought too many years for their respect to risk that. She wasn't going to give it up because she'd missed a few nights' sleep in order to return to the States in time to follow the lead she had been given and to complete her mission.

"Man, I need a cold beer, a warm woman and a soft bed," Aaron said, sighing as he leaned against the elevator wall, his brown eyes reflecting the same weariness they all felt.

Diane snorted as she leaned against the wall as well and waited for the tenth floor. "Cold beer, warm shower, and that soft bed." She sighed.

The thought of a warm man slid through her mind and she immediately, forcibly, pushed it back.

"Here we go," Thor breathed out in relief as the doors slid open. "I'll let you know about that accountant, boss."

"I'll be there," she promised. "Once Wyatt hears my report we'll probably be heading out for that vacation we've all dreamed of."

It was the only distraction she had to use to explain her own disappearance once she gave the impression of having given up on this mission.

She wasn't about to give up.

The girl she was looking for was too important and there were too many forces converging around her for Diane to give up now.

"Night, boss." Thor headed in the opposite direction to his room.

"Night, boss," Malcolm echoed as he crossed the hall to his room.

"See ya, boss." Aaron followed Thor, and headed farther up the hall, his shoulders drooping just a bit.

Aaron got his wish to head home to see his parents. Brick could pick up with the woman he'd been living with for the past few years, while Malcolm had a sister he intended to visit. Thor kept talking about budgets, accountants and balancing the books. She threw a careless wave over her shoulder to her men as she headed down the hall to her room. Reaching the door, she nodded to the Breed Enforcers assigned to guard the floor of the exclusive D.C. hotel reserved for Breed VIP visitors to the city.

Tonight, it was home.

She could feel the grime of the past three days on her body, and the long hours spent in the middle of the desert before that hadn't helped. And it seemed no matter the direction she went, the information she was searching for was always one step ahead of them. Just as the woman was.

◆   ◆   ◆

Lawe stepped from the stairwell entrance, preferring it over the elevator to help alleviate some of the tension that tightened his muscles.

As the door closed behind him, the ping of the elevator had him pausing as the doors slid open and Rule stepped into the hall.

Dressed in black, the Lion Breed Enforcer insignia on his right shoulder and his black hair pulled back from his face to reveal the strong features and brilliance of his topaz eyes, he didn't look like Lawe's twin. There was a resemblance, though, one strong enough that the genetic line wasn't in doubt.

He paused as he turned and saw Lawe, a frown marking his brow.

"Jonas didn't mention you were scheduled to be here."

Lawe's lips tightened.

"Do you ever get tired of his machinations?"

Rule snorted. "Don't we all. If it weren't for the fact that killing him would only cause more problems, I would kill him myself."

It was a regular refrain from damned near every Breed that came in contact with the director.

Rule tilted his head then as he stared back at Lawe questioningly. "Why are you here?"

"Because Jonas is playing games with us," Lawe growled. "He knows she's my mate, Rule."

Rule nodded sharply. "It would be hard to miss. She carried your scent when I first met her. I wondered if you would tell me when it happened and why you walked away from her."

The curiosity in his twin's gaze was impossible to miss. Lawe had been ignoring it for months, and didn't intend to explain it now either.

"I haven't mated her." Lawe's teeth clenched at the speculation in his brother's eyes. "Jonas sent you to try to push me to it."

Rule's lips thinned. He didn't like Jonas's games any more than anyone else, but Lawe could see something more swirling in his brother's gaze. Something that had him tensing at the possibility that his brother could become a problem where Diane was concerned, just as Jonas was becoming one.

"No mating huh?" Rule asked softly. "Tell me, Lawe, what do you think of Jonas and Ely's position that if a Breed doesn't claim his mate, then a genetic relation, or brother, may have that chance?"

Lawe's nostrils flared with his attempt to hold back the instinctive anger that shot through his system because of the question.

Jonas and the Breed specialist, Dr. Ely Morrey,

seemed to be under the impression that if a female wasn't physically mated, then the first stage of mating heat made her vulnerable to other males.

That first stage, when the minute quantities of the hormone appear on the fine hairs covering a Breed's body, or when something as simple as a brush of his lips to her flesh could infect her with enough of the hormone to activate her ability to become a mate. That combined with an emotional response, Ely had hypothesized, could allow her to mate another Breed.

Lawe had no idea if it had ever happened in the past, but he'd be damned if he'd allow Rule and Diane to prove it.

"Don't go there, Rule," Lawe warned him softly. "I don't think your horoscope declared today to be a good day to die."

Rule reached back and rubbed at his neck as he gave a heavy sigh.

"Jonas wants you out of this," Rule said as he dropped his arm back to his side. "I agree with him. You don't want her, you don't want the mating and I understand why. That doesn't mean she should be left vulnerable to any Breed looking to complete it. A Breed perhaps unable or unwilling to utilize her strengths."

"Use them you mean?" Lawe questioned with icy disdain. "Don't sugarcoat it, Rule. We both know Jonas doesn't want to lose her and her team. He knows I'll pull her off active duty the second I can."

Rule shrugged. "She's a hell of a warrior. You'll destroy her if you do that, Lawe. On the other hand, I think I could handle it."

Lawe couldn't help but laugh, though the sound held little amusement. "Go find your own woman. This one's off-limits to every other Breed with the mistaken intention to even attempt such a thing."

"But you're not claiming her," Rule pointed out softly. "You know, Lawe, we're brothers. Identical twins, despite the differences in our looks. I don't want to love a woman to the point it marks my soul. If you don't want your mate, give me that chance. I'd take care of her."

Was he serious?

Lawe stared back at Rule and once again was struck by the strange chill that had entered his brother's eyes in the past months. There was the chance that his brother was entirely serious.

"Why don't you just run on home while I consider your request?" Lawe grunted though he felt that dark-animal corner of his being awakening and attempting to overtake his humanity.

Rule's lips quirked. "While you're considering it, I'll just step in here and get things started, why don't I?" Despite the amusement, there was an edge of warning in Rule's tone.

The snarl that curled Lawe's lips and flashed his canines was the first indication that the animal genetics were slipping the leash he kept on them.

Rule didn't back down. His brow lifted instead as he crossed his arms over his chest and stared at Lawe. "You don't do that often," he pointed out coolly. "You're letting her get to you."

"No, you and Jonas are getting to me," Lawe growled. "What the hell makes you think you can force a mating? Even Cabal told us he'd had no attraction for his twin, Tanner's, mate. What makes you think it would be different for you? Hell, what makes Jonas and Ely believe such a thing could even be considered?"

"Because they were created differently, Lawe. We're actually twins. Fraternal perhaps, but still the genetics are stronger than Tanner and Cabal's, and we share a bond they didn't. It's worth finding out if those genetics would allow me to claim the woman you don't want. Besides, it's information Dr. Morrey may be able to use in the future if my ability to be her mate is possible."

Lawe almost shook his head, hoping to force a level of belief into his senses. To actually accept that his brother would consider such a thing.

"You would take what's mine?" Lawe asked, unwilling to admit to the confusion.

"You're not claiming her, Lawe," Rule growled. It was a low, rumbling sound that hinted at the same internal anger Lawe was feeling. "You don't want her. I don't want a mate that could destroy me. It seems a fair enough exchange to me."

"You don't want her either. Not as she deserves. So what the hell makes you think it would be worth the fight I'll give you? Get the hell out of here, Rule." There wasn't a chance he was going to let his brother around his mate. "Get out of here before I do something we'll both regret."

His brother started to turn and move up the hall toward Diane's room. Lawe could see his intent, feel it, and he wasn't having it.

He was moving even before he was aware of the impulse. For that brief moment of time the animal inside him rose up and acted before he could rein it in.

Rule was against the wall as Lawe pressed his forearm tight and hard into his brother's throat. The Breeds standing guard farther up the hall stepped forward then deliberately restrained themselves from moving from their posts.

The VIPs they guarded were more important than their feline curiosity or instincts concerning the violence rising between the two brothers. But they still watched curiously and Lawe was still very much aware of them.

"No!" he said with a snarl in his brother's face. "Don't destroy the bond we've had since our birth, Rule. Back the fuck off."

Rule's lips curled in amusement despite the powerful arm Lawe had pressed into his throat.

The mocking amusement he'd had moments before returned to his gaze. "The scent you put on her can be washed away eventually," Rule warned him. "It's not strong enough to do anything but cause a Breed to pause and then assure him she's Breed compatible. If I don't take my chance, then another Breed will. Which would you prefer, Lawe? That another mate her or that one you know will protect her with his life has her?"

"Another Breed won't get the warning you're getting. I'll fucking kill him. Stay the hell away from her or I'll make damned sure you wish you had."

Before the animal raging through his senses could strike out and harm the brother he had pledged to protect, Lawe jerked back before stabbing his finger on the elevator control panel.

The ping of the elevator sounded before the door slid open.

"For both our sakes," Lawe stated quietly with much more restraint than he actually felt.

Their gazes locked in silent confrontation, each gauging the other's intent and the strength behind it before Rule finally gave a slow nod.

"This time," Rule stated softly. "This time, Lawe. But before I see another take what I know should be yours, I will step around you and claim her myself. One way or the other, no matter the enmity it may cause between us."

Lawe clenched his fists at his side and forced himself to hold back the anger that pounded through his veins and kept his animal instincts on a sharply honed edge.

He hated that feeling. That feeling that there was another entity rising inside him and threatening to steal the control he'd honed over the years.

His gaze remained locked with his brother's until the elevator doors slid closed and the small cubicle carrying Rule made its return journey to the lobby of the hotel. He stood, watching the numbers on the digital display count down the elevator's progress until it reach the lobby.

He made himself stand there, watch, and wait as he fought the primal instincts tearing through him.

He'd managed to keep it at bay during the past months since he'd rescued Diane and realized she was his mate. He'd reined it in and assured himself that he could deny that savage impulse to claim her. Each time they'd come in contact, each time the battle became harder, but he'd still managed to walk away.

As he stalked to her door, that control he'd had most of his life was fading away. The animal part of him was clawing its way to the forefront of his senses, and its attention was locked on a single, subtle scent.

The scent of its mate.

The mate that even now the rational, logical part of his brain was screaming to deny. He couldn't have her. He wouldn't allow himself to risk her. But he could ensure, at least for a little while, that the scent he placed on her was strong enough to keep even Rule at bay.

For a little while.

◆   ◆   ◆

Diane had finished dinner and cleaned up her mess when she suddenly paused just inside the kitchenette, her gaze slicing to the door at the sound of a keycard sliding through the lock.

The soft hiss was a sound most people would have

never detected, but most people hadn't been trained by her paranoid uncle.

Perhaps paranoid was the wrong word to use. Her very cautious uncle.

In that second, her weapon cleared the holster she wore at the small of her back. The small laser-powered personal defense handgun had the look of the old-style Glock the military once issued, but it contained all the power of the adjustable laser-powered rifles.

The bursts of fiery energy could knock a man off his feet or put a hole in him the size of a bowling ball.

"Put your weapon down, wildcat. It's just me."

Diane froze, the weapon still held at her thigh by both hands as the door swung open and he stepped in.

Just me. Just—there was no "just" where Lawe Justice was concerned. There was nothing so simple as that word implied.

Confident, powerful, a supreme male animal and as fucking alpha as he could get, he stepped into the suite as though it belonged to him.

He was complicated, powerful, mysterious and rakish, wicked and seductive, and her entire body seemed to flood with warmth at the sight of him.

Diane remained still, her jaw locked in a deliberate attempt to exert control over herself and her reaction to the sound of the dark, sexually intent tone that had her body wanting to melt.

There were nights when the thought of him, of the touch she ached for, tormented her to the point that she wondered if perhaps he didn't own a part of her already. At the very least, he owned her fantasies, her erotically charged, sensually tormented fantasies since the first moment when she had opened her eyes to find him standing above her.

Tall, his shoulders broad, his body powerful, the

thick, heavy length of his black hair was much longer than it had been the last time she had seen him. He looked as dangerous as she knew he was. As primal and as savagely intense as she sensed he was.

Denim encased long, powerful legs and rode low on his hips to be cinched by a leather belt at his muscular hips. A white cotton shirt, the arms folded to the elbow covered wide shoulders and an impressive chest. Heavy Western boots covered his feet, a silver chain riding low around the heel.

He looked good enough to take a bite of, and her mouth watered to do just that.

The dark overnight growth of a beard shadowed his lower face—most Breeds couldn't grow a full beard, but that rakish, next-day growth was the norm for those who allowed that sexy to-die-for look. And that was exactly the look Lawe was going for tonight. The look that stripped her down to bare bones, hard-core sex and the need to ride him until they were both exhausted.

Not that it would take her long to reach exhaustion after the past three months and a search that had driven her bat-shit crazy. But what a way to go.

"What are you doing here?" First replacing the weapon, she then unclipped the holster before walking through the suite. Passing the small living area as Lawe stepped into the room, she moved to the bed where she laid the weapon on the bedside table before turning to face him.

"What I'm doing here should be rather obvious." Midnight black brows formed a V between the intense ice-cold violet blue eyes that swept over her.

Cold, cold eyes. She could never see what he was thinking, and she sure as hell had no idea how he felt from one second to the next. But she wanted to. There had been times she would have given anything to see behind the ice in his gaze.

"If you say so," she agreed with a hint of mockery. "I've arrived safe and sound, Lawe, so you can go back to your own room, your own place or wherever you're sleeping now. I'll give you my report when I give it to Jonas in the morning. I'm too tired for the third degree tonight."

She often wondered where he slept. And with whom. Rumor was, Lawe spent very few nights alone and his sexuality sure as hell didn't rest.

She knew the Bureau had several apartments in town, as well as a safe house, where he and other high-level Enforcers stayed while in D.C.

What the hell he was doing here this late simply made no sense. Lawe Justice rarely, if ever, stayed in hotels unless he had the Presidential Suite. And she knew the three Presidential Suites were in use by the Russian Wolf and Coyote Pack leaders, as well as the Russian Feline Pride leader.

"I would have worried about you if I hadn't known you arrived safe." He surprised her with his reply. "Damned good thing I did too. You've just arrived and I can see how little you've taken care of yourself. What good did it do me to rescue you from certain death if you're just going to commit suicide slowly?"

Never let it be said that the Breeds didn't protect their assets to the best of their ability. They did. Even to the point that he was here tonight to ensure she had arrived and was tucked safely in her room.

"You prefer I do it quicker? That eager to be rid of me, are you?"

He snorted. "Beats watching you waste away day by day."

Why, how sweet, she thought with savage mockery.

Yeah, right, that was why he was here all right, to check up on her health.

Bullshit.

He was there for the same reason she couldn't get him out of her mind. Because neither of them had the self-control or strength of will to stay away from the other. And that terrified her. In the ten months since he'd rescued her from a Middle Eastern hellhole, he'd consumed not just her fantasies but also her thoughts and her determination not to care for anyone but Rachel and Amber.

She didn't need this. Not here, not now, not at a time when she was trying so very hard to make too many decisions where her life was concerned.

As she turned back to face him, she watched as his gaze shifted from her to the bed, then back.

The bed was turned down invitingly, ready for them if either had the guts to push it.

The shower awaited. They could share it, she thought, though it would be a tight fit. The thought of heated water sluicing over his hard, naked body had her knees weakening in arousal and the need for touch.

Just for touch.

As he had touched her in England just before he left to return to the States after rescuing her. The way he had stroked the backs of his fingers along her cheek.

Or just after Brandenmore had finally been captured by Jonas Wyatt. He'd found her in New York that night before she had flown to Turkey for another job.

He hadn't taken her. He had just touched her, his calloused fingers playing over her body as though the sensation of her flesh beneath his touch was an ecstasy all its own.

She had never been undressed and neither had he. He hadn't touched her below the waist and he hadn't given her the release her body was crying out for. But he had made her ache.

Hell, she shouldn't want to want him like this. She shouldn't allow herself to want him like this.

She could be in the bed sleeping off the jet lag and frustration if he would just leave. She could hurry and masturbate, make use of the vibrator hidden in her bags and then rest for a few hours before she had to meet with his boss.

"Fine, I'm safe and sound," she finally said, breaking the tense silence growing between them. "You can stop protecting me now and let me get some sleep before I face the big bad prick in the morning."

Not that Jonas was really that bad, but it wouldn't do to let him know she actually liked him. She had a feeling he would take such deliberate advantage of that fact, it wouldn't even be funny.

Just as Lawe would take full advantage of the sheer fascination she had for him, if he knew of it.

Letting him know would be the biggest mistake she could possibly make.

Lawe kept watching her. His gaze was like a dominant, powerful caress she couldn't evade.

The sensation of that invisible touch never failed to leave her off balance and nervous. She could feel her blood beginning to rush through her veins, her heart rate becoming spiked and elevated. Her clit swelled with aching hunger and sexual desperation. Damn, she needed him to leave, then she could at least have him in her fantasies.

"Why are you still here, Lawe?" she asked. He was destroying her nerves with the violet blue intensity of his gaze and her certainty that there were indeed emotions roiling beneath the layer of icy calm.

"You should know why I'm here."

She shook her head in a tight, jerky motion. Oh God, now wasn't the time for this. Not while she was so tired, and so weak. "I have no idea, and I really don't give a damn."

God help her, he was killing her.

If she had to be fascinated by a man at this time in her life, why did it have to be a Breed? And why did it have to be this particular Breed? There was a level of the independence inside her that he frankly terrified and she knew why.

He was protective.

He would smother her with layers of protection if she allowed him to do it. That was what he would do with any woman he called his own. Hell, even his lovers had been known to complain of his insistence for bodyguards and heightened security. They complained of their inability to shop, to lunch with friends, to enjoy their lives.

For a minute, for the shortest amount of time, she might enjoy it, but Diane knew herself and knew it would destroy her. Her and Lawe. He could never accept danger to his woman, and he sure as hell could not accept danger to the woman he thought was his mate.

And he thought *she* was his mate.

She almost shivered at the thought.

"You need to leave, I'm tired and I need a shower, and I can't deal with you tonight," she retorted, forcing herself to confront the only man she had ever fantasized about wanting in her entire life.

She was thirty years old, for God's sake.

She'd gotten used to the accusations of being frigid, lesbian, unfeeling, robotic. They had ceased to offend or wound her long ago. In most cases, they sincerely amused her.

For the men she knew, bedding a woman was no different from hunting a particular buck with a trophy rack. They used the same instincts and often the same finesse.

But this man, he made her feel something. This Breed. He made her heart race and her body feel flushed. He made her clit swell, her nipples harden, and oh yes, she knew damned good and well he sensed it.

He was a Breed, after all. All those nifty powerful senses. The sense of smell, hearing and eyesight that was like four or five hundred times that of a normal human.

He could probably smell her pussy dampening.

His nostrils flared as she allowed her brows to arch mockingly.

Oh yes, he could smell it.

"You were late arriving from the airport," he stated as she realized his voice was much deeper than she was used to hearing. It had been since the moment he had spoken earlier. As though the animal genetics he carried were suddenly coming alive in ways they never had before.

She shivered at the thought.

"I'm really tired, Lawe." She didn't have the time or the heart to engage in the battle she knew he wanted. "Can we postpone this until tomorrow?"

Exactly what "this" was she truly hadn't figured out yet. All she knew was that if she allowed herself to take what she wanted, if she reached out and grabbed at him with both hands, she would be making a supreme mistake. One that could end up destroying her.

She didn't want a keeper or a jailer, and that was what Lawe would become. She couldn't bear the thought of it.

"Funny, each time we're together and the scent of your arousal begins to fill the air, it's suddenly cut off just as quickly," he mused, shocking her with the comment. "How do you manage it, Diane? Give me your secret, love. Maybe then I could control my own hunger as easily."

"I remember quickly what pricks male Breeds can

be," she informed him sharply. "Do you think for a minute I'd put up with it without shooting you? Then Jonas would have to shoot me. Rachel would probably cry—" She shrugged as though she had gone far enough.

His lips tilted in amusement. "You have it all figured out I see."

"I like to be prepared." Hooking her thumbs in the belt loops of her pants she continued to watch him carefully. "What's the saying? Better safe than sorry? I must prefer nice, safe non-Breed males. They don't hassle me near as much and let me come and go as I please."

Oh boy, big mistake. She watched his gaze narrow dangerously.

"And how many of those non-Breed males have you preferred, Diane?" His voice dropped as he began to move closer, becoming silky and dark, seductive. He could talk a woman out of her panties with his voice alone, she thought with an edge of searing hunger. And once he turned the heat up, how the hell was she supposed to resist him?

She stood perfectly still as he moved to her. He eased between her and the wall until he stood directly behind her.

She should have run, but that would have been the same as admitting defeat. Besides, he was a Breed male—the worst thing a woman could do was run. She became the prey then. An erotic delight that Lawe would ignore.

"Does it matter?" She had to force herself to remain still as she felt his cheek brush against her hair.

"Oh, it matters." That was definitely a growl in his voice. "More than you know."

She definitely heard the low, dangerous snap of his teeth behind her as he finished speaking.

"What the hell are you doing?"

She gave in. She moved to jerk away, overwhelmed and unprepared for the effect he had on her.

His hands clamped on her shoulders, holding her in place as a sharp breath expelled from her lungs.

"I want to bite you, Diane," he growled. "I want to come behind you, fill your sweet pussy with my dick and lock my teeth in the side of your neck while I feel the tremors of your release shaking through your body. Be damned careful, baby, because trust me, it would be something neither of us will recover from." His body tightened further behind her, his hips dipping, rolling, grinding his cock against the crevice of her rear as she felt her knees weakening.

One hand fell to her hip, holding her in place as Diane tried to pull free once again, her breathing rough and uneven as pleasure began to tear through her body.

The other hand stroked from her arm to her lower belly, pushed beneath her T-shirt and between one heartbeat and the next curved around the swollen, sensitive flesh of her breast as his fingers found and began to play with a tender nipple.

"Lawe!" Breathless, thick with a sudden, overwhelming pleasure and uncertainty, her fingers gripped the wrist at her hip as she felt her breathing lock in her chest for precious seconds.

Between her thighs her pussy clenched and spilled its juices as her clit began throbbing furiously.

The need to come was screaming through her body, drawing her muscles tight as she fought to find enough sensation against her clit to send her flying into release. Maybe then she could find her control again.

This was the closest they had ever been, the most they had dared to touch. Each of them knew what mating heat would do to them, just as they knew it was there, between them, banked but ready to flare out of control.

Something was definitely flaring out of control now. Like a wildfire burning everything in its path, the sensations and the hunger for more burned away her resistance and her common sense.

"Lawe," she whispered his name this time, the whimper of agonized arousal an indication of the heightened sensations flaring across her nerve endings. "Please. Don't do this to me."

She couldn't bear the throbbing desperation any longer. No amount of tightening of her thigh muscles was easing the ache. It was beginning to pound out of control, the piercing need shattering her defenses and stealing her ability to breathe.

It was terrifying. Exhilarating. It was the most dangerous thing she could allow to happen.

"Let me show you what you'll never find with another man, Breed or not." Savage, fierce, he growled the words at her ear as his hand stroked from her hip to the closure of her jeans.

Tearing at the snap and zipper of her jeans until they parted and his fingers were able to push inside.

She should stop him, she knew. She should have never allowed it to go this far. She couldn't allow herself to sink so deep into this morass of sensations.

But it was happening.

Her thighs parted as his fingers met the soft tuft of curls between her thighs.

He hadn't kissed her. But at that moment every thought was centering on what he was doing, not on what he hadn't done.

There were very few preliminaries, but she didn't need them tonight. When his fingers found the saturated, sensitized slit of her pussy and the swollen folds of flesh between her thighs she wondered if she somehow lost her mind in that moment.

Because there was no way that any man's, or Breed's, touch could really feel this good.

She really didn't feel sensation suddenly snapping through her body as something so far beyond pleasure tore through her senses.

A cry slipped past her lips. Rough, ragged, it was one that echoed with a building ecstasy and the need she couldn't control.

She didn't want to control it.

"Lawe, this is dangerous!" Her voice filled with the need for more, the fear of more, the exclamation came just as his fingers stroked around her clit, gripped it and began plumping it.

Her knees weakened as she arched into the sensually charged, erotically painful pleasure. She could barely gasp for air, the sensations were so brilliant. It was all she could do to spread her thighs farther apart. Tilting her hips closer, Diane reached back to hold on to his neck as his fingers released the tight bud, slid lower then sank inside the clenched, tight depths of her pussy.

She moaned. Her inner muscles clamped on his digits, flexed and convulsed around them.

"Feel your body milking my fingers." The growl in his tone, animalistic and primal, had her womb clenching with pulse after pulse of erotic excitement. "That's how you'll grip my dick, Diane. All sweet and hot. Like a tight little fist wrapping around it and sucking my cock until I'm exploding inside you." His fingers pushed in deep, the feel of them rough and calloused. "Until I'm pumping my come so hard inside your pussy we're both dying from it. Locked so tight inside you we'll wonder where one begins and the other ends."

And she wouldn't care.

She was so close.

She wouldn't care where he began and she ended.

All she cared about now was the pleasure and the need for release that beat inside her bloodstream like a fever.

"So silky and hot." His fingers eased back before thrusting inside her again, hard and deep and drawing another ragged cry from her lips.

"I want to taste you, Diane." His voice was more guttural, rougher than ever. "I want to fuck you with my tongue, taste all your sweet juices and feel you coming for me. I want to taste your pleasure until I'm drowning in you."

"Lawe, please." She couldn't bear it. The need for release was growing, tightening, burning inside her until she felt as though flames were licking through her body. "Just do it, damn you."

"Mate you?" His fingers were deep inside her, stroking, caressing, rubbing against nerve endings never touched before and too sensitive to bear it for long. "Should I mate you, Diane? Give you my kiss and let you go crazy with the heat that will fill both of us?"

"Why are you doing this to me?" She moaned as reality threatened to intrude.

A whimper built in her chest as the sensations began to coalesce into a white-hot conflagration that she no longer had any control over.

She could feel her release building, feel her womb, her pussy, her clit tightening, reaching, rushing headlong into ecstasy.

"You're mine," he whispered at her ear as his fingers stroked, rubbed, thrusting into the clenched tissue. "My scent covers you. It's my touch you ache for and only mine that will satisfy that sweet, hot little pussy."

His fingers were moving harder inside her. Faster. She could feel it beginning to pour through her, like a wave rushing out of control, pounding at her, building, surging—

She wanted to scream.

"Why are you doing this?" she cried out, desperate for release as he tormented her. "Please, Lawe . . ."

"Don't think to let another have you, Diane," he snarled at her ear, nipped it. "Because no other will ever give you this . . ."

Harder.

His fingers fucked inside her with a rhythm that had her gasping at the savagery of the pleasure, reaching, crying out and giving herself to every white-hot sensation he unleashed inside her.

When the ecstasy hit she could do nothing but lift to him and gasp for air, her pussy clamped down on his fingers, convulsing, spilling more of her juices as she shot into her release with a power that left her spinning out of control.

She had never known anything so intense, so erotic and primal. An orgasm had never tossed her so violently into rapture, into such an ecstasy that there was no control, no denial or reality but that of Lawe and the culmination of his touch.

With Lawe, there was no way to throttle back, no way to ease anything or control it.

She was his.

Dependent upon him to remain standing and not sink to the floor.

Dependent upon him to hold her against him, to share his warmth, his heartbeat, to protect her for the few fragile moments she was defenseless and unable to protect herself.

She was dependent upon Lawe to ensure she came back to her own body after flying through space and time. To ease her past the savagery of each aftershock, to croon her name at her ear, to bring her slowly back to earth before he eased his fingers from the tight, convulsive grip of her sex.

Slumping against him as he turned her in his arms, one hand pressing her head against his chest as the sound of his heart raging in his chest beat at her ear. Beneath the furious beat a primitive male growl rumbled as a sob nearly tore from her chest.

His hold, the way he all but wrapped himself around her, the way he dared her to ever allow another's touch, even as he gave her a pleasure she knew she would never reach without him, proved every fear she had ever had of him.

He would own her.

If she allowed it, Lawe Justice would steal every ounce of her independence, every chance of being the woman she had always fought to be.

She could be herself, or she could be his mate.

Standing in his arms she battled the tears filling her eyes.

She could never be both.

"I can't be someone I'm not," she whispered painfully, not bothering to hide the conflict inside her, just as she didn't bother to hide the pain.

There was no way to hide it deep enough to keep him from sensing it. She was simply too weak, and too torn.

"How do you know the extent of who you are?" His hand stroked gently down her back as he posed the question softly. "How do you know, Diane, that fate hasn't given you an escape you were unaware you needed?"

She stiffened, her head cradled against his chest as she blinked back the tears and accepted the knowledge that Lawe would never accept the fact that she was exactly who she had been all her life. The fight for justice, the feeling of being a part of that fight, of simply making a difference, just a difference, had always run to the very core of who and what she was.

"I know who I am." Just as she knew he couldn't

accept it. "I know what fate meant for me, Lawe. You're the one who doesn't want to accept it. You don't want to accept me."

Yet, she had accepted him. Every part of him. The arrogance. The genetics, the Breed strength and phenomenal confidence he possessed.

She accepted everything he was, and there was nothing she wanted to change.

Nothing except his refusal to see who she was.

His mate.

So much more than a biological match, or even an emotional tie. A mate was more than a wife, a willing fuck or the survival of the Breed species.

She was his feminine equal.

The other half of him.

His right hand, his left if that was what he needed.

His sword.

Warrior to his warrior.

And all he wanted her to be was the toy he took out for amusement whenever he had the time.

She stepped back and stared up at him sadly. Her body still vibrated, her sex ached and the hunger for him burned hotter and brighter inside her.

He was her other half as well.

Her right hand.

Her warrior, her partner, her strength as well as her weakness. Anger bit at her soul that he refused to accept her as she accepted him.

"I need to be alone—"

"No, Diane . . ."

Her hand snapped up as she moved farther away from him. "I need to think, Lawe. I need to know I can be what you need before this goes any further."

"It's too late to deny it." His heavy and brooding gaze speared hers. "Mating heat doesn't work that way."

Her chin lifted.

Like hell.

"Nothing rules me, Lawe. Not mating heat, not emotion or need. Not even you. I'll accept it willingly, or it will not be a part of my life. And I need to consider what I can and cannot accept." She stalked to the door and opened it slowly as he followed. "Please leave."

"We're not finished."

She took his parting words as a statement of intent.

"We haven't even started," she informed him. "And we won't, until I decide I'm ready.

"I should have just kissed you."

"And I should have never returned here," she snapped back. "You're not my boss, nor are you my jailer. Now please, leave. At least allow me the chance to accept what can't be changed here and to go on from there."

His lips thinned. He didn't answer. He stalked past her, striding into the hall before turning and heading toward the elevators once again.

As Diane closed the door, she knew her life had just taken a turn. And it was, quite possibly, a turn for which she wasn't entirely ready.

CHAPTER 4

Somewhere between point A and point B, she had managed to lose her fucking mind.

Somewhere between Lawe moving behind her and a release that had erupted like a volcano inside her, her common sense had taken a vacation and left her libido in charge.

Bad idea.

Very, very bad idea.

Because her libido had no common sense and it sure as hell had no self-preservation instincts.

Standing beneath the pounding spray the next morning, her eyes closed as water sluiced over her body, Diane admitted that she may have made the worse mistake of her life when she allowed herself those few moments of pleasure.

Yes indeed, allowing Lawe Justice a window into a woman's greatest weakness was a no-no. His touch was

her greatest weakness, his kiss her fantasy, his possession an aching hunger that tore at her senses.

And he would be her destruction if she allowed it.

Last night had to have been some sort of break-
down. That was the only way she would have allowed
it to happen, she assured herself. After all, her common sense was normally firmly intact. Her uncle hadn't
raised her to be no man's dummy or his favorite pet.

And she could so easily see Lawe attempting to turn
her into his favorite little pet.

She shuddered in horror at the thought. But it had
nearly happened last night. She had allowed him to do
far more than touch. She had allowed far more than the
weakness that came with a moment of pleasure.

He had actually made her regret her unwillingness
to be a Breed pet for all of—how many seconds had
she been locked in her orgasm? Okay, for however long
the rapture had held her in its grip, that was how long
she had regretted it.

The sensitivity of her flesh this morning was irritating, though. The feel of a phantom caress against
her tender nipples, the need for his kiss tempting her
senses. All those things were something she simply
didn't need right now.

Because she knew exactly what it was.

It was mating heat.

She let the water hit her full in the face, wondering if
she could possibly wash away the knowledge that somehow those savage animal genetics Lawe possessed had
chosen her as his mate.

Should she be honored?

How insulted would he be to know she wasn't, she
wondered as she smacked the shower wall and let a
more human growl of outrage pass her lips.

She so, *so* just did not need this.

She wasn't about to deny it, though, and see herself in much more trouble than she was actually in. Denying the fact that mating heat was ready to begin burning like a wildfire through their senses was the worst thing she could do.

Denying it would only cause an even larger mistake to be made. Perhaps a kiss to be shared, or even the ultimate transgression—that they would actually have sex and then the agony of the heat would sweep through her and Lawe with a strength that would be destructive to them both.

Diane shivered at the thought. A wave of weakening hunger swept through her, causing her knees to dip at the very thought of having that primal male moving over her.

Moving in her.

Stretching her inner flesh—

Taking her—

Fucking her like a man possessed by the beast his genetics were derived from.

Oh yeah, she could so get into the pleasure.

It was the thought of that ultimate possession that had her completely freaking out, though.

It was the thought of being bound. Helpless. Watching death steal those she knew, those she loved, and being unable to stop it.

Her parents, because she had been too young.

Her uncle, because he hadn't trusted her to help him.

And Padric. Padric with his smiling eyes, his devil-may-care grin and his love of poetry. She hadn't been able to save him because neither he nor her uncle had heeded her warnings that the past would never completely go away.

Giving her head a hard shake, Diane stepped from the shower and quickly toweled dry before dressing in

jeans, a white silk sleeveless camp shirt and the scuffed,
worn leather half boots she preferred.

Fixing her hair was a simple matter of running her
fingers through it as she spread a light gel and arranged
the heavy waves as they fell to her shoulders.

The primping wasn't exactly normal for her, but at
the moment she needed all the feminine self-confidence
she could steal. Facing Lawe at that meeting with Jonas
was not going to be easy.

As a matter of fact, it was going to be killer arous-
ing. It was going to flush her entire body with heat and
cause every erogenous zone in her body to light up like
the Fourth of July.

Dammit.

All she was going to be able to think about was riding that hard, powerful body. Moving above him. Taking him inside her. Feeling him working the engorged
length of his cock into her—

Controlling all that exquisite, exceptional, male
power—

She shivered again, glanced in the mirror then grimaced at the completely feminine image she saw in the
mirror.

In the eyes of the men she fought with and commanded, there was a difference between being weak
and feminine weakness. Just as there was a difference between being a woman and possessing a girlie
side that had never affected her ability to lead them,
and being a submissive woman. And submissive was
something Diane knew she could never be. So it hadn't
affected their willingness to follow her.

A light application of makeup followed, just a dust-
ing of a powder foundation. She spent more time on
smoky hues of shadow applied to her eyes and a light
application of mascara to lengthen and thicken her

lashes. A coating of gloss to her lips, then a light misting of her favorite perfume.

The woman that stared back at her wasn't the woman who had checked into the hotel the night before. Worn, exhausted and struggling to haul her bags to her room, she had felt as though she would never get enough rest.

This morning, rested, bright-eyed and approaching a clear mind, she drew in a deep breath and gave a brief nod to her image. Her determination to never allow his touch may have been compromised, but so far, she was dealing with the consequences of it.

Her pussy was wet and heated, longing for his touch.

Her nipples were tight and hard, aching for his lips, the stroke of his tongue, the sucking heat of his mouth and the rasp of his teeth.

Every cell in her body longed for the warmth of his, but it wasn't agonizing. It was irritating. Damned irritating. It was close to a compulsion, but she was handling it.

And she would continue to handle it, she promised herself. Staring at the image in the mirror, she decided she was now ready to face the day.

Or Lawe.

A flush raced over her face and down her neck at the memory of the searing pleasure that had shot through her body at the culmination of his touch the night before. A pleasure that had suffused her entire body. It had been so unexpected, so hot, she'd been helpless against it.

It had weakened her, heated her, marked a part of her she couldn't explain.

And the release . . .

Was that a moan that slipped past her lips?

Gripping the counter tight, she breathed in sharply and fought back the insidious ache that insisted on tormenting the most feminine parts of her body.

She had to stop.

She could feel her pussy dampening, clenching, preparing for the ultimate possession by the ultimate male animal.

And she had to stop it from happening.

Now.

She could not go into this meeting with Jonas Wyatt smelling of sexual need and the inability to concentrate.

She couldn't allow Lawe Justice to turn her mind into mush like this.

There was too much at stake for that, not just for the Breeds but for her sister and her niece too.

The serum that the medical research giant Phillip Brandenmore had injected her niece with was so unknown that they had no idea what it would do to the child.

Diane knew there were changes in Amber. She could see them when she spent more than a few weeks away from the baby. And then there had been the night when Rachel called her on a secured sat line while Diane had been out of the country on a mission.

Rachel had been sobbing.

Her daughter was purring, she had cried, and the other children hissed and snapped at the babe whenever she was around, causing Amber to cry.

Amber wasn't a Breed, but she was acting like a Breed, and she was becoming frightened of the other children because of their reaction to her. She was withdrawn, whimpering whenever Rachel took her around the other children because of their reactions to her. Amber was now frightened of all children, and she was barely eight months old. She was too little, too young, to have to face such an instinctive and primal reaction from others her own age.

Rachel had been nearly hysterical and trying to hold back her pain and fear from her mate, Jonas. Rachel had called her sister instead and spilled out the pain build-ing inside her and the pain tormenting her.

The agony tearing her apart as the changes in her baby became more noticeable was destroying her. Sob-bing, she had begged Diane to just make what was hap-pening to Amber stop, when they both knew that if it could be stopped, then Jonas would have already done whatever was necessary to put a halt to it.

The mother inside her sister had splintered and wept for the changes in her baby. Changes that were so uncertain and unknown.

Brave, strong, resilient Rachel had waited until her mate had left for D.C. and then she had broken down. It was then she had finally called her sister and told her what was happening to Amber after Brandenmore had attempted to kidnap her that night.

Diane had rushed back to the States in the middle of a mission despite her men's anger, and returned to her sister's side.

What she had seen for herself had shocked her to her very core, and terrified her.

At five months old Amber had watched her with an intelligence and understanding that Diane couldn't seem to process.

Amber wasn't talking yet, but Diane had had the most intense feeling that Amber would have known exactly what she wanted to say if she could have spoken.

The fear that Amber would be harmed in the future was ripping those who loved her apart. So much so that Diane had begun immediately investigating Phillip Brandenmore in the search for the scientists that had helped him create the serum.

Jonas had his own investigation going, but, as she had told him, Amber wouldn't have been his first victim. A scientist never used his most important research subject for the first trial. And Amber had been very important for some reason. A reason Diane had yet to find.

There would have been others.

Diane wanted answers and she was in a position to push buttons and go further than the Breeds. They were watched with the same intensity as any experiment under a microscope. They could only work in the shadows, but the type of social interaction Diane was an expert in, they hadn't really been raised to do. That type came with the life Diane had been born to as a child and lived until she was a teenager.

She could charm, bribe and threaten people the Breeds had a harder time getting to in those more social settings. And she could do it without having to kill later. After all, there was no way to hurt the Breeds by going after her. They would only hurt her sister. And themselves, if the world learned they had harmed the wife of the director of the Bureau of Breed Affairs.

Diane had found in the past three months exactly what she had suspected. She had found proof that Brandenmore had done the same experiment before, and more than once. The first test subjects had been more than twenty years ago, and terminated when the serum had resulted in feral fever. With the second set, there had been success, of sorts. At least, there would have been if he hadn't lost the test subjects he had used to help create his serum.

The same serum he had given Amber.

Three children. A male Bengal Breed, the daughter of a young woman who had been thrown out by her influential family when she had been diagnosed HIV positive, and a child reported to have been kidnapped from her very influential military family and held for five years. Those had been his second test subjects.

The Breed and the child of the homeless woman

were to have been terminated once the experiments on the serum were considered a success and the scientists moved on to adult subjects. The daughter of the military family had been returned to her family, free of the rapidly spreading, fatal leukemia she had been diagnosed with at age two.

It began with those children. Children who were now adults and, according to an anonymous message she had received via a contact she'd found in New York before leaving for Argentina, were still living. They were doing more than living—they were thriving. And they held the answers to the dangers, and the changes, Amber now faced. Moving to the sitting area of the hotel suite, Diane grabbed the backpack she carried wherever she went and headed to the door.

She was reaching for the doorknob when a heavy knock sounded on the other side. She knew that knock. Thor wasn't exactly timid.

A grin tilted her lips as she pulled the door open and met the gazes of the four men she had led since her uncle's death five years before.

And that damned warning that had been slipped beneath her hotel door haunted her.

There was a spy close to her. These four men were the closest and the only people, besides her sister, that Diane trusted. And she couldn't discount the fact that each time she had thought she had found someone who would know something, and she had shared that information with her men, something had happened to her sources.

"Had a feeling you'd be ready to roll before a humanly decent hour," Thor grunted, his gaze clear but his demeanor his early morning normal. Grouchy as hell.

That was the problem. She couldn't imagine any of her men betraying her. Hell. She felt like a traitor herself for even considering one of them could betray her.

"Did you miss your coffee this morning, Thor?" she asked archly as he glared back at her silently.

"Come on, I hear Jonas has Rachel in town with him. She always makes sure he has excellent coffee at his office." Closing the door firmly behind her she moved out ahead of the others as she ignored the hope that lightened his morose expression.

"Any new information come in, boss?" Brick asked as they headed for the elevators. "I'm ready to head home for a little vacay if not."

Diane had put out a few feelers before leaving Argentina. She had found several of the scientists and research technicians that had worked at the Omega lab in the Andes as well as one that had worked briefly in a little-known lab in Alaska in the Denali mountains.

Getting any of them to talk once she had managed to slip away from her men hadn't been simple, though. Fear was a hell of a silencer and working around it wasn't often easy.

Blackmail was such a dirty word, and so very effective when those scientists and research assistants were terrified of the world learning they had worked with Brandenmore or the Genetics Council.

It was then that Diane had learned of the three research subjects from Brandenmore labs who had disappeared. Research subjects who had been treated for years with the serum Brandenmore had created.

If those three had lived, that meant the answers she needed for Amber were out there as well. That night, Diane had found the warning note in her room. A location and the warning that she was being betrayed by someone close to her. It had been signed, *The Executioner.* The Breed rumored to be killing the scientists and some researchers who had worked in the secretive Brandenmore labs assigned to Breed research.

"Evidently not," Thor answered, his tone disgusted when she didn't speak. "It's like they dropped off the face of the earth, Diane. There's not even a hint as to where they could be."

Oh, there was a hint, Diane knew, but she just couldn't share it yet. Not until she managed to check it out herself and figure out exactly what was going on.

She hated distrusting her men, but she wasn't stupid either. There was something that simply didn't feel right since her capture in the Middle East sixteen months before. Something that had never set just right with her.

Her uncle's enemies should never have found her while she was in Syria. They hadn't known what she had looked like. She had used a fake passport and credentials, and she had none of her own contacts there. She hadn't reached out to any of her uncle's contacts either.

So how had they known not only where she was, but also who she was pretending to be at the time?

She'd had a feeling she had been betrayed then, but only her men had known where she was that day, and what she was doing. No one else had known, and she sure as hell hadn't given up her location herself.

Her thoughts were cut off as the elevator door opened, depositing them out into the busy lobby of the hotel.

"Too damned bad that fucker Brandenmore died," Malcolm muttered behind her. "We could have just beaten the information out of him."

That had been Malcolm's suggestion from the beginning. Hell, his Christmas wish had been for two minutes with the dead man to ensure he suffered before he killed him again.

A grown man who still made Christmas wishes. It never failed to amuse her.

Just as the thought of Brandenmore never failed to piss her off.

Brandenmore had been in bed with the Genetics Council well before he'd even realized it. His father and his grandfather both had supported the Genetics Council and hoped to benefit from the experiments and creations the Council had conceived.

Through his connection to them and the revelation of the aging retardation with Breed matings, Brandenmore had been drawn in to research the phenomenon.

A phenomenon he had found reason to suspect could not only retard aging but would also cure any human diseases the human mate may have.

Once any female child given the serum hit puberty, Brandenmore had theorized, then she would possess the ability to mate with any Breed as well. That the serum would slow her aging once she hit her sexual maturity, cure any disease, and also ensure Breed hybrid conception and possibly help Brandenmore find the cure to the cancer that ran in his family

Which wasn't exactly true, as Diane understood it. Mating heat did much more than Brandenmore's serum, and much less, if his files and the information Rachel had given her were anything to go by.

Breeds mated for life, Rachel had told her. The Breeds known to have lost a mate and survived that loss lived sad, miserable lives. The serum wasn't a mating. It couldn't ease or cure a mating. And in Brandenmore's case, it had caused a painful and horrifying death.

"Wyatt is sending a car for us," Aaron informed her as they crossed the lobby and headed for the front exit. "It's supposed to be waiting outside the hotel."

Diane nodded rather than making the scathing comment she would have at any other time.

This meeting with Jonas was too important to chance any transportation other than the Bureau's. She just hoped he had gotten the hint and found a way to distract her men before the meeting began.

"One of my contacts called last night." Thor leaned close as the other men moved ahead. "I need to meet with him tonight. He may have some information where General Roberts and his daughter are concerned."

She glanced up at him, suddenly aware of the fact that he was ensuring no one heard him but her.

"How reliable is your contact?" she asked Thor, once again patting herself on the back for making him her lieutenant. If what he was telling her were the truth and not a betrayal.

He'd become an information magnet since achieving the small raise in pay. Suspicion aside, he had never failed to find whatever they needed, no matter the mission they were on.

"Reliable," he said softly. "But I'd prefer to keep this between us for the moment. No sense in disappointing the others while they're dreaming of vacations," he snorted.

Diane forced a grin, though she had to admit, the others were anticipating that vacation if Jonas himself hadn't learned anything.

Would a man determined to betray her be so eager to escape her presence?

"Let me know when you leave," she told him quietly. "Do you need backup?"

"I shouldn't," he answered. "But I'll let you know once I check a few things out."

That was odd for Thor. He rarely went without backup, and never had she seen that dark glimmer of suspicion that she saw in his eyes now. Despite the excuses he was giving, there were other reasons he wasn't informing the others of the meeting he was setting up. Looking at each man, she couldn't imagine any of them betraying her, though she knew, to the soles of her feet, she knew some-one had betrayed her in Syria. She also knew she was being watched in the past months. That suspicion, an itch at the back of her neck, wouldn't go away.

Moving through the exit, Diane paused, her gaze moving up and down the crowded D.C. street as a frown began to pull at her brow.

Jonas was never late, and neither were his Enforcers or drivers.

"Car's not here," Thor muttered, his confusion and his concern evident in his voice as well.

"Traffic jam maybe?" Malcolm queried as he too began to tense.

Diane felt it then, that peculiar itch at the back of her neck, that early warning that wasn't so early.

Riding fast on its heels was the feeling of having a target painted on her head. Right between her eyes. A finger on the trigger and that finger wasn't going to wait.

Live by the sword, die by the sword, she'd once read. When the hunter became experienced enough, they became immediately aware of becoming the hunted. Her uncle had told her that just weeks before he was killed in that warehouse explosion.

She wasn't just being watched. She wasn't just being tracked. That finger was literally tightening on the trigger.

"Move!" She screamed the order even as her gaze was whipping around, ascertaining the innocents in the line of fire as she moved to push one older lady to the safety of the hotel doors.

The sound of the bullet whipping past her head was a whine of danger and death just before it exploded into the cement and stone wall of the building behind her.

Screams began to ricochet around the sidewalk as another burst of gunfire sounded and it began raining bullets. Cries of shock and fear began to fill the busy early-morning crowd that rushed to work or errands. They were now rushing to save their lives as another barrage of automatic gunfire began to spatter through the busy streets.

Car horns were sounding, the crash of metal against metal and the screams of hysteria echoed through her head as she scrambled to pull a terrified teenager from the side of the street and into the hotel entrance.

Diane was scrambling for the entrance, holding the door open as she pushed the kid in, then watched Malcolm and Thor suddenly grab Aaron under the arm as a bloom of red began to soak the fabric of his slacks over his thigh.

"Move! Move!" Diane yelled to the bystanders, ducking as the large window at her side exploded and glass began to rain around her.

The bastard was shooting at her.

She was only distantly aware of the shouts, sirens and more gunfire.

It was a crowded street no more than blocks away from the White House. The immediate response that would converge on the area would be thick with secret service, ATF, FBI and any other law enforcement alphabet agency currently based in the city.

But the bullets were still whining as Diane yelled at Thor to move his ass while she dragged a young professional through the door and hysteria threatened to overwhelm the young woman.

As she turned, searching for her men to ensure they had made it to safety, she was suddenly grabbed around the waist, hauled against a hard chest and tossed through the entrance as shards of cement exploded around her. The side of the building where her head had been looked like an iron fist had slammed inside it. Then she was flying through the air and thumping against a hard chest on the lobby floor.

"Thor!" She was aware of Lawe jumping to his

feet in a graceful feline move she highly envied as she rushed for the wounded Aaron. "How is he?"

"I'll fucking live," Aaron snarled, his rough face tight with pain and fury.

He was stretched out on the floor as Brick fashioned a quick tourniquet around his thigh with a belt.

Cries, shouted orders and Breeds were filling the area. Cold, hard-eyed, armed and swarming through the hotel and onto the street before disappearing entirely as Diane turned, her gaze going to Lawe in narrow-eyed knowledge.

"They were shooting at me." And she wasn't armed. "Dammit, I told Jonas I needed that public weapons permit."

Anger suddenly suffused her as she stared around at the wounded, weeping and shocked victims that had found safety inside the hotel.

"What the fuck is going on? What did you find, Diane?" Lawe was suddenly in her face, his canines flashing, and for once, his icy blue eyes weren't icy.

They were burning. An inner blue flame flickered inside his eyes burning hot and furious as he gripped her shoulders and gave her a tight little shake.

"The hell if I know," she yelled back furiously as she jerked away from him and scrambled across the floor to her men. "Where was my driver? If Jonas had his shit together and my driver had been out there, then I wouldn't have been fucking shot at and my men wouldn't be wounded."

Aaron wasn't the only one who had been hit. Brick and Malcolm were both bleeding, though Aaron's wounds appeared to be the worst.

All three had taken rounds in their legs. Aaron's hit was in the thigh, Brick's appeared to be a flesh wound, while Malcolm was tying off a tourniquet on his lower leg. None of the injuries were life threatening, but they were definitely enough to ground them for a good while.

Lawe grimaced, his expression savage as he once again stared around the room while the sound of sirens outside grew shrill. "The hell if I know, but I promise you I will find out."

The sound of gunfire had ceased, as though with the chance of picking her off with one of the bullets gone, the shooter had found better things to do than play with his gun.

"How bad is it?" she questioned Thor as she moved closer to check out her men.

"Bad enough." Disgust filled the behemoth's voice. "All three of them are out of commission. They'll be getting that vacation whether they want it or not."

It also ensured if any of the three were attempting to follow, or betray her further, that their efforts would be delayed.

Aaron, Brick and Malcolm didn't look happy either. They were glaring at her, lips pressed tightly together, their gazes shuttered. "What the fuck is going on, boss?" Aaron growled.

Diane gave a quick shake of her head. "I don't know, Aaron, but I intend to find out."

"You won't be doing anything," Lawe snapped behind her as his fingers suddenly gripped her arm, pulling her to a stop. "The five of you are out of this. The rest of you go home." Then he turned to Thor. "Take Diane to Sanctuary. A heli-jet will be here within the hour to transport you there, and then the pilot will fly you wherever you need to go."

Diane froze.

Her gaze met Thor's as Lawe began shouting orders to the Breeds still in the lobby. Most of those orders centered around protecting her.

Like hell.

She was aware of her men watching her. Brick, Aaron, Thor and Malcolm remained silent as she stared back at them.

She could feel the sudden distrust, see a glimmer of it in their gazes.

She wasn't going to be protected. It had taken far too many years to prove to her men that she could lead *them*. That she could protect *them*.

Unfortunately, for the moment, she needed them away from her. Until she found out what was going on, it was for the best.

Lawe stalked away as though his orders were all that mattered.

"Boss?" Thor questioned her softly. "What do we do?"

"Sounds to me like we're heading home." Brick snorted as he shot her an accusing glare.

In that second, so easily, Lawe had damaged the very foundation of her life.

"Boss?" Thor asked again, his pale blue eyes narrowed.

"We haven't found anything yet, Thor," she stated, keeping her voice low. "If we don't have more information before morning, then it sounds like vacation time."

Her smile was tight. She felt icy inside. Frozen.

She knew where she was going. She didn't have to turn over what she knew; it could wait. If she found who or what she was looking for, then she could call Jonas in. Perhaps by then she would know which of her men was the traitor. Not that there was a chance of gaining any help from them now. Lawe was another story.

How dare he think he could rule her life so easily? That he could make such decisions and force her to follow them.

"Since when do we obey Breeds?" Malcolm bit out

furiously as Thor's nostrils flared and Malcolm cursed under his breath, while Aaron laid back, his eyes closing in disgust.

She was very aware of their perception of her, but even more, Diane was aware of her perception of herself, and her determination to never be weak again. Let them believe Lawe could weaken her, for the moment anyway. Until she found out what she was dealing with and what the hell was going on, then it was for the best perhaps.

"Looks like we're all taking a vacation," she stated. "There's nothing we can do with the three of you wounded anyway." She nodded to the three stretched out on the floor.

"He's weakened you," Aaron muttered without opening his eyes. "Hell of a way to be taken out of the game."

"Is that what you really think?" she asked, her chin lifting as she deliberately kept her voice soft, her expression clear.

"What else could I think?" he grunted, refusing to even give her the consideration of opening his eyes.

"You could think, 'I hope you have a nice vacation, boss. See you when we're all healed,'" she told him softly before informing him, "You'll get your pay when we're back to work."

Once, long, long ago, she had been weak. She hadn't been able to protect herself or Rachel, and she hadn't been strong when it had mattered the most.

She had sworn it wouldn't happen again.

Never again would she allow herself to be so weak and so dependent on someone else that if they failed her, then it could destroy her.

Hell, maybe she should have just let Thor carry her bags last night after all. Then she could have gotten used to that edge of suspicion in their gazes.

She couldn't deny the charge though. The sudden opportunity the wounds provided her couldn't be wasted. That didn't mean she had to take Aaron's insults.

His eyes opened slowly. "If you were a man . . ."

"What?" She actually laughed at him. "I kicked your ass the last time, Aaron. You're stronger, but I'm smaller, and your balls are damned vulnerable. Remember that one."

His nostrils flared with instinctive anger before he glared at her with silent resentment.

"Anyone else?" She met each man's gaze steadily.

"That's all well and good, Di," Brick said softly. "You control the money and you can put us on the ground, we get that. But there are other ways to be weak, and right now, those Breeds are making you weak."

Diane shrugged. "Your opinion. Now, I hope you all enjoy your vacation. I intend to enjoy mine."

"We will." Malcolm nodded slowly, the amused quirk at his lips only slightly mocking. "We might be available when you call us back."

"Your choice," Diane assured him, as though she didn't doubt for a moment they would all jump at her command.

Turning her gaze to Thor she lifted her brow inquisitively. "You have anything to say?"

Thor nodded slowly as he watched her, his eyes narrowed, the icy blue intent, thoughtful. What that nod meant, she wasn't certain and she wasn't about to ask.

"I'll be waiting, boss," he finally stated. "I suck at vacations, just like the rest of these morons do." He nodded at the other men. "But today ain't my stupid day, so I'll just say we'll miss you."

She almost grinned. Damn smart-ass. At least they didn't suspect her of having plans of her own. After the meeting with Jonas, she would head out and see if

Honor Roberts was where she suspected her to be, without anyone being the wiser.

If Lawe wanted to convince himself that she was on her way to Sanctuary, then hell, whatever helped him sleep at night, right?

But she wasn't going to Sanctuary.

She was going hunting.

And she would go alone. Her uncle had trained her how to protect herself first. How to track alone, hunt alone, how to slip out of sight and do what had to be done if something happened and his men weren't with her.

Working alone wasn't her preferred course, but the only man she trusted at this point was Lawe. And Lawe would never allow the hunt for which she was preparing.

Malcolm drew her attention. "I wonder how long your Breed has been watching your back. I wondered how we were all so damned lucky these past six months. A few of those jobs you took us on should have been suicide missions. His Breeds were protecting us though, weren't they?"

"Not to my knowledge at the time, Malcolm, but if he and his men want to save us from a few bullets, then that suits me fine."

Malcolm gave a mocking snort. "Didn't save us this time, did he? Makes me wonder if maybe he didn't arrange it. Keeps you out of the line of fire, doesn't it?"

It did.

"Only for the moment," she told him shortly. "That I promise you, only for the moment."

• C H A P T E R   5 •

Lawe had been watching her all along.

She hadn't been protecting herself and her men as she had assumed. Her careful preparations and alternate plans could only lend confidence to her men if no one interfered.

Lawe had interfered.

That knowledge swept over her once she had her men taken care of and returned to their rooms with medics.

The old-fashioned bullet wound was cleaned and the bullet dug out of hard male muscle and flesh and bandaged within the hour. The Breed heli-jet was on its way from Sanctuary and it would fly her men home before returning to fly her and Rachel back to Sanctuary.

Or so Lawe and Jonas thought.

She sat back in the wing-backed chair in the living area of the lower-floor penthouse suite Jonas and Rachel had taken at the hotel, after the attack on Diane and her men. She knew other high-level Breeds were now in residence as well. It was becoming a damned Breed military stronghold. With one boot-shod foot propped on the coffee table, her elbow propped on the arm while her chin rested in her palm, Diane watched silently as Jonas and Lawe talked on the other side of the room.

Her sister stood next to her mate, and unlike Jonas and Lawe, watched Diane worriedly. Her sister knew her. Diane's lips quirked at the thought. Rachel would know damned good and well that Diane wouldn't be going anywhere near Sanctuary.

But Rachel hadn't come over to her since they had arrived in the room either. She stood next to her mate, silently aligning with him, and for the first time, Diane realized that her sister no longer turned to her first.

Lawe had a team of highly trained covert Breeds trailing her for—she didn't know how long, she thought as she watched them.

Oh yes, she did know. Because she knew how long it had been since she had so much as scratched herself during a mission. She hadn't been wounded on a mission since the night Lawe and a very small team of men had rescued her from the Middle East dungeon she had been held in. Bar fights, though, were another story. Diane had been recovering from a bar fight in Asia when Thor had told her about Brandenmore's nearly successful abduction of her niece.

Come to think of it, she had taken a few brawling injuries since her abduction and what she suspected was Lawe's decision to place a team on her for protection. Those injuries had involved bar fights—usually begun by Malcolm the hothead.

Diane had immediately pulled out of the current job, returned the client's advance and walked out on his screaming insistence that she make the scheduled pickup Thor had arranged. She had flown straight to the States and immediately begun shadowing her sister.

It had been weeks of hell afterward as she attempted to follow Rachel and provide backup for the Breeds attempting to protect her.

Thor had replaced the stitches in her leg more than once, cursed her for her stubbornness and railed at her when she had collapsed in exhaustion.

And when Lawe had found out, he'd nearly gone ballistic.

She clearly remembered walking away from him as he growled in rage at the two Breeds who had been part of her team at that time.

Those Breeds had since left and joined Sanctuary. She'd been smart enough to confront them and demand their loyalty when she'd learned Lawe expected them to tattle on every move she made. That demand had been one they had been unable to meet. Their first loyalty, they had informed her, was to their people. Diane suspected they had already assumed she was Lawe's mate. That meant their highest priority was her protection.

Diane had already begun to suspect there was something drawing them together that wasn't entirely normal.

Mating heat.

And she'd made it a point, just as it seemed he had, to steer clear of any chance of it flaring to full, burning life.

How long had it been since he had taken her out of that hellhole? Sixteen months? There were times she still felt as though she were recovering from the weeks she had been held and questioned about her deceased uncle and his activities before his death.

And since that rescue, she hadn't been wounded once conducting a mission.

It was no damned wonder the Bureau of Breed

Affairs was coming up short on Enforcers to spread around on the missions they were contracted for. They were sending their Enforcers on too many damned personal missions, she thought caustically.

And she hadn't put two and two together and come up with four by herself in all these months. She felt the sting of self-disgust at that thought.

She had seen the looks in her men's eyes earlier and she knew they too had sized up the situation correctly.

Lawe had had a team covering her without their knowledge too. Which meant they were more than damned good.

They were damned fucking good.

The number of "accidents" had increased though. The knife wound during a bar fight, a fall from a cliff when her equipment had mysteriously failed.

The first time Rachel had needed her, just after she had learned she was pregnant while in Switzerland, Diane had been in Syria having the shit beat out of her.

The second time, when Amber had been taken by Brandenmore that evening, Diane had been recovering from a knife wound inflicted during a bar fight.

The third time, when that deadbeat bastard who fathered Amber was attempting to legally take Amber from her mother, Diane had been recovering from injuries sustained when her equipment had failed during a mountain climb.

Strangely her so-called accidents coincided with events that had involved her sister or her niece at a time when they had needed her most.

And she was piecing this together finally why?

Because only this past week, after the Executioner—which was what they called Gideon Cross—left that message for her in Argentina had she begun to suspect that one of her men could be attempting to ensure she was no longer a part of her sister's life, or her protection.

She simply couldn't make herself consider Thor, for the simple fact that he had been the one to pull her ass out every time. But, neither could she make herself completely trust him either.

"Did you know they were on my ass?" she asked Thor as he stood silently behind her, his arms crossed over his chest as he too watched the small group.

"Nope. Didn't," he said shortly.

He was pissed, but he wasn't the only one. The rest of her men were as well.

Aaron, Brick and Malcolm were in the other room. Aaron had taken a bullet to the thigh, Malcolm had taken one to the back of his leg. Brick had taken one across his outer thigh, a flesh wound that required advanced skin patches along with two stitches. He had stated he was just too damned disgusted to put up with Breeds tonight. Thor had insisted on staying with her. As though she needed someone to protect her.

Had her command already begun breaking down, or was Thor more concerned with any information that he may miss?

He was the one she trusted the most. He helped plan every mission, knew every move she made and was the one most insistent that she never went anywhere, or did anything, alone.

And she had a spy close to her.

"I didn't even suspect they were there until they started pouring out of the woodwork like cockroaches today," she muttered resentfully.

"That's not the only problem we have," Thor said softly. "I don't like surprises. I checked our rooms while they were treating the others. We were bugged, and they weren't Breed devices."

So that was why he had slipped away from the rest of the group.

"Why?" she asked. "What made you suspect we were bugged?"

"Because whoever the fuck was out there trying to put a hole in your head knew exactly what time to be waiting on you." Low and rumbling with fury, his voice rasped above her. "We never leave at the same time, we never take the same exits twice. There's no fucking way to predict your movements, boss. That's why we follow you rather than lead, because only you know which way we're going."

That had been her uncle's way as well.

"Were you able to identify the device?" she asked.

"Not yet, but I'm working on it," he told her.

She nodded slowly as Lawe's head suddenly jerked around, his blue eyes narrowing on her and Thor.

"You're not going back to Sanctuary," Thor stated, the suspicion in his tone assuring her that he didn't entirely believe the plan she had given him.

"Yes, until more information comes in."

She hated lying to him. Thor was the one she knew the best. He was the one who had arrived with her uncle when her parents were killed, the one who had helped her uncle slip them out of the States and into Africa when her and Rachel's safety had been at risk.

She frowned at that.

Her uncle, Colt Broen, had taken her and Rachel to the only place he'd been certain they would be safe while he investigated their parents' death.

"I'm meeting with my contact at midnight. He called. There's a report you have a shadow on your tail," Thor told her. "He heard about the shooting and informed me someone is trying to separate you from your team but we haven't sussed out the reason why. Something's not right here, Di, you know that."

"Let me know before you leave and I want your report the minute that meeting is over," she ordered. "Keep working on why someone wants to separate me from my men."

"I'm all that's left to cover your back, Di," he stated worriedly. "Don't do something stupid and run off on your own."

If she knew Thor, then he knew her just as well. That could become a problem when she made her own move and headed west.

"Don't worry, Thor," she murmured, covering her lips with her fingers as her sister looked back to her once again. "I'm trying really hard not to do stupid things this month."

He grunted in disbelief at the comment.

Lawe moved from Jonas and Rachel before she could say anything more, striding to where she sat and stopping only inches from her as he stared back at Thor with icy intensity.

"I guess he wants me to leave, boss," Thor drawled, his tone thick with sarcasm.

Diane let her lips curve into a cold smile.

"We'll finalize the arrangements later, Thor." She covered their conversation, her voice low as she remained locked with Lawe's gaze. "Make certain you have the accounts in order and let the accountant know we'll have to change our appointment to tomorrow evening."

They didn't really have an appointment yet, but it was the best she could do on such notice. "Got it, boss." Thor nodded sharply, gave Lawe a hard glare then turned and walked quickly to the door.

One of the two Breeds guarding the inside of the room opened the doors for him, then closed and locked them as he left.

Looking past Lawe, Diane met her sister's worried gaze across the room, and understood completely why Rachel hadn't, and most likely wouldn't, say much to her for the time being. Not until she knew exactly what Diane was planning. Or more to the point, not until Jonas and Lawe figured it out.

It hurt. She felt as though her baby sister had deserted her. As though the one person she had always depended upon was suddenly more loyal to others instead.

She didn't bother to hide her feelings as Rachel met her gaze. Diane let the hurt, as well as the disbelief, fill her eyes before deliberately turning her head.

To meet Lawe's gaze. She almost sighed. That look was brooding and intense as though if he looked hard enough, deep enough, then he could read her plans in her eyes.

There was no way she would allow that.

Breed senses were much too primal. The least hint of a lie or subterfuge and Diane would have so many Breed guards on her ass that it would be impossible to peel them off. The only way to hide it was with anger. She had a damned good reason for being angry too. One of her men was betraying her to the point that she suspected her past accidents had not been accidents at all. Someone was trying to put a highly fatal hole in her head—*and* her sister was deserting her.

"Ignoring your sister isn't a move guaranteed to please Jonas," Lawe told her as she stared back at him silently.

Diane shrugged. "Did she know you had Breeds on my ass?"

No doubt she did. Diane knew her sister, and she knew how Rachel worried. She wouldn't blame her, but she could definitely use it to her advantage. Just as Rachel would expect her to.

"The team was my decision," he growled as his gaze flashed with something akin to regret. "You were nearly killed in Syria, Diane."

"Oh, no doubt," she said, mockery filling her voice. "I rather doubt either Rachel or Jonas sicced them on me, Lawe. For some reason, both of them seem to believe I'm perfectly capable of leading my team on my own and saving my own ass whenever needed."

"Neither of them saw you the way I did in that Middle Eastern dungeon either," he snapped.

Diane came out of the chair, anger pushing her to her feet at the chastising tone of his voice.

"You are not my fucking keeper," she informed him furiously as one finger poked firmly into his chest before her hands went to her hips. "Get that in your head, Lawe Justice. I haven't had a keeper since I was twenty-one years old, and I refuse to accept one now. Especially one as high-handed, arrogant and completely superior as you appear to be."

His gaze narrowed. "We're definitely going to have this fight," he informed her. "But Jonas wants your report first."

"There is no report." Crossing her arms over her breasts, she was confident that the scent he was searching for when his nostrils flared wasn't there.

There really was no report. She wasn't about to tell them a damned thing. Not in this lifetime. Not as long as she risked losing control of the mission she considered still active. The one she considered her personal responsibility.

"You told Jonas you weren't comfortable sending information electronically," he reminded her, his tone become cold, hard. "If there was nothing to report, why bother?"

She sneered back in his face. "Because I was being

watched. For some reason, dumb little ole me thought it was an enemy or one of those pesky little groups that thought they could get to the prize before I did. Do you think I wanted them to know I couldn't find a damned thing? I do have a reputation to consider, Lawe. And I'm also sick of the confidence displayed by the Council when it comes to finding subjects they don't want us to find."

She'd learned while the two Breeds were with her team exactly how to lie to a Breed. Hell, they had even helped her learn how to do it.

A fierce frown furrowed Lawe's brow as a snarl lifted the sides of his lips. "That's why the rogue they call the Executioner was shooting at you. Because he thought you knew something, Diane." He bit out his words, the ice in his tone barely covering the anger. "Why the hell are you risking yourself and your men that way?"

"Let him keep thinking it then." A toss of her head and a wave of her hand should be enough to convince him she really didn't give a damn. "I hope the bastard has nightmares about me getting there first. Wherever the hell 'there' is."

He raked his fingers through his hair as he turned from her, took two steps then turned back suspiciously. "You were gone three months," he reminded her. "You found nothing?"

"Oh, I found plenty," she informed him. "The files are in my bag." She flicked her fingers to the leather bag she'd carried downstairs earlier. "Brandenmore and his scientists were some coldhearted monsters, but you already knew that. They were determined to make the Genetics Council's scientists look like cuddly teddy bears. But none of them knew where the Roberts girl or the other two earlier subjects were. As far as they knew, the Bengal and the remaining girl had been terminated. If they knew any differently, they weren't telling."

She hadn't expected them to know differently. She'd hoped one of the techs who had befriended the girl, or perhaps one of the scientists' assistants, would have come forward, but none had.

"Son of a bitch," he growled, the exclamation an animalistic rasp pushed between his teeth.

"None of the information I found applies to her," she informed him. "And you know what, Lawe, I'm tired of looking. Especially considering the fact you've had a team just waiting to push me out and take over."

The look on his face assured her he would have done just that.

"I didn't know you were on that mission," he finally told her, his voice harsh. "I had the team covering you, nothing more, in case your uncle's enemies found you again. They hadn't even notified me that Jonas had sent you out. As far as I knew, you were still on that security detail in California."

The expression of self-disgust on his face had her suspecting he just might be telling the truth, but it didn't really matter. Once he had learned what she was doing, he would have still pulled her out of it.

She snorted at the excuse. "Whatever helps you sleep at night, asshole. And that security detail? I'm not a friggin' moron. I knew it for what it was while I was there. A damned pat on the head and a safe little corner to stand the weak little female in." She flipped her hand carelessly as she stared back at him in disgust. "Now, I have reports in triplicate to write for your boss and a few vacations to arrange for my men. I have paychecks to write and bills to pay. Deposit my damned fee in my account so I can get that done." Her voice rose in anger. "And leave me the hell alone."

While he was speechless, or at least not speaking, she pushed past him and stomped across the room to the door. She threw a very human, more than furious snarl at the guard standing inside.

There were two more outside and two more at each end of the hall. The mated wife of the director of the Bureau of Breed Affairs was in attendance, so the security required was no less impressive than that of the alpha's mated wives on the next level.

That didn't mean there was a single damned Breed in the place that she wanted anything to do with at the moment.

Jerking her key card from the back of her jeans Diane swiped it through the electronic lock and pushed her way into the room.

As she knew they would be, her men were waiting, still and silent, their gazes narrowed as she came inside.

"Boss, I don't like these fucking Breeds tellin' us what to do," Brick bitched immediately as she closed the door behind her, his dark face creased in a scowl. "This ain't no fun for me at all. And I sure as hell don't enjoy getting my leg trashed by some bastard out to keep secrets from them. I say we ditch this hellhole and go back to our real jobs."

Their real jobs. Military and private engagements that of course paid much better, but despite the sniper earlier that day, was still a hell of a lot more dangerous. And those jobs were guaranteed to keep her away from her sister and her niece if they ever needed her again.

Malcolm and Aaron mumbled in agreement as Thor stepped forward and laid several electronic listening devices on the long narrow table beside her.

Diane stared down at them.

"Hell," she said, sighing. "When did you find these?"

"When we came back in," he said softly. "Someone slipped in here while we were out, boss."

"You're not safe here," Aaron said with quiet anger. "And these damned Breeds ain't doin' a damned thing to protect you."

She turned and glanced at the door. "There are Breed guards up the hall," she stated. "How could someone have slipped in?"

"If they were dressed as hotel staff even a Breed could have gotten in here," Thor pointed out. "The Enforcers are far enough up the hall that no scent would have reached them."

"What about the ones at the elevator?" She shook her head in confusion. "They're not Breed devices."

She knew every design they used, even the covert ones. Jonas had made certain she didn't risk removing one the Breeds had placed while she was tracking Brandenmore's scientists.

"Hotel staff," Malcolm said once again. "All they had to do was look, act and smell the part."

"Unless they didn't show you all their listening devices," Aaron pointed out. "Just in case they decided to watch you closer." He was glaring at her. Aaron and Thor were the two strongest personalities in the unit and were usually the ones to argue with her or approach her with any disagreements the other two had.

Diane bent closer and stared at the one Thor had taken apart. Taking the magnifying glass Thor offered her, she surveyed the internal components silently.

The electronics didn't look Breed, but anything was possible when it came to the men and women created to be more cunning, more vicious than any other species on earth.

Diane started to shake her head again, only to have

a firm knock on her door interrupt her. She dropped her chin instead and blew out an irritated breath.

She should have known better than to think they would just let her escape.

She knew who it was. Sure as her name was what it was, she knew who it was.

Rather than speaking, she turned, leaned back against the table and waited until Thor reached the door and threw it open.

Lawe and Jonas. She hadn't expected Jonas.

Thor glared down at Lawe.

Not that he had far to glare. At six-two, Lawe wasn't much shorter than Thor. At six-five, Jonas was exactly the same height.

"Thor, we'll talk later," Diane told him warningly before glancing to the other men. "The four of you get some sleep. Your checks will be ready by morning and we'll all head home."

Thor grunted in disapproval as the others rose from their seats. Aaron pushed himself up, grabbed the crutches Thor had somehow managed to find and with the other two limped to the door.

"Later, boss."

"See ya, boss."

"Damned busybodies," Thor muttered before pushing the other half of the double door open and moving through it.

Brick slammed it closed as he and a limping Aaron left the room last, leaving her alone with Jonas and Lawe.

At least they hadn't suggested they stay and protect her, she thought angrily. No thanks to Lawe. He'd ensured her men had every reason to question her orders as well as her competence.

Bracing herself against the end of the table and crossing one ankle over the other, Diane waited.

The doors closed as both Jonas and Lawe entered the room, stopping at the seating several feet from her.

"I can smell the irritation." Jonas's lips curled in amusement as he watched her from those eerie silver eyes.

"I imagine you can see it fairly easy as well," she drawled, her gaze flicking to Lawe before returning to Jonas. "I'd really prefer not to fight with the two of you at the moment. So leave."

Jonas's head inclined in mocking agreement but didn't comment as he and Lawe watched her silently for several long moments.

"Rachel's concerned," Jonas finally admitted. "I'm here to see if I can fix the situation."

Diane's lips thinned. She shot Lawe a furious glare before turning to the director.

"So tell me, Jonas, why would the Bureau feel the need to spy on me and my men? When did you decide we couldn't be trusted?"

"You weren't being shadowed because you couldn't be trusted," Jonas responded sharply, his own irritation creasing his expression. "You should know that."

"I'm not talking about your Breed goons," she snapped. "And you should know it."

If she didn't know better, she would have sworn he had no idea what she was talking about. He and Lawe glanced at each other before she sensed the tension that suddenly filled the room and stretched between them.

"What's happened, Diane?" It was Lawe that rasped out the question, not Jonas.

Her brow lifted.

His brows lowered into a brooding frown. "Keep giving me that look, sweetheart, and I promise you'll have reason to suspect a hell of a lot of things, but my motives won't be one of them."

"What about the bugs we just found in the room? Placed here while I was conveniently busy in Jonas's suite? Tell me, Lawe, do you think, compounded by your Breeds following me, that may have aided my suspicions where your motives are concerned?"

Lawe's head jerked to the side, his gaze cutting as it sliced to Jonas, almost in accusation.

"Not me." Jonas lifted his hands in denial as he faced Lawe's wrath. "Hell, Lawe, you're the one I give the order to if we bug someone. Did I give you an order?"

Lawe's lips thinned. "Where are they?"

Silently, she pointed her thumb over her shoulder and watched as each man moved around her to the tiny devices that had been left on the table.

Neither man touched them. They bent close, their gazes trained on the devices as she watched silently. Her eyes locked on Lawe's bent back and she swore she could feel her mouth watering for him.

Her timing was incredibly bad, to say the least. The very fact that her libido was kicking in now, when she was furious with him, was enough to flat piss her off.

She didn't need this. She didn't want this. She didn't want anything to do with it.

At least right now.

She and Lawe Justice were like oil and water.

She was independent and he wanted a lap kitty for a mate, wife or lover. She wanted a man who trusted her abilities and the lifetime she had spent training, adapting and learning to protect not just herself and her men but those she was hired to protect and/or rescue.

She wanted a partner for a lover, and Lawe would never be a partner to his mate any more than he had been one with his lovers. Even the Breed lovers he'd had were forced to either stay behind the walls of Sanctuary or do without that perfect, hard, incredibly sexy body.

She bet he even growled when he fucked.

The thought of hearing that dangerous rasp in his throat as he came over her, inside her, was enough to send a shiver of anticipation surging through her.

And if he were her mate? There would be the barb, that extension her sister had told her about that emerged from beneath the wide crest of a feline Breed male's cock when he found his release inside his mate.

The flush that mounted her sister's cheeks and the gleam of remembered ecstasy in her eyes had been enough to immediately bring Lawe to Diane's mind.

She turned away from him quickly.

She had to do a hard reverse where such thoughts were concerned or—

"Too late, he can already smell your arousal." Jonas's voice had her swinging around with a frown to glare back at him.

Both he and Lawe were watching her closely.

"Do you expect me to blush?" she asked as she crossed her arms over her breasts, more to hide her hardening nipples than out of confrontation. "Sorry, boys, I stopped blushing in my teens. I would like to know where those bugs came from, though." She indicated the devices, then flashed Lawe a tight smile. "Any scent I may have, I can't smell, so I can ignore."

Lawe's brow arched. "As long as you don't expect me to ignore it."

"I may not be able to ignore the fact that the mating heat is there, but I can sure as hell ignore any scent of need that I, myself, can't detect," she informed him firmly. "And you can ignore it too, Lawe, because it's not going to happen. Period. You're arrogant, imperious, and your attitude where women are concerned just piss me the hell off. We're not pets, and I'll be damned if I'll play your little lap kitty, for even a second. Now take your toys there and get the hell out of my room. I'd like to get some sleep before I have to decide how the hell I'm going to repair the damage you did to my team when you showed them you've had your little purr boys watching over me rather than respecting my ability to protect myself."

"As you did in that little village in Syria last year when your uncle's enemies got their hands on you? Where were your men then, Diane? Let me tell you where they were," he informed her as he cast a hard and brutally iced look. "They were nice and safe and not risking their asses because Thor and the two Breeds with you at the time had the good sense to contact Sanctuary. Do you have a fucking clue the danger it would have represented if your captors had had a clue that they held the sister-in-law to the director of the Bureau of Breed Affairs?"

Lawe could feel it. That loss of control that signaled Diane's determination to challenge him in both words and deed. He could smell her intent to push him, see it in her gaze and in her expression as she stood there glaring at him.

"What about those Coyotes that pierced your hide with their bullets last year?" she charged as her brow lifted mockingly, anger glimmering in her dark brown eyes. "Neither of us exactly lives a safe life. Stop trying to pretend you're the only one who does."

"And I'm supposed to stand aside when I have the ability to hedge your chances of surviving?" He could feel the growl threatening to edge into his voice.

Damn her, he could feel the animal inside wakening at her determination to place her life in danger. As though she were daring the enemy to strike. Daring him to make his move and challenge her.

"What you should have done was left my Breeds on my damned team instead of taking them away from me and giving me the *choice* to contact you when I needed them." Her voice rose along with her anger as she glared back at both of them.

"The shooter today was Gideon," Jonas informed her quietly as he broke in on the battle getting ready to flare to life. "He's been following you for weeks, Diane. The team tracking you has had signs of the shadow on your ass but they couldn't verify. All they had was a sense of it. Catching sight of him has been impossible despite their efforts, and you know my men are damned good."

She knew Gideon, the Executioner, had no intention of killing her, despite appearances. Not once had she herself been struck by one of the precisely aimed bullets. But three of her men had been. Three she couldn't be certain weren't betraying her.

"And if your men hadn't been between me and him, perhaps he would have taken the advice I left for him at my previous location and actually come out of the shadows and arranged a meet," she suddenly yelled at him as she threw her hands up in fury.

In her room she'd left an answer to the message she'd received in Argentina. She'd done everything possible to draw the Executioner to a meeting after he had left her the warning that she was being betrayed.

"My God, Jonas, do you realize how many times your men, by his order probably, stood between me, my contacts and my damned missions?" She stabbed her finger in Lawe's direction as a haze of disbelief filled her mind.

She was furious.

There was no scent quite as intoxicating as feminine fury, unless it was female lust. And the lust was definitely there, Lawe thought as he felt that instantaneous, burning hunger suddenly sear his mind.

She wanted to hide it. She wanted to deny it. She would have denied it to hell and back if he confronted her over it. She would cut her nose off to spite her face and they both knew it.

She was so determined to be alone, to push him away, that she ran in the opposite direction of him every chance she had.

"Both of you stand down," Jonas ordered, his tone harsh with irritation.

Turning to him, Lawe realized the other man hadn't taken his eyes off the devices lying so innocently on the pristine gleam of the table.

"Why don't you take your handler and leave," she ordered him, the command grating on the animal instincts threatening to take over. "Then the two of you can moon over the electronics together."

"These aren't just electronics," Jonas said as he reached into his pocket to extract a handkerchief before carefully wrapping it around the three bugs and pocketing it before turning his gaze back to them.

"Really?" Her arms slid down to allow her hands to prop on her hips defiantly. "Are they aliens disguised as electronics? Didn't I see that movie already?"

Jonas's lips quirked. "Only if you managed to find a copy that I couldn't. That movie is over forty years old and harder to find than *Casablanca*. But these little babies are like fingerprints. I've only seen them twice before, which means if Gideon put them in place, then I may have a way of tracking him."

Diane focused her attention on him rather than the anger demanding action as it rose inside her.

"Such as?" Diane asked.

Not that she cared. Come daylight she would be after far different prey. "Such as the same signal that he used to pull information into these babies can be used to pull information out of them," he told her. "I'll explain it tomorrow when we meet with the Leo, Leo Vanderale. He'll need to talk to you as well as Thor in regard to where you found them and how they were connected to their power source."

Oh yeah, she was going to be at that meeting. Besides the fact that she had no intention of being in D.C. come morning, she also had no intention of facing the First Leo, the rumored first ever successful melding of human and animal DNA, more than a hundred years before.

"Speaking of that information, I'll have it before I leave."

Autocratic, demanding and arrogantly certain of himself. She would have expected Jonas to demand the information, not Lawe. Diane laughed at the pure Breed confidence he had in himself and his certainty she would be led so easily.

"You can get the information at the same time Leo and your alpha do," she snorted. "I don't explain things twice, Lawe."

And he knew it.

It was a test. Had she told him, then he would have known she had no intention of making that meeting.

His eyes narrowed.

"The meeting's at ten," Jonas informed her as she and Lawe were locked in a silent battle fought only with their eyes.

"Fine. Now you can leave." She had no intention of speaking to Leo Vanderale the next day. Once the first glimmer of light had made its debut, she intended to be on her way to Window Rock, Arizona.

Giving a brief, sharp nod, Jonas turned to Lawe. "I'll contact Callan and Leo tonight. When you're finished here..." He paused before his lips edged into a grin. "Or should I say instead, sometime tonight, you should contact Rule and let him know we'll need every Breed in the vicinity on grounds when the heli-jet arrives in the morning."

"I'll take care of it," Lawe promised, his nod sharp as Jonas headed for the door.

When the door snicked closed and locked behind the director, Diane turned back to Lawe.

"You need to leave with him," Diane stated, her chest tight and aching as she battled tears that made no sense. She was stronger than this, she told herself. She was no ninny to cry over a man as though he were essential to her life. But for some reason, the betrayal she felt was tearing at her heart.

Lawe felt himself still. With his gaze locked with Diane's, he had a feeling the battle of wills beginning was one that could end up destroying them both.

As she suggested, he should simply leave with Jonas. Staying here, accepting that challenge was the worse decision he could make, but that was exactly what he was doing.

"After last night, you really think it's going to be that easy?" he asked with silky smoothness.

Diane's gaze flickered with a glimmer of excitement and anticipation that he could feel her attempting to fight.

Attempting.

Lawe felt his own body preparing, his cock hardening, lengthening, the glands beneath his tongue swelling and the faintest hint of the unusual taste of spiced, candied pears.

He hadn't expected that.

He'd heard the hormone tasted of cinnamon, spring

rain, even summer heat. But he'd never heard of candied pears.

"I don't want this." The surprising statement had him fighting every instinct he possessed to ignore her.

Jonas had suggested he just mate her and get it over with. Mating her hadn't been his preferred course of action until he'd seen those bullets slamming into the cement wall above her head.

Until he'd almost seen her die before his eyes.

His mate.

She was his, and other than those stolen moments the night before he hadn't touched her. Even then, he hadn't kissed her. He had felt her sweet heat, but he hadn't tasted it. He was dying for it. He wanted to lick the heated flesh of her pussy, taste the slow glide of her juices as they met his tongue.

He wanted her with every cell of his body, with every breath he could drag into his lungs.

"Don't look at me like that, Lawe." There was an edge of breathlessness in her voice that had sweat popping out on his forehead and along his back as he fought the need to kiss her. To share the erotic taste filling his senses.

The head of his dick throbbed imperatively and the need that had it stiff and aching wasn't something that was going to go away any time soon.

That order, though, that female arrogance as she demanded he deny himself even the pleasure of looking, had that dominant animal inside him rearing its head in furious denial.

"I can look at you however I want," he growled, moving closer to her, aware that she wasn't backing down; she wasn't edging away from him.

A woman as wary as Diane should have been running to protect her virtue, because his intention was to steal every ounce of it.

And once he had her virtue, he would have her submission. His hands actually ached to grip the curves of
her ass, spread them apart, show her an erotic hunger
that would lead to the full, feminine acknowledgment
that he was her mate, her protector.

Diane drew in a slow, deep breath and he could almost hear the thunder of her heart. He could definitely
see it in the fierce throb of blood in the vein at her neck.

"You think you can intimidate me?" she asked.

"I'm not trying to intimidate you." Intimidation had
nothing to do with what he had in mind. Hell no. He
wanted to fuck her until they both passed out in exhaustion, but he had no intention of intimidating her.

Unless he had no other choice.

And only after he sated the hunger tearing at his
senses.

She stared up at him now, the nervousness that
flowed through her senses based more in her need for
him, a need she was fighting desperately to deny. And
he could feel the fight, the desperation, and though he
could understand why she fought it, even approved the
fight, he refused to allow her to be any less helpless
than he.

"Fighting it doesn't work," he murmured as he moved
around her, his head lowering, his lips at her ear. "It only
makes the body hotter, the need more intense. It only
makes you hungrier, doesn't it, Diane, especially after
having some small, tempting taste of it."

Her breathing accelerated.

He could smell her heat then, burning hotter and
wilder than ever before. It was blooming inside her,
overtaking her control and reaching out to him as he
stopped behind her and allowed his hands to settle
at her hips, his fingers curling over the fragile bones
lightly.

"Right here," he breathed over the fiercely throbbing vein in her neck. "I could take the gentlest of bites and it would begin. It would burn through both of us, making the hunger impossible to deny, impossible to walk away from."

Her hands curled over the top of the chair in front of her then. A hard, desperate grip as he felt her fighting to hold on to the last of her control. The same as he was fighting to hold on to his.

"I won't wait much longer," he warned her, knowing he couldn't deny that instinctive, desperate edge of need beginning to tear at his senses.

"And that's supposed to make me step into line?" The denial, the defiance, was still there.

"I could only hope." He couldn't resist brushing his lips along her neck.

Just his lips.

He didn't lick them first. He didn't place a layer of the hormone between his lips and her flesh.

And the animal inside paced in fury because he hadn't.

She jumped against him, suddenly moving to tear away from him, to escape his grip as she whirled around to face him.

"No."

No.

His lips quirked. No was no. It was intrinsic, whether it was a game or not. It had the same meaning.

He would heed it. This time.

"We have a meeting with Jonas, Callan and Leo tomorrow," he told her instead. "You'll be there to give your report."

She nodded sharply, the scent of her heat nearly drugging him with the nearly overpowering need to taste her as only her mate could do.

Turning, he stalked to the door and left without a good-bye, without a hint of the primal response to her that he was quickly losing control of.

One second more. So much as another breath scented with the flowering lust that wrapped around her and he would have forgotten she said no. He would have forgotten that edge of fear he'd sensed inside her.

He would have forgotten it all and he would have taken his mate.

✦ C H A P T E R 6 ✦

"I'm sorry, Diane," Rachel spoke from her bed where she lay curled around the little girl who blinked back at Diane as she stood beside the bed.

Amber awakened even before Diane had disabled the digital window lock and wiggled through the narrow opening. Her little head had lifted, her eyes focusing on the window as Diane had stood on the ledge outside considering the lock and the occupants of the room beyond the window.

She watched the baby now as a sleepy little smile curled her tiny lips. Tugging at a soft curl beside her face, Amber watched her, gaze somber, as though she could sense her aunt's heavy heart.

"Why turn on me, Rachel?" Diane asked softly as she sat down on the mattress, her fingers reaching out to touch her niece's downy cheek. "Why didn't you speak to me tonight? Why couldn't you stand *with* me rather than against me?"

Why had her sister turned on her? She had shown her loyalty was with Jonas and Lawe by standing across the room in hushed conversation with them rather than standing next to the sister who had been with her all her life.

"Was it because I wasn't here when you needed me? When Amber needed me?" Diane asked, the ragged pain of that memory tearing at her when her sister didn't speak.

"God no," Rachel exclaimed, her voice still hushed and now filled with tears and pain. "I could never blame you for that, Diane. There was nothing you could have done when Brandenmore struck."

Rachel's eyes closed briefly as her hold on her daughter seemed to tighten.

The pain of that memory still had the power to bring tears to Diane's eyes, as well as sending a shaft of pain striking at her heart. Her gaze slid to Amber. She was so sweet and innocent, and Diane was well aware that she had failed the child.

As Diane watched, she saw the glimmer of tears on her sister's cheek a second before a tiny, almost silent little rumble of a purr emitted from Amber's tiny chest.

The only sign Rachel gave that she heard it was a brief tremble of her lips as Diane gave a surprised start. It was the first time she had heard the sound and found it to be completely endearing. But with her mother's reaction, a whimper left Amber's lips as they puckered in the threat of tears.

"Jonas says she can feel it when we're frightened, or if something causes us pain," Rachel's voice was jagged, obviously causing the confused cry and the tears that dampened the little girl's eyes.

For a moment, Diane wished she could still berate her sister as she had when she was a child. Unfortunately, they were far past such recriminations. The need to ease Amber's confusion was one she didn't have to ignore though.

"Look at Mommy, getting all upset over a little ole purr, Ambie. She just doesn't realize how special that makes you does she, sweetie?" Diane chided the baby as she leaned down and rubbed her nose against her niece's little button nose.

Amber's smile trembled for a moment before a baby laugh parted her lips and Diane lifted her from Rachel's arms. Cuddling the little form close to her own breast as the small head tipped back to stare up at her had Diane's heart melting with such a surge of love it was painful.

"She looks like a mini-you," Diane whispered in awe as she glanced at her sister for only a second, her eyes drawn back to the baby. "She's more beautiful every time I see her, and every time I see more and more of your features when you were a baby. They are coming alive inside her. Mom and Dad would have melted for her."

Her sister sniffed as a tear slid down her cheek. "And you look more like Mom every day, Diane. Sometimes, I swear, it's like having her here."

She couldn't help but laugh.

Diane tickled Amber's little belly where it peeked out from her pajamas. Chubby legs kicked as baby laughter filled the darkness. Grasping little fingers found Diane's shirt, grabbed and held on tight as Diane leaned down and brushed a kiss over her forehead. That little sound came again, the cutest little purr, stronger, almost teasing. A sound of happiness as Diane hugged the baby against her and blew another kiss against her baby-scented neck.

Rachel's hand pressed to her lips as she fought back

a sob, the pain and fear trembling through her body as Amber suddenly tensed. She struggled against Diane until she could turn and stare back at her mother in confusion.

"Ignore Mommy," Diane advised her and tickled her belly again, bringing a hesitant little chortle before Amber looked to her mother again as though asking permission for such a simple joy.

Diane lowered her lips to Amber's ear, her gaze meeting her sister's. "Mommy forgets that was a nasty old Breed-type serum that bad old doctor gave you," Diane reminded the mother rather than the child she was talking to. "What did she expect, hmmm? Wolfie growls maybe?"

Rachel shook her head. "It isn't funny, Diane."

"Well, you know, we need to make it funny, or our little chimp here is going to think we don't love her as we should." Diane lowered her head further and growled against her niece's little shoulder.

Amber's little gale of laughter was followed by that cute little purr. The second the sound slipped free her gaze moved quickly to her mother once again. Rachel hadn't heard it that time, she had been concentrating on the baby laughter instead, the fear fading away as her daughter seemed to enjoy this moment of unexpected pleasure.

"Rachel, you have to enjoy the changes that aren't harmful to her," Diane chided as she continued to draw the little chuckles from the baby. "Every time she purrs or makes a sound you consider odd, I bet you're crying. Becoming frightened."

"Diane, it's wrong," Rachel whispered raggedly.

Once again Amber gave a frightened little start as her lips puckered and she turned to her mother for solace.

"I wish I could smack you." Diane sighed in disappointment. "You're letting your own stress affect her and steal her childhood. Give her some laughter, Rachel. Play with her. Let her purr or growl or whatever she needs to do. She's so precious. Too precious to be made to feel unaccepted."

Diane continued to speak with gentle affection as she tickled, petted and teased the baby. Finally, she had Amber's attention once again as Rachel watched her with sudden understanding and agonizing regret.

"How are the other children reacting to her now?" Diane asked, knowing Rachel had mentioned problems a few months earlier.

"They growl at her, snap at her without thinking." Rachel reached out and tickled Amber's tummy as she kept her tone soft.

Amber was no dummy. She watched her mother somberly for long seconds before Rachel was able to draw a smile from her.

"Those little hybrid brats giving my girl a hard time?" Diane whispered as Amber curled closer to her and gave a sleepy little yawn.

"They don't mean anything—" Rachel began to protest.

"Geez, Rachel, I know they don't mean anything by it." Diane sighed as she rocked the baby gently. "It's the changes in her scent that frightens them perhaps? They're just babies too."

She wanted to give her sister something to hold on to, something to ease the fears Diane knew tormented her.

"Not David," Rachel whispered as she ran her fingers lovingly over Amber's heavy curls. "Callen and Merinus's son isn't a baby, Diane. He growls at her if he doesn't stop himself first. Just having her around seems to irritate him. Low, involuntary growls rumble in his chest before he becomes angry and simply leaves the room."

Rachel's voice trembled painfully. "He's being groomed for his father's position, trained to take over. He's the children's alpha, do you know the implications of his rejection of Amber?"

Diane smoothed her hand down the baby's back as she made a tiny sound of distress once again. "What are the implications, Rachel?" she asked gently, though the look she shot her sister was berating. "David is in puberty, he's going through maturation of not just human hormones but also the animal ones. He was Jonas's favorite before Amber. Subconsciously, perhaps he resents her for the love Jonas has for her, and his animal DNA is simply reacting."

Jonas loved children, but David had been his favorite before Amber's arrival. Once Rachel had given birth, Diane heard Jonas had fallen head over heels for the infant. Nothing in this world mattered as much as Rachel and the child he claimed as his own. Though Diane knew David still received quite a bit of attention from the director.

"When it's all said and done, he's still human," she reminded her sister. "Have you told Merinus?"

Rachel rolled over to stare at the ceiling, one arm across her stomach as she scowled heavily.

"Rachel?" Diane urged her.

"I'm not going to Callan or Merinus," Rachel muttered, though this time, she kept the anger and any pain she felt out of her tone.

"Why not, Rachel?" Maybe her sister couldn't, but she could.

"And you won't either." Rachel's head snapped to the side, her expression fierce as she stared back at her.

Diane's lips thinned. She hated it when Rachel could so easily guess her intentions.

"Why can't you go to Merinus?" Diane asked rather than arguing. "She's David's mother, she can talk to him. If not Merinus, then Callan."

Rachel sniffed as she rubbed her hands over her face before starting back at Diane heavily. "Because I refuse to play tattletale on a child." She sighed wearily.

Diane had to laugh. "But, Rachel, it's children you're *supposed* to tattle on."

Her sister's lips almost twitched in amusement.

"Laugh, Diane." She sat up and it was then Diane saw the tears glittering in her eyes. "I'm not going to play the bitch mother and beg Merinus Lyons to please make her son stop being so mean to my baby."

Diane was confused now. She stared back at her sister, wondering what the real problem was here.

"I all but went to school with you for the first six years because the older kids liked to bully you," Diane reminded her sister fondly. "I yelled at teachers and I argued with principals. Then Uncle Colt came in, glared at them all and even visited their parents and all but threatened them. But what happened to stop it, Rachel?"

"This isn't school, Diane." She sighed. "Kicking the bully in the balls isn't going to fix this."

And oh how her baby sister had kicked the bully and left him crying. Diane loved that memory.

"No, it won't," she agreed reasonably. "But if you don't speak to Merinus, Callan or David, I don't care which, then I will."

Ignoring Rachel's scowl she laid the now-sleeping Amber back in the bed beside her mother.

"Let it go," her sister ordered.

"No. Find the cause and fix it, or I'll do it for you."

Diane shrugged, unconcerned with her sister's arguments. "And you know I will, Rachel. That's my niece and she's too young to have to endure a teenager's temperamental attitude. I won't have it."

"It's not that easy," Rachel whispered. "They're Breeds, not human children, Diane. Just as his father is. There's more involved than puberty or teenager temper."

"Bullshit." Diane was in her face, nose to nose, leaning over Amber and glaring in her sister's eyes, though she kept her tone soft, gentle, without a hint of anger or emotion that would awaken Amber. "It's that easy. You find David, you ask him what the fuck his problem is. You get to the bottom of it, or I swear to God I will."

Rachel's eyes widened at her sister's tone. "You're serious."

"Why so surprised, Rachel?" Diane asked between clenched teeth. "I protected you when you were little. I fought for you. Do you think there's a chance in hell I'd not do the same for your baby? My niece?" Diane reached out, touched the tears on her sister's face, wanting to cry herself. "Rachel, you're my sister. We've been through hell together, and I'd walk through hell for my niece. Don't you realize that?"

Rachel shook her head and Diane realized her sister feared the same things now that she had feared as a child. That her actions would hurt someone else she loved or somehow offend someone she respected.

"Jonas is a big boy and David's parents are reasonable adults," Diane told her sister gently. "Your mate is as alpha as his leader is. Does he even know what's going on?"

"Not fully," Rachel answered.

"Fix it, Rachel," Diane ordered as she leaned close and hugged her gently. "Fix it for Amber, or I'll do it for you."

Diane moved from the bed and headed for the window she'd used as an entrance.

"You're leaving, aren't you? To find the Roberts girl," Rachel whispered, a vein of fear filling her voice. "Alone."

Diane turned back slowly. "You have Jonas," she stated firmly, her voice low. "Your loyalty is to Jonas and his causes, and that's how it should be." She forestalled her sister's protest with a firm look and a quick raise of her hand. "I have my own battles to fight, Rachel. There are things I have to do and I can't do that if I'm shackled to your side, or locked inside Sanctuary."

"I don't want you to risk your life for us," Rachel cried suddenly, the softness of her voice made hoarse by her tears. "That's what you're doing, Diane, and I can't bear it. I'd die inside if anything happened to you because of us, because you feel you have to protect us."

Diane shook her head. "That's not what I'm doing, Rachel."

"It is." She heard her sister moving from the bed. "You're still chasing information on Brandenmore, aren't you? You're still trying to save Amber." Those tears were thicker in her voice now. "Trading your life for hers. That's why you won't accept Lawe—"

"No." Diane turned quickly, furiously. "I'm not his pet, Rachel. I'm not a child he can lock in a room for my own safety. I fight." It burned in her gut, it flamed through her mind. "I do what I need to because that's who I am. That's what I am. And he wants to take it from me."

That hurt. It broke her heart. It tore at something she wasn't even certain she recognized. It tore at her sense of justice and her sense of self.

"He wants you to be here for us," Rachel whispered, her voice hesitant and concerned.

"Even if I'll die confined, Rachel?" she asked painfully. "You always dreamed of a family, of a place to settle down and have babies. Jonas and Amber, they are your dream. This was what you always wanted." Moving to her sister she caught Rachel's hands and held them firmly, staring into her eyes, desperate to make her understand. "What about *my* dream? Did you ever ask yourself what my dream was or if I had the right to it?"

"You do it because of Mom and Dad and how they were killed. Uncle Colt convinced you—" Rachel cried. "That is why you fight."

Diane shook her head again. "No. I fight because that's my dream, Rachel. I don't want a jailer or a protector. I want a partner. I want someone who will let me fight when I need to fight and let me rest when I need to rest. I don't want to be told when I need to do either one because, trust me, I know what I need and I know when I need it. And what I don't need is to be handcuffed or locked away in Sanctuary where everyone is happy and satisfied because I'm safe." She wanted to cry with her sister. She wanted to howl at the pain for never being accepted for what she needed, yet always giving as much of herself as possible. "Rachel, let me be me," she whispered with a desperation she hadn't realized was trapped inside her. "If I can't be me, then there's no reason to even exist or to fight to live. Don't you understand that?"

Rachel's arms were suddenly around her, holding her tight as Diane wrapped her own arms around her sister comfortingly.

"I'm so sorry, Diane." Leaning back she stared up, allowing Diane to see the true regret in her eyes.

Diane swiped at her own tears. "I wish we could be kids again. That the innocence we once knew was still a part of us."

"But it is." Rachel's lips trembled as she tried to smile. "I see it in Amber. I see your eyes, Dad's grin, Mom's brows. I see the children we once were and I know the happiness I want for her. And I see everything Brandenmore could be stealing if his evil manages to take her away from us."

"I won't let that happen," Diane swore. "I'll find them, Rachel. I swear I will."

"Help me," Rachel whispered then, her lips trembling now. "Help save my baby, Diane." A silent sob shook her sister's fragile body. "I don't know if I could survive losing her."

Diane had to fight her own tears as they held on to each other; fear was eating at them while hope continued to burn inside them.

"I'll find Honor Roberts," Diane swore. "Whatever kept them alive, I'll do everything in my power to make certain Amber has it."

Rachel swiped at the tears on her face. "I know you will." She sniffed. "And I'll help you however I can."

"Just believe in me, Rachel," Diane requested painfully. "Don't help them tie me down. If we're truly sisters, believe in me as you did when we were children."

In her sister's eyes she saw the regret, the love, and the fear. The fear that had been there ever since Rachel first learned Diane was joining their uncle's team. That her sister would be risking her life in the line of fire.

"I'm sorry," Rachel whispered. "I stood with Jonas because I'm terrified of losing you. Of losing the only person I know besides Jonas who would face hell for me. But I'd face it for you too. I'd face anything to see you safe and knowing that safety isn't what you want terrifies me."

"I know." And she did.

"But safety would kill you faster than a bullet would," Rachel guessed.

It was the truth. It was the truest thing in Diane's life. She met her sister's gaze as they both blinked back tears.

"Then do what you have to do." Rachel released her then and stepped back with a tearful smile. "Do what you have to do, Diane. I'll never stand against you again."

That was an admission Diane knew wasn't easy for her sister.

"Thanks, Rachel," she whispered. "For being my sister. If you need me, if anything happens, I'll tell you where I'm going, if you swear to keep that secret to yourself."

She knew her sister. Rachel would make herself insane if she didn't know where Diane would be. And she knew Lawe would find her eventually, either way.

Leaning close, she whispered the information in her sister's ear, just in case Jonas had left an electronic listening device on the chance Diane slipped into the room.

Rachel nodded as Diane gave her one last hug before pulling away and forcing herself to leave.

Moving to the window Diane managed to shimmy through the narrow opening onto the ledge beyond before making her way across several window ledges to the corner and the drain pipe that followed the line of the building down more than twenty stories.

She knew Rachel was watching as she slid the gloves from her pockets and then clipped a metal latch hook to her belt and to the rope she had already prepared. Looping it around the metal pipe, Diane made her way to the ground below. Crouching, she moved quickly to the heavy shrubbery that decorated the lawn and led to the parking lot beyond.

It took only minutes to make her way to the Land Rover she'd had delivered for her journey. Slipping inside she breathed out roughly, started the vehicle and pulled out of the parking slot.

Leaving like this, without her men, without backup, was unfamiliar but strangely satisfying. She'd always fought with a safety net. There was no net now. Just her, her training and her instincts.

And her goal.

Saving her niece. And maybe she would prove to Lawe that she was strong enough to not just walk beside him, but to fight beside him. Without that acceptance, without her ability to do what she had to do, Diane knew, a part of her soul would die.

Then, she wouldn't be of use to anyone.

Especially a mate.

◆   ◆   ◆

Watching the vehicle pull away as the first rays of dawn began to stretch fragile light across the sky, Rachel breathed in deeply and made a decision she prayed she wouldn't regret.

She knew Diane, perhaps better than her sister liked. She had seen the pain in her eyes, heard it in her voice when she had sworn she would die if she couldn't fight. When she had whispered with aching hunger of the partner she needed.

And Rachel knew Lawe. The Breed cared for her sister. Hell, he loved Diane, he just wasn't ready to admit it. But, what he didn't realize was that he loved Diane because of exactly who and what she was, not for what he thought he wanted her to be.

If Rachel allowed Diane to go off on her own and, God forbid, she was harmed, then Lawe would never forgive her for not telling him where she was heading.

She would never forgive herself.

First, she had to figure out how to tell him without Diane feeling betrayed.

It took a while, but she had a plan.

Smiling, she showered, called the Feline Lioness who had taken the position of nanny and prepared to invade the meeting for which Jonas had left their bed.

Her sister was stubborn as hell and just as willful.

It would take careful maneuvering, of both Diane as well as Lawe, but Jonas had taught her quite a bit.

Rachel was extremely confident she could pull this off. That she could ensure the mating of her sister and the Breed commander. Rachel was determined to see that her sister had the life she dreamed of and the happiness she deserved.

✦ CHAPTER 7 ✦

Diane was late.

As Jonas filled in the alphas of the Prides and Packs, including the two who had traveled from Europe to represent the growing number of Breeds coming out of hiding there, Lawe felt his frown deepen.

It was three quarters after ten. She was late enough that if she wasn't there within the next quarter hour then he was going hunting for her.

He should have already done so, he thought impatiently as he felt the restless energy beginning to sizzle through his body. His instincts were that heightened, a sense of awareness prodding at him, warning him.

Something wasn't right.

Diane was never late. What had possessed him to allow Jonas to convince him that she was simply irritated with them all and making them wait for the hell of it.

That wasn't Diane's style.

He could feel the tension flooding his body, a warning that it wasn't right and he should go now, that he should head straight to her rooms and find her.

Her men had flown out hours earlier, each heading for a different area of the United States. Even Thor was gone.

She wouldn't go out alone—

The hell she wouldn't.

Why hadn't he seen the clues?

Straightening from the position he had taken against the wall, Lawe moved to leave the room and check on his too-independent mate.

He hadn't even taken that first step when a hard, demanding knock sounded on the door and the scent of Jonas's mate reach his senses.

Lawe's gaze moved to Jonas as a sudden knowledge flooded his system. Animal genetics surged to the forefront of his senses as he bit back a growl and forced himself to remain in place.

A Breed Enforcer moved to the door and opened it quickly. Rachel Wyatt swept into the room in a cloud of heated anger and resentment as she moved to her mate, the director of the Bureau of Breed Affairs.

Jonas turned to the door as the delicate figure of his mate entered the room.

Jonas's mated wife was lovely, compassionate and intelligent. With her quiet femininity and iron-strong will, she was the perfect counter for his icy, sharp-edged son. There was little Jonas managed to pull over on her, yet there was also little that she wouldn't forgive him.

Long, dark brown hair was pulled atop her head in a classic twist, thin-framed glasses perched on her nose as her gaze locked on her husband's. Her expression was tight, her lips thin and the scent of her anger drifted through the room like the scent of hot, rich sugar.

"Rachel?" The question in Jonas's tone, gently voiced and curious still had the power to surprise those who had only known the hard lash of his tongue before he found his mate.

As though the animal inside Jonas, always pacing restlessly, furiously, had suddenly found solace and a sudden, overwhelming peace. That peace descended over Jonas as his wife moved to him and took the hand he reached out to her.

"What have the two of you done to my sister?" she asked him, her voice low, her tone accusing and distressed as she stared up at her husband.

"Nothing as of yet," Jonas assured her as Lawe ignored the look of retaliation in the director's eyes. "Though I'm certain Lawe has a few things in mind."

Rachel gave a brief, less-than-feminine snort to the statement. "I rather doubt he's going to get the chance to do anything. Whatever you said to her last night, she packed and left before dawn this morning. I've missed my sister, Jonas, and you allowed him to run her off as though she were some criminal with no rights and no ability to choose her own fate. Since when was the decision made that a suspected mate should become a prisoner?"

She wasn't pleased. And her displeasure was centered more on him than on her mate, Lawe knew as he felt his own fury beginning to tighten through his system. The pain that pulsed and burned inside her reached out to slice at each man in the room, and to remind him of his basic responsibilities to his mate.

That of her happiness.

Lawe could feel the condemnation in each glance directed his way.

Then, Jonas turned and glared momentarily at Lawe for having the temerity to do anything to displease Diane and, in effect, displease her sister as well.

"The hell she has." Lawe fought to hold back the growl rumbling in his chest.

He knew he should never have left her alone. The night before, something had warned him not to take his eyes off her. Not to trust her. But he had never imagined she would dare attempt to leave without backup. Without her men. Especially after her capture and near death not so long ago.

Ignoring the looks Jonas and the others cast his way, Lawe quickly began trying to figure out which way she was heading and why.

The girl, Honor Roberts, no doubt, he thought furiously. Diane had no intention of letting it go or of allowing anyone else to take over the completion of that mission. Jonas could feel a growl building in his throat at the low rumble of anger that left Lawe's throat. As though he refused to believe Diane Broen would dare to leave without his permission. Even Jonas had expected this move, yet Lawe had done nothing to stop it.

The Breed was too certain of himself, too assured of his hold over Diane despite the lack of mating between them. It amazed Jonas. Where had his friend, the man he considered more intuitive than any other, disappeared?

"The hell she definitely has." Rachel crossed her arms over her breasts and turned to Lawe with narrowed, angry eyes. "I just talked to her a few hours ago, Lawe. Even I was unaware she was leaving until she slipped into my room to tell me. I watched her shimmy down the metal gutter twenty stories down as the sun rose, because it was easier to slip away from the goon squad you put on her. What did you do? Pull the big brave Breed act on her again?" She didn't bother to hide the sarcasm in her voice. "Didn't I warn you that you were going to frighten her away?" Unshed tears rasped her voice now and glittered in her eyes. "You can't chain her.

You can't force her to be some timid little pet. You're going to get her killed by forcing her to focus more on her fight for freedom than on protecting herself."

"She's going to get herself killed because of her own damned stubbornness," Lawe all but snarled as Jonas attempted to hide his wince.

That wasn't the response that should have come out of his mouth.

Rachel's brows lifted in derisive, angry surprise. "So she should just play the helpless little female for you like your other conquests do and let you go out and play all by yourself then?" A sharp laugh left her lips. "Really, Lawe, I thought you were smarter than that. Just because you gave up active military status for bureaucratic bullshit and the logistical planning you love, doesn't give you the right to imprison her."

Lawe glared back at her.

Jonas wondered if he should commiserate with his soon-to-be assistant director or kick his ass. He saw the way Lawe was staring at her, his eyes glittering with fury, and the look had a warning growl vibrating in Jonas's throat.

"Keep trying to protect her, Lawe," Rachel said painfully. "All you'll do is keep her running. And each time she runs she'll become harder to find and more determined to suffer the heat alone rather than attempt to make it work with you. She's worked too hard to give up her independence or to allow any man, especially a Breed, to control her. You'll only make her hate you."

"So I should allow her to continue to risk herself as though her life doesn't matter?" Lawe was furious, his icy blue eyes were snapping with anger as his expression tightened to a furious hardness, the impression of feline savagery intensifying.

"That, or learn how to fight beside her," she suggested with an inner pain so agonizing every Breed in the room felt it. Especially Jonas. He could feel it lashing at him, burning straight to his soul and searing him with his mate's tormented fears for her sister. "Because if you become the reason why I no longer see my sister, or my daughter grows up without her aunt, then I promise you, I will do everything in my power to make damn sure you pay for it."

Lawe growled, a low, deep rumble of such intense male confusion that if it weren't for Rachel's pain, the other Breeds in the room would have been more than amused at the sound.

"Rule!" Lawe snapped out his brother's name. "You're with me."

"Am I? I don't know if I want to go with you, Lawe," Rule stated from across the room. At the look of fury his brother directed his way, he sighed with weariness rather than his normal mockery. "Fine, but I think it would be in my best interests to stay here. This mating stuff is becoming contagious and I'd just as soon remain uninfected if it's all the same to you. Unlike you, I'm still avoiding the issue and doing my damnedest to remain free."

Lawe turned, and though Jonas couldn't see his expression any longer, he watched Rule sigh in resignation as a grimace tightened his face. "Fine. Fine," he groused. "But if I end up infected, I'm gonna kick your fucking ass and will do everything I can, every time I can, to make sure you're cock blocked."

Lawe swung back to Jonas. "I'll contact you when I've found her."

Pure Breed arrogance and a touch of male superiority filled his gaze and his voice. Jonas could have warned him then and there he was headed for trouble. But hell, he knew the other Breed wouldn't listen.

Some things, a Breed just had to learn for himself.

And the lessons Diane was getting ready to teach Lawe were those he would never forget.

As painful as those lessons might be, as certain Lawe was he had no need of them and would never bow to them, Jonas knew it would be an adventure Lawe would never want to miss.

After all, Diane was his mate. A perfect match, heart and soul, to the man he was. Could he have expected his mate to have been less of a warrior than he?

"Yeah, you do that," Jonas said with a snort as Lawe and his brother headed for the doors.

Lawe jerked one of the wide panels open, stalked through it and didn't look back. Rule followed more slowly and as he reached the door turned back to Rachel. "I'm certain you arranged this somehow," he stated knowingly, his gaze narrowing on her as Jonas caught a hint of some unknown emotion, a scent he didn't recognize. "I don't think it was very sporting of you, Rachel. I have problems of my own you know. I didn't need to borrow his."

As the door closed behind him, Jonas turned back to his mate and arched his brow at her in question as she leaned against the table and smiled complacently.

The anger was gone. She was still hurting, but Diane was her sister, a sister who constantly placed herself in danger for some reason, in battles that weren't hers, for men, women, children and creatures that would never offer the first word of thanks.

He was aware of the alphas behind him muttering, whispering and preparing to leave.

"What have you done?" he finally asked his mate, his voice low as he stared down at her in contemplation.

Rachel smiled sweetly, innocently. "Let's just say I've hedged my own bets where my sister is concerned. Let's just hope Lawe is smart enough to cash in the marker I just gave him, and he learns how to be my sister's partner rather than her jailer."

Ah, his little mate was far wilier than he gave her credit for, it seemed. And God knew, he gave her plenty of credit for that wily side of her nature.

"Playing games, sweetheart?" he asked in amusement, amazed as always that this perfect woman was his. That she loved him. That she was the woman God had created just for him, when his creators had told him that such a superior being would never claim him and would definitely never send such a ray of sunshine into his existence.

"And here you thought you were the master manipulator." She gave a low, light laugh as he lowered his head to rub his cheek against hers. "Darling, you may know your Breeds, but I know my sister," she whispered at his ear. "She'll have him bagged and tagged before they ever return to D.C. or Sanctuary. He'll be mated more firmly than any Breed you'll ever meet and loving every minute of it."

With that, she turned her head and pressed her lips to his cheek, bestowing a kiss of such warmth that each Breed in the room was suddenly longing for his own mate.

It wasn't a longing born of lust but a longing born of the gentleness and the sudden softening they glimpsed in the Breed they had once sworn had been created with a machine for a soul. A true, flesh-based robot.

As she stepped back moments later, her gaze was filled with warmth as she glanced out at the other men. A small grin tilted her lips.

"Where has she gone, sweetheart? Holding that information back isn't something you can do. And it's not debatable."

They had an understanding and he gave her the

phrase that indicated it wasn't a situation where she could deny him the information he needed.

"And you'll tell him, of course." She grimaced as she sighed heavily. "She's going to take him home, Jonas. Diane's heading to Window Rock. Right in the heart of his family, I believe."

Yes, it was.

The past, the present and the future were coming together and Jonas knew the pain of it would affect Lawe even more than Rachel could guess.

"Pride Leader Lyons?" Her tone was formally polite, causing Callan's brows to arch before his gaze narrowed.

Lifting a hand, he rose to his feet and indicated that his second-in-command, Kane Tyler, should follow him, then he moved to Rachel. Not that it would keep the others from hearing them speak, but her tone had warned him that facing the room with what she had to say could be uncomfortable for her.

"Rachel?" He stopped in front of them as Jonas watched his mate warily, suddenly certain she was prepared now to take his advice and to speak with Callan concerning their daughter.

Rachel lifted her chin and stared directly back at him. "I would prefer you speak to your son before I do." She kept her tone incredibly soft. So soft, that perhaps the others couldn't hear her after all. "The next time he frightens my child and shows the others his refusal to accept her by growling and snapping at her, I will take the matter up with his mother. At his age, he may prefer that any discussion of the problem come from you first."

Callan's brows lowered. "How long has this been going on?" he asked, careful to keep his tone below the anger level.

"As long as my daughter has been in Sanctuary," she informed him. "His refusal to accept her is affecting the other children, I believe." She quickly blinked her tears back. "This is the reason I no longer come to the main house when invited and no longer join activities with the other wives. I can't leave my daughter alone with them, Callan. Especially if David's in the house."

Callan was eerily silent. A muscle ticked at the side of his jaw, and for a moment, Jonas considered pulling his mate back from his alpha. Until Callan sliced a look of disapproval at him, as though sensing Jonas's thoughts.

"Forgive me for not seeing a problem existed, Rachel," Callan said softly. "And I do appreciate you bringing this to me, though Merinus will be contacting you soon, I'm certain. We'll discuss the matter with David before the three of us meet with you and your mate, if that's acceptable?"

Jonas felt Rachel's hand brush his. Twining his fingers with her delicate ones, he gave her the support she suddenly seemed to need as she realized the alpha of the Prides was perhaps much more understanding than she had believed.

"Thank you," she whispered. "I'm certain we can be available whenever you need us."

Callan glanced at Jonas once more. "Your mate is too good for you," he stated with an amused twitch to his lips. "And far more intuitive. You should have come to me sooner, Jonas."

"Don't blame him." Rachel shook her head. "He's stayed quiet at my request, Callan. I wanted to wait. I didn't want to cause strain at a time when I know other matters are far more important. But, Diane isn't near so patient I'm afraid. She made me do it."

Amusement at the almost childish proclamation drew a chuckle from Callan.

"I'll thank her personally when next I see her," he promised. "And thank you again."

Rather than kissing her cheek, shaking her hand, or any other form of touching that could have caused her discomfort, Callan instead lowered his head to hers and rubbed against it briefly.

The acceptance, respect and affection inherent in the gesture wasn't missed by Jonas or any other occupant in the room. From that day on, Rachel would always be considered a member of Callan's personal Pride, and his inner circle of family.

"Gentlemen." She nodded to the others gracefully as Callan stepped back. "I'll let you return to your meeting now. And if I were all of you, I would prepare for the fallout when they return."

She didn't explain the fallout, but she didn't need to. If they returned with the former Brandenmore victims, then it would be self-explanatory.

Without another word she walked gracefully from the room, nodding to the Breed guard who opened the doors and then closed them behind her.

Jonas turned back to the alphas who had deliberately found something else to watch.

All but Leo, the man biology named his father. Amber eyes watched him thoughtfully, his lips quirked with a hint of knowing amusement.

He'd watched each moment of the exchange and, Jonas suspected, heard far more than either he, Rachel or Callan wished. But his gaze had softened as his expression reflected a respect Jonas rarely saw in the other Breeds' gaze.

It was then that Leo nodded back at him before stating, in a tone that reflected surprising fondness, "I think she scares me."

Jonas sighed in resignation though his chest seemed to weaken with his love for her. "Yeah," he drawled. "I think that makes two of us."

· CHAPTER 8 ·

Gideon watched the window of the hotel room carefully through the scope of the rifle. The gold jewelry that Scott had been kind enough to keep in the safe had purchased the sniper rifle and highly sensitive scope from the black market contact he'd made years before, during one of his brief escapes from Brandenmore's labs.

It was an old-fashioned weapon, one powered by the ammunition loaded into it, rather than the kind that used a laser box for power before each shot.

The soft sizzle of the box powering up the laser rifles were easily detectable to most Breeds if they were within a certain distance. But even easier for them to discern were the two tiny pin lights at the side of the box. Those pin lights could be seen from miles away by a Breed's sensitive eyes.

This weapon, though, with its dull steel and the

shaded glass of the scope, was all but undetectable to Breeds or humans.

Until it was fired.

This weapon, unlike the laser-powered variety, was loud enough to alert even the densest of the human population that violence was being committed.

It couldn't be powered back to wound rather than kill or to burn rather than pierce. It couldn't be deflected by the reflector glass or comparable material. There were few things that could stand between a man and a bullet.

Or a woman and a bullet.

At the moment, the woman in question was sitting comfortably in the chair she had moved to the side of the bed, directly in front of the window. The curtains were open and gave him a clear line of fire as she propped slender, jean-clad legs on the low table in front of her. Scuffed boots looked worn and comfortable, as did the faded jeans and the sleeveless, snug camisole she wore.

And she was staring straight back at him, her gaze meeting his in the scope of the rifle, daring him to fire.

Gideon had to smile.

He was almost becoming fond of this woman after the past three months.

She had a backbone, a daring no other adversary he'd known possessed. She was bold, confrontational, and mysterious. And she was damned intelligent.

Intelligent enough to know she was being followed and cunning enough that she had almost lost him more than once. Gideon had never come so close to losing prey as he had this woman since he'd begun following her.

She was a damned fine adversary, and he had no doubt she would make some worthy man a damned fine lover.

If she survived the little game they were playing at the moment.

He almost envied the man that would share her bed. No doubt it would be the Breed whose scent he'd detected on her clothes when he slipped into her bedroom earlier.

That Breed would have a woman most men could only dream of having. A woman that would be his partner. She was one who would go into battle with him, soothe his soul, mend his wounds, and drive him crazy in bed once the danger was over.

She couldn't cook worth a damn, he'd heard one of her men say, but she commanded four powerful, territorial, less-than-courteous bastards who lived for war. Three of them followed her willingly, loyally.

The one who wasn't completely loyal still lived because Gideon had only managed to identify him in the past twenty-four hours. If he were still traveling with her, then Gideon would have already killed him. This woman deserved more than the traitor who had sold her to her uncle's enemies, she deserved more than the supposedly careless accidents used as attempts to get rid of her. Someone wanted her out of the game. They wanted to keep her from aiding her sister's mate in protecting her sister and her sister's child. According to the rumors swirling, now that she was so firmly aligned with the Breeds, someone wanted to ensure that if Colt Broen ever resurfaced there would be no one he could reach out to for assistance.

Someone was very frightened of the combination Diane Broen and her uncle represented. So frightened that once they realized she either didn't know where he or the Leo's home base was located, or was strong enough to keep her secrets, decided they were better off with her dead.

Alive, she represented a threat. A threat someone wasn't willing to take.

Gideon doubted she realized how often three of those men stood between her and laser fire. If any of them were there now, he had no doubt they would be standing between her and his rifle. As her uncle and her ex-lover had tried to stand between her and the enemies that followed. And they had paid for their efforts in blood.

She was alone now. She had left her men behind, just as he had suggested she do in the letter he had left for her in Argentina. At the time, Gideon hadn't yet uncovered the identity of the traitor on her team.

Now, he knew. He knew who had been the cause of her lover's death, who had betrayed her uncle, and who had betrayed her.

For what? For a secret her parents had taken to the grave with them. The secret of the location of the Lion's Den, the home of the first Leo.

She had sent them all home, three of them wounded by Gideon's bullets. At the time, there had been only one Gideon was certain she could trust. It was only in the past twenty-four hours that the traitor had shown his hand and Gideon had identified him. That one was a danger to her. The bullets Gideon had used to take the three he suspected out of the game had been a warning to each that they had struck, and it was one the bastard had best heed. Neither man nor Breed could serve two masters, and that one was making the possibly fatal mistake of attempting to do so.

Still, she intrigued him.

She'd surprised him with the answer she'd left him in reply to his warning in Argentina.

Come out and prove my enemy is near. Stalking me is only pissing me off. I much prefer to talk rather than continue looking over my shoulder. If what I

*suspect is true, we're working toward the same goal.
Combining our efforts would be far more effective.*

And now, she was giving him the perfect opportunity to discuss whatever he pleased with her. She had given him similar opportunities after running from the Breed who was determined to claim her.

Too bad he wanted only to use her, just as the traitor within her group did. He had no intention of identifying himself to her. He would only follow her to the prize for which she searched, and he would ensure he possessed it before she could take possession of it.

None of that changed the fact that Diane Broen confused the hell out of him though.

She was an enigma to Gideon, but she wasn't a fascination. It wasn't this woman who hardened his dick when he thought of her. The Breed whose dick she did harden would be here soon, though.

Gideon knew he was only perhaps hours ahead of the Breed following her. And that Breed was pissed. Lawe Justice had roared his rage the second he'd left the Bureau of Breed Affairs and stomped to the black SUV awaiting him outside the Bureau.

Gideon had watched him from the shadows across the street, and his gaze narrowed, wondering if he should chance a grin as the Breed stopped and stared toward the area where Gideon had hidden himself.

As though Commander Justice knew he was watched. Knew, and knew the direction from which it came. Like the woman, he would make a fine adversary, but a much more dangerous one if Gideon dared to attempt to harm her.

Unfortunately, they just may become enemies if she threatened to step between him and his quarry, rather than leading him to her. Gideon couldn't allow that.

And he had a feeling the Breed wouldn't be able to keep her from doing it.

It was regrettable that Gideon needed her to draw Judd, Fawn, and Honor from their chosen identities.

Unfortunately for the Enforcer, though, he'd been delayed in his quest for a while. A flat on the SUV before he cleared the block. That was a stroke of genius and luck, Gideon thought. The nail that had pierced the tire had been put in place the moment the call came down to the garage for the SUV.

Gideon had taken the call, prepared the vehicle, then slipped out to prepare the area for the small projectile.

He'd found it incredibly amusing that he'd been able to slip into the garage of the Bureau so easily. He'd not been able to get any farther, into the bureau's offices, nor had he been able to sneak a weapon inside. The sensors were too sensitive and impervious to sabotage.

But he had gotten close enough to determine the vehicle Lawe Justice had called down for. Close enough that the garage attendant had tossed him the keys, believing him to be a fill-in for the Breed who'd called in ill.

Duplicating the security badge had been a bitch. It had taken more than twelve hours straight to prepare one that would fool the sensors as well as the guards and the garage attendant.

Luck.

Luck had been on his side for a minute.

The young woman centered in the scope arched her brow curiously as though questioning his inattention to her. His delay in pulling the trigger.

Daring him.

When she dared her mate in the same way, she would learn the consequences of such impulsive foolishness, he thought with an edge of regret. A shame, really, that she had already been marked by the Breed's scent.

If times were different, if he were the Breed he had been at nineteen, or hell, even twenty-seven when he had been recaptured by the soldiers from the Brandenmore labs. Even then, he'd had hope; he'd remembered what it was like to laugh, to lust, to dream of freedom.

If he were still that Breed, then he would see if a mate could be charmed from her mate.

Once, he could have accomplished that goal, he thought. Or he would have at least had a chance. He would have given it a hell of a try, and had a considerable amount of fun in the attempt.

The woman in the view yawned as though bored and tired of waiting. She gave a little shake of her head and a chiding smile, as though she were berating him for merely watching her rather than confronting her.

What made her believe he would ever confront her?

What made her imagine he would pull the trigger?

He caressed it. His finger stroking over it as he would a lovers flesh as her lips quirked just a bit at the corner as though in a grin.

"Live by the sword and you'll die by the sword, my uncle always said," she had commented with a laugh as she had walked with her men days before from the airport in D.C. The Swede who walked with her had shaken his head at her response to his advice that she should proceed with care once they met with Director Wyatt.

She hadn't heeded his advice. Instead, she had sworn to him that she would find the three they had been sent to collect and she would regret her actions later. This job, she had claimed, was too important. Her niece was too important for her to fail.

She would find all of them once she found Ms. Roberts. They would be with her, Gideon knew, and this woman would attempt to take them back to the Breeds to perform more tests. More brutal treatments.

A knife slicing through flesh just to see what hurt the most.

Gideon knew what they would see, though. He wouldn't allow it. He hated the woman he was after more than he hated any scientists he had encountered. But even for her crimes, admittedly, a crime a child had committed. As terrible as it had been though, he wouldn't allow that brutality to happen to her.

Ms. Broen was moving into the area where his prey was suspected to be located. Moving in to take from him the vengeance he'd lived and breathed for far too many years.

He couldn't allow it.

He wouldn't allow it.

He'd waited too long, fought for too long. And he wouldn't be cheated of it now that the end was so near.

His sanity depended on keeping the vow he had made to himself so long ago.

He knew the general area where they were, and he'd given this woman the location. She would get there before he did, but, he would be close, and he would be watching. And once she found the prey, he would be there to steal it from her. If he remembered Judd, and he did, then he knew that the girls would be very well hidden. Very well protected.

Perhaps even sharing his bed.

He had to force back a roar of rage as he focused on the woman once again. Focused on what he knew rather than what he suspected.

He knew once Commander Justice arrived, Justice would be distracted by the past that would haunt him there in the form of the family his birth mother had been taken from.

The same family that had aided Judd and Fawn after Gideon had disappeared into the darkness on the night of their escape.

Terran Martinez had arrived, just as Judd had said he would. An arrangement Scott Connelly appeared to have been a part of. Because Fawn was his daughter.

His teeth clenched as a growl escaped before he could bite it back. He wouldn't accept that. He couldn't accept it.

He frowned and glared through the scope as the woman arched her brow imperiously.

Oh yes, she knew he was there. Watching. Waiting. She wasn't daring him to pull the trigger, she was daring him to take what they were both after.

"Good night." Did she speak the words or simply allow her lips to form the shape of them?

Regardless, she rose from the chair and strode to the curtains, which she pulled closed with a jerk, shutting out his view of her and leaving nothing to chance. She tucked the bottom edges of the curtains into the window frame, ensured there were no cracks an assassin could use to target her, then turned off the lights to the room.

Gideon sighed at the loss. There were times in the past three days as he followed her, that he hadn't felt so alone in this quest. He had felt that someone, who might even understand his desperation, was there with him. Her battle to save her niece was a noble one. And one he understood. Unfortunately, it was also one she could possibly lose.

She was unique, even to him, and learning more about her would be imperative before he struck to take the prize she would find for him. He didn't kill innocents.

Even the medical assistants in the Brandenmore labs had been spared. He hadn't held them responsible for the horrors suffered there. They had fought on many occasions to ease the agony or delay the tests, to allow him a chance to recover before they were repeated.

Several had conspired to aid his escape more than once, only to fail. One had died in the attempt. Another had died when they were caught attempting to ease Judd's pain. It was their lives or the orders they were given. Gideon never held it against them when they reluctantly followed those orders.

Diane Broen, like those assistants, was innocent of the crimes he found punishable. There was no cruelty in her. Unlike many, though, there was a fierce, burning need to survive and to protect those she loved. Though there were very few she loved. Her sister, her niece. Of the four men she fought with, he saw loyalty from her; he didn't see love.

With the Swede, though, he saw friendship, respect. Yet, he knew she would die to protect any of them. They were her responsibility, and therefore, under her protection.

Sighing briefly, he lowered the weapon and waited, carefully gauging the darkness and the shadows before moving. There had been other eyes watching her until he'd put a stop to it. The Coyote Breeds employed by the research scientists still attempting to carry on the Brandenmore legacy had tracked her as far as Tennessee before he'd had enough and cut their throats.

They had sent a two-man team to follow her. Their orders were, when and if she found the Bengal who had escaped nearly twelve years before or the two girls, they were to take them before the Bureau of Breed Affairs could move in to protect them.

Gideon had taken care of them instead. This woman

he would allow to live, but those Coyotes had deserved only death.

He would allow no other adversary to track or to attempt to harm his prey or the warrior woman tracking them. That was his prerogative alone.

His teeth bared at the thought of it.

The memory of copper-rich blood flowing over his hands sharpened his senses and had a growl threatening to rumble in his throat.

Not yet, he told himself as he broke the weapon down to its individual parts and stored it in the case next to him. Then he donned the hat he had worn earlier. A beaten, stained cowboy hat that shadowed the mark on his face and went with the scuffed-up boots he'd stolen along with it. The scent on the clothing would keep any Breeds from accidentally figuring out that the individual they might pass had no scent of his own.

It was becoming a hassle, that lack of scent. It was an immediate alarm to any Breed who detected it. It required Gideon steal used, worn clothing rather than the nice, new clothing he would have preferred.

His prey would pay for that as well, he promised himself as he picked up the case and began moving quickly to the path that led down from the rise across from the hotel and back to the parking lot.

He was moving past the pickup he had bought days before when he almost stiffened, almost gave himself away. The vehicle pulling in and crossing his path was far too familiar for him to be comfortable.

Keeping his pace, he moved across the blacktop to the metal stairs that led to the third floor and the room he'd taken two doors down from Ms. Broen's. He'd actually taken two rooms: the one he entered and the one that sat between him and his quarry.

The rooms, connecting as they were by two inner

doors, had made it possible for him to slip into her room and position the three electronic listening devices he'd put together leaving D.C. He wasn't seen entering her room from the cameras outside, nor by anyone who may have slipped by his notice to watch her.

Two of those devices, she had found immediately. He had to give her credit for it because he had actually attempted to keep that from happening this time. The third, he believed, would remain hidden, undetectable by either the Breed detectors or the ones John Thorsson, the man the woman called Thor, tinkered with to pick up the homemade or "silent" listening devices, which could record in deactivated mode for short periods of time.

Gideon was counting on that listening device to give him the current identity of the young woman he was searching for as well as the Breed protecting her. He would have to work past the Bengal Breed he had only known as Judd to gain his revenge.

They were the same age, he and Judd. They had, for a short time, shared the same cells, the same tests, the same hell.

Then, the termination order had come through on them all. They had escaped during transport to the termination facility. Somehow, Judd had managed to free himself before Gideon had and overpowered the guard in the back of the van. Gideon had gone after the driver, but the bastard had managed to flip the van, causing the incisions from an exploratory entrance into Gideon's side to reopen and begin spilling blood.

He could have died then. He'd prayed for death often enough that he hadn't cared if he died. Hell, he would have welcomed it with open arms.

She had cared though.

Gritting his teeth, Gideon fought back the memory. She had cared to see him living, to see him tortured further. To see his hell extended in ways none of them could have envisioned.

He found it strange that Judd hadn't told him who had aided them by slipping the other Breed the keys to his chains. Gideon had always wondered how Judd had managed to gain his freedom, but his injuries and the result of Judd and the girl's attempts to save him hadn't allowed for a question-and-answer session.

Gideon's fists clenched as he moved to the window, standing to the side to gaze through the narrow crack at the side of the curtain. There he watched as the doors swung open on the black SUV and Lawe Justice and his brother, Rule Breaker, stepped from the interior to gaze up at the room Ms. Broen had taken.

Two other vehicles pulled in on each side, both similar to the one Justice and his brother were in. There were three Enforcers in each of those vehicles, a total of six to complete the eight-man team commanded by Justice and his brother.

Ms. Broen's Breed was taking no chances with her safety. Seeing them, though, recognizing the threat they represented forced a growl from his throat. He'd known they would arrive soon, but the complication and the animal that threatened to overtake him sent a punch of adrenaline and feral fury surging through him.

They dared to attempt to get in his way? To attempt to steal the only solace he had, the only hope he had of finding the girl and gaining his vengeance? He wouldn't allow it.

He would kill them all before he would allow them to steal all he had worked for or the only chance he would ever have at finding peace.

Lawe moved up the steps while Rule held back, staying close to the SUV. Gideon stepped to the table where the small receiver and headphones were set up.

The commander, Lawe Justice, was known to be the right hand of the director of the Bureau of Breed Affairs. If the director knew something, then Commander Justice knew it. He was curious as to what information could be gleaned in this meeting. Or if the woman inside the room would kick the Breed out as quickly as he had entered.

He'd known Justice would follow the little female mercenary. There was a scent on her that he had left. It wasn't mating heat, and it wasn't that brand of ownership male Breeds placed on their mated females. Still, though, it was a scent that warned other male Breeds away. One that lingered on her and assured a Breed that touching her would be territorial invasion.

The primal genetics that were so much a part of Gideon had drawn back in discomfort, uncertain about nearing the female any farther than he had when he'd brushed against her at the airport the other night.

Justice hadn't mated her.

He'd done something far, far more primal.

Lawe Justice had somehow managed to mark her with just enough of his scent to ensure that any other Breed recognized his intent to mate her. She belonged to a powerful, dangerous primal being.

A Breed who would kill to keep what he had marked as his.

✦　✦　✦

Lawe unlocked the door and eased it open. Slowly, he stepped into the hotel room Diane had taken for the night and glanced around the small room.

The sound of the shower running and the soft scent of her wafting from the bathroom assured him she was currently standing beneath the running water rather than watching from some shadowy corner, waiting to spring a trap.

She was actually damned good at that. She was as quiet as any Breed, just as capable and, when needed, just as merciless. She lacked only their strength. Their strength and their ability to call upon the DNA that added the extra surge of power, the rush of adrenaline infused with a feral hormone, which added to their strength and their lack of mercy.

The scent of her, beyond the artificial soy and almond scent of her soap and shampoos, reached out to him, causing him to close his eyes as a grimace of hunger pulsed in the engorged iron-hard length of his dick.

God, he swore her scent was that of peace, of solace. Whenever she was near he could feel those qualities attempting to slip past his guard.

The scent of her was like a beacon. She smelled of a spring rain and summer heat, which pierced him with a bolt of pure lust that tightened his balls and filled his cock with a furious, burning sexual need.

She smelled of promises, and only God knew how he figured that one. It was a scent he couldn't pin down, one that filled with warmth that went beyond lust and had his arms aching to hold her.

Just hold her.

To find and give comfort.

Comfort was another quality he'd never truly known and had no idea how he managed to identify it.

As he turned the dead bolt on the door, the bathroom door opened and a rush of steam spilled into the room. Before Lawe could draw in a breath, Diane stepped out and for a few precious seconds stole any chance he had of breathing.

Water beaded on her shoulders. A small rivulet

coursed across her collarbone. Beneath the towel, her legs shimmered with a satiny smoothness that bespoke regular visits to salons for exfoliation. There were no razor marks, no redness from waxing. She was particular when it came to her body. She was rounded but toned, healthy but without the current fixation on being skinny.

She was, to the male and to the animal, perfection.

Arousal hit him instantly, throwing his senses into chaos as her soft freshness lanced through his control. He'd never imagined there was a break in the shields that kept emotion from weakening the formidable drive and determination he'd once had to never feel for another being.

In that instant, he learned differently. He felt those emotions tearing through him, rushing his senses and throwing his beliefs to the wind. And for a second—for one unbelievable second—he imagined fighting at her side, sharing their triumphs and hearing her laughter at their successes.

A growl rumbled in his chest, hoarse and unbidden as he fought to keep from crossing the room and jerking her to him. To keep from taking what he so desperately needed her to give him.

◆　◆　◆

Diane froze as she reentered the bedroom. A flush mounted her cheekbones, filled her gaze. She could feel the warmth washing up her face before increasing to pure flaming heat and rushing south to send a surge of sensation burning through her pussy. At the same time, her chest clenched, emotion swamped her and the saddened realization that she could have him or her freedom burned like a blaze through her mind.

Oh Lord. She didn't need this. She didn't need the emotion. She didn't need something else, or someone else, to lose. And with Lawe, there was no other course. She could have the man she longed for, or the freedom that was the same as the air she breathed.

Her thighs clenched as her clit began to ache, her vagina spilling the heated, slick moisture that made her pussy feel swollen, her clit more sensitive.

The arousal that tormented her whenever she thought of him kicked into overdrive.

But she didn't have to think of him now, her aroused, overheated body screamed. He was here. He was aroused. There for the taking. Ready. Willing.

A silent groan and that tingling urge to rub against him had her juices gathering further, easing past the swollen folds of her pussy to dampen her thighs as well.

Diane could feel her body softening, her thighs weakening. She tightened her grip on the towel. Her fingers clenched in the material between her breasts, holding on to it as though it were all that was holding back that insane need to touch him.

To be touched by him.

How did he do it to her? How did he make her feel so vulnerable and needy? How did he make her want him so desperately when she hadn't ached for a man in years? She had never ached for anyone like this, she realized. For that "something," that ethereal promise of "more." That satisfaction, satiation and pure contentment she'd seen in other women who had mated with Breed males and found their fulfillment.

Her sister. Lyra Jordan. Megan Arness. Merinus Lyons. Faith Arlington, and even Storme McKenzie and Ria Warrant. Strong, vital mates to arrogant, dominant and yet loving Breed males who had accepted their mates were more than vessels to continue the Breed legacy, or porcelain dolls that needed to be smothered with protection.

Here was a really good one. Why the hell was she so willing to throw away her pride and her independence for a momentary pleasure? Why, in that second, did she suddenly wish she were less independent and more like her sister, Rachel, just to please the brooding, somber Breed standing before her.

He made her dream. That small voice, so filled with hope, whispered inside her as the memories of all she had lost over the years rose to torment her.

He made her dream honest-to-God vivid-color dreams of a future colored in more than blood. She had begun dreaming of a man that the woman, the part of her that was a warrior and the part that was still a frightened little girl desperate to find control and freedom, could hold on to. Hold on to and still be herself.

"Why are you here?" she forced the words past her lips, forced herself to ask the question rather than moving to him and begging him to fuck her.

Or to allow her to fuck him.

Whichever could be achieved and her orgasm reached in the quickest amount of time.

Instead, she filled her tone with irritation to add to the unwelcome glare that she forced to crease her expression.

"Why are you *here*?" he repeated the question with a heavy emphasis on her location. "You were not told to resume this mission."

The wrong thing to say and he knew it the moment the words passed his lips. Unfortunately, there was no way to call them back.

Diane smiled back at him sweetly as she stepped across the room, and Lawe couldn't help but watch her warily. She was damned well trained and quick as hell and he knew it.

But she didn't move for him. Attacking him obviously wasn't on the agenda tonight. At least, not yet.

Watching him warily Diane moved past the bottom of the bed, keeping her gaze on him, her body tense and ready to run as she moved to the backpack lying on the mattress.

One hand stayed knotted in the towel covering her. If wishes alone could rip it from her body, then it would have already been lying on the ground in shreds.

Nearly holding his breath he watched, his gaze centered where she held the towel securely. He wished it from her body, every muscle in his body tensing as he willed her to drop the material and give him a glimpse of that perfect, beautiful flesh.

The head of his dick throbbed, pounding furiously beneath the material of his jeans as he felt his balls drawing tight to the base of the thickened shaft in the need for release. Just beneath the engorged crown of his erection, the flesh seemed to stretch tighter, hotter as it pulsed in need.

The barb was there, stretching just enough to assure him of its presence. To assure him that this woman was indeed his mate.

Beneath his tongue the glands that held the mating hormone was swollen as it throbbed, ached. The need to push his tongue into her mouth and demand she engage in the sensual, heated kiss that would spill the hormone to her senses, was overwhelming.

"Stop looking at me like that." The demand was made as the scent of her arousal began to intoxicate him, to fill his senses and the glands beneath his tongue with the mating hormone.

The confrontation she seemed determined to initiate wasn't helping, and neither was the fact that those were clothes she was pulling from her bag.

Yoga pants, a T-shirt, panties that were little more than a triangle of silk.

Gripping the clothing in one hand, keeping her death grip on the towel with the other, she moved to skirt around the bottom of the bed and, Lawe knew, to return to the bathroom to dress.

He stepped in her way, blocking her escape as effectively as steel bars as he ensured she would have to make close, personal, intimate contact with his body to get by him.

She stared back at him warily as she paused at the bottom of the bed.

"That's the hell of it where these little rooms are concerned." He glanced around the small cheap hotel room as he allowed a rueful grin to tug at his lips. "Two people can't move around it at the same time without brushing or even stroking against one another. Whereas the more expensive suites that most Breeds prefer have plenty of room to move around and avoid contact, if that's what they wish."

As he spoke, he crouched down, one knee on the floor and the other bent as he loosened the laces of the combat ankle boots he wore.

She eyed him warily now, a hint of desperation filling her gaze as he shifted to the other boot, loosened it, then straightened and pulled each off.

"What the hell are you doing?" she gasped out, knowing full well exactly what he was doing. And her body knew. She could feel her sex growing wetter, hotter, flushing the sensitive folds and causing her clit to swell tighter.

"You ran from me, Diane," he growled as he pulled the thin, black temperature control socks from his feet. Then his hands moved to the utility belt of his pants, his fingers working it loose.

Breeds had different growls for different emotions: irritation, aggravation, an angry growl, a furious growl.

And then there was this growl. It rumbled deep with lazy, hungry intent. This one echoed through her nerve endings and caused her vagina to clench as she swore the sound echoed in her tender depths.

"And I'll run away from you again." She swallowed tightly as she defied him, nervously, her grip on the towel tightening until her knuckles turned white. "I'm not your puppet, Lawe."

"You're my mate." He heard the growl in his own voice, hated himself for the primal dominance that vibrated in his voice.

"I'm not yours to control nor did you purchase a shining new toy you can sit on the shelf until you decide to play with it."

If her pussy wasn't heated, flowing with the sweet, soft juices he was dying to taste, then Lawe might have paid attention to that hint of desperation in her voice. The apparent fear of his touch, of the mating heat, and he would have forced himself to turn away.

It wasn't fear despite the appearance of it, though. He smelled desperation, hunger, confusion. She wanted him; she ached for him with the same clawing hunger that he ached for her and that was all the animal rising inside him recognized.

They were dying for each other, yet she thought she could run and he wouldn't give chase?

The animal DNA inside him demanded he do just that. That he give chase. That he become the hunter, the dominant force that would bind her to him.

What made her believe she could place herself in danger and he wouldn't stand in front of her? That he wouldn't protect her with every last ounce of strength that he possessed? That he wouldn't give his life and the life of every Breed ever created to see to her safety, to the continuation of *her*.

"Placing you on a shelf is the last thing I want to do, sweetheart," he promised silkily. "But playing with you is definitely in the cards."

Rather than removing his jeans after the belt loosened, Lawe shrugged the thin jacket from his shoulders, then tugged the black sleeveless shirt from his body and tossed it aside.

Her little tongue, pink and tempting, reached out to flicker over her lips.

The gleam of moisture on the sensual lower curve had his balls clenching, the need to take her pounding through him.

He was so hard he could barely stand to breathe as he unsnapped the metal tabs of the jeans and, as she watched, stripped them from his body.

"Did you think you could run from me without consequences, mate? I'm a fucking Breed. Run and I *will* give chase. Challenge me, Diane, and I *will* accept it. Do you see me as some poor castrated animal you can control so easily?"

"Castrated?" Her gaze flickered to his erection. "Not really. But I've been assured by Jonas several times that you're really quite domesticated. Do you purr on command, Lawe? Or does only Jonas have the power to give that order?"

She was insane, Diane decided, certifiable. Her uncle had made that prediction more than once during the years before his death.

He was obviously right. Only a crazy person dared to manipulate a Breed in such a way, no matter how harmless it was.

But both Lawe and Jonas deserved every moment of it.

Jonas for daring to play his games with her, and she knew he had been. She hadn't figured out how, but she knew him for the calculating, manipulating monster he was when it came to ensuring every capable Breed mated.

And Lawe, for making her feel. For making her want. For refusing to be a partner and a lover.

She didn't want or need either to feel the emotions tearing her apart or to ache with such need for any one man. She hadn't asked him to step into her life and throw all her beliefs and the life she'd resigned herself to into chaos. And she sure as hell hadn't asked her brother-in-law to help him. She'd begged Jonas for a way to make Lawe understand how it would never work to pressure her into giving up the life that made her feel valued. Instead, he'd suggested she resign herself to giving it up.

He'd warned her about yanking Lawe's chain more than once.

He had warned her that Lawe was not a domesticated housecat but a fully trained Lion Breed in his prime.

Just as he had warned her that Lawe didn't take orders worth a damn and he sure as hell didn't purr on command.

And the last warning had been that the animal Lawe shared his skin with would one day overcome his determination to hold it back, and it would take the mate it sensed waiting.

If the look on Lawe's face and his stiff, jutting erection were anything to go by, the animal and the man were pretty much in agreement that it was the time to claim the mate and they were prepared to prove it.

Icy blue eyes flared, then darkened, as his expression tightened and primal dominance suddenly marked it.

This was it.

They had been dancing around each other for more than a year now, deliberately easing in, then pulling back at the slightest hint of emotion, only to be drawn back again.

She'd teased, and she'd forgotten the warnings Jonas had given her.

She'd run from him, fighting to escape what she'd sensed was the inevitable. Jonas had warned her about running. He'd warned her about the predator living inside Lawe, the dominant animal that would move heaven and hell, kill or risk being killed, to possess his mate. And he would give her whatever she needed, whatever he knew instinctively she had to have, just to be happy.

For more than a year he had stayed away. He'd ignored the hunger, just as she had. He had ignored the need and let her run from all the emotions she couldn't handle, and the knowledge that accepting him meant accepting the cage he would build around her.

Had he somehow sensed the monsters that rose up to slash at her emotions each time she'd fought to escape him, because he'd always let her go. Or had he been concerned with his own monsters and the battle to slip past them instead?

Whichever it was, he'd obviously decided it was time to do something about the hunger clawing through both of them.

Diane exhaled in a breath of surprise as Lawe moved for her, catching her around the waist as she turned to evade him. Gripping her hips, he jerked her back, bringing her ass against the hardened length of his cock as he pressed against her, firm and dominant, the stiff stalk of his erection rubbing against the cleft of her ass.

And she couldn't keep from pressing back, from feeling him, heated and poker hard. She could feel him against her from her shoulder to her thighs. She could feel the rasp of his flesh, feel those tiny, tiny, almost invisible hairs that covered him from shoulders to ankles like a pelt of roughened silk.

"Living dangerously, baby?" He nipped at the lobe of her ear as her hands fell to his wrists, her grip desperate as she fought to push back the desire, or the fear. She had to let one go because he obviously wasn't going to allow her to let *him* go.

The desire wasn't budging from its position, it was only growing. The fear was holding on with bloody fingernails and faltering further beneath his touch as she felt the incredible, sexual heat sizzling up her spine.

"Scared, little wildcat?" he whispered against her ear, the warmth of his breath a caress against the sensitive shell of her ear.

"Of you?" The bravado in her tone was at odds with the vulnerability she felt, not to mention the inferno of lust building in her womb. "I think you know better than that, Lawe."

Even as she denied that charge, Diane knew it for the lie it was. A soft exhalation parted her lips as his fingers tightened, his nails rasping over the skin of her hips as he pressed against her more firmly, grinding his cock harder against the cleft of her rear.

Pleasure whipped across her nerve endings, sending sharp flares of sensation rushing through her system.

Fear fell back as the warmth of his body seemed to penetrate the chill that wrapped around her earlier. But it wasn't gone. She wondered if it would ever go away entirely.

A shudder raced through her with the touch of his tongue, like a roughened rasp against the sensitive flesh just beneath her ear. In that second, the fear was gone and pleasure overshadowed every nightmare that had ever chased her.

Need was a sharp-toothed demon tearing at Lawe's

cock, but even that couldn't hold back the animal senses that drew in the scent of his mate's desire, the heat of her need, and the chill of her fears easing away beneath the onslaught of pleasure.

He felt the animal genetics rising to the fore inside him. Each Breed carried the genetics of the animal he possessed. Some carried their animals closer to the skin than others, and for some the animal instincts were impossible to control when mating heat rose and sank its claws deep inside the primal alpha-male core of his psyche.

The need for her was tearing through him. He tried to control it. He fought it. But in that moment, Lawe knew he had lost the battle.

Pulling her around, his fingers burrowed in the back of her hair. Gripping the strands, he tugged her head back and before he could think or consider his actions, his head lowered and his lips covered hers as instinct had him pushing his tongue between her lips and burying it in the heat of her mouth.

Finding her tongue he rubbed against it, feeling the glands beneath his as they began to swell and throb further, pumping the spicy heat of the mating hormone suddenly spilling from him into the woman the animal inside had chosen as his mate.

Lawe had heard of the animal part of a Breed male taking over. How it rose to the forefront of desire as the mating hormone began spilling from the glands to mix with the adrenaline, the hunger and the lust coursing through him and into his mate.

Now, kissing Diane, touching her, Lawe felt the exquisite bite of a need unlike anything he had ever known in his life. A pleasure he realized he didn't want to miss, not anymore. That empty hole in his soul had disappeared. That dark, bitter, unknown pain that always lingered inside him had been easing away since the moment he realized what she was to him.

Holding her head in place with one hand, he used the other to caress the soft, heated flesh of her lower back, then along the rise of her buttocks.

Diane lifted against him, arching, a small whimpering moan leaving her throat as he felt her hands press against his chest, her fingers curling, nails rasping.

He was burning for her. The tiny hairs that covered his body seemed so sensitive, so brutally alive as she stroked against him that he swore they were directly attached to his nerve endings.

Hunger clawed at him. A sexual hunger impossible to deny, creating an urgent, intense wave of lust that had him only distantly aware of his actions.

Diane whimpered as the heated, unique taste of him spilled to her tongue, her senses and, she swore, her soul.

Spicy, sweet, like candied pears. The taste of his kiss was spiked with the most addictive elixir. The taste seemed to permeate every corner of her awareness.

And it made her hungrier. Made the need so sharp and intense she could only whimper in distress as it struck repeatedly at her clit, at the tender depths of her pussy.

Jerking his head back with another animalistic growl, Lawe tensed, the hard ridge of his cock throbbing imperatively. Still immersed in his kiss, Diane let her hand travel down his bare chest, his abs, until she was running her palm along the heated ridge of the heavy erection.

"God, Diane." He palmed the back of her head as she pressed her lips to his chest, allowing herself a taste of the hard flesh that covered the tight, flexing muscle.

"You're going to push me too far." His voice was so rough it was animalistic, sending a wave of sensual pleasure rushing through her.

"It's okay for you to push me?" Diane whispered against his sensitive skin before her tongue licked out to taste him once again.

She had to press her thighs together, the muscles tightening convulsively at the sight of the heavy flesh strained out from his body.

She couldn't help herself.

She'd fantasized about him for so long. Since the night he had rushed into a Syrian camp where she had been held by her kidnappers, her leg broken, her face swollen, her collarbone fractured from the beatings she had endured.

She had taken one look at the savage features of a Breed she didn't know from Adam, and for the first time in far too many years, she had been more than a soldier. More than a hired gun.

Bloody, in pain, certain she was going to die, and for one heart-stopping, irrational moment, she had been a woman and had wished she'd met him at time when she had a makeup bag handy.

A nice dress.

Heels.

And she had never worn any of the three since high school. She hadn't found a chance to.

Now, with her tongue flicking over the salty male flesh, the heavy length of his erection throbbing beneath her fingers as she stroked along the thick shaft, that need was there again.

The need to be a woman.

To be Lawe's woman.

It had always been there, but as the taste of candied

pears filled her system, it amplified, bombarding her system with need.

"Sweet, sweet Diane." He groaned, his hands fisting in her hair. "I've dreamed of touching you. Dreamed of fucking you."

A moan whispered past her lips.

"I dreamed of having your lips on my dick, watching as I fuck your mouth, stretching your pretty lips."

Her gaze jerked up, meeting his as his fingers tightened farther and began pushing her down. "Give it to me, baby. Give me your pretty lips. Wrap them around my dick as I've dreamed . . ."

Pressing her forward, pushing her to her knees Lawe watched as Diane licked her lips, parted them and leaned forward to take the thickly erect head of his cock between them and into her mouth.

Lawe froze immediately.

His entire body tensed, his fingers flexing in her hair. They tightened as she let herself become accustomed to the heated width filling her mouth, the fierce throb of power and life beneath her tongue.

Holding the base of the shaft with one hand, her fingers were unable to wrap around the thickness as she held the stiff flesh steady for each exploratory lick and stroke of her tongue.

It had been too long. It had been too many years since she had known the strength and heat of a man's desire. And she had to admit, she'd never known a strength or thickness like the one that filled her mouth.

"Diane. Fuck, yes. Suck it, baby. Give me that sweet mouth." Strangled, his voice torn, the pleasure in the hoarse, ragged tone of his voice had her tongue lashing beneath the sensitive crest with renewed hunger.

Each stroke was met with a fierce throb, a subtle

taste of powerful heat and the male he was. He embodied strength and male hunger, and she found herself becoming intoxicated on it. She was nothing if not adventurous, if not courageous. If not daring.

If not determined to destroy herself by having this man and tempting a possession she knew would destroy her.

CHAPTER 9

Suckling the thick crest of the heavy cock filling her mouth as deeply as possible, Diane let her tongue rub and caress the underside with languorous pleasure. At the separation of flesh at the top of the flared iron-hard crest, she felt a heavy throb as it seemed to flex, expand and retreat.

Her heart beat faster. The knowledge of the barb located there, feeling its warning pulse, the threatening stretch of the flesh, stole her breath.

Rachel had told her about it, but details had been amazingly sketchy. Diane knew what to expect though, and the thought of it had her tightening the grip she had on him as she laved the area again.

"Ah yes, wildcat." Lawe groaned above her. "So fucking good. So sweet. Sweet, sweet fucking mouth."

He buried his hands in her hair and his fingers clenched in the thick strands. The slight pinch of the pulling action was more erotic than it should have been. It sent flares of incredible striking pleasure piercing her womb, clenching it as her clitoris throbbed in painful need.

"Suck it, baby," he growled, the erotic rasp of his voice stroking over her senses as a whimpering moan vibrated in her throat.

She had had only two lovers, and neither of them had been vocal. To hear Lawe's rough voice whispering encouragement, hearing the pleasure in it, had her riding the edge of orgasm and he had yet to even take her.

"Diane, sweet baby," he whispered above her as she stroked the heavy shaft with her fingers, ran them lower and allowed the tips of her fingers to play over the smooth, silken flesh of his balls.

The fine, barely there, invisible body hair Breeds possessed was said to be as soft as silk beneath a woman's fingers. It was softer, Diane decided as she let her fingers caress to his thighs. Almost like a downy pelt created for a woman's sensory pleasure.

His fingers tightened in her hair, pulling at the strands as Diane swirled her tongue around the heavy crest of his cock, tasting the head and relishing the male taste of his flesh.

Each lick only seemed to make her hungrier for him. With each little taste, she swore she could taste the faintest hint of sweet pears mingling with the taste of his flesh.

It was an addictive taste. She wanted more. She wanted to fill her mouth with him, taste him, experience every ounce of pleasure that could be gained from it.

Between her thighs her clit was swollen, throbbing with furious abandon as need flooded her system. She could feel the muscles of her pussy convulsing, clamping together as hunger overwhelmed her.

Her juices flowed from the sensitive flesh, dampening the folds between her thighs and sensitizing her clit to the point that pleasure rode the edge of pain.

"Enough! God, Diane, not like this." The rough edge of his voice had a shiver racing up her spine as his fingers tightened in her hair and pulled her head back.

"No. Lawe, please." Frustration, need and hunger converged as strong fingers gripped her upper arms and pulled her to her feet.

Before she could protest further, his lips were on hers again, his hands sliding to her rear where he gripped her, lifted her, then turned and pressed her against the wall.

Lawe could feel his hands trembling, feel the control he prided himself on melting from the inside out. He was losing it. Losing it in a wave of heat and pleasure that made no sense, even within the bonds of mating heat.

He had his mate backed against a wall, her knees gripping his hips, the soft, velvety heat of her cunt rubbing against the shaft of his dick.

He could feel the dampness of her juices, slick and wet. He rolled his hips, the luxurious softness against his sensitive flesh bringing a grimace to his lips, baring his canines as he lowered his head.

He wanted to taste her. He wanted to touch her.

"Ah God," he whispered just below her ear. "I need to fuck you, Diane. Like air, like breath, I need you."

He felt as though he would die if he weren't inside her soon. And at the same time, if he didn't touch her, didn't consume her, then he would die from that need as well.

He licked the soft flesh just beneath her ear and felt her breathing escalate further as her hips shifted, the hard little bud of her clit raking against his cock.

He rubbed his tongue against her, much as she had rubbed hers against the hidden barb on the heavy crest of his dick. A slow, tasting rub. A consuming caress that filled his mouth with the taste of her and the taste of the mating hormone. And both were similar. Both filled his senses with the taste of sweetened spice, of juicy summer pears causing him to nip the delicate flesh with a compulsive bite.

A moan rippled from her chest. A breathless little sound that tightened every muscle of his body as his fingers speared into her hair, his palm cupping her scalp as he turned his head to her lips.

He simply touched the soft curves with his own lips first, let himself feel her, breathe her air as she stared back at him with a vulnerable hunger that sank clear to the soul he had been trained to believe he didn't have.

"I could consume you," he growled against her lips as he licked them first.

Her lips parted, those incredible dark brown eyes opening, her lashes fluttering as her gaze met his.

This wasn't the warrior who stared out at the world with such suspicion and wariness. This was the woman he would give his very life to protect. The one that made his guts tighten with fear at the thought of her facing bullets.

"You're just staring at me," she whispered against his lips as that steely determination he normally saw in her gaze flashed in for an instant.

"You mesmerize me." It was nothing less than the truth. "You destroy me, Diane."

Her lips parted to say more and Lawe found himself helpless to do anything but take advantage.

His tongue sank past her lips, finding hers as he felt the ache and throb of the glands beneath his tongue as it hit the warmth of her mouth.

That spicy summer taste filled his senses again as her lashes drifted closed and an aching moan whispered from her once again.

His free hand slid from her hip to the curve of her breast, turning to cup the delicate flesh as his thumb raked over a hardened nipple.

As badly as he wanted her kiss, he wanted that nipple too. He wanted to pull it into his mouth, lave the tender bud with his tongue and suckle her with an erotic hunger he felt he was starving for.

"Lawe," she whispered his name as he felt his lips moving down the slender column of her neck. "This doesn't change anything. I won't let it. I won't let you chain me."

He nipped in retaliation, drawing another moan from her as he then licked the erotic little wound.

"It will change everything," he assured her. "And I never wanted to chain you."

It would change them both, whether they wanted it to or not. Just as it would chain them both.

Holding her slight weight to him, Lawe turned and bore her to the bed. Placing his knee in the mattress he lowered her to the comforter, his gaze narrowing as her eyes opened once again, staring up at him with a dazed pleasure that awed him.

He'd always pleased the women he'd had in his bed, he'd made certain of it. But seeing that look in his mate's eyes had his stomach tightening and his cock swelling harder, impossibly larger, with a male pride that made no sense to him. He hadn't even brought her to her orgasm yet. That pride should be saved for her completion, yet here it was, rising in response to the pleasure he was giving her.

Lifting his hips from between her thighs, he allowed his hand to stroke from the rounded curve of her breast then down her curved waist, to her hip, to slide between her slender thighs and the humid warmth between them.

Hot, slick, the moisture gathered on the silken folds of her cunt, lying thick and heavy, easing the way for his fingers as they slid through the narrow slit.

Her hips jerked, a small, throttled cry falling from her lips as her hips arched, lifting to him as he let just the tip of his finger circle the hardening little bud of her clit.

Silken, throbbing with arousal, the little nubbin reached out for his fingers as Diane's hips twisted and writhed against his touch. The scent of her cunt, heated and female, drew him, making his mouth water for her taste as his lips moved from along her torso, easing closer to the humid dampness mesmerizing him.

Between his thighs his cock was a solid ache, throbbing against the comforter as he sought to draw as much of her in as possible.

His.

Mine. The word echoed through his head in a primal thought, a silent roar of primitive possession as he let his cheek brush against the curls between her thighs.

Neat, feminine, barely shielding the soft folds, those curls were dewed with her juices, a sweetened elixir he was dying to taste.

With a gentle lick, a touch as soft as a breath, he licked over the droplets, feeling her still beneath him.

Not out of fear.

Out of anticipation.

A ragged, animalistic sound rumbled in his throat as he let his tongue ease into her slit, working up, gathering the wet silk to his tongue and tasting pure ecstasy as he drew it to him.

"Lawe! Oh God . . ." Diane arched, blinded by the surge of pleasure that tore through her system like a kaleidoscope of pure light and color.

Tightening her fingers in his hair she fought to hold him in place, the feel of his tongue, just a bit more of a rasp than human, caused electric currents to pop and zing through the little bud as they sent snaking fingers of rapturous sensation to attack her womb.

Back arching, her head thrown back, she bent her knees and pressed her feet into the bed as her hips pressed closer. She couldn't get close enough, she couldn't get enough sensation, enough pleasure building at just the right moment to send her surging over that edge of ecstasy awaiting her.

It was just out of reach. So close it tempted and tantalized as each stroke of his tongue threw her closer to that edge without allowing her to fly over.

"So good," she moaned as a surge of heat pierced her clitoris, wrapped around it and burned with sensual flames. "Oh God, Lawe. I can't bear it . . ."

She needed to come. Just once. Just enough to ease the ever tightening conflagration burning through her.

Instead, he stoked it, stroked her, and sent her racing into a storm of pure sensation while holding her back from the orgasm she was fighting to reach.

A rumbling moan of pleasure vibrated against the sensitive bud as she felt his fingers, the calloused tips stroking from the inside of her thigh to the swollen folds of her pussy.

She lifted again, her hips grinding into his lips as she fought to breathe, then held her breath as she fought for release.

A ragged moan, so unlike her, filled with pleading and with a hiss of agony and pleasure escaped her throat as she felt those teasing, tormenting fingertips at the entrance to her vagina.

Not just one, but two. Broad, strong, they rubbed and caressed as he pressed her thighs farther apart with his free hand. Spreading her legs wider she arched to him again, certain she couldn't bear such an intimate touch without exploding in pure need.

Yet he managed to keep her poised on that edge even as his fingers began to stretch her entrance. Rubbing, caressing, easing inside her as Diane felt her juices gathering and flowing harder as the pleasure rose with impossible heat.

Rachel hadn't mentioned this, she thought hazily as that imperative need began to burn brighter, hotter than before, higher than she could imagine it.

Mating heat.

Rachel had told her it was impossible to fight once it began.

She didn't want to fight it. Unfamiliar territory rose before her, more dangerous than any mission she had ever attempted. Adrenaline raced through her system, sang through her veins and the taste of candied pears and spice filled her senses as she felt those broad, male fingers penetrate her with a sudden, dominant thrust.

Lightning. It rushed through her pussy, clenching the inner muscles with involuntary spasms as a cry tore from Diane's lips. Heated and heavy, his fingers stretched her and sent a sensual pinch of painful pleasure through the delicate tissue.

Her juices flowed through the narrow channel as she writhed beneath him, working her hips to stroke the length of his fingers inside her as she relished the invasion.

"Lawe!" Crying out his name, she tightly wound her fingers in his hair again as she felt both of his fingers pull back, then push inside her forcefully.

One knee bent, her body suddenly desperate for more, fighting without conscious thought to slip over that magical edge of release, Diane arched closer. Tried to force his fingers deeper.

Lifting her leg back to prop her foot on Lawe's shoulders, her hips worked on his fingers as he fucked them inside her. The rasp of his harder, rougher flesh against the delicate inner tissue had her nerve endings screaming with pleasure. Perspiration layered her flesh as the pleasure expanded inside her, racing through her veins, flaming through her. As his lips released her clit and only his tongue, just the roughened rasp of his tongue, began to rub, flicker and caress her with quick, driving licks, Diane felt the world itself begin to unravel.

Pleasure was such a tame word. Ecstasy didn't even come close.

A supernova of such intense sensations that she couldn't make sense of them exploded inside her with a starburst of energy. Color and light whipped through her mind, exploded behind her eyelids as a wail of violent ecstasy burst from her lips.

Lawe came over the shuddering form of his mate, his teeth clenched, primal pleasure and power tearing through him as he rolled her to her stomach and lifted her hips to him.

Her fingers curled into the comforter. The scent of her cunt, a soft, feminine sweetness that filled his senses drew him, possessed him. Gripping the base of his dick, he moved in behind her, one hand gripping her hip as he lined the swollen head of his erection with the wet silken folds of her pussy and began pushing inside her.

Delicate inner muscles gripped him immediately in a hold that stopped just short of pain. Milking the thick head to pull him deeper, her grip tightened and released, her juices flowing and easing his way as he fought to hold back the primitive response to his mate's pleasure.

He hadn't anticipated this.

He had known it would be an animalistic response.

He'd known that once he got between her thighs she would loosen the control he'd fought for all his life.

But not to this extent. He hadn't anticipated this. Hadn't anticipated the animal inside him taking over completely or stealing away the control necessary to ensure he took her with the gentleness, with the depth of aching pleasure he so wanted to give her.

He was an animal, and God help him . . .

He clenched his teeth tight as he fought and failed to hold back the primal response.

A snarl of hunger tore from his throat as he pressed inside her, pushing, thrusting into her as he worked his hips, pushing his cock inside her with short, shallow thrusts.

He couldn't ease in. Despite the desire to take her slow and easy. Despite the vow he'd made to himself that he would take her in such a way, still, he took her like the animal he was.

Gripping her hips he came over her, his lips at her shoulder, his kisses meant to soothe her as he buried inside her to the hilt, over and over. The fierce grip of her pussy pulled him deeper, fluttering against the sensitive flesh of his cock as he felt the pleasure–pain of the barb throbbing just beneath the swollen crest.

He nipped her shoulder, then growled in self-loathing at the fierceness of the bite.

"God, yes!" Her cry was as much a shock to his system as the loss of control was.

Her hips moved into each thrust, her cunt clutching at him, clenched tight on every fierce stroke inside the moist depths as her slick, honeyed juices eased the raw possession.

Not that the animal inside him cared. It was on fire for her, so hungry for her that for the first time in his life, Lawe was helpless against it.

"Mine!" he snarled at her ear, overtaken by the sense of possession that ran hot and deep inside him. "Do you understand me, mate? You. Are. Mine!"

He had to imprint it on her as deeply as possible. He had to show her, convince her, make her see that she could never run from him again. Ensure that she could never overlook her safety as she had in the past.

His survival depended on hers.

"Tell me," he growled as he thrust inside her harder, faster. "Tell me, Diane. You're mine!"

"Fuck you!" she cried out. Her scent whipped around him, lust, hunger, fury and a need that made no sense to his primitive brain.

"Oh no, baby. Let me fuck you!" he snarled back at her as his head lowered to the vulnerable crook of her neck, the sensitive flesh where her shoulder met her neck, and he licked her with erotic hunger, forcibly holding himself back from the bite he needed to deliver.

His hips slammed against the rounded curves of her ass. Perspiration covered both their bodies, the wet slide of flesh and the primal joining creating an erotic, animalistic coupling that sent his senses reeling.

Control. He'd always had the control to never take a woman in such a way.

He'd always had the consideration, the knowledge of what his strength would do to them.

And still, he was helpless in taking his mate.

Helpless, filled with such hunger for her that each throaty cry from her lips, each proof of her pleasure only spurred him further, pushed him to take her with all the hunger that had burned inside him since the day her scent had slapped the animal inside him awake.

And it was awake now.

Her pussy tightened impossibly further, the burning grip of her muscles intensifying, the fluttering response that vibrated in the depths stroking against the throb of the barb beginning to emerge from captivity.

Lawe was certain he couldn't lose control of the animalistic urges inside him more than he already had. He was certain he couldn't mark her deeper, certain the pleasure couldn't blaze higher or hotter.

He should have known better than to tempt his genetics with such thoughts. As her cunt began to ripple tighter around his dick, as her juices flowed hotter, her pleasure peaking to an explosion he could sense rippling through her, Lawe lost that final edge he maintained on his control.

Turning his head as he pushed the hair from the back of her neck, his lips parted over the vulnerable nape of her neck, and he bit.

He tasted her blood as his canines broke her flesh. Tasted the hormone flowing from his tongue as he felt his cock twitch, felt it swell thicker, harder, as his semen began spurting from the tip with violent ecstasy.

Immediately, a growl from his chest as the barb emerged from its position just beneath the flared head at the top of his dick, stretching his flesh, throbbing, swelling inside her and locking into that hidden curve deep in her cunt to spill its own release.

Fluttering against the ultrasensitive female flesh there, finding the bundle of nerves just beneath her clitoris and pressing inside it, the barb locked him inside her and increased the ecstasy for them both.

Rapture exploded over and over inside them.

Beneath him, Diane convulsed again, the second wave of release more intense than first, fueled by the barb spurting and fluttering against the sensitive curve it held in its possession.

Lawe growled against the nape of her neck, his hips

jerking, his release spurting inside her again, blinding him with the pleasure of it until the last eruption sent a shudder racing through him.

His teeth were still locked in place, his tongue licking, stroking, easing the sting that might have existed if it weren't for the hormone spilling into the womb.

The mating hormone.

Easing his teeth back from the shallow bite, he laved it again, this time with more languorous licks as he felt the final pulses of the hormone easing from the glands beneath his tongue.

Covering her, Lawe felt her body relax into the bed, exhausted, sated, her ragged breaths matching the pace of her still-racing heart.

Still buried inside her, locked in place to allow his seed every chance to find fertile ground, Lawe too fought to simply breathe.

A part of him felt shattered. An emotion much too close to terror began to grow insidiously inside him.

He could lose her. Even now, over twenty years after the vivisection that had killed his mother and her mate, there were still those scientists who used the pure blood groups and other various Breed enemies to secure live research specimens for them.

Mates.

Those Breeds who found the one whose unique biological, chemical and pheremonal makeup came together to ensure they stayed together as long as they lived. Because each was the perfect match to the other to ensure conception and the survival of the species.

He'd heard some say God had adopted them.

The reverend he knew said God had touched man's creation and bestowed the Breeds with a soul to show man, once and for all, that only God could give life.

And still others said they were no more than a fluke of nature, like a reptile. Soulless, capable of nothing but survival and dark evil.

And there were those who would give their own children to possess a hybrid Breed, a child of a mated pair, to learn the unique secrets the Breeds could one day possess.

Proof of any of their abilities would almost certainly ensure the destruction of the Breeds if used the wrong way.

This was all that contained the information. Keeping it confined to mates for the most part. Men and women who understood exactly what they had to lose if the world ever knew.

This.

Their souls.

"Diane," he whispered her name as he clenched his eyes closed for the impossibly long moment it took him to bite back that dark emotion threatening to engulf him.

He'd get her back behind the protective walls of Sanctuary, deep in the middle of the compound, surrounded by the cabins, tents and lairs of the unmated Lions and Lionesses, Wolves and Coyote Breeds that constituted the Breed community.

Once there, she would be safe from the fanatics as well as her uncle's enemies. The men who had taken her nearly a year before had been but one of the teams searching for her. They were the only ones who knew who they were searching for or at least knew the face of the woman they believed could lead them to the man they were seeking and the secrets they believed he held.

Secrets she was rumored to hold as well.

"You're heavy, Lawe," she answered moments later, her voice drowsy, lazy.

She would sleep well tonight.

She didn't always sleep well, Jonas had informed him several months ago after Diane had spent a few days in the new wing of the main house, which had been built for Jonas and his mate.

Jonas was a member of the Pride family, whether he liked it or not, and his Pride leader half brother, Callan Lyons, had insisted on building the new wing to house Jonas, his new mate and their daughter. The main house was connected to a series of underground protected rooms and tunnels that had once been used for Breed research. It was now used to protect the mated wives and children on the few occasions the compound had been attacked.

Lawe knew that a wing of the main house was something he would never want himself. He'd never aspired to such things. He preferred a measure of privacy, and Lawe knew Jonas often chafed at the lack of it at times.

Lawe's home was located close to the main house, though, less than a half acre away. As the head commander of the Bureau of Breed Affairs, his position necessitated a close proximity to the Bureau director as the commanding force behind the Bureau's teams of Enforcers.

He worked with Jonas on each phase of every operation and mission going out of the bureau and ensured Jonas stayed up to date on each one.

Diane would be as protected as any of the Prime family, he would ensure it.

Forcing himself to ease from her, the barb finally retracting back into its position beneath the hood of his cock, Lawe collapsed beside her, exhaustion weighing his own muscles down.

He hadn't been able to close his eyes in the nights past since the shooter had attempted to take out Diane's head with one of the outdated sniper rifles he'd used.

Outdated, yes, but the bullet-propelled weapon was also entirely more effective, if highly illegal. The laser-powered weapons afforded more control, but their response time was much slower. Waiting for such a large weapon to power up before firing in succession didn't leave much room for error.

A compulsion entirely foreign to him had him pulling his mate close to him, tucking her against his chest and shielding her with his body.

He made certain to lie between her and the door and window. Just in case.

Just in case anyone was stupid enough to come through the door or attempt to slip into the room. Just in case he wasn't fast enough. He shielded her, giving her a chance to live, a chance to escape, and perhaps . . .

His jaw clenched and the fear he'd fought back earlier returned.

Just in case she had conceived his child.

"Diane, you know this isn't going to work."

Lawe watched as Diane cleaned her weapons. Efficiently, smoothly, and with an ease that bespoke far too many years of practice.

"How long have you been breaking down and cleaning your own weapons?" he asked when she didn't comment on the previous statement.

Her expression softened then. The look was one filled with longing and memories she often cherished.

"Since I was barely seven and staying with Uncle Colt while my parents were out of the country on their various *business* trips," she remembered with a gentle laugh. "They were spies you know. CIA agents. They met while they were both at Langley, just after they joined while in college. And they died together."

"There's a lot of missing information regarding Raymond and Esmerelda Broen's lives," he stated as he

watched her double-check the cleanliness of the barrel
of one of the weapons. "Their deaths and what they
were chasing are two of those missing links. Did Colt
tell you what happened?"

She looked up for a second, her expression stilling
somberly.

"He told me." She sighed heavily. "We had a deal.
Once I managed to successfully command my first mission, then he would give me the information. Just after
I did so, he told the others we were celebrating family-
style. His idea of family-style was to take me to the
mountain in Kandahar where my parents died. They
were ambushed and killed while tracking the identity of
a man rumored to head a network secretly transporting
files, genetic material, Breed DNA formulas, cryogenic
embryos and possibly many of the infants and young
Breeds that were missing at the time."

His brows arched. "I was unaware the CIA was
working on the behalf of the Breeds. The last records
we had, many of their agents were actually involved in
the training and information control of the various labs."

"My mother left a diary," she said, "several of them,
actually. She knew many of the agents who were working in just such capacities, but they were also slipping
information out to those they knew were working to
reveal the brutality the Breeds lived under. There were
opposing interests in the CIA, according to her. Only a
few substations were actually involved with the Genetics Council. Langley was actually trying to verify
the rumors, track down the labs, and aid the Breeds'
escape. I gave Rachel the diary last year and I believe
she turned it over to Jonas."

Lawe nodded. "Yes, I read it. From what I read, your
parents were far too reckless for a couple with two children depending upon them."

It was a trait they tragically shared with her uncle, Colt Broen. As a mercenary, Colt had been in the perfect position to funnel information back to the States or to ensure that U.S. interests, as well as the CIA's, were preserved.

Raymond and Esmeralda Broen had coordinated their trips with their missions, ensuring that if they weren't home to protect their young children, then Raymond's brother would be. Still, they had died while their children were young, and according to the reports Diane turned over after she came into the Bureau, their parents' enemies had immediately gone after the uncle, as well as the children.

She didn't comment on his criticism, nor could Lawe detect any emotion other than regret. There was no anger toward her parents or her uncle, and no resentment for the life she had led.

But then, he had no doubt she was able to, and definitely would, hide any emotion she didn't want him to see.

The Breeds who had been a part of her group until the past months had taught her how to bury and conceal her emotions. As they had explained to Lawe, it had become a game between them and their "commander" to detect her moods, her emotions or other various states of being that she experienced.

In the end, Diane had become far more adept at it than either of them had imagined she would.

"Are they the reason you followed your uncle into war?" he asked her finally.

"Their enemies took care of that," she stated, her voice hardening as she glanced up at him. "They attacked children, Lawe. They came after us like a plague and refused to give up for years. As though they would tell *children* any secrets they had kept from their superiors over the years."

"If they manage to capture you again, and kill you without the information they're looking for, do you think they would then go after Rachel and Amber?" he asked her.

Diane wanted to roll her eyes. He obviously believed he was making a point. It was a point she had no intention to acknowledge. He never lost an opportunity, never allowed a relaxed moment to be preserved.

"Ignoring me isn't going to solve the problem facing us," he finally warned her as Diane fought to keep from clenching her teeth.

"I'm not trying to ignore you," she assured him as she finished reassembling the small, handheld, laser-powered personal defense weapon she usually carried strapped to her thigh.

She was lying through her teeth and he knew it. He didn't need to smell it.

"Do you think I'm going to allow you to continue this search, Diane? To risk you against a rogue we know so little about, as well as whatever assassins have been sent out to eliminate Brandenmore's research projects? If they're even still alive." It was the wrong way to go about it, and Lawe knew it, but he was damned if he could figure out a better alternative.

She laughed at him, though the sound carried no amusement. What it did carry was disillusionment and a sense of pain. He could feel her pain as though it were his own. And for the first time in his life, Lawe ached for more than his own inability to be anything or anyone other than what his past had shaped him into.

"Do I act as though I need your permission to do anything?" she asked as she repacked the weapon and turned back to him, disdain reflected clearly in her gaze. "Really, Lawe, I'm a big girl now. I don't need your permission to stay out after dark."

Technically, she was right since she reported directly to Jonas.

"I'm quite certain Rachel was smart enough to warn you about the effects of mating heat," he stated instead of tying and gagging her as he wanted to and forcing her back to Sanctuary. "You can't just return to the same life as before. It doesn't work that way."

He couldn't let her continue this mission either. She wasn't just facing a rabid Breed in what was suspected to be the throes of a medically induced feral fever but also a team of Council-loyal Coyote soldiers searching for the same prey. And if the Breeds who once fought with her were right, she was also dealing with a traitor within her own ranks.

None would hesitate to kill her if she dared to attempt to interfere with their acquisition of the Bengal Breed Judd, Fawn Corrigan, or Honor Roberts. And they knew she was doing just that, as was evidenced by the attempt on her life before she slipped away from him in D.C. And if they didn't kill her, the Council scientists would surely love to get their hands on a female experiencing mating heat.

"I can damned near do anything I want to do, Lawe." Getting to her feet, she packed away the cleaning materials before storing them in her ammo bag and securing it firmly.

She kept her back to him, which was something else he hated. Diane was fairly skilled at lying with her lips and keeping the scent of it covered, but she hadn't yet perfected lying with her eyes.

It was the only way he would have of detecting her emotions for now.

While she was able to hide certain emotions and their scents, she couldn't use it as a reliable shield against Breeds for long. Especially not from Lawe.

"Any Coyote who detects the scent of your heat will make it his job to kidnap you and turn you over to the Council and their scientists," he argued. "That's not a pleasant place to be, nor is it a pleasant way to die."

He was restraining himself and the effort to do so was about to snap his back teeth as he clenched them so tight his jaws ached. If he were human, he had no doubt they would have already been ground to the gums.

He had never clenched his teeth so often or as tightly as he did whenever he and Diane faced off in a disagreement, which was pretty much every time they came in contact.

"You should have stayed in D.C. rather than following me," she told him as she lifted one of her duffel bags to the bed.

Disillusionment covered her. As though there had been some glimmer of hope that he would allow her to continue? The sad part was he had tried. Hell, he was still trying, yet all he saw each time he tried to formulate a plan to allow her to complete the mission, was her blood. Her screams. Her death.

Pulling down the heavy tab of the zipper, she opened the luggage and began packing the few items she had used the night before into the bulging interior. It was evident she had no intention of listening to him.

Which only left Lawe with that idea of tying and gagging her.

"Don't push me like this, Diane." Anger had the mating heat boiling inside him. Strong emotion, especially anger, had the effect of intensifying the rush of the sexual hormones and sending them surging through the body. "You won't win."

At that point, she did turn and face him, her gaze clashing with his as he got a glimpse of the burning emotions she was still keeping tightly reined.

He was amazed at her ability to do so. The deep brown of her eyes held a darker, almost burgundy tint. Rage had to be eating her alive for her eyes to have turned such a startling color. Yet not so much as a hint of the scent drifted to him.

"What will you do to force me to obey you, Lawe?" Her head tilted to the side as he watched her visibly struggle to keep the emotions reined in. "Will you beat me? Tie and gag me before dragging me back to Sanctuary? Because those are your only options."

"I would never harm you," he managed, fighting the urge to snarl in outrage. His fingers tensed, the desire to clench them almost overwhelming as he faced her and the suspicion in her gaze. "And you know I would never strike you."

"Then that leaves tying and gagging me." Her hip cocked, a delicate hand resting on it, and the scent of her fury finally drifted to him for the briefest second.

It was viciously hot, nearly searing him and making him want to take a step back from it as the edge of pain slapped his senses. God, what emotions did she hold back on a normal basis for such intensity of feelings to slip past her careful control?

The animal side of him flinched at the thought that he could be the one hurting her. That his need to protect her, to ensure her life could possibly have created such a well of agony.

"Those are your only options," she stated. "Because I refuse to return to Sanctuary to be kept locked away like a favored pet."

A favored pet?

Lawe felt his jaw bunch and his dick jerk with an imperative demand as she confronted him. He would fuck her into exhaustion if it weren't for the fact he'd be doing the same to himself. Throughout the night she had proven she was more than a match for his sexuality, and his hunger.

Just as she was more than able to keep up with him in other ways.

"Better a favored pet than a mate tortured to death. Do you know what the Council scientists, Brandenmore's research monsters or even the government's so-called Breed geneticists would do if they got their hands on you? Do you have any idea of their preferred means of learning how mating heat changes the body? How horrifying a vivisection is? What it would do to me to be forced to watch such a thing happen to you?" he questioned, hearing the harshness, the guttural quality of his own voice. "And you. Could you bear to hear my screams as they dissect me alive? Perhaps more than once? Over and over again? Because, baby, I would sure as hell scream. Even the strongest of us eventually break when they lay the knife to our guts."

Diane wanted to turn from him. She wanted to hide the painful, horrifying knowledge that she was very well aware of what any scientist would do to either of them now.

"I've seen it." Agony raged in his eyes as he crossed to her, his fingers curling around her arm as he pulled her to him. "I watched, Diane. Forced to pretend disinterest. Forced to show no fucking reaction." Animalistic, filled with horror, his voice rasped with the words. "I watched as they first cut into the Coyote commander who made the mistake of mating one of the breeders in the lab where Rule and I were confined. Then, I watched as they cut into his mate. My mother. The woman Rule and I fought to find freedom for since we were barely old enough to realize we were captives. I couldn't roar in rage. I couldn't beg them to cease, because if I did"—his expression was filled with tormented memories, dragging a muffled sob from her lips—"if I did, then three others in that lab would have died. It could have been Rule. Or the young Cheetah female they kept separated from us. Or another of the young that Morningstar Martinez reached out to in their dreams."

Her lips parted in surprise. "In their dreams?"

Lawe released her slowly and stepped back. Pushing his fingers through his hair he drew in a hard, painful breath. "In our dreams. As far back as we could remember. Morningstar came to the children she was fertilized with in vitro. She rocked them. She sang to them. She painted pictures of the place she called home, the family she was certain was searching for her, and all the joys she had known as a child."

Diane watched, silently, feeling the tears that would have fallen if she hadn't had so many years of practice holding them back.

"Her life was a living nightmare, yet she brought us joy whenever she could. And because the Coyote commander found joy in her and mated her, they died in the most horrifying way possible."

He had seen the nightmares he feared she would face. It was no wonder he was so determined to lock her away in cotton batting. If only she could survive it.

He and his brother, Rule, had been forced to watch, as though uncaring, forced to watch as though unconcerned as their mother was murdered in just such a way.

"It would kill me." She knew she lost the battle to hide the emotions tearing her apart inside when Lawe's head jerked back, his nostrils flaring as he drew in her scent. "To know I was the cause of such a fate for you, Lawe. It would destroy any part of my soul that was left at the second I faced death."

Yes, she hurt. She had nightmares about the lives

she knew the Breeds had endured. The very thought of what they had gone through was often more than she could bear contemplating at length.

"Then don't do this," he snarled, his canines flashing as his lips pulled back from his teeth furiously. "Give this up, Diane, and let the Bureau's Enforcers track her down instead."

"It would kill me," she said again. "But being locked away, unable to be me, would make me hate you, Lawe. I would hate you and any Breed I ever came in contact with again."

She had fought too long, endured too much. Her freedom, her existence and the reason she followed in her parents' and in her uncle's footsteps and followed war was too deeply ingrained inside her.

"Why?" Fury, pain, they raged inside him like a volcano threatening to erupt.

"Because I won't be powerless again," she whispered. "When my parents died I was just that, Lawe. I was powerless. When my parents' murderers beat my uncle to our home, Rachel and I were alone with our babysitter." She shuddered, the memory tearing through her with a force that never eased. "I didn't watch my mother die, but I heard the screams of the person Rachel and I considered more than just a babysitter. Uncle Colt's fiancée died swearing to them we weren't there while I ran with Rachel and hid. I had to listen to her screams as she did the only thing she could do to protect us because no one, no one," she cried out furiously, "had taught her how to fight. How to survive. And if you lock me away, then every time I hear of a Breed death, every time I hear of a mate being murdered so savagely, I will blame you!"

Because her parents had fought for the Breeds. Her uncle had fought for them. And the secret they had all died to keep was still one Diane knew had to be preserved. She had information even Lawe didn't have. Something she knew that Leo feared she would reveal each time he caught her gaze.

She didn't expect her answer to cause such a reaction in Lawe, though. Before she could avoid him he displayed the incredible speed of his feline DNA and crossed the room to grip her arm and jerk her to him again.

His arms were like steel bands around her, holding her in place and keeping her against his chest despite her initial attempt to place distance between them.

Staring up at him, eyes wide, her senses churning with both anger and an arousal that felt as though it were burning out of control, she glimpsed the torment that raged in his blue eyes.

"Better your hatred than your death. Or the horror of watching you taken apart piece by fucking piece." He spat his words.

There was no fear at the display of dominance.

Anyone who was around Breeds very often learned to live with such displays and such arrogance. The torment that burned in his gaze did affect her, though. It struck through her heart, tightened it, and left her throat thick with the unshed tears she refused to free.

"You could trust my abilities as I trust yours," she yelled back at him, her emotions driven by her anger, both for him and against him, as he displayed his complete inability to ever consider her a worthy partner. "Tell me, Lawe, does your life go on hold with this mating too, or just mine?"

She knew the answer to her question. It wasn't hard to guess exactly who the mating affected and who it wouldn't.

His expression did no more than confirm her suspicions. She gave a bark of scornful laughter. "Don't bother answering, because I can see it in your face. It doesn't. You'll still fight, you'll still risk yourself and you'll still expect me to sit in the little cage the Breeds have made for their mates and play the dutiful wife. Should I be barefoot and pregnant too?"

The flicker of his eyes, the glimpse of the sudden longing that crossed his expression before he could hide it, had her stomach tightening. With longing, or with pure rage, she wasn't certain.

"So you'll just go out, have your fun, then return home to fuck me before you pat me on the head and ride off into the sunset again." Oh, she so didn't think that was going to happen.

She wouldn't allow it. Not even for a second.

She had never allowed herself to play any man's doormat and she wouldn't start now. She would be his equal partner, or she would be nothing. Nothing less was acceptable.

"At least you'll be alive," he bit out, the icy storm in his gaze almost frightening as he stared down at her.

"The hell I will." Pushing against his chest she tried to escape his hold, only to become aware of just how firmly he held her without appearing to. "No, Lawe, I won't be alive. I'll just exist, and I'll hate you for it. I will not be there waiting for you. I'll be doing as I've trained to do all my life and I'll do it alone if that's what I have to do. I won't let you cage me!"

"I won't allow it." One hand moved from her back to push into the hair at the back of her head as the vow slipped past his lips.

He wouldn't *allow* it? As though she would ever let him have any say in the matter as long as he was doing so in such a manner. As though he owned her.

The pain of that realization had her body tightening

until she was on the verge of shaking, the pain, anger, and incredibly, the fear racing through her to mix with an arousal she couldn't force away.

She wanted him. She wanted him to touch her, to hold her, to share his kiss and the incredible taste of spiced pears that filled it. She wanted him to accept her. To stand beside her. To allow her the happiness she needed to make that decision for herself.

And she wanted to kick his ass for ever imagining she would allow him to make such a decision for her.

"Sorry, Lawe, I won't allow you to kill her as surely as the Council would."

The shock of the words coming from the deep, normally booming voice of her second-in-command had Lawe moving. Before Diane could stop him, he had thrown her behind him as Thor stepped into the room, twirling the key between his fingers as he stared at them, a tic of anger throbbing at the side of his jaw. "Having fun alone again, boss?" he asked. "I thought we agreed that wouldn't be happening this time."

He was pissed.

Lawe's blue eyes were icy. His broad, masculine features looked carved from stone and anger had his normally full lips tightening as she knew he held back every smart-assed, purely male arrogant insult he could have thrown her way.

Thor completely ignored the fact that Lawe had one of the snub-nosed, laser-powered, rapid-burst hand guns trained on him, his finger riding the activation lever a little too firmly. But he wasn't ignoring the fact that Lawe was attempting to shield her. The action earned Lawe one of Thor's famous, sarcastic sneers. A lifting of his lip at one side as disgust filled his gaze.

"For God's sake, Lawe, get the hell off me!" She pushed at the back of his shoulders as he continued to hold her behind him with the seemingly effortless strength of one arm.

Dammit, she could kick the asses of men that were twice his size and pure muscle. But she couldn't budge him.

"What is he doing here?" Lawe's voice was an animal's growl.

"Move!" She finally managed to lever a few inches between them before he slowly, very damned slowly, allowed her her freedom.

She shot him a look filled with the promise of retribution.

She was not going to put up with this. "This is the number one reason most partners involved in any kind of military or covert work end up divorced," she snapped furiously.

"Mates don't divorce."

"Be careful, Lawe," she suggested, her voice raspy with the sheer depth of her anger. "You'll be the first."

"I get to sell the tickets." Thor's smile lacked any amusement or warmth.

"You're supposed to be on vacation," she snapped at the oversized Swede that stood in front of the now-closed door.

"And you're supposed to be visiting your sister before you head to Sanctuary with her." Thor's brow arched with mocking curiosity. "I guess we both lied, huh?"

Yes, she had lied. Something she had never done to Thor as long as she had known him.

"And I had a very good reason for it," she informed him as she moved to go around Lawe, only to have him catch her arm and hold her back silently.

He hadn't said a word. He stared back at Thor with lowered brows and narrowed eyes, his entire body tense and ready for action.

For God's sake, his very demeanor, so dominant and forceful had her pussy creaming furiously despite the disgusted irritation the action earned him.

She decided she hated Breeds.

"Reasons don't matter." Thor shrugged. "Just the action."

Diane grunted at his standard no-forgiveness stance.

"Were you following me?" Suspicion suddenly rose inside her, dark and ugly.

Thor had been the one who had arrived with her uncle to tell her of her parents' deaths. He had held her when her lover, her uncle's second-in-command, had been killed, and he'd been the one who had sat and prayed at her hospital bed after her rescue from that Syrian hellhole.

Suspecting him of anything seemed nothing short of a sin.

Yet there it was.

"I wasn't following you," he stated with a bite to his voice. "I've actually been tracking your shadow. I just wanted to see who he was tracking when I caught sight of him sneaking around the hotel the night before you left. I didn't know you were his quarry until I heard you and the Lion here arguing inside. It makes sense, though, considering the fact I *warned you* someone was out to kill you." He turned to Lawe as he crossed his arms over his wide chest. "Your Breeds are falling down on the job, prick. They weren't at the door as they should have been."

"For a reason," Lawe snapped irritably. "We knew you were following her. The only reason you got to the door was because you're not considered a threat."

Diane was more concerned with Thor's revelation than the argument between him and Lawe. She had left before daylight. Gideon Cross had been watching for her and she had known it. Just as she had known he was tailing her, despite the fact that she hadn't been able to catch sight of him.

One of these days, perhaps she could catch up with him and convince him to teach her that little trick.

Keeping one step ahead of her mate as well as her enemies might well be in her future. He didn't appear to be out to kill her. She just hadn't figured out exactly what it was he did want. Evidently, Lawe was paying close attention to Thor, especially the part about Gideon shadowing her and the rumor that there was a price on her head. Just what she needed, for Lawe to become more protective than he already was. "Let me go before I have to kick your ass," she muttered, her fury downgrading to simple kick-his-ass anger as he slowly released her.

"That threat is getting old," he told her quietly. "Either kick it or find another part of my anatomy to consider abusing."

She almost rolled her eyes. She wasn't even going to touch that one.

Pushing her fingers through her hair, she stared back at the window beside the door. The curtains were still carefully closed and tucked in close to the wall to ensure not even a shadow could be revealed.

She had known last night that a weapon was trained on her. Right between her eyes as she sat in the chair that she had thankfully moved this morning. If Thor was unaware of who the tracker was following, then he couldn't have seen her the night before making herself a willing target.

"Did you catch sight of him?" she asked Thor.

For long moments Thor stared back at her in mocking disbelief that she had even asked such a question.

He indicated her window with a jerk of his head. "I managed to catch sight of him with the long-range binocs we procured from those Coyotes last year." The binoculars were a hell of a lot more than long range, with night vision, heat sensing and several other tricks Diane hadn't yet been able to try out. "He has a nice, powerful sniper rifle trained right in here is my guess. I saw the shadow and the rifle, but I couldn't get close enough to glimpse his features or keep him from pulling the trigger." The last was snapped out furiously. "What the fuck were you doing propped up in front of the window daring that fucker?"

She rolled her eyes at him, before her gaze turned wary at the sound of the rumble of pure displeasure she heard vibrating in Lawe's chest.

"Stop that." She hissed the order as her nerves went immediately on edge.

She did not like that sound.

"I'm ready to imitate him," Thor bit out in irritation. "For God's sake, Diane. You have no idea what you're dealing with here."

"Wonderful." Diane propped her hands on her hips again and stared around the room as she said mockingly, "And here I was hoping he would settle for binoculars to watch my girlish figure."

Not that either man took her mocking amusement for what it was.

"That assassin is still tracking you and you insist on remaining on this mission?" Lawe turned to Diane, incredulity shooting past any control he could have considered enforcing on his scent. "Have you lost your fucking mind?"

"Well, he hasn't shot me yet." She ignored the flash of a wicked incisor at her exclamation.

"Well, fucking give him time," Lawe suddenly yelled at her. "He's only made his first attempt. If at first you don't succeed—right?"

Her eyes widened.

She had never heard Lawe yell, and she had seen him and Jonas go head-to-head on more than one occasion. Lawe was always calm, collected and cool. The three C's. She'd always envied the hell out him.

All three of those C's were gone this morning, though. That Breed standing before her was ready to blow with the force of the anger raging through him.

"You need Valium," she stated in irritation. "If he wanted to kill me, then you would still be cleaning my brain matter from the side of that hotel in D.C. Get a clue, Lawe. He didn't want to kill me. He wanted to get me away from my team to keep me from getting killed by whoever is betraying me. The best way to do that was make certain they couldn't follow me." She glanced at Thor. "It's a damned good thing you're the only one I know I can trust. But I want to know who it is. I was hoping to convince Gideon to join me long enough to tell me."

She turned to her second-in-command. It was too late to hide anything from him now.

A sizzling curse slipped past Thor's lips a second before his expression turned to stone.

"I'll kill the bastard," he swore, his voice rumbling with near Breed violence, and he was stone cold serious. "When I find out who he is, he'll be dead fucking meat, Diane. He'll only wish I had turned him over to your mate, because there's no Breed on Earth that will make him suffer as I will."

"Fine, you make him suffer," Lawe snapped as he gripped Diane's arm and pulled her around to face him. "What the *fuck* made you think you could trust anything a feral Breed had to say? And just when did he inform you of anything—"

"And why the hell didn't I tell you about it when it happened?" she asked sweetly as she batted her lashes at him and affected a passable Southern Belle accent. "Why, Lawe, could it be because of all those raging Breed hormones going nuts inside your body right now? Or could it be the fact that little ole me could handle it just fine by myself?"

"Oh did you now?" All teeth. His smile was frankly disconcerting. "Well, Mate, let's see how well you handle me, now that I know about it. And I promise you, it won't be near as easy as you've had it the past. You can fucking bet on it."

◆   ◆   ◆

Gideon pulled the slim wireless receiver from his ear and tossed it to the table before wearily wiping his hand over his face. He almost smiled.

Damn, she was smarter than he had given her credit for. But, when it came to her mate, she wasn't showing the most sensible manner in how she was handling him. Challenging a Breed was simple idiocy. Especially a Breed male. That was the height of idiocy. Especially when it came to their mates.

Hell, maybe he should have met with her before Commander Justice arrived. But it had been his intent to save the information for a more useful time. Perhaps when he needed to distract her after stepping between her and his prey. Well, their prey.

Truth was, he'd wanted to meet with her. He'd wanted to see if he could draw any information from her, perhaps trick her into telling him more than he already knew, but he had a feeling it wouldn't happen. Useless effort had never appealed to him. It would have been amusing though, he thought as he held back a chuckle. They would have both been playing the same game. It would have been interesting to see if either of them had won or if it had only come out a draw, as he suspected it would. He actually respected her. Her strength and daring were almost legendary, her integrity unimpeachable. Like her uncle before her, Diane Broen led her men on missions that never harmed innocents, only saved them. She went after the monsters in the world and tried to make living just a little bit easier for those she helped.

Gideon despised treachery and traitors, and Diane had a traitor in her midst. Someone she trusted had been feeding her uncle's enemies information until they had finally caught up with her in Syria and managed to kidnap her.

Gideon had been in the area tracking down one of Brandenmore's clerical assistants when he'd caught wind of the abduction. He'd made certain Thor had the information and knew where he could find a Breed team that may be willing to help.

He'd owed her uncle that much.

Funny, how small the world could be. It had been her uncle, Colt, who had helped him during one of the few times he had managed to escape Brandenmore's labs.

Gideon had been in Europe when he had run into the team of Coyotes searching for him. Colt Broen had been following the Coyotes on a rumor that they were after a very special research project. His curiosity had been dangerous. It had also ended up being the reason for his death.

At that time, though, the mercenary had helped Gideon and even allowed him to join the team and share in the payments. Hell, he should have stayed with them rather than believing he would find safety at Sanctuary at the time.

He hadn't even made it to the small town of Buffalo Gap before he was ambushed, proving that even Sanctuary wasn't safe. Because only he and the Breed he had talked to there had known he was coming and the route he was to take.

He had paid for that escape. It hadn't stopped him from trying again, though. And again. And again. Except, Colt hadn't been there to rescue his ass. Perhaps it was for the best, he thought. Not that Thor would recognize him now, nor did he know who he had met with the night Diane had fled D.C. Shadows were wonderful things sometimes, and Thor was just smart enough to be suspicious, and intuitive enough to put the information Gideon had given him together.

She would need the Swede, he was afraid. Gideon couldn't protect her, and he was afraid Lawe would be too intent on forcing her to safety to watch for her little tricks when it came to slipping away from him.

The sound of voices raised in anger from the earpiece drew his attention back to the confrontation in the other room.

He knew what the outcome would be, though he was certain Commander Justice had no idea he was going to lose this round.

Diane wasn't a woman any man or Breed could protect by locking her away from the world. She was a woman that would always feel the need to find a way to fight at her mate's side. If the Breed had wanted a wallflower, then he should have mated some shy little miss and stayed the hell away from the warrior he'd found.

Because there was no doubt in his mind that the woman would find a way to freedom. And if she couldn't find her own way out, then the men who were loyal to her would find it for her. Especially the one they called Thor.

◆ ◆ ◆

Lawe pushed his fingers through his hair as he rounded on Diane once again. Disbelief spiked his blood pressure—who had ever heard of a Breed with high blood pressure—then mixed with the arousal already biting at his balls, to create a conflagration that threatened to explode within him.

He stared at his mate. She was as serious as hell when she stood and discussed a traitor in her group as though she hadn't nearly died sixteen months before because of his betrayal.

And she was discussing it with one of the very men she should have been suspecting.

He was thirty-four years old and he'd never been so close to losing his control as he was now. Even as a babe, or cub as they were called in the labs, he hadn't been so close to complete mindless rage as he was now.

He had watched friends and littermates die.

He'd been betrayed over and over by his trainers.

He'd been betrayed by Breeds he'd believed were his friends.

He'd watched his mother die by vivisection and had seen countless Breed children suffer until their deaths were a mercy.

And still, he'd maintained his control because he'd had no other choice. And now, when that control was even more imperative, he could feel himself losing his grip on it.

"There's no way to set a trap when the last thing I need right now is to have any of them know what I'm doing." Diane shook her head at Thor's suggestion that they find a way to trap the traitor within their group. "Besides, it can wait. I want to concentrate on finding Brandenmore's research subjects right now. As far as the others know, I'm at Sanctuary and Rachel will cover for me if by chance one of them attempts to contact me."

"You know where she's hiding then?" Thor asked as he leaned against the wall, arms crossed over his chest and watched his commander somberly.

Diane breathed in slowly. He could sense the battle she waged within herself for a moment before resignation settled in. Her shoulders straightened as her head lifted proudly at whatever decision she'd been silently contemplating.

"I know where they're at." She nodded. "Window Rock, Arizona. The night the Breed they called Judd and the young human girl, Fawn, were supposed to be terminated, Judd somehow managed to cause the guard to wreck the vehicle and took the girl and ran with a Native American who had been contacted by an anonymous source several days before. He found them, hid them for several days, and then took them to Window Rock."

"And just how do you know this?" Lawe could feel himself tensing, the pit of his stomach tightening at the look in her eyes.

"Because I'm smart like that," she drawled mockingly. "And once I had that bit of information I began investigating him. He's known for disappearing regularly and he's known for his habit of attempting to help Breeds. He was also near the area where Judd and Fawn Corrigan were being transported for termination the night they escaped."

Lawe stared back at her.

He could feel the ice battling against the mating heat to take over once again. To wrap around his soul, to freeze the emotional abyss waiting to spread through him and destroy him once and for all.

Window Rock, Arizona. A Native American who

would be willing to help Breeds. One Lawe knew for a fact had been searching for a particular young woman who had been kidnapped decades before by the Council. Terran Martinez, his uncle. But neither Terran nor his father had been there for Morningstar Martinez. His sister.

Lawe's mother.

"All the evidence we have verifies the termination," Lawe pointed out.

"Because no one was left living to un-verify it," she reminded.

"Remains were found in the cremation unit," he argued. "Enough to prove there were at least two bodies."

"And every guard in the building was dead," she reminded him. "Did you find teeth? Bone matter? Anything to verify the DNA? Sex? I know how thorough Breeds are. There was nothing there or I would have known about it when Jonas gave me the file on Honor Roberts."

"And how did you hear about this?" he asked, his tone grating. "That information hasn't come up anywhere else."

To which Diane smiled. "No one could verify their deaths, not even the Brandenmore scientists and research assistants I managed to talk to. I was probing into the suspicion of their escape when Gideon left his little note for me in my hotel room informing me that I had a traitor on my team and if I wanted to find who I was looking for, I should head to Window Rock and pay close attention to Terran Martinez."

"And you trusted this information?" Thor asked, surprised.

She didn't blame him; she was normally the most suspicious person she knew.

She breathed out heavily. "There had been too many accidents, Thor. I was already suspicious. And once I began checking into the information and Terran Martinez's past, it began adding up."

"Why didn't you give Jonas this information in your report?" Lawe grated. "You didn't tell me?"

Diane smiled back at him knowingly. "Because I didn't trust the encryption for the digital files and I wanted to make certain the Martinez name or Window Rock didn't get picked up by the wrong ears or listening devices. When I saw you had no intention of allowing me to complete the search for her, then I kept it to myself. This is my job, Lawe. Gideon Cross may be a killer as well as a feral Breed, but whatever caused him to give me that information kept me alive. Someone wants me out of the way so Amber or Rachel, possibly both, will be more vulnerable. Each "accident" has coincided with an event where Amber has been in danger. She needs all of us, not just Breeds, to protect her."

"Have you considered the fact someone could be using you to draw your sister out?" Lawe demanded, his voice rough, tortured. "For pity's sake, what in the hell makes you believe you can trust a Breed that's carving up Brandenmore scientists like pork at a picnic?"

She rolled her eyes. Lawe had a tendency to become irritatingly caustic as he grew angrier.

"I didn't say I trusted him. I said so far, he hasn't lied to me," she pointed out.

"Why tell you anything about the Roberts girl, or about the Breed?" Thor mused.

To which Diane stared at him then back to Lawe with knowing mockery. "Because he wants them too. For whatever reason, he's after the same goal and he obviously believes I have a much better chance of drawing them out. He'll shadow me. Watch me. He'll try to get to them first once they're identified. And I intend to keep that from happening."

"How?" Lawe snapped. His patience was seriously wearing thin.

"I'll let you know when I've figured that one out." She shrugged in unconcern. "Until then, I'll just do what I do best, Lawe. I'll question, watch, listen, and pull my facts together. If all else fails, I'll introduce myself to Mr. Martinez as his future niece-in-law and see if that helps."

She was joking.

Unfortunately, Lawe wasn't in a joking mood.

"Don't even try it." The growl in his voice sent shivers racing down her spine. "If you treasure that independence as highly as you claim to, Mate, *don't even fucking try it.*"

She had a feeling facing the past was the last thing Lawe intended to do and the very thing that would end up happening before this mission was completed.

Just as she had a feeling, a very bad one, that before it was over with, her heart just might end up broken, or perhaps her neck instead.

Lawe had to turn away from Diane. Drawing in a deep breath, he pushed his fingers through his hair and contemplated the cheap picture hanging on the wall in front of him.

Terran Martinez. Morningstar's younger brother. The brother who had been searching for his sister, or proof of her death, for more than thirty years.

So what had happened to the proof of her location, which Lawe had sent to her father, Orin, the week before she was killed? Lawe had kept up with the family after his rescue but neither he nor Rule had ever approached them.

He'd never gone to Window Rock to meet them, nor had his brother, as far as he knew. He'd never discussed his mother or her death with anyone, though he knew Rachel had most likely filled Diane in on the details. They were close like that. And he had never reached out

to let his mother's father know what had happened to
his daughter or the fact that she had been cremated and
her ashes thrown to the mountains around the termination facility in upstate New York.

He still heard his mother's screams in his nightmares. He could still here the certainty in her voice
that her father would have his vengeance, that her family would punish them all. And just as he had silently
predicted, no one had struck out at the Council to make
them pay for her death.

Or had they?

It was days later when the Breeds in that lab had been
liberated. The force sent in to free them had reached the
Breed labs hidden in the mountains just outside New
York City, and the Breeds had been released from the
harsh captivity and inhuman training they were sub-
jected to.

Tightening his fingers at his hips for long moments,
he forced himself to turn around and confront Diane
once again.

"There are no Bengal Breeds in Window Rock," he
told her. "The chief of the Navajo Nation is Ray Martinez, Diane. My birth mother's older brother. I keep
up with them. I would know if there were any Bengal
Breeds there."

Diane's gaze was somber. Lawe could feel the comforting warmth of her compassion reaching out to him.
He almost wished she had maintained her anger because
without that it was damned hard to maintain his.

Of course, she would know the facts of his history.
The Breeds who had fought with her before Jonas had
mated her sister had most likely answered any questions
she asked. Her men had a hard time telling her no, it
seemed. And they had seemed particularly enamored
with her.

"Judd's Breed genetics were recessing before his escape," Diane reminded him. "It was the reason he was slated for termination. Somehow the drugs they were giving him had begun to have the appearance of reversing the Breed DNA."

Lawe frowned at the information. "Where the hell did you hear this?"

Her lips quirked. "Argentina, Lawe. Several of the scientists and researchers working with Brandenmore escaped there when they received word the FBI and the Bureau of Breed Affairs were preparing to serve a search warrant on the facility and to enact Breed Law against anyone found there."

Lawe nodded tightly. "Argentina revoked their agreement of extradition against Breed researchers and participating individuals with the United Nations for crimes against genetically altered beings. We suspect they receive quite a hefty yearly payment in return."

Diane suddenly rubbed at her upper arms as though chilled as she nodded in agreement. "I was there for three weeks. Several of the research assistants I talked to were informants for the U.S. on the group of scientists living there. One of my contacts managed to set up a meeting with several of them. Once they knew I had no intention of giving the Bureau their names, they were very cooperative."

And Lawe had no doubt he knew who several of those informants were. They may play at wanting assurance that the Breeds were unaware of them, but the truth was, they were only still living because they were giving the Bureau the same information or more than they were giving the U.S. government.

The knowledge that she had talked to them gave birth to another suspicion, though, one that had his shoulders tightening.

His gaze shifted to Thor as he remained silently at the door, his arms crossed over his broad chest, his expression brooding as he listened to the conversation.

The knowledge that Diane had gone out without him obviously didn't set well with the other man.

"Do your men know who you talked to?" The Bureau couldn't afford to lose any of their informants in Argentina. If the spy in her group knew who she had talked to—

The look she gave him was filled with disdain, but she slid a silent apology to Thor. "I had already received the warning from Gideon. Though at the time, he called himself the Executioner. I didn't risk it. I slipped out at night and met with them. Give me credit for knowing how to protect my contacts."

"I give you credit for far more than that, but whoever's betraying you is damned effective at it. And having him out there makes this situation much too explosive, especially considering the mating heat. We're going to be too distracted by its symptoms to be effective in either the search or the protection of whoever we find there. If we find anyone. We can't continue this." He sighed, knowing he was wasting his time.

She would never return to Sanctuary with him until this was finished and he knew that accepting anything less could mean her death. He knew it, and the knowledge burned in his gut like acid. That was an option he couldn't face.

"Once the mating heat eases," he began, forcing the words past his clenched teeth, hating the fact that he was lying to her now. "Once we can think again, we can revisit the option of returning here and finding them."

Her lips lifted slowly, the shallow curve of a smile filled with pain as she watched him too closely.

"By then they'll be fucking dead or locked in

research cells," Thor muttered as Lawe flashed him a quelling look.

That won't happen, Lawe promised silently. He would send a team after them, a team he knew would ensure any of the three still living survived and arrived at Sanctuary safely.

"I won't let that happen," Lawe growled.

Thor's brow arched in mock amazement.

The bastard had no intention of standing down, and he wasn't a Breed. There was no way Lawe could enforce any order he gave.

"Do you think I'm stupid, Lawe?" Diane asked him softly. "You'll send someone after them and then they'll run the second your team enters the reservation and they get suspicious."

"And they won't run when you arrive?" he scoffed. "They'll run just as fast, Diane, if not faster."

"She knows what she's doing, Breed," Thor broke in as though she needed a protector. *She has a fucking protector,* Lawe thought furiously. "And she knows how to find people without making them feel like prey. If she didn't, the team would be broke."

"Dammit, Thorsson, you're talking like a man who wants to see his commander dead rather than showing your loyalty and seeing to her best interests," he snapped at the other man.

Thor smiled, his expression icy and cutting. "It's a good thing for you that my commander would go crazy without you, Breed. Otherwise, we'd discuss those words. Violently. I've always had her back, and I always will."

"It's your place to protect her, not endanger her further by encouraging her to continue this search under the present circumstances," Lawe snapped again.

Thor laughed as Diane frowned and crossed her arms over her breasts as she watched them.

"You mean, while she's in mating heat?" Thor asked with an amused snort. "When she was sixteen she broke two of my fingers to win a fight she had to win in order to travel to Nicaragua with the team to oversee communications. Brick still carries a scar on his wrist where she sliced it open to participate in a hostage rescue in California, and her uncle's former second-in-command found himself bouncing on his ass at least weekly whenever he made the mistake of suggesting she stay out of a mission. She's won all the battles she needs to win in my eyes. She's my commander. I follow her orders and I watch her back as she watches mine. You mating her won't change that."

When Thor said she had won all the battles she needed to, Lawe knew he was referring to the battles to secure his loyalty.

There was no scent of a lie coming from the other man, but then again, like Diane, Thor had probably learned from the two Breeds who had been a part of the team how to control certain scents. A lie being the most important.

Diane had proven herself in battle to her men, there was no doubt of it, or they would have killed her themselves for trying to take command. She had proven she could protect her men and herself. She had proven her ability to plot, plan and guide them through any number of situations where her ability to lead exceeded theirs. She still had a traitor in her group, though. A traitor who meant to harm her. The question was, was that traitor Thor?

"Then I'll tie her up and gag her before I throw her on a heli-jet," Lawe snarled rashly as he ignored Diane's snort of mockery.

Hell, he was never rash. He never, ever made empty threats until he had come against Diane's stubborn will.

Any other woman and he would have had a team of Enforcers abduct her and transport her to a secure location until the situation was resolved.

But Diane wasn't any other woman. She was his mate. Besides, she would probably shoot his kneecaps off at first opportunity for the insult.

"And you'll make her hate you as well as make an enemy of her," Thor warned as his gaze snapped with fury. "Because you'll have to kill me, Breed, to pull that one off. And trust me, I'm her favorite."

Her favorite? Lawe's eyes narrowed on the mercenary as he began assessing any other threat Thor may represent. At the look, Thor flashed a confident, taunting smile.

Lowering his head, Lawe was only distantly aware of his lips curving back at one side to display the canines there as a growl sounded in his throat.

The danger, the threat that the other man might represent, had the primal animal that lurked inside him rising dangerously.

Diane stepped forward at Thor's smile and the answering, savage sound vibrating in Lawe's throat. She could hear the anger in Thor's voice. That anger was something he rarely showed, and the fact that it was bleeding from him was an indication that the confrontation needed to stop now. Because he was intent on pushing the one button he knew would only piss Lawe off.

Even more dangerous, though, was that totally feline, completely enraged sound Lawe was making. She had never heard that from any Breed, and she'd fought with two of them for several years before Jonas and Lawe had made it impossible to keep them on the team.

"Leave, Thor," she ordered him, making certain her tone brimmed with authority. She had to separate the two before she had more trouble on her hands than she could deal with.

Thor glared at Lawe accusingly for long moments before turning back to her, his shoulders tense, his expression tight with outrage as he glanced at her. "Are you sure, boss?"

"I gave the order, didn't I?" The lash of command that hit her voice before she could stop it had Lawe's gaze slicing back to her.

Thor grimaced tightly before turning back to Lawe. "Don't make me your enemy," he warned Lawe. "Take her by force, and I promise you, I'll retaliate."

"Thor! Now!" The last thing she needed right now was Thor playing his games with Lawe.

Thor threw Lawe a look that even Diane clearly understood. A look that assured Lawe he wouldn't hesitate to strike out if he felt he had to. It was a side Diane had always sensed in the other man. Thor followed her, he respected her abilities and her command, but he would always see her as a female first and a soldier second. It was his one fault as far as she was concerned, and one of the main reasons she had already ruled him out as the traitor. Thor had had far too many opportunities to kill her and make it look like an accident if that was what he wanted to do. He didn't have to play games.

"Do I really have to say it a third time?" Third time meant cash from his account to hers. And a hefty amount it would be too.

"Fuck, fine. But it's not the damned money. It's the ass kicking that goes with it," Thor bit out as he turned quickly, opened the door with a furious jerk, then paused. Looking over his shoulder, he glared at Lawe. "She can't really kick my ass, you know, but she plays fucking dirty and goes for the balls," he said before striding out and slamming it heavily behind him.

She flinched as the metal door met the frame hard enough to rattle the windows.

"Teenagers," Diane muttered as she glared at the door, then at Lawe.

She swore men were no more than overgrown teenagers.

Glaring at him she had to restrain a sigh. She had fought the good fight and she knew she had to ignore the heat blazing through her body while Thor was there. The tormenting waves, the lash of hunger and the overwhelming urge to rub against him were nearly impossible to deny, though.

The sensitivity of her nipples and breasts, her clitoris and even her flesh made her feel as though every nerve ending in her body had turned erogenous. She wanted to take him. She wanted to feel him. She wanted to burn the anger and pain from his eyes and for just a few moments, she ached to be a partner, if only sexually.

She didn't have time for this. She didn't have time to be some Lion Breed's sex kitten. She had a mission to finish, but all she wanted to do was crawl over his tight, hard body and feel him against her. She wanted to rub on him.

Hell. She wasn't doing this. This was not the way to prove she could handle mating heat and the mission.

And she had no choice but to prove it or she would have to back off and give Lawe exactly what he wanted. The end of her freedom.

Lifting her hand, she pushed it beneath her hair and rubbed at the sizzling sensations that seemed to pulse just beneath the skin there.

The bite Lawe had given her ached with a sizzling sensation and almost brought a moan to her lips as she touched the wound.

Jerking her hand back, she glared at him before turning to the bed and grabbing her bags.

Pulling the short hiking boots from the closet along with the clean socks she had pushed into them the night

before, Diane threw them on the bed as she prepared
to leave.

"You can go with me or you can haul your ass back
to D.C., I don't really give a damn which," she told him
as she prepared to leave.

Liar. Liar. The inner sex kitten was chanting the
word as her body screamed for sex. For mindless,
erotic, nasty sex and another one of those primal, primitive bites at the back of her neck.

She turned to inform him exactly what he could do
with his protective possessive attitude and his refusal to
consider anything but his own way, when he was suddenly right there behind her. He gripped her arm and
hauled her against the exciting heat of his much larger
body, his arms surrounding her, the heat of him seeming to penetrate through her flesh straight to the core of
the arousal blazing higher at his nearness.

Her breath caught in her throat.

"You want to be fucked so bad you can't stand it, let
alone protect yourself and that arrogant behemoth you
fight with," he snarled down at her. "And still you would
walk away from me?"

"In a heartbeat," Diane flung back at him. "If you're
so damned stubborn and chauvinistic that you can't
accept the fact that I can't be anything but what I am
any more than you can, then you're damned right I will.
I won't beg you to be my partner, Lawe. You should be
intuitive enough to want to be."

She would die of arousal before she would beg him
to allow her to be anything but herself. She was who
and what she was and she wouldn't apologize for it. Just
as he could be nothing other than who and what he was.

She didn't ask him to change and knew he couldn't
even if she did ask it of him.

He had no right asking it of her either.

"You can barely walk for the need to fuck," he charged again, lust and anger burning in his gaze, darkening the blue of his eyes and intensifying the hunger she knew he already felt.

Mating heat was nothing if not demanding. And exacting.

"So fuck me and get it over with." Going on tiptoe she pushed her nose almost into his, her gaze locked with the wicked, sexual fire in his as she felt his cock pressing into her stomach. "Come on, Lawe, if you're not going to go with me, then at least give me a quickie for the road."

She had never been so furious with anyone in her entire life. Even Padric, her uncle's second-in-command, and for such a brief time, her lover, hadn't made her this angry during the years he had helped train her.

No one or nothing had ever made her as furious as Lawe could. Just as nothing or no one had ever made her want him as he made her want his touch.

"A quickie for the road?" Incredulity filled his voice and his rich blue eyes. "Have you lost your fucking mind? As if a quickie would ever be enough for either of us."

Tilting his head, Lawe forced her head back by simply burrowing his fingers in her hair and pulling.

The prickle of the pleasure-pain attacking her scalp seemed to echo straight to her pussy. Her lips parted on a gasp of rising excitement as his lips suddenly covered her own. His tongue pressed forward demandingly, possessing her mouth and controlling the kiss as Diane rose to him and sank beneath the pleasure.

The addictive taste of spiced pears filled her senses as the mating hormone began to spill from him. Immediately nothing else mattered but that kiss and the man giving it. Nothing mattered but holding him to her, sharing the kiss, and stroking Lawe to that point of no return, just as he was pushing her.

Even without that hormone Diane had a feeling she would never be able to say no to him. There was something about Lawe that made it impossible for her to ignore. Whether it was the pure dominance that challenged every inch of her independent streak or the primal, sexual knowledge that gleamed in his blue eyes and filled his demanding nature, she wasn't sure.

Whatever it was, he had been a fascination for her since the night he had rescued her from that hellhole. And ever since that night she hadn't been able to decide if she should kill him or fuck him.

She didn't want to kill him.

She wanted to tie him to her bed and have her way with him. She wanted to stroke every inch of his broad, muscular body before riding him into exhaustion. She just wanted him to need her as she needed him, and accept her as she accepted him. For once in her life she wanted to be a part of something rather than someone attempting to manipulate her into accepting only a lesser portion of what she deserved.

"God, Diane." Lawe groaned as he pulled back from the kiss, his blue eyes blazing with need and an inner torment that sent a shaft of aching regret to clench her chest.

She could see the conflict raging inside him.

She could feel it, and she knew it would likely destroy both of them before it was over.

Because he only knew how to be protective of her.

And she only knew how to be the woman her uncle had created when he allowed her to see what had been done to her parents' bodies.

In the same heartbeat she realized he was jerking her shirt from her jeans. She felt the pure, primitive hunger raging through him and knew she couldn't do anything but meet it head-on.

Lifting her arms a moan escaped her lips as the material cleared her head and Lawe's lips covered the tight, violently sensitive peak of her breast.

The muscles of her pussy clenched. Her womb spasmed with greedy hunger and a wave of heat raced over her flesh like a wildfire out of control.

As he bent to her, his mouth drawing on her with an intense male hunger, his fingers were jerking her belt loose and efficiently disposing of the metal buttons of her jeans.

It was a damned good thing she hadn't put her boots on yet, she thought with dazed pleasure as he began pushing them down her hips. Otherwise, they may have had problems.

The anger had intensified the arousal already amplified by the mating heat, and the need to have him inside her clawed at the muscles of her pussy.

"Hurry," she begged as she clawed at the T-shirt he wore as well, tugging at it, jerking it up his back until his head lifted and he was tearing it from his body.

Her hands moved to his belt, then to the button and zipper of his jeans, as she kicked her jeans away.

Lawe dealt with her panties quickly. He just tore them off her legs before his arms went around her. Gripping her ass Lawe lifted her to him as she lifted her knees, clasping his hips as he positioned his dick at the heated, slick entrance to her sex.

It was only seconds before she felt the engorged head of his cock pressing inside her. Thick and hot, the wide flesh pushed against the snug entrance as Diane's head tilted back and shudders of pleasure raced over her body.

"There's a bed." She gasped, her nails biting into

his shoulders as the head of his cock suddenly pressed forward.

Pinpoints of light exploded behind her lashes as the crest forged inside her. Within the next heartbeat, the next thrust, he was stretching her further. The sensations, so close to ecstasy mixed with the pain of the thick penetration to become the most pleasure she had ever known.

The gift of mating heat, her sister had once told her. It had taken hours to get the information out of Rachel. *It's like being suspended within pure bliss, heated bliss. It burns, energizes and leaves a woman too weak to protest whatever touch is given, and too hungry to ever deny it.*

And Diane couldn't protest. She had no desire to deny.

"Oh God, yes," she moaned as he continued to forge inside her. Diane could feel the snugness of her inner flesh, as though he hadn't spent the past night, nearly all night, buried inside her.

Tightening her legs around his hips, she arched her back and moved against him, forcing the engorged crest deeper. Each pulse and throb of the thick flesh stroked sensitive nerve endings as adrenaline raced through her body.

It was like being high on the danger of a mission, only better.

The feel of his cock moving inside her, impaling her with short, quick strokes, was driving her crazy with pleasure. Each inner caress caused it to build and tighten inside her with violent intensity.

"There, baby." Lawe groaned as he turned and stumbled to the wall, putting his back to it to brace himself. His knees bent as he held her in place and pushed in hard. The fierce thrust caught her off guard. Pleasure lashed at her body as the sudden biting pleasure-pain of the impalement had her gasping for breath as perspiration began to sheen her flesh.

"Ah hell, yes, tighten on my dick just like that, Diane. Like you're sucking it with that snug little pussy."

Sensation slammed through her womb. The piercing, fiery surge of clenching reaction detonated with a flash of heat inside her. The eroticism of the moment and his words went so far beyond pleasure that she had no idea how to describe it.

Moving again, Lawe turned her to the wall, braced her back against it and with a hard push of his hips stroked to the hilt between her thighs. The rasp of his flesh inside her, the sensation of it stretching her so tight, revealing nerve endings unused to such sensation, had a cry tearing from her lips.

It was so good. Oh God, it was so good.

How could she live without him, live without this, for even a day?

Her head lowered, her teeth raking his hard bicep before gripping it desperately to hold back the words that would have given him everything he wanted.

Please don't leave.

Please don't lose another chance to feel not just the pleasure, but the emotions suddenly whipping through her as well. Because only when he held her, when he took her, when he gave in to his own needs did Diane feel as though he were giving her more than just the release he spilled into her body.

Her hips writhed, her pussy clutching at the thick flesh as Lawe pounded inside her.

Diane felt her juices spilling, her muscles milking his erection each time he forged his way past the snug grip of her pussy.

The feel of his cock buried so deep, the engorged head throbbing in the depths of her had her senses reel-

ing, her pussy creaming wetter and slicker. His hands
gripped the curves of her ass, his fingers flexing into
the rounded flesh as Diane felt her sex rippling around
at the thick invasion, attempting to tug him deeper
inside her.

"Lawe," she whispered his name a shattered moan as
the need continued to claw at her senses.

"I'm here, baby," he rasped as his head lowered, his
lips moving to the slender column of her neck.

His teeth raked against her shoulder as she felt the
change that slowly came over him. Tension tightened
through his body as Diane shifted her hips, lifting herself then returning as he growled against her neck.

That growl vibrated through her, causing her hips to
jerk as she felt Lawe thrust against her once again.

She couldn't seem to make herself remain still. Her
hips rolled and thrust against him as he began to move
inside her. Pulling back then surging deep and hard, the
engorged crest and hardened shaft caressing and stroking sensitive inner nerve endings and pushing her closer
to ecstasy.

Her knees tightened at his hips as she lifted and
lowered herself against him. Her head tilted to the
side as his lips traveled to that point between her neck
and shoulder. His lips settled there, his tongue licking,
his teeth scraping over her flesh. There was a hungry
roughness to his touch that sent fiery trails of sensation
racing through her, the pleasure becoming a hungry
greed she couldn't deny.

Her pussy gripped his shuttling dick with desperation.
The need for release tightened through her with a violent
hunger that sent her pulse racing. The need for his kiss
was overwhelming, an addiction she couldn't fight.

One he seemed to sense.

With a last rake of his teeth against her neck, Lawe's

head lifted, his lips covering hers as he pressed her closer to the wall, holding her tighter as he began moving with a strength that had Diane crying out with a pleasure that tightened with painful force.

"Lawe." She wanted to scream his name, but it only rasped from her throat.

The force of the need rose inside her and began to shudder through her body. Arching in his arms and straining against him, her nails scraped along his back, need beginning to tear at her, to tear through her as the overwhelming hunger surged hard and fast through her body.

Tearing his lips from hers, Lawe scattered kisses to her jaw, along the edge of it, down her neck. Tiny bites, the scrape of his canines; then, as the burning sensations rushing along her nerve endings suddenly exploded in an inferno, she felt his teeth pierce the vulnerable line between her neck and her shoulder.

Her orgasm erupted through her in a series of rushing waves that threw her into a place of pure, exacting ecstasy. She was lost in it. Surging through the tidal wave of it as Lawe buried inside her deep and hard, his cock throbbing, expanding and spurting inside her as the barb suddenly emerged. It became fiercely, thickly engorged, rippling against the tender, sensitive flesh it was locked inside. Diane felt the heat and burning rapture of the increased pleasure that amplified and heightened the sensations that overtook her senses.

There was a part of her that realized, distantly, that each time her orgasm rose and expanded from the surging pleasure Lawe gave her, she felt a part of herself weakening, opening. As though her heart, her soul or something was opening despite her determination to keep that part of her closed off. To remain safe from the emotional abyss that she knew would be awaiting her.

Collapsing against him, shuddering, her breathing gasps of both ecstasy and the agony of emotions tearing free, forcing her to acknowledge them and to acknowledge the fears she had held back for so long.

She held on to him, terrified something or someone would jerk him away from her. Certain that the disagreements they shared were going to blow up in her face.

There were too many explosions that threatened to blow out of control inside her. Too many emotions she couldn't control nor push back enough to give her the chance to control them.

Instead they rose, pushed at the shields that held them back and almost broke free.

Diane was only distantly aware of Lawe's lips still at her neck as he licked and lapped at her flesh.

Marking her.

Everything he had done in the past months had been to one purpose and she knew it. To force her to release what she held back from him. What she refused to give him.

Her entire heart. The part of her soul that only the man who owned her heart would ever have.

And Diane had sworn to herself that no man would ever hold her heart and would definitely never open that part of her soul.

She was terrified if he owned that part of her, then he would control her. Because if Lawe could change her, if he could force her independence to give way to his need to protect her, then he would do it in a heartbeat.

"The thought of losing you destroys me," he suddenly whispered at her ear. "When I saw you in that filthy cell, beaten, almost broken, so delicate and so determined to live, you stole a part of my soul."

Shock held her silent. To hear this strong, always so emotionally cool Breed say such a thing. Lawe wasn't a man prone to give in to emotion. And most certainly, even for a Breed, he had seemed even more unwilling to experience emotion than most.

Keeping her eyes closed she could only hold tighter to him. There wasn't a chance of hiding what she felt from him. His ability to smell emotion and recognize it was too good.

And she knew what he could sense from her.

The denial, a rejection of what he was offering her and the pain of being unable to reach out for it and hold it close to her.

"Why?" he suddenly asked, his face still buried in her neck. "Why don't you want what I have to offer, Diane?"

She felt the tears that tightened her throat, and though she couldn't smell scent as he could, and the pain wasn't in his voice, still, she could sense it. It tightened her chest and sent an ache to burrow so deeply inside her that she knew she would never escape it.

"Because you refuse to accept who I am," she whispered hoarsely. "You're rejecting me as well, Lawe. The rejection is just deeper. I accept you for who you are. You refuse to do the same for me."

His head lifted and drew back.

She was still pressed to the wall, his body still a part of hers and the pleasure . . . The pleasure still throbbed inside her from the presence of the barb as it kept her mate locked to her.

"Do you accept me for who I am?" he asked quietly, somberly. "If you did, Diane, then you'd help me." His fingers touched her cheek, the backs of them caressing her flesh gently. "You'd help us both find a way to compromise. Instead, you run. And running will do nothing but destroy us both."

As she stared back at him and battled the tears she

had no experience with, Diane felt the barb slowly releasing her, retracting back into the hood of his cock and taking with it the echoes of rapture that held her in its grip. That held Lawe in her grip.

"Do you compromise, Lawe?" she whispered. "Because honestly, I haven't seen any give in you that would indicate the ability."

Dropping his head to her shoulder he bestowed a gentle kiss before slowly helping her to slide from him as he pulled the still semi-hard shaft from her pussy and stepped back.

"We'll go to Window Rock," he said softly, and Diane had to swallow past the hard surge of emotion that tightened her throat at the chill in his voice, because when he stared down at her, she could see the torment blazing in his eyes. "Be careful while we're there," he said as he released her fully. "Remember what happens to me, Diane, if anything happens to you, and vice versa. Because regardless of what you believe of me, from the day I realized you were my mate, I stepped back from active status. Because nothing meant more to me than your life, your health and your safety. I would have never fought again."

He didn't mention her happiness. Strangely, the fact that it was forgotten had the power to pierce her heart.

He didn't give her a chance to reply. She couldn't have replied anyway, because she was too shocked, too uncertain about the implications of what he had just told her and the emotion he hadn't mentioned.

To a Breed, nothing was more important than the battle for safety, the battle to ensure that the Breeds, as a people, survived.

So much so that all unmated Breeds vowed an oath to protect, even at the cost of their own lives, all mates, male or female, until they too found their own unique biological, chemical and pheromonal match.

Unmated Breeds composed the majority of the Breeds' fighting force. Once mated, they pulled back to operations rather than active status, or to the protective and security ranks of either the Feline Breed base of Sanctuary, the Wolf Breed base of Haven or the nearby, newly created Coyote stronghold of Citadel.

It was information she had to process, and Diane knew as she watched Lawe gathering her clothes together before he gathered his that now she had no choice but to face the decisions she had been running from.

The choice of accepting Lawe as her mate, and in doing so also accepting the loss of her freedom, or she could deny them both and eventually, sooner rather than later, perhaps be the cause of both their deaths.

• CHAPTER 12 •

"How do you know Thor isn't the traitor in your ranks?" Lawe asked as she lay sprawled against his naked chest, exhausted, limp and drowsy as the sun rose bright and warm the next morning.

"Because I know." She yawned, wondering if she had time for a nap.

They'd had breakfast earlier, then they'd had each other for a bit of early dessert. She was at least two days behind schedule and rather than rushing to pack and leave, she was instead considering a late morning nap. If only Lawe had been kind and had not begun questioning her.

"How did he find you, baby?" he asked. "You didn't tell him you were leaving. You didn't tell anyone."

"He followed Gideon, remember?" She wished he would just drop it. Defending Thor wasn't on her agenda. She needed a nap, then possibly dinner before she hit the road with two grouchy, territorial, overprotective men.

"That's not an answer." And it was obvious he wasn't going to drop it.

"He offers to carry my gear."

Well, that shut him up. Maybe she should have tried that explanation sooner.

As the silence continued she allowed herself to settle closer into sleep.

"He does what?"

Well, it shut him up for a minute anyway.

Exhaling in resignation Diane forced herself to sit up and stare down at him as she pulled the sheet over her breasts. "I said, Thor offers to carry my gear."

"And that proves his innocence how?" he asked as though the answer couldn't possibly make sense.

Pulling her knees up and wrapping her arms around them, she stared back at him directly. "A man doesn't offer to carry a woman's gear if he sees her as a soldier." She was aware of the disgust that lay heavy in her tone. "Thor follows me because I can strategize and cover the bases while he and the others do the grunt work. He gets to do the accounting he loves, watch his bank account grow and take a vacation once a year. He's not going to risk that."

"Diane, you may have to explain this a bit further." He cleared his throat carefully as Diane hid a smile. "Someone on your team is betraying you. They've put your ass on the chopping block and they all enjoy the same benefits."

"But not all of them will take a bullet for a woman they don't know or risk their lives to slip into an enemy village to leave food on a widow's doorstep. The last of his rations, I might add." She shook her head at the thought of it. "And no one but Thor deliberately ensures he's literally covering my back on every mission we take. He sets himself up to take a bullet for me, just as he did with the teenager we rescued last year, that bloated old CEO we extracted when he was stuck in a country he shouldn't have been in, or the teenage boy kidnapped the year before last while on vacation with his parents in Jordan. The others have never done that, but Thor does."

"You put too much faith in him." He shook his head at her explanation. "Just like that damned Gideon. What made you think you could pull him in?"

Lawe watched her lips quirk in amusement. "Gideon took out all but Thor. He shot Brick, Aaron and Malcolm. He was taking the players he suspected off the field. He obviously didn't suspect Thor. Or you." She ticked the reasons off with her fingers. "He left not just a warning of the traitor in my group, but also the location where he suspected Honor Roberts, Judd and Fawn Corrigan to be. He also led me in the direction of several contacts in Argentina that were able to verify the information as well as add to it, possibly giving me a few clues once I get there, where to start looking for her."

He grunted at that, but the explanation made more sense than he wanted to admit.

"What makes you think he wants to talk?"

"He didn't shoot me." She shrugged. "And he's been following me since I was in Argentina. That's the reason it's taken me so long to make it to Window Rock. I wanted to know what he wanted."

"So you just laid yourself out like a fucking piece of raw meat to an animal?" he charged, his expression incredulous. Diane doubted anyone had seen incredulity in Lawe's expression in his life.

"If he wanted me dead, then he would have killed me in Argentina," she assured him caustically. "Give me a little credit, Lawe. I'm not exactly stupid. If I were, you would have already had to help me."

So even he had to agree she wasn't an idiot, because she was obviously still alive.

"Diane." He wiped his hand over his face.

Diane laughed aloud at the reaction. It would have been endearing if not for the fact that it showed a complete lack of faith in her abilities to do her job and to protect herself.

"Diane, he's a male Breed suspected to have been forced into feral fever," he growled. "If even half of what I know is true, then we are well aware of the fact that he's not completely sane, at the very least. Whatever his agenda is, he has no intention of helping anyone except himself to whatever goal he has in mind."

"And, of course, I couldn't possibly be intelligent enough to use him as well," she pointed out reasonably.

"That wasn't what I meant," he snapped back at her. "Gideon is a master strategist, Diane. You'll think you're pulling him in until he has his bullet buried in your brain or his scalpel peeling your flesh from your body. It's a little late to consider the error of your beliefs then."

It was enough to make a woman want to gnash her teeth in irritation. Hell, she *was* grinding hers. His arrogance just pissed her off.

"Whatever you want to believe." It hurt more than words could ever describe that he hadn't extended the same faith to her that he would have extended to any other Breed who may have given him the same explanation. Or any other man period. Gideon thought he was playing her, she was aware of that. She had her own plan as well.

He hadn't given her the possible location of Brandenmore's former victims for nothing. He knew where they were, or where they might be, what he wouldn't know, despite the time he had spent in the labs with them, is what they looked like now. Twelve years was a lot of time. The girls would be twenty-four or twenty-five. Judd would be in his thirties. Maturity could have, and most likely had, drastically changed their looks.

"This isn't personal, Diane." Lawe's expression was tormented as he watched her, and he probably did sense how much his lack of faith hurt.

"Fine, Lawe." She was too tired to argue with him, too disillusioned to attempt to justify or explain her own intentions. "I need to pack . . ."

"I'd prefer to wait to leave, Diane."

She turned back to him slowly, suspicion rising inside her. "Why?

His lips thinned. "I sent Rule and Malachi to Window Rock to request permission from the Navajo Council to conduct the search for a rogue Breed in their territory," he revealed. "That doesn't happen overnight."

How stupid did he believe she was?

"Bullshit, Lawe," she said wearily. "You sent a team to Window Rock to find Gideon or to lay a trap, didn't you?"

"No, I did not." Anger tightened his expression as he came out of the bed, his blue eyes icy as he pushed himself from the bed. "I did exactly as I said I did. I sent a team into Window Rock when I realized where you were headed and what you were doing."

"When I told you where I was headed you sent a team ahead of us to capture Gideon," she accused him knowingly. Hell, she wasn't even surprised. "Is that what this is going to be, Lawe? A series of games you play to keep me one step behind you and always under your thumb?"

She should be angry. She should be raging. But,

surprisingly, she was more amused. Too amused to really be hurt, though she was certain that would come soon. The very fact that he thought he *had* to notify the Navajo Nation Council astounded her.

"Had I thought I wouldn't irreparably damage the mating relationship I want to build with you, then that's exactly what I would have done," he snapped back at her. "Instead, I'm trying to clear the way for you. It wasn't that hard to trace the calls on your sat phone to the reservation. Especially after you made your reservations with the Navajo Suites just before I arrived here. You didn't have to tell me where you were going, I knew. How you had tracked the Roberts girl to this area was what I was unaware of."

"And that was all you did—you just tracked my phone?" She was highly suspicious.

"That's all I did." There went the hand over the face again.

"And you thought you would achieve what by waylaying me here?" Pulling her jeans and shirt from the floor, Diane dressed quickly, aware of the feeling of being at a distinct disadvantage with him by standing before him naked. "How did delaying me benefit you, Lawe?"

It was hard to attempt to make him see that she was more than able to complete her mission, hell, to get him to even give her the chance to prove she could complete it, without the feeling of vulnerability that being naked gave her. Besides, he was still hard, his cock still very interested in a little mating sex.

It was impossible to deny her own renewed interest in the sexual pleasure found in his arms as well. Fortunately, the interest was tempered, the mating heat sated for now, leaving only the natural desire they shared between them, which was strong enough without adding a hormonal, pheromonal, biological and whatever else it was reaction to each other.

"I wasn't trying to achieve anything, Diane." He sighed as he pulled his pants over his hips and zipped them casually. "I was trying to give us a bit of time together as Rule cleared the way for our investigation in the area. The Breeds count the Navajo as one of our greatest proponents and supporters. We can't do anything to jeopardize that. Conducting a secret investigation in their territory could only piss them off and I'm not enough of an optimist to think we can do it and get away with it."

"And I don't need your damned help," she told him. "I already had permission to be in the territory from the Bureau's base office in the Nation. That's all I needed."

The base office was manned by three Breeds and a member of the Navajo Nation Law Enforcement. "As long as I had permission from base, I was fine."

"Base can't give you permission to investigate Breeds or Genetics," he gritted out.

"No, they can give me permission to investigate other areas though. Areas such as the peaceful resolution of the casino conflict outside Window Rock. For God's sake, Lawe, didn't you even consider the fact that I had laid my own fucking ground work? Once I was here, I could have used that to explain to anyone and everyone I spoke to. And then I could fall back on it to explain how I may have stumbled upon the identities of the girls. I'm good like that." Frustration roughened and colored her voice as complete disbelief flooded her senses. "You took the confrontational route, I took the effective one. One of the differences between me and you."

Here they went again, arguing over whether or not she knew how to do her job. She had known eventually he would go behind her back and when he did, she had known it would be in a way that would completely drive her crazy.

At this point, there wasn't even any sense in getting angry. Pulling her own hair out was an option though. Or his.

She wasn't arguing over it any longer. She was tired of pointing it out, tired of begging him to give her a chance to prove it. She didn't have to prove a damned thing, she had already proven it with five years of command and the fact that she had survived this world since before she had graduated high school.

"I'm heading to Window Rock," she informed him as she tucked her shirt into the band of her jeans before sitting down to pull on her socks. "You can stay or you can go, I really don't give a damn which."

She could feel his gaze narrowing on her as she pushed the last few items into her bag and zipped it with a furious jerk of her wrist.

"Diane, we're a government agency of sorts," he stated with obvious forced patience. "We don't just waltz in on their land and begin conducting an investigation, especially against a Breed that could possibly carry the genetics of one of their own. Even Jonas doesn't fuck with the Navajo Nation, for good reason."

"And it could have nothing to do with the fact that you're desperate to make certain I'm wrapped in cotton batting and protected from a fresh breeze," she retorted.

"You make it sound as though the bastard hadn't just finished taking potshots at you and your men last week," Lawe bit out angrily. "I was there, I know what was going on, Diane, and that bastard could have killed you as easily as he wounded your men. There's more on his agenda than giving you a helping hand."

Duh. No kidding. This wasn't her moron week, no matter what he wanted to think.

She shrugged again as she continued to gather her things together. There was no point in staying any longer, just as there was no point in attempting to convince him that she was trained well enough, that she was intelligent enough to do what had to be done.

"Would you listen to me." He grabbed her arm as she turned to move her bags to the door. "You don't have to do this."

Diane stared back at him, seeing the worry in his gaze but also seeing the fact that her future would be as bleak as hell if she gave him what he wanted, if she left with him and returned to the safety of Sanctuary.

"I do have to do this, Lawe," she stated softly, the growing anger dropping away in the face of his concern and the conflicting emotions she could see darkening his gaze. "I don't have to do it for you or even for myself. It's for Honor Roberts. It's for Fawn and for Judd and the other Breeds that were tortured in those labs. I'm doing this, Lawe, because no one else cared enough or knew enough to protect them when they needed it. I do this for my niece." Tears filled her eyes at the thought of Amber. "For the consequences she may pay for Breed research after that bastard injected her. I do it for what they did to you, to the others and for what they'll continue to do. God, Lawe, I do this because it's who I am."

Lawe stared into her eyes, saw the conviction there, saw the woman she knew herself to be as well as the woman he knew she could be. "You only see the warrior you are, Diane." He sighed, feeling as weary as she had sounded moments ago. "You don't see the rest of you, but I sense her. I hope you find her, before you destroy both of us."

Mating heat was so much more than a sexual hunger that brought a couple together. Lawe knew it for the emotional abyss it could be as well as the thriving, beautiful relationship it could become.

Staring into her eyes, he tried, God knew he tried with everything inside him, to still the dominance that was so much a part of him. To tell her what he felt and know it wouldn't give her the encouragement he was certain she would get from it.

He'd felt her hurt, knew what he'd done to hurt her and he hated himself for it.

Without a thought he'd attempted to wound her self-confidence just as he'd attempted to weaken her belief in herself.

He'd done it without thinking, without a moment's hesitation, and she'd seen right through him. He'd seen it in her eyes, in her expression. She'd known even before he had what he was up to. And she deserved so much more.

She deserved much more from him.

"Before I destroy both of us." She sighed as she turned away from him. "There is no 'us,' Lawe. There's still just you and what you want."

She looked alone, bereft. Staring at her, Lawe couldn't believe the gift standing before him or the incredible strength and will she possessed. She was as strong as the woman who had given him birth. And he knew beyond a shadow of a doubt she would die for him the same as Morningstar had died for her mate, Elder.

"After my escape from the labs I avoided every woman who I felt, even remotely, could have been my mate." The surprise on her face was nothing compared to his own as he heard himself speaking.

Reaching out Lawe touched the side of her face with the backs of his fingers, brushing her hair back as he did so. "Not because I didn't want you." He cupped the back of her neck as that remembered ache of hunger shot through him. "Because I did, Diane. With everything I am, everything I was, I wanted my mate. I wanted to hold you, to have you hold me. I wanted to laugh and feel the contentment I knew other Breeds felt with their mates. I wanted to sleep with that sense of peace others spoke of. But even more, even more than that, I wanted to ensure that the evil I knew existed in this world never touched you. Because I knew the dangers, I knew the pain and horrors that I could bring to you. And I wanted nothing more than to vanquish all your dragons. And here I was, the greatest of all those dragons."

She turned her head away, blinking. Damn, she was blinking back tears?

"Tears," he whispered, amazed. "I never wanted you to have reason to shed tears or to feel the helplessness that rages through me when you do." To know she hurt enough to cry made him crazy. It made all the animal genetics that raged inside him threaten to overtake him once again.

"You can't hold back life, Lawe," she stated, the frustration eating at her, and raking at the control Lawe was fighting to hold on to as he sensed it.

"I know I can't hold back life," he agreed as he pulled his hand back rather than tightening his hold on her. "I don't want to hold back your life. I want to fucking share it. Damn it, Diane, I just want to ensure that nothing takes us from the other. We're mates. If you die, then I may as well die with you. And if I die . . ." He shook his head, the other side of mating suddenly clearer to him than it had ever been. "If I'm gone, then you'll be always alone. Always, Diane. Always suffering that loss because you'll be unable to bear to have another man touch you. You would be completely vulnerable. You and any children we may have unless you're in Sanctuary. Unless you're protected and you understand that need for protection."

Watching her face, watching the pain that flashed in her eyes, and the fear, he suddenly wondered if those Breeds who were still unaware of the true depth of it, would allow it to begin if they knew the truth. He knew that fear. The fear of being enclosed, of being imprisoned. She was terrified he would find a way to cage her, and Lawe couldn't swear to her that the day wouldn't come when it would have to be done.

Lowering his head he pressed his forehead against her temple, inhaling the scent of her. The mating heat, a spicy, fruity scent, a combination of him and her, a merging of who they were.

That was the mating scent. It was what mating did. It merged two beings, it merged their scents, and sometimes, when needed, it merged their dreams along with their hearts and souls.

"You are more than a soldier," he promised her as he let his lips brush against her hair, as he inhaled the scent of both of them merging. "You are more than a mate, more than just a woman, a sister or an aunt. You can't fight this fight alone, Diane, and that's what you're trying to do. Nor can you fight against rogue Breeds who can smell you coming a mile away. Or Council Coyotes who can smell your scent and know it for what it is. And if you're taken because of it, if you're taken, you become the same as the other mates the Council has captured. You become a science experiment." Screams echoed in his head now. "Vivisected, screaming, begging and dying as they compare your organs, compare the changes to them, against those they've murdered in the same way before you."

Pulling back, he stared into her tormented gaze and

wanted to roar out his rage and his pain at what he saw there.

A woman fighting not just her hunger but all the dreams and all the needs she had never had to deny herself before. Dreams and needs he was asking—no, demanding—she give up. She was more than just a soldier, she was his mate. She was the woman he'd always dreamed of having and the one whose sheer bravery terrified him.

"Lawe." She touched him. Her palm against his jaw, her fingers against his cheek. "Sanctuary is attacked at least once a year. I know of two attempts against the community during the social events Callan and Merinus are forced to throw throughout the year. Snipers have been caught twice attempting to get into position and Callan was nearly killed at an event thrown by a Breed supporter. Sanctuary isn't safe either. And each time it was attacked, each time a Breed, a mate or any member of the community was harmed I'd die inside. I'd always feel I could have helped. I'll always feel responsible."

He tried to protest, only to have her fingers press against his lips to hold the words back.

Her hands weren't silk and satin, but neither were they calloused and rough. They were a true woman's hands. She used them. She worked with them. She touched him and he swore she breathed life into his soul the night he rescued her.

"I can't be more than a soldier, Lawe. Even for you. It's all I've dreamed of being. And, until you, it's all I've dreamed of having. I don't want a protector or a jailer. I want a partner. And that's what I'll have or I'll have nothing or no one at all. Even you." She stepped slowly back from him even though he could feel, sense, her need to crawl into his body and stay there.

And that was where he wanted her. Buried so deep

inside him that he knew every breath she took. That he felt it. That he could reach out at any given time and assure himself of her safety, of her happiness.

As he watched her, she slung the strap of the duffel bag over one shoulder, the strap of the backpack over the other, then hefted the black duffel bag that contained her weapons. Lawe almost shook his head in bemusement. The gear looked far too heavy for her to manage on her own.

Yet she did manage it. It weighed heavily on her slender shoulders, pulled at her arm, yet she went out the door and slammed it behind her.

His eyes narrowed.

Turning back to the room, Lawe took his time and finished dressing. There was no gear to pack or collect. It was all stored in the back of the SUV Rule had left in the parking lot before heading out to Window Rock with all but one of the team members who had driven out with them.

He pulled on the sleeveless black shirt that matched the same-color mission pants, then the long-sleeved light shirt that buttoned over it. He laced his protective black ankle boots snugly and clipped the holster that held the laser-powered handgun. Finally, he tucked the sheathed knife he carried at the small of his back.

He moved unhurriedly to the door, opened it and left the room. Stepping out onto the covered walkway and glancing down at the parking lot where the SUV and the feline Breed Enforcer waited.

With his mate and her second-in-command.

Diane leaned against the front of the vehicle, and even across the distance he could smell the complete fury raging through her and spilling out to scent the air with the smell of sweetened heat and flaming ambrosia.

Damn, his dick was steel hard.

He'd gone from semi-hard to a full, engorged erection in about a quarter of a second. The glands beneath his tongue began filling with the mating hormone, the spice and sweet taste flooding his senses as he gave a resigned sigh.

She was pissed as hell and the knowledge of it sent adrenaline rushing through him as she stared back at him in challenge.

And it was definitely a challenge.

The soldier was facing him. The hardened expression, the flattened line of her lips, the stance as she saw him. She straightened, her hip cocking, one hand resting against it, her fingers outspread.

She wasn't tapping her foot. She wasn't tapping anything. She was standing still, her gaze locked on him, her eyes burning into him.

The expression was all soldier, but that gaze, that was the woman's gaze. It was filled with anger, with unrealized dreams, with a woman's emotions. A mate's battle for independence.

Mating and life with a Breed was hell on an independent woman. It was hell too on Breed women who were independence, strength and reliance personified.

Diane could have been a Breed female. She had trained from an early age, but rather than being abused or treated cruelly, her uncle had instead fought to teach her to protect herself and her sister. To react with instinct as well as years of training. To strategize and foresee all possible angles and problems that could arise.

She had killed to keep from being killed. She had fought in the darkest, deepest hellholes and in the concrete jungles where civilization should have ruled. She had moved in to take command of four of the meanest bastards in the independent military communities and she'd ensured all their bank accounts were well-padded and drawing excellent interest.

She wasn't just a soldier and a commander either. She was a hell of an investor.

Breaking his gaze from hers, he turned and moved along the third-story walk to the metal stairwell in the middle of the long building.

He could feel the hairs at the back of his neck tingling. He almost paused to search out the cause, but it wasn't a feeling of imminent danger as much as it was of being watched, studied.

If he paused to search out the cause, then he would be allowing his unknown enemy to know he was aware of him. Far better to surprise Gideon should he decide to attempt to catch Lawe off guard.

For now, he had his mate to deal with, along with a trip to Window Rock.

As he stepped to the concrete walk the sat phone at his side vibrated demandingly. His senses alert, his gaze still on his mate, Lawe pulled it free and brought it to his ear.

"Enforcer Justice," he answered.

"We have a problem." Rule's voice was strained. That in and of itself was unusual.

Lawe picked up his pace to the SUV.

"Report," Lawe ordered, his tone declaring his full attention to his brother.

"We had a situation here," Rule stated. "Malachi mated a Martinez. Our little cousin, Isabelle, and her mate had a stalker. The stalker shot our favorite little Coyote, Lawe, Ashley Truing. They don't know if she's going to make it."

Ashley Truing. She had colored, highlighted and streaked blond hair; perfectly manicured, painted and

decorated nails—nails as false as the color of her hair.
She had so many pairs of shoes it was said her entire
room was lined with shelves to hold them. Not that
he believed it. She gave the impression of self-interest,
conceit and laziness, but she was one of the most dangerous female Breeds ever created.

Lawe's gaze went to Diane's as he moved faster.
Instantly, she straightened and moved for the side of the
SUV where she threw open the passenger door as Thor
moved just as quickly to slide onto the passenger seat
behind her.

The Enforcer Josiah was in the back rather than taking the driver's seat as he often did, his Breed senses
picking up the sudden sense of haste Lawe could feel
surging through him.

"We're heading in," Lawe assured him as he grabbed
the driver's door that Diane had thrown open for him.
"I'll call you when we're near."

"Be sure to," Rule stated harshly. "Gideon took out the
stalker. We should have told Malachi who we were looking for, Lawe. He knows him. Hell, he knows a lot about
him. Ashley's in surgery, Dr. Armani and Dr. Sobolov
are with her. I'll contact you again when there's more."

The line disconnected.

The call was long enough to fully apprise Lawe of
the situation but not long enough for an enemy to lock
onto or to track.

Diane had taken the electronic starter from Josiah
and had the motor running and ready as Lawe slid into
the driver's seat. Throwing the vehicle into gear, Lawe
pulled out of the parking space.

"Ashley's been shot," he informed them. "Gideon's
already in Window Rock. He took out the shooter and
then disappeared." Glancing at Diane, he couldn't help
but fear that one day she could be in Ashley's place. "It

looks like we're going to get that permission to investigate after all. Let's see how quickly we can get this taken care of and get Gideon contained." He glanced in the rearview mirror. "Notify Sanctuary we're heading in and I want my regular team out here ASAP. It's time to go hunting."

A Breed hunting a Breed. Lawe had never imagined he would be in this position unless one of the Council's malevolent Breeds were concerned, or that he would need to hunt a Breed who had known the most vicious of hells during his confinement.

Quickly, he explained the information Rule had reported, brief though it was.

Gideon was in protective mode, a far different role than he had been playing in past months. He had saved Malachi's mate, Lawe's first cousin, and he was known by Malachi. Rule was right; Lawe should have told the team the full identity of the Breed they were chasing rather than giving the minute details he had passed along. He should never have assumed Gideon was unknown by the team traveling with him.

They had searched for months for a Breed who had known the assassin. One who could give them some sense of the Breed they were searching for.

He wouldn't have expected Malachi.

He wouldn't have expected Gideon to protect a human, especially another Breed's mate.

But he sure as hell hadn't expected the vivacious, energetic and completely efficient Ashley to ever have been targeted or caught off guard by a stalker.

God help him if he ever had to face the day Diane became such a victim, because Lawe knew that if it happened, the animal would control him. And the animal was by far more savage than the man could ever be.

CHAPTER 13

Ashley Truing's perpetually tanned flesh looked so pale, washed out and dull that Diane could actually detect the dark roots that were beginning at her scalp.

Normally, the professional color she had applied to her hair looked so natural, so well colored and streaked that it was impossible to tell it was artificial.

It was also not natural to see her this quiet, almost lifeless, as though the exuberance and vivacious life force that was so much a part of her had drained out with the blood she had lost from the laser-shot wound.

All but silent, almost always deadly when set to its highest setting, laser hand weapons could emulate the old-fashioned bullet-loaded weapons but with much more deadly results.

Thankfully, Ashley had had a med tech well versed in immediate care of such wounds. It had kept her alive long enough for the Breed doctors to get to her.

Just as her Breed genetics and amazing inner strength had helped her live through a wound a mere human wouldn't have had a chance of surviving.

Diane watched through the window of the ICU room as Lawe stood at Ashley's bedside listening to Dr. Armani and Dr. Sobolov fill him in on her condition.

The Pride alpha and his prima, Callan and Merinus Lyons, had already been there and were currently in their suite awaiting Lawe and Diane at the Navajo Suites along with the Wolf Breed alpha and lupina, Wolfe and Hope Gunnar, and the Coyote Breed alpha and his coya, Del-Rey and Anya Delgado.

The nurses had reported that the Coyote alpha had to force the coya from the hospital. Ashley was one of her dearest friends, and she was inconsolable with worry.

"They lost her twice during surgery."

Diane swung around to face Rule, the current commander in charge of the teams that had been sent to Window Rock ahead of them.

"Will she be okay?" Diane turned back to the glass looking into the dimly lit room as she shoved her hands into the pockets of her jeans and watched Lawe.

His expression was pulled into lines of worry as he stared down at Ashley. His arms were crossed over his broad chest, his eyes burning with fury.

Ashley looked like a little doll tucked into the hospital bed. A pale, still, lifeless little doll.

"The doctors say every hour she's breathing is a reason for hope," he said with a sigh. "It was a bad hit. Too close to the heart, and she's small."

The reflection of his casual shrug was at odds with the heavy sadness in his voice and in his expression. It was rare that she saw Rule showing any tender emotions. He was good at anger, sarcasm and mockery, but it wasn't often he allowed himself to feel anything more.

"He's going to get worse." The quietly spoken words had her tensing as her gaze touched on Lawe again.

"What do you mean?" Was he aware of the struggle she and Lawe were involved in?

"Lawe saw you almost broken when he rescued you in Syria," he said softly. "I saw his face when I and the team met him at the hospital you were flown to. He knew you were his mate. He saw you at your weakest. You're not going to take that image out of his head."

She glanced at his reflection once again, her gaze meeting his in the glass as she recognized the emotion that swirled in the darker topaz of his eyes.

"You don't like me much, do you, Rule?" Her lips twisted at the thought.

"Actually," he said, exhaling roughly, "the problem is, I do like you, Diane. I liked you even before I knew you were his mate." He nodded toward his brother. "What I don't like is the fact that you're not willing to keep him as safe as he's willing to keep you."

"And that's how you see it," she murmured.

He nodded firmly. "That's how I see it."

How little his brother knew him, but hell, how little he knew himself actually. Lawe may have pulled back from active status, meaning he was no longer taking the worst of the worst missions, but he was still there, working side by side with the bogeyman of the Breeds, Jonas Wyatt.

Her lips quirked at the thought, a mocking acknowledgment of her own thoughts. Lawe wasn't being shot at, but he was still in danger.

"He's not exactly back home on the farm planting vegetables, is he, Rule." A bitter reminder that Lawe hadn't retreated to Sanctuary to build cabins, work base security, public relations or the political positions that were kept open for those Breed mates pulling back from active status. "He's still directing the missions and dining on adrenaline. But you expect me to tie on an apron and bake bread, don't you? That's what you and Lawe both expect from me." Sarcasm dripped from her lips and she knew it. At the moment, she excelled at it.

His head tilted in acknowledgment. "It would make life easier on the rest of us." His gaze flicked to hers in the glass. "Unfortunately, I don't think it would be edible."

Diane almost smiled at the comment, though her heart clenched in pain at the reminder that Lawe wouldn't give a damn as long as she was out of danger.

Before she could pull the emotion back and take control of it Lawe's head whipped around in the middle of his conversation with the doctors, his gaze narrowing on her, then on his brother.

Rule clucked his tongue behind her. "See what I mean? There he goes, getting all protective. The second he senses your hurt feelings, he's ready to battle."

From the corner of her eye she watched Rule's image in the glass as he gave his brother a mocking little finger wave. She had to roll her eyes. Brothers were brothers whether they were Breed or human. Alien brothers were probably the same she thought ruefully.

Evidently, the taunt reassured Lawe because he turned back to Armani and Sobolov, though he did shoot his brother a warning glance as he did so.

She was about to hate men. She could see it coming. They were irritating, overconfident, arrogant and just plain assholes. At least the good ones were. She sighed in resignation at the thought.

She'd actually given due consideration to the subject of giving up the day job as Lawe lay napping the previous night. God knew she didn't want to see him distracted at the wrong time, and she didn't want to see

him hurt or dead because she couldn't take a backseat
and return to Sanctuary with him. It was in the middle
of the night that she realized there wasn't a chance in
hell he would stay there with her. Not for long anyway.

Like Jonas, he would go back and forth. But Rachel
was Jonas's personal assistant, and when possible, she
traveled with him. She shared the job with him; they
often talked shop together and he valued her opinion.

She simply couldn't see Lawe doing the same. He
wanted too desperately to forget that she was a soldier.
That she was nothing but his mate.

Dr. Sobolov adjusted Ashley's blanket, smoothed a
wisp of hair back from her cheek and stared down at the
silent form for long moments.

"Her attacker was killed?" Diane asked.

Rule nodded sharply. "Gideon killed him. Holden
Mayhew was attempting to kidnap Malachi Morgan's
new mate. She and Ashley are friends and Ashley was
caught in the middle."

Diane knew Malachi. The former Enforcer, who
had been pulled into public relations for his exceptional
ability to read expressions and detect conspirators, was
quiet and intense and, for a Coyote, quite likeable.

"And his mate?"

"Bruised, beaten, though not severely. There were two
Council Coyotes waiting at the stairwell exit outside for
them. He was selling them a Breed mate. We found the
two Council Coyotes this morning, skinned out and gutted
in the desert. Gideon can be a savage bastard, it seems."

Diane suppressed a shudder at the thought of what
those Coyotes had suffered, but words her uncle used
to mutter drifted through her mind: "Live by the sword,
die by the sword."

"Lawe said Malachi reported knowing him?" Surprising enough.

Rule nodded. "They met during one of Gideon's escapes, his first one. Gideon worked with a small group Malachi was leading until they reached Amsterdam where Gideon decided to go his own way."

"And there he was betrayed by a prostitute," Diane murmured.

"Yes, he was." Rule sighed. "Malachi's mate is Chief Ray Martinez's niece, though. The attack convinced them to give us permission to begin the investigation to search for him."

Diane stilled for a long second before turning to Rule, uncaring that Lawe or anyone else for that matter would detect her displeasure.

"That's not why we're here," she reminded.

"We are not going to get permission to investigate the missing research projects, and we're not going to inform them that's why we're here," he told her, his tone steely now as he lowered his voice. "I can give you the reasons why later, in private, when I update Lawe. Suffice to say, our story is that we're searching for Gideon for fear that the feral fever he's slipped into could cause an unwarranted death. That's all they need to know. The Navajo don't want bodies to begin piling up in Window Rock, especially after Isabelle Martinez's attack by a man her father once trusted."

She swung back around and glared at Lawe now. He'd turned, his gaze meeting hers, his stare brooding as it flicked between her and Rule.

"You shouldn't have come here to begin with." Gritting the words between clenched teeth she shoved her hands in the pocket of her jeans to keep from trying to strangle him. "You caused an incident where none was needed."

"Then Malachi wouldn't have found his mate," Rule pointed out, as though that somehow validated the decision.

"You and your brother just piss me off." Diane

turned back to him, the irritation churning into anger. "Your arrogance and complete lack of consideration for others never fails to amaze me, Rule."

The corners of his eyes shifted and his brow arched. "What did we do this time?"

"You found a way to argue a decision you knew was wrong to begin with. Gideon knows you're here, and now he knows it's not just him you're chasing but the Brandenmore Research projects he's after as well. You've just forewarned him."

"The Genetics Council believes we're searching for him." His voice grated.

"He's not stupid," she retorted. "By allowing him to believe you even know where he's at before letting me arrive first was all he needed. You're not dealing with the Council or their Coyotes. You're dealing with a Breed whose intelligence rates at the genius level and whose ability to coordinate and carry out what others considered suicide missions when he was only a teenager should have been *your* warning. He knows, and now he'll stop at nothing to ensure you don't get anywhere close to them. I just pray to God he doesn't consider killing them a viable option to losing them to you."

Better yet, she was to the point that if it weren't for her own niece, she would hinder their search in any way possible. Fortunately for them, Amber needed the girls. The answers to what the serum had done to them as they matured, especially Honor Roberts, was vitally important.

For some reason, the contact she had found in Argentina had believed it was Honor who may hold the answers to what Amber would be facing as she grew older.

The changes in her niece were astounding. She had been walking for the past few weeks, despite the fact that she was barely eight months old. She was purring when she found something that pleased her, if she believed she

was alone. And her sister swore her daughter understood
far more than she should for her age. The few moments
Diane had spent with Amber before leaving D.C. had
assured her Amber did know far more than she should.

Jonas was convinced of it, Rachel had told her during
an earlier discussion. She often caught Jonas talking to
the toddler, giving her directions, then watching her carry
them out when she thought her "da" had left the room.

Rachel was terrified that the advanced intelligence
was only the first sign that her daughter would follow
the same path as the monster who had injected her. That
her brain would deteriorate, just as Phillip Brandenmore's had after he had injected himself.

"Diane."

Lawe caught her arm as she paced up the hall. Her
only thought was to get away from him and his supreme
confidence that he had done the right thing. Any moron
would know this couldn't possibly be the right thing. It
would have been far better to allow her to handle it alone.
Gideon wouldn't have been nearly so worried about her,
because he believed she would be weak without her men.
Everyone she met believed that, believed she was no
more than a figurehead to the group of mercenaries.
"We're going to destroy lives here," she whispered without turning around, the certainty that they couldn't do
anything less if they continued was searing her conscience.
"We know he's here to find them as well. That's the only
reason he would have given me the location he suspected
they were in. For whatever reason he believes I'll have a
better chance of identifying, locating or convincing them
to reveal themselves. But what does he intend to do once
that's accomplished? Why go to these extremes?"

Her only thought was for her niece. She and her sister had gone through years of torturous testing to cure
them of their diseases, and according to the scientists

in Argentina, they had nearly died several times after being given the serum that was eventually concocted.

According to one of her contacts, it was possible Amber would never survive past her second year without the help of the two girls that had been in the labs, especially Honor. Regret had filled his gaze when he told her that Honor Roberts was her only chance, because Fawn Corrigan had died with the Bengal Breed they'd been experimenting on, known as Judd.

Just as he had warned her to be careful of the remaining Breed that had been in the labs. The one they had possibly driven past the point of sanity.

Gideon's fury was becoming the stuff of legends already. The suspected feral fever that drove him had made him one of the most vicious assassins to come out of the creations science had dreamed up.

She had wondered why he was helping her. She had let herself believe it was out of concern for the three who had been imprisoned with him, but a part of her had known better. She hadn't believed the man known as the Executioner—but also known for never harming an innocent—would strike out against the victims he'd shared the Brandenmore labs with. She still couldn't believe it.

"He has no reason to kill them." Gripping her upper arm lightly he began steering her to the elevators as Rule followed. "And we were petitioning the Navajo Council for this investigation. We can't operate on their lands without apprising them of it. It will break the agreement we have with them and we'll lose far more than we'll gain. Even doing it your way would be seen by them as dishonest and cause sanctions to be slapped on us immediately. Ray Martinez does not tolerate Jonas's games and he doesn't care who it effects once he learns he's being manipulated. There would be no way to convince him that Jonas wasn't behind this."

"There's more going on here than Gideon is allowing us to see," she bit out as the doors opened and he led her into the empty cubicle, followed by Rule. "He knows Malachi. He knows it was Malachi's mate he saved from being taken by Council Coyotes. That means he's watching. And he's listening. I knew he wasn't giving me the information I needed out of the kindness of his heart, but I can't find any other reason for the aid he's given us."

"What was his relationship with the others?" Lawe asked.

Diane pushed her fingers restlessly through her hair as she exhaled helplessly. "Apparently good. The four found ways to help each other, often. There were several lab techs that attempted to help them whenever they could as well. When the order for termination went out, Honor Roberts had already been returned to her family. No one knows what happened exactly. The termination facility was destroyed but there was evidence more than one body had been placed in the cremation chamber that night. There wasn't a guard or assistant left alive to verify it, though their computer files show the three were logged in and Judd and Fawn were terminated. Brandenmore decided Gideon must have found a way to escape and destroyed the facility. And Gideon was excellent with computers. He could have found a way—easily—to have falsified the entries."

But why hadn't she considered his motives sooner? She should have. God, she should have. She was just certain she could work around them. That she could find a way to take Fawn, and hopefully Honor, out of Window Rock without Gideon realizing what she had done until it was too late.

She knew why she hadn't considered them before.

Every thought had been consumed with her niece, with saving the child whose innocence and sweet smiles made her remember what she was fighting for.

Lawe was silent. But she could almost hear what he could have said.

He had warned her. He had warned her she couldn't possibly know what was in Gideon's mind. And she didn't. Was he there to harm or to help? Did he have a grudge or an atonement driving him? Was she risking the very people who may well be Amber's last hope?

She had expected an argument, a confident denial and assurance that Lawe knew what he was doing, yada, yada, yada. She could have almost spit the argument out for him, she'd heard it so many times from other Breeds.

Instead, he remained quiet as the elevator made its way to the main floor.

She didn't risk glancing at his face, she didn't dare. She knew she wouldn't be able to bear to see that arrogance, that confidence that he was always right in his expression.

She should have thought of this sooner. The moment she realized Lawe had been following her, she should have known what he would do. She should have known he would have warned Gideon they were searching for him. Knowing that, Gideon would be much harder to anticipate, and much harder to slip away from.

"The plans were already in place," he said quietly. "Before you ever told me what you knew or who had told you. I figured it out, Diane. That's my job. It's what I do. It's what I was trained for. To take the smallest of details concerning an operation and put them together, like pieces of a puzzle. Once you ran from me, and I realized the direction you were going, it came together."

Yes, that was what he was trained for. And yes, he would have put it together. But she should have realized he would notify the Navajo Nation of who the Bureau was searching for.

And just to begin with, she should have realized she couldn't run from him, she couldn't hide from him.

He'd sat back in the past months and had left her alone. She had believed he would do so again. She had never truly believed he would follow her to Arizona when he hadn't followed her to any other mission since he'd rescued her.

She'd been prepared to avoid his goon squad, but not him. Because there was no avoiding Lawe.

Now, Gideon knew they weren't just after the others who had shared the hell of those experiments with him. He knew they were also after him, and that would make him a threat to them all. The sense of hopelessness that filled her was almost overwhelming.

What had she done?

Lawe ensured that he and Rule placed themselves in position to protect Diane as they exited the elevator and then the front of the hospital.

The SUV was waiting at the door as he ordered. Rule opened the back door, his gaze flint hard as he scanned the area while Diane pulled herself inside and Lawe followed.

He could feel that sense of hopelessness radiating from her and he knew he was the cause of it. He had no idea how to fix it. The pain she always kept buried so deep inside radiated outward with it, assuring him that whatever she was thinking had sliced deep inside her soul.

Feeling that hopelessness coming from her had his fingers clenching into fists of need unlike anything he'd known before her. His own helplessness rose like a demon inside him as he realized there was no way to stem the pain she was feeling. There was no way to ease it.

"Commander Justice, Director Wyatt and Pride Leader Lyons and his prima request that you meet with them when you arrive. A meal is being prepared as are reports for your arrival."

"Please inform them that as soon as we've settled

into our room we'll contact them," he replied as he kept watch on Diane from the corner of his eye.

Neither her expression nor her emotions changed. She didn't react in any way that he would have imagined she would. She simply stared out the window, a light frown on her face as she watched the small city from the confines of the vehicle.

What was she thinking? Sometimes it was impossible to decipher her thoughts. Other people Lawe found easy to read, even Breeds. Diane, though, he'd never been able to accurately predict and that had the power to irritate the hell out of him.

She wasn't angry, and she should be, he admitted. Had she admitted to him that she had worked him so easily, or that she had attempted to interfere in one of his missions then he would have been furious. With himself as well as her.

It hadn't been easy to do, but he had given her just enough rope to hang herself, Gideon and the three individuals they were searching for.

Did she realize they were even working toward the same end? The survival of a child too small and too vulnerable to understand the changes going on inside her or to explain to anyone what those changes were?

He couldn't allow his feelings or his pain for her to become involved in his decisions. If he allowed himself to sympathize or to understand how the three from the Brandenmore Labs would feel about being dragged into this war, then it could alter his ability to do the job Jonas had entrusted to him. And it could affect the survival of the Breeds as a whole. There were too many changes evolving in mating heat, too many children who were displaying unexpected anomalies and changes as they matured, to allow emotion to sway what had to be done.

His loyalty was to his mate, to his Pride leader and to

the Breeds. In that order. He couldn't allow anything or anyone to change that.

God knew he wished there had been no victims to the Council's madness or to Phillip Brandenmore's insanity. But there had been. Thousands of them. Every child kidnapped as genetic material, every woman taken as a vessel to grow the creations they envisioned and every Breed created had been a victim.

For more than a century research had evolved. Jonas actually believed the research had been going on for over a hundred and fifty years. One hundred and fifty years of the horror that had evolved to the lives they now lived.

He couldn't allow himself to turn his back on it, or on those depending upon the decisions made now to preserve the future.

"Josiah, is the director's mate with him?" Diane directed the question to the Enforcer driving.

"Yes, Ms. Broen. Mrs. Wyatt is traveling with the director, as is your niece, Amber. Your sister hopes you'll attend the coming meeting this evening as well."

Lawe watched as she lifted her hand and rubbed at her forehead wearily.

The scent of her hopelessness had slowly eased away, but it hadn't been replaced by other emotions as it would with anyone else. There was only the scent of the woman, a fresh, summery scent that had altered only the slightest with his own and the mating hormone. The scent of the mating heat was there, but that altered mated scent hadn't evolved as it should have.

He controlled his frown, his confusion. Each couple developed a unique scent, a combination of both of them that they carried after mating heat began. Its habit was to completely change each individual scent to ensure that the mates were one scent, just as they were one complete unit. Yet Diane's scent was still uniquely her own. It was tinged with his scent, similar to that of an impending storm, but nothing more, and he found the primal genetics reacting to that with a wary lifting of the hairs at the back of his neck.

A warning of danger or an instinctive response to a situation that the animal sensed wasn't quite right, Lawe acknowledged. He barely caught the growl that would have rumbled in his throat. He barely held back the sudden, raging need to have her or the scent of that need from filling the interior of the SUV.

He wanted her. Naked, willing. He wanted her arching to him, the heat of her pussy enveloping the engorged shaft presently tormenting him, and he wanted her to accept him.

To accept that he couldn't face the danger she was so determined to challenge.

Lust was rising hard and fast inside him, and Lawe silently admitted the meeting with Jonas and Callan Lyons would have to be delayed for it. Locking his mate to him was a priority he couldn't ignore much longer. The knowledge that she was somehow, emotionally and forcibly, refusing the mating had his senses in an uproar. Ensuring she carried his scent, if only for the few hours it lingered on her skin after he possessed her, was raking at his balls with merciless talons. The hunger for her was a fever in his blood, one that was rising beneath his flesh as each second without her touch went by.

The glands beneath his tongue began swelling, the hormone filling it and sinking into his senses with heated demand. There would come a point when denying it wouldn't be possible. When he would have to have her, immediately, without the control needed to ensure he touched her, held and loved her as he ached to do.

It seemed that every time they came together it was with a flaming hunger that stole his ability to drive her to the edge of sensual madness with just his touch. The mating hormone fueled a different kind of hunger, ensnared them with the addictive, sexually charged fever they both found impossible to delay.

As though sensing the hunger tearing through him, Diane's head jerked to the side to stare at him rather than the passing scenery.

Lawe had to clench his fists; his entire body tensing with the need to fuck her as the scent of her emotions finally reached him. Or rather, the scent of her hunger.

It slammed into him, as though the act of glancing into his eyes, seeing his need burning there for her, had opened the floodgates to her own.

And she ached. She needed.

She wanted him as he wanted her, fast and hard, with a pleasure so incredible it would burn them to the core and meld them to each other, heart and soul.

Nothing mattered to Lawe but holding her, feeling her wrapped tightly around him, crying out his name, her sharp little fingernails piercing the flesh of his back and shoulders.

That was what mattered.

Just one more time. Before he met with Callan and Jonas, he needed her, just one more time before reality intruded any further and attempted to steal her heart from him.

If he even had it at all.

The question was: Could he survive without the heart of the woman he longed for? Or would he experience the slow, agonizing death of his own soul because of her rejection of him?

Or because of his refusal to accept her?

CHAPTER 14

Diane always had the feeling she was on the outside looking in. Even before her parents had died. She'd been different. She had been different and she'd always known it. She had never felt accepted until the team had allowed her on that first mission. Until every last man had voted her in, not because her uncle was their commander but because they had trusted her to watch their back. They had trusted her to do her part and theirs if needed.

She'd found her niche in a world of blood, violence, and to her, ultimate justice. She'd been accepted, but there was still a part of her searching. A part of her that had looked around and wondered if that was all there was.

Until the night she had opened her eyes to see Lawe standing over her. To see him cutting the ropes from her, felt him pick her up and carry her out despite her protestations that she could still walk.

She would have fallen flat on her face and he had known it. She had known it. And he had carried her to safety while ignoring her protests.

Even then, barely conscious, dazed from the pain and the beatings her captors had inflicted, Diane had recognized that "something" she had searched for. She had realized it wasn't a thing, but someone. A feeling, an emotion she had shied away from since the night Padric had died.

It had been love. That first look, the touch of his fingers against her cheek, the low croon of his voice as he promised her she was safe.

She had been waiting for Lawe.

The second time she saw him, she had looked at him and realized how hopeless having him might be.

He wasn't just powerful, he wasn't just dangerous. He was supreme male power with advanced fighting skills. But he wasn't willing to share his world with her. She had seen it in his eyes, heard it in his voice. Felt it in the tightening of her chest and the feeling of being restrained, held back and protected.

He wanted her to forget her own needs, her training and her hunger to make a difference. He wanted to hold her back, for her to always know there was more for her and yet to know that she couldn't have it and have him as well.

No, she would always have him. Mating heat ensured that they would never let each other go entirely. What she couldn't have was any peace in it and still be herself. She couldn't be complete.

She would always be on the outside looking in, and she hated that feeling. She would watch him leave to do whatever he would be doing. Overseeing missions, of course, or perhaps the rumor she had heard that Jonas intended to promote him to assistant director wasn't just a rumor. Whatever his particular role, he would still be a part of the missions; he would still be commanding, directing, fighting for what he believed in. And she would still be on the sidelines wishing she were there. Wishing she had at least that much to remind her that she wasn't a drain on oxygen. That she was helping.

As the SUV pulled beneath the hotel's wide canopy Diane knew this would be her last mission if Lawe could arrange it. And there was no doubt in her mind that Lawe would definitely arrange it.

Waiting as Rule jumped from the front and opened Lawe's door, she could feel the protectiveness suddenly closing around her, threatening to smother her.

She could feel Lawe's gaze as she slid across the seat rather than jumping from the other side as she would have normally done.

Could she handle it? she wondered. Could she actually find a way to live with it?

Sliding from the vehicle, Diane was aware of Josiah joining them, moving in just behind her as Lawe placed his hand at the small of her back and urged her forward. As though she needed to be led rather than do the leading herself.

"Where's Thor?" she asked as they moved through the automatic doors and across the wide receiving area to the short flight of stairs that led to the lobby.

"I've teamed him with Emma and Sharone," he told her as they stepped up to the lobby. "They needed the stability right now."

Emma was Ashley's sister, and Sharone was the same as a sister. A littermate who had been trained alongside Ashley and Emma in Russia. They were close, and no doubt suffering the pain and fear that they would lose the vital, laughing young woman they relied so heavily on to vanquish the sometimes dark fears that haunted their lives.

"Stability?" she asked as they headed to the elevators, wondering if perhaps one of the girls' rage was in danger of giving way to feral fever.

She felt closed in, as though the walls were moving in on her, as though she were being deprived of air, of freedom, and the only way to survive it was to find a way to push it back.

"They're reeling from Ashley's attack." His hand moved to her hip, tightening, seeming to pull her closer as they stepped into the elevator. "They're looking for revenge for Ashley and there's no way to attain it. I'm hoping he can keep them out of trouble."

"He's good at that." Diane concentrated on the digital display of numbers as the elevator rose.

She remembered a time when vengeance had been all she had thought of. When Padric had been taken from her and the team and Thor had been there for her as well. He had let her fight. He had let her take the lead and he had made certain when the grief had overtaken her that she hadn't been alone.

"How long will he be with them?" Had Lawe taken him out of the equation because he had sworn he wouldn't allow him to restrain her freedom?

Of course he had. He knew, if push came to shove, he would have to fight Thor, and she would never forgive him for it.

"Not much longer," he told her. "The girls will return to the Citadel, the Coyote base, with the coya—she's here at the moment to oversee Ashley's progress. She's close to all three girls and refuses to leave Ashley while she's in the hospital."

Diane nodded slowly, aware of Rule and Josiah

glancing at her and then to Lawe, their expressions concerned.

What were they sensing? she wondered. It couldn't be any emotion rising from her, because she made certain her emotions remained locked as deep inside her as possible.

But the deeper she tried to bury them, the higher the physical ache centered in her womb seemed to build. Like a fire blazing out of control and overtaking her with a heat she couldn't avoid.

Thankfully, when the elevator stopped on the twenty-fifth floor and Josiah stepped out, the tension seemed to ease. A second later, a brief nod and Lawe's hand was pressing against her back, guiding her firmly out of the elevator and down the hall.

There were Breed guards stationed at every room along the wide, elegantly carpeted hallway.

She saw Callan and Merinus's personal guards, as well as Wolfe and Hope's and Del-Rey and Anya's. Each alpha had four personal guards while the second-in-commands, heads of security or other high-profile Breed leaders or Pack alphas normally only traveled with two.

Unless they were mated. If mated, those Breeds were assigned no fewer than four Enforcers for security to ensure they weren't struck in retaliation or kidnapped for research.

"Here's our room." Lawe stepped to a set of wide double doors, slid the key card through it, then opened the door and moved aside.

Rule and Josiah moved ahead of her and then Lawe. Going through each room, checking for listening devices or any other electronic or digital threats.

And Lawe thought he was going to keep her standing at the door?

Her lips tightened as she determinedly strode past him and headed into the living area while Josiah entered the double doors that led to the sleeping area, and Rule went in the opposite direction to inspect the kitchenette and dining area.

Luxuriously appointed and opening to a balcony shielded with long, gauzy curtains, the soft dove-gray carpeting sank beneath her boots while the cream-colored walls, decorated with their subtly colorful paintings, gave a relaxing, peaceful air to the living area Diane stood within.

She felt anything but peaceful, anything but calm.

Moving to one side of the beautiful glass and wrought-iron balcony doors, she carefully, and with a sense of regret, closed the heavy, room-darkening shades.

The view of the man-made lake outside, the ducks swimming peacefully on the water and the tranquil breeze blowing gently across it should have been a sin to cover.

She could have used the breeze blowing across her face, filling her senses for a moment. But the risk that came with the Breeds' lives didn't make it worth it. Because it could all be blown to hell with one well-placed bullet.

It was too high a price for the experience of enjoying the perfect scenery.

"Inform Callan and Jonas that I'll notify them when we're ready to head to the meeting," she heard Lawe murmur to either Josiah or Rule as they reentered the room.

"Will do," Rule answered. A few seconds later the door opened and closed again, signaling their departure.

Diane moved to turn around to face Lawe, only to find him at her back, his head lowering, his lips suddenly at the base of her neck as he pushed her hair back, his tongue swiping over the mating mark left there.

A shudder of pleasure raced down her spine. Closing her eyes, she felt his arms wrap around her waist, pulling her to him as his lips moved to the side of her neck to the second mark he'd left on her.

A slow, leisurely lick over the small bite had her knees weakening and a whimper leaving her lips as frissons of excitement traveled through every cell of her body.

Diane couldn't help but tip her head back to his shoulder, one arm lifting to allow her hand to curl around the back of his neck to hold him in place. Her eyes closed, her weight leaning into him as she surrendered herself to the exquisite sensations. Because she needed this, she needed him. Nothing else mattered and no other pleasure could compare to it.

"You're breaking my heart," he whispered, his lips caressing her, sending little flares of sensation to attack her nerve endings as he spoke. "The scent of your pain is killing me."

She had to swallow back the need to spill out the anger she was working so hard to conceal.

He couldn't help the instincts driving him any more than she could help her own needs, her own hunger to be more than just a mate.

She could only hide it within herself, arch closer to him and let the pleasure have its way as she hoped it covered the scent of whatever pain she wasn't hiding effectively.

The hand that curled against the back of his head delved into the length of thick, cool black hair. It wasn't as silky as it looked. There was a hint of coarseness to the feel of it, just rough enough to feel unusual, to remind a woman she wasn't with a normal male.

Just as the rake of his teeth against her shoulder, the feel of his tongue, just the slightest rasp against her flesh, was just different enough, just exciting enough to sent a hard rush of sensation to ripple through her womb and clench around her clit with erotic pleasure.

Breathing in roughly as his hands slid around her waist and pulled the shirt free of her jeans, Diane barely restrained the moan that would have slipped free.

His hands touched the bare flesh of her midriff, flattening against it to stroke upward and curve around the aching rise of her breasts. The roughened pads of his thumbs stroked over the material of the bra, feathering over the hardened, sensitized tips sent erotic sensations slamming to her womb.

"I need you," Lawe whispered, his lips trailing up her neck to her ear where he worried the lobe, first with the flick of his tongue, then with his teeth. "Let me have you, love."

He didn't have to ask. Surely he knew she couldn't tell him no. Even if she wanted to. But even without the heat, Diane knew she couldn't have denied him.

The very things that made her insane where he was concerned were the things that drew her to him. The strength and arrogance, the dominance and protectiveness, the honor that was so much a part of him.

He was so much more than just a man, and he held so much of her heart and soul that she wasn't certain how to survive what he made her feel or the sacrifices she knew he wanted from her.

Turning in his arms, Diane waited for Lawe's kiss. The warmth of his lips covering hers, his tongue flickering against them as the spiced-pear taste tempted her senses. The need for that taste, for the adrenaline-fueled arousal that would pump into her system, had her lips parting, her tongue waiting, flicking against his as her lips closed around it. Tucking beneath his tongue, hers rubbed and caressed, her lips tightened, drawing the hormone rich taste from the swollen glands as she moaned at the strength of the pleasure filling her.

The contradiction between the man himself and the taste of the mating hormone never failed to amaze her. He was one of the darkest, one of the strongest, Breeds she knew. Yet the taste of his mating kiss was sweet with a hint of spice. A taste of summer pears but with a hint of that vast well of sensuality he possessed that he kept hidden from the world.

Wrapping her arms around his neck, her fingers spearing into his hair to hold him to her as she arched closer, Diane allowed the emotions she kept such a tight rein on to rush through her senses.

There was no need to fight it now. There was no need to hide from him, no need to worry that vulnerability inherent in those emotions could be used against her. Because Lawe was right there with her. Lost to the hunger that flared through them, lost to the emotions that mating heat wouldn't allow him to fight.

The feel of his erection beneath his pants, pressing into her lower stomach was a heated reminder of the pleasure to come. His hands, drawing her shirt upward, pulling it from her as he broke the kiss only long enough to dispose of it, was a sensual enticement.

Lowering her hands to push aside the light black jacket he wore, Diane tugged at the sleeveless black shirt, dragging it up his chest and pushing it higher as she tore her lips from his.

"Take it off," she commanded, panting for breath as the need for him tearing through her, racing like a blaze billowing out of control, left her helpless against him. "Now. Get it off now, Lawe."

He tore it off.

The broad, golden bronze expanse of his flesh drew her fingers, her flesh aching to touch him, to feel the sensation of the invisible, silken hairs that covered it, caressing her palms with a lush, erotic sensation.

"Get those fucking boots off," Lawe growled as he pulled her back, then lowered himself to the wide, comfortable chair to the side to pull at his own.

She had hers off first. Then her jeans. Pushing them over her hips and thighs and kicking them to the side before he surged to his feet, his pants just clearing the heavy erection they had covered.

As he pushed them down she was there but not to help him undress. Her fingers curled around the thick stalk of flesh, stroking to the base. Lawe suddenly stilled, his body tightening as he gave a harsh growl.

Diane stared up at him. His expression was tight, his blue eyes like a living flame in his bronze face as he stared down at her, his jaw flexing, tight with the obvious effort to restrain the need to assert his control of the sensual battle.

Holding his cock with the fingers of one hand, the other lifted, the tips of her fingers trailing down his chest, the darkened flesh rippling as the muscles beneath tensed. The hard flesh pulsed in her grip. With each hard throb of blood through the heavy shaft it seemed to widen further as her mouth watered to taste the primal strength she held.

A growl, harsh and grating, escaped his throat as Diane bent, her head lowering, her lips parting to allow her tongue to swipe over the engorged crest, to taste the damp flesh, the salty male taste of his pre-cum before sucking it slowly into her mouth.

With her fingers stroking the thick shaft, Diane tightened her mouth around the head of his cock and sucked at it with slow relish.

Heavy veins throbbed beneath her fingers as he finally managed to shed his pants from his legs. His fingers buried in her hair, clenching in the strands and sending pinpricks of pleasure racing across her scalp as he tugged at her strands. His pleasure in her touch was obvious. Every muscle in his body was strung tight as those in his muscular thighs flexed powerfully, his hips jerking and burying the engorged flesh deeper between her lips.

"You make me weak." He groaned. "Diane, sweetheart . . ."

He growled again as she tucked her tongue beneath the head and rubbed at the smooth flesh there, feeling the pulse and throb of excitement beneath it.

Sucking at it again, her head back, lowering over it, taking him as he moved in shallow thrusts against her lips, fucking her with a slow, heated rhythm that had the breath tightening in her chest.

She wanted him. Wanted to feel him covering her as he had before, taking her, his teeth at the back of her neck as he held her in place. She wanted to feel him losing himself with her, inside her, pumping inside her, that wicked, pulsating barb sending flares of sensation to erupt through her clit, her pussy, reducing her to a mass of pure pleasure.

She'd never imagined she could gain such pleasure from the act. That without the stimulation of having him touch her body that she could be burning so intensely for him.

She wasn't blaming it all on mating heat, though she knew it played a part. She blamed it on the man.

It was all Lawe's fault that the tug of his hands in her hair sent a pulse of sensation to tighten around her clit each time he tightened his fingers. That the rasp of his nails against her scalp had her womb clenching with a surge of pleasure.

She wanted him. With a power she hadn't known a woman could feel, she wanted him like she had never wanted anything in her life. Like she had never known she could want a man. Or a Breed.

She tried to suck him deeper, take as much of him as she could. To give him as much pleasure as possible before they both lost control.

And the loss of that control was coming.

She could feel it in the way his fingers were kneading her scalp, pulling at her hair. Each swirl of her tongue around the head of his cock had it throbbing harder, seeming to thicken further in her mouth. And each reaction had her feeling the flames burning higher in her own body.

Her juices eased past the swollen folds of her sex, heating and dampening her clit as she tightened her thighs, desperate now for enough friction against the bundle of nerves to spark the release she was aching for.

The need clenched her vagina, the sensations, the building hunger for touch there, for the burning stretch of his penetration, accelerating her need until she was moaning with each shallow thrust of his cock past her lips.

With one hand wrapped around the thick flesh, the other moved between her thighs, stroked across the swollen, wet folds and found the aching bud throbbing between them.

"Enough."

Before she could stop him Lawe pulled back, forcing her to release his cock as he drew her up, his lips covering hers again.

The kiss wild, his tongue pumping into her mouth before pulling back, his lips slanting over hers as he kissed her with hungry insistence. His hand tightened on her hips, then slid around, down, gripped her buttocks and lifted her to him.

Diane gripped his shoulders with desperate fingers as she tried to lift herself closer, going to her tiptoes, the need to have him inside her burning through her nerve endings. Every cell in her body ached for his touch, to feel his hands stroking over her flesh, his body stroking against her, his cock stroking inside her. The feel of the silken hairs that covered his body rubbing against her. She ached for the strength of his arms around her.

She ached for him. "God, Diane," he whispered as his lips moved over her shoulder, his teeth raking with sensual intent before he took another heated nip.

Sensation ripped at her nerve endings, pleasure burgeoning inside her belly as she arched against him. Bending her knee she drew it up his thigh as she stood on tiptoe. The slickened folds of her pussy rubbed against the base of his cock, parted and exposed the swollen bud of her clit to the hot shaft.

"Your pussy's so fucking hot. So wet and slick." He groaned, the explicit words sizzling across her nerve endings as she felt him bend just enough that the head of his cock raked over her clit.

A shudder zapped along her spine. Her nails dug into the flesh of his shoulder as his lips were suddenly on hers again, his tongue against hers. Before she could capture his kiss, capture the tormenting stroke past her lips, Lawe pulled back. His tongue stroked down her neck laying a path of sizzling pleasure to her shoulder once again.

A nip at the curve, his teeth raking over her skin had a cry escaping her lips.

"Come here. I can't wait, Di. Ah hell. Come here, baby. Fuck me. Fuck me, Diane," he growled as he shifted, moved until he was settling into the chair once again.

Gripping her thigh with one hand he lifted it, pulling it over his thigh as Diane straddled him, the other gripping the base of his dick as his hips shifted and he pulled her to him.

"Take me." He groaned as she straddled his hips, lowering herself and feeling the wide, blunt head of his cock as it parted the swollen folds of her pussy and began to press inside her.

A shiver raced up her spine.

"Too slow." She moaned. She wanted more, she wanted all of him, and she wanted it now.

His hands tightened on her hips as he pushed upward, penetrating enough, stretching her far enough that her head tipped back, a desperate cry falling from her lips.

Lawe took swift advantage of the arching of her body. Leaning forward just enough to swipe his roughened tongue over the tip of her breast, licking and laving it as she twisted against him, forcing him deeper inside her.

His hands stroked from her hips to her back, pulling her closer, his lips surrounding her nipple, pulling it into his mouth and surrounding it with tight, fiery suction. As his tongue lashed at the tender, over-sensitized tip, his hips surged upward, burying himself to the hilt inside her as she cried out at the pleasure flaming through her.

His hands clenched at her rear as he began to move her, his hands lifting her then pulling her down, his hips surging upward, impaling her hard and deep as talons of sharp sensation blazed across her senses.

His cock stretched her, throbbed inside her, pushing her closer to that abyss of pure ecstasy that she could feel beginning to build around her.

Another harsh, deep-throated growl sounded from his throat as she felt her pussy tightening on the heavy flesh invading it, desperate to hold him inside her, to feel the throbbing caress deeper inside her.

Heat built around her, built inside her.

Rising and lifting herself, his hands gripping her ass, moving in rhythm with him, Diane felt the hunger building. The pinching stretch of his cock moving inside her pushed the need deeper, hotter. With each thrust through tissue sensitized by his touch, by the heat, by the arousal that seemed to climb further inside her with each thrust, Lawe marked her, took her with a hunger she knew she couldn't live without now.

She was close, so very close, when he moved. Lifting her from him despite her sudden cry of protest, he turned her, pushed her to her knees in the chair and then moved behind her.

Between one breath and the next he had her where she had hungered to be. Covering her, his cock pushing inside her as he came over her, his lips taking stinging kisses of her neck as he began to fuck her with driving strokes.

The slap of damp flesh, the feel of him moving inside her, stretching her, thrusting powerfully into the tightening grip of her pussy, had her nails digging into the upholstery of the chair as she cried out in rising bliss.

She couldn't hold back the sounds, she couldn't hold back the loss of control. The ability to restrain herself, to rein in the sensations that pierced her, that urged her to give herself to him, all of herself to him, was gone.

It wasn't mating heat. It wasn't just the pleasure. It wasn't the fear of her loss of independence or the fear of the loss of herself. It was the man. The Breed. It was the pleasure she had instinctively known was coming amplified by his insistence that he build on it. That he force her deeper into the blaze, that he brush her hair back from her neck, lick over the too-sensitive wound, then slanting his head, his canines pierced it once again.

Diane erupted into a release so blinding, so burning hot she lost her breath. She couldn't scream. She couldn't cry out his name. She could only hold on as ecstasy exploded over and over as she felt the barb extend, felt it vibrating inside her, pushing over another blazing edge of sensation that only amplified the release.

She was a creature of pure, sensual sensation.

She was lost in him. Lost in a feeling that locked them together more firmly than the barb locking them together. Held her tighter to him than any bonds, either natural or man-made, ever could.

Clenching, spilling her release to his, her pussy rippled around the penetration of his cock and the locking bliss of the barb. The sensations, the release that seemed to never end, then the clenching, pleasure-pain of her womb contracting as her vagina milked the flesh locked inside her, was overwhelming.

As it slowly eased, ever so slowly gave her back her breath, Diane found herself slumped over the back of the chair, fighting to breathe, each intake of air harsh and overloud. Lawe shuddered behind her, his cheek against her shoulder, his breathing as labored, his hands kneading her hips as she felt his cock still throbbing inside her, though without the iron-hard strength it had possessed previously.

She was exhausted, drowsy, sated.

Limp, her eyes closed, she wanted to stay there until the world righted itself, until there was no need for protection, no danger to haunt them. She wanted to hide forever, right here, just like this, locked in his hold, shuddering with sensations too overwhelming to fight and too heated to conflict.

She wanted to ignore the world outside, ignore the problems she knew would rise between them again, and she wanted to ignore her inability to settle for what she should take rather than what she didn't know if she could live without.

"I love you, Diane," he whispered behind her, causing her breath to still for precious seconds at the declaration. "If there has been anything, or anyone, I have ever loved in my life, then it's you. To the point that if something happened to you, then I would cease to exist alongside you."

Tears filled her eyes.

She didn't want to hear this.

She didn't want to face this. Not yet, not until she had a handle on her own emotions, a handle on the decisions she knew she had to make.

"And I know you love me." He kissed her shoulder gently. "I can feel that love, I can smell it when you forget to watch your emotions, to hide them from me. Just as I can feel your pain and your indecision." Another kiss at the base of her neck, a gentle lick over the tender wound he had inflicted once again. "If I could give you what you need to survive, then I would, in a heartbeat," he whispered, his tone deepening, becoming rougher with regret. "If I could do that one thing for you, and still live with the fear, then as God is my witness, I would."

But he couldn't.

The message was there, and Diane heard it loud and clear.

"If I thought I could survive without it, then I would," she said, keeping her own voice soft as her breathing hitched on a sob. "If I could, Lawe, I would, just for you." And the first tear slipped from her eyes. "Because I love you so much it breaks my heart. You break my heart . . . daily."

Her eyes closed as she fought back more tears, feeling him withdraw from her, that bond breaking as his cock eased through tender tissue then slipped from her entirely.

As he helped her to her feet, Diane stepped back, knowing what he would have done, and knowing she couldn't bear it. Her hand lifted in an instinctive gesture, palm held out, in a silent denial.

She couldn't bear it if he did as he had before. Cleaning her so gently, and with such obvious enjoyment, did something to her that made it harder each time to fight against his need to protect her.

"I'm going to shower." Her voice was rough, from her tears, from the cries that had been torn from her as the pleasure exploded around her. "I need to think."

"What's there to think about?" he stared down at her, his expression dark and forbidding as he watched her. "We can't deny what we have, Diane. The mating heat won't allow it."

She gave her head a hard shake. "Later, Lawe. We'll fight about his later. After we've found what we came looking for, after Gideon has been neutralized. Give me that much at least."

"And if I can't?" The question was voiced harshly, as though the words were torn from the very soul of the creature that lived inside him. "If I can't let you do this, Diane, then what?"

She felt tormented, tortured. As though the pain that lived inside her soul was raking at her with jagged claws.

What would she do if he didn't allow her to finish this? If he didn't stand beside her rather than in front of her and let her find the three individuals who were once injected with the same, or very similar, serum that her niece had been injected with? If she didn't learn from them what had happened to those who had died from the injections and the facts surrounding those deaths?

Could she live with the failure?

"If you love me," she whispered painfully. "If you really love me as you say you do, Lawe, then you'll stand by me." The tears she battled edged closer to winning the war when another ran down her cheek. "Because you know I won't be able to bear it any other way."

He may as well lock her in a cage, she thought, as she moved quickly to the bathroom and the shower she so desperately needed. She needed the escape worse, though. The few precious moments she could steal to think, to weigh her options and consider the future. Because the time was coming when she wouldn't be able to run any longer. The time was coming when she wouldn't be able to hide anymore.

The time was coming when a decision would have to be made.

✦   ✦   ✦

Gideon stared at the wall across from him, a frown on his face as he heard Diane all but beg her mate to believe in her.

Lawe Justice was a hell of a Breed soldier, as was his brother, Rule Breaker. Gideon didn't think much of their choice of names, but they did seem to rather suit them.

This, this bothered him, though.

Not that he should care either way. Hell, the more conflicted the two were the easier it would be to keep them distracted and to learn more about them.

The fact that they had missed the new electronic bug was pleasing as well. Keeping ahead of their little bug detectors was getting harder by the day. This one wasn't as strong as the others, and there was a lot he missed of any conversation. White noise, which Breeds most always used when discussing missions, would completely incapacitate it. But information such as this was damned useful as well.

Lawe and Diane weren't at their peak fighting abilities because of mating heat. That would make them weaker, slower. And they were the leaders, the commanders. With any luck, the others wouldn't feel the need to work over or around the two. They trusted them. And Gideon was trusting them to remain immersed in each other while he found Fawn.

Her big dark eyes, so filled with tears. "Give him my blood," she sobbed out to Judd. "Don't you let him die!" she had screamed at the Breed as the chill of the night air seeped into Gideon's bones. "Don't you dare, or I swear, I swear I'll make you pay."

And Gideon had been dying. He had wanted to die. God knows it would have been such a relief, to slip over that edge of nothingness and find eternal rest.

She had denied death to him. She had begged and she had ordered, until Judd had found a medical kit in the transport vehicle. As fate had had it, there was a transfusion kit too, and she gave him her blood.

They had saved him, and he hadn't wanted to be saved. He'd been too weak to stop them, too weak to do anything but glare at her in hatred.

He'd known that by saving him, she had only extended his horror. He had been right.

He'd tried to forgive her. He'd fought to get the memory out of his head. Then, a decade later, he was forced to allow his recapture to get into the labs once more to destroy the records kept on Judd, Fawn and Honor. To ensure that no DNA matches could be found when he'd learned the Brandenmore Labs were once again searching for them.

The suspicion that Judd and Fawn weren't dead revived every few years, but this time, General Horace

Roberts, desperate to find his only child, had demanded they search until Honor was found. That they search until it was proven that the others had died. He was certain his daughter would never have run away without help and the only friends she had known had been Judd, Gideon and Fawn. Gideon had planned it perfectly. He was certain he would have at least a few weeks before the testing began again.

Then, they had tested his blood. He had immediately been restrained, the paralytic pumped into his body, and then, they had killed him themselves. There on the autopsy gurney, as he screamed and begged, they had cut him open to investigate the changes found in his blood. The additional strength he'd acquired over the years had been strange enough, even to him. But after he'd died on that table beneath their scalpels, after they'd transfused him again, using the blood they had taken from her years before, the changes had begun multiplying.

Not that they had found answers after cutting him open. There was nothing there. No reason for the anomalies showing up in his body until he'd begun experiencing brief episodes of full-blown feral fever.

The thought of death had been wiped away. The pain that clawed at his insides didn't mean he couldn't extract vengeance, though. That was something he had never wanted. He hadn't wanted to live, to develop a fever so agonizing the animal inside him had been forced free to pull him back from the brink of insanity.

As the man huddled in blessed silence within his body, the animal had raged and roared; it had clawed at the walls and snarled at the guards. It had stared at the scientists, remembered the girl, the blood the scientists had used as they laughed at him and he had sworn vengeance.

Her blood had destroyed him. And she was gone. He hadn't been able to find her in ten years, and several times, he'd actually searched for her and Judd, then for Honor once he'd learned of her disappearance.

It was as though they had simply ceased to exist.

When he had returned to the wilderness where he had left the night he'd awakened after that first transfusion, there had been no sign of them. He had brief memories of the termination facility. A small metal building, a cremation vault and the bloodied bodies he'd thrown inside it. There were flashes of images of guards, looks of horror on their faces, the taste of blood overriding his senses.

The animal had raged inside him, for how long, Gideon had never been certain.

When he'd finally come to himself and made his way back to the scene of their escape, it was to find it all gone. The wrecked vehicle, the two guards, Judd and Fawn.

It was only later he'd begun to suspect the lie of it. Only later that the animal inside him had begun to dream of dark eyes in an adult's face. But the features of that face he never saw in the animal's dreams.

She would pay for that demand that he live. For whatever her blood had done that had changed him, that had stolen the time he needed to ensure she was never found. She would pay for the additional agony. And when he was finished with her, maybe, just maybe, he would put them both out of their misery.

CHAPTER 15

Amber was changing.

Diane stood next to her sister at the end of the crib and stared at the sleeping child. In just a few brief days, even she could see the changes. Tiny, so very tiny, for her age.

Her dark brown hair was longer, hanging down her neck in little ringlets. Her lashes had always been long, feathering her rosy cheeks. Soft baby lips were slightly parted as she lay on her back, her breathing slow and easy.

She looked picture perfect. A babe, innocent in her slumber, dreaming whatever bright, happy dreams happy babies had. But there were changes.

Her face was thinner, the features altered almost imperceptibly and appearing almost feline. Her hair was lighter, with soft black and reddened streaks showing themselves amid the golden brown.

There was the faintest point to a tiny ear and every so often a very distinct purr.

"She's running a fever," Rachel whispered, her voice husky with tears. "She's been running one for the past two days. It's spiked on us twice, going over a hundred, and Dr. Morrey has tried everything to bring it down. Nothing works. Then it will just go away on its own."

"Should she be here?" Diane wanted nothing more than to reach out and pick her niece up, to cuddle her, to hold her closely and keep whatever was tormenting her from ever hurting her again.

"Dr. Morrey is in the next room," she answered. "With Callan and Merinus traveling here as well, they decided it best to bring Amber. That way, she's with us if needed."

Another little purr left the baby as a small frown wrinkled her forehead before easing away.

Lawe stood behind Diane, his hand resting against her hip as he too watched the baby. She could feel his concern. Just as she could feel Jonas's as he stood behind her sister.

"She's healthy," Jonas whispered. "Ely keeps a daily check on her. She's not hurting."

But that was little comfort today, when tomorrow it could all change.

"Did you get my report from the doctors in Argentina?" Diane glanced back at the director.

He gave a sharp nod. "The main scientists working with the girls were killed by Gideon, though."

"Before I could get to them," she agreed. "I only had their assistants that I could talk to."

The information they had given her had terrified her. The girls had survived, obviously, but those assistants hadn't understood how, or why. Because the stages of agonizing pain and adjustment owing to the serum had had the children begging for death more often than not.

Had her sister seen those reports?

"She's so tiny," Rachel whispered. "She's not growing properly, even Ely admits it. If she goes through one of the stages those girls did . . ."

Fawn Corrigan and Honor Roberts had been older. They hadn't been infants when the experiments had begun, nor had they been healthy children.

"Ely will be there for her," Diane promised. "And we'll find the girls, Rachel. I promise you we will. They'll have the answers we need."

She prayed they'd have the answers needed, if nothing else, the memory of what the scientists had done. Honor Roberts's mother reported her daughter had possessed a photographic memory. There was nothing she heard or saw from that time that she had forgotten. She remembered it all, in blinding detail.

Those details had been what had convinced her mother to help her run. When the scientists had come to General Roberts to request he return his daughter to the labs, she had known she had no other choice. Because her husband believed her daughter had somehow been infected with Breed genetics. Genetics he wanted out of her.

"She's not in pain now, Rachel," Jonas whispered at her ear. "So far, she's been relatively free of anything but our worry. Let's pray it stays that way."

Diane glanced at the director. He should have never shown Rachel those reports, but somehow she had known he would. Rachel hadn't been raised as Diane had been, amid the blood and horror the world could spawn. Diane and their uncle had done everything possible to protect her, to ensure her life was more settled, that it was safer.

Diane was older, and she had longed to follow her uncle into his chosen career. The night their parents had died it had been Diane who had used the few tricks her uncle and her parents had taught her to save herself and her sister.

Just in case, they had always reassured her. She had never suspected their trips could carry the risk of their deaths, as well as her and Rachel's. She had never known their secrets, their rescue of certain Breeds and aid in transporting them to a hidden base in Africa could have come back to destroy the lives they lived.

Rachel hadn't been prepared for the life she had been thrust into.

Diane had sensed, and then known, she thrived within it.

"Come on, sweetheart." Jonas kissed the top of his mate's auburn hair. "Let's let her rest. We can talk in the living area."

They eased quietly from the room.

"This is the first day she's napped in weeks," Rachel said as Jonas closed the doors carefully behind them.

Her sister was beginning to look exhausted. Exhausted and worried out of her mind.

"We also managed to secretly kidnap one of the researchers involved in the testing at the Brandenmore labs, Jenny Austin-Carrew," Callan Lyons, alpha of the Feline Prides, stated as he stood from the small table when they reentered the room. "She was a higher-level research assistant, and we're hoping she actually worked extensively with the head scientists."

"Have you questioned her yet?" Diane asked.

He gave a shake of his head as his wife, Merinus, moved to his side.

"Ashley was wounded before Jonas could begin questioning her regarding her work. We came right out here with her sisters, Dacey and Marcy. They were still at Sanctuary."

Ashley's sisters. The Truing sisters were true sisters. Sharone Bryce hadn't been conceived by the same mother or the same genetically altered sperm that had been used to fertilize her each time she had conceived.

They were all littermates though, created in the same lab and overseen by the same scientists.

There were no records concerning how the sperm had been altered or who the main donor had been. The five girls, Emma, Ashley, and twins Dacey and Marcy, looked nothing alike, though. They could have been born of completely different genetics rather than from the same donor with the same animal genetic profiles.

"The twins are at the hospital with her," Merinus stated. "Sharone and Emma are . . . hunting." Merinus's pause had Diane shooting Lawe a hard look.

"What or who are they hunting?" she asked.

"They're with Thor searching for any signs that the Coyote team that bribed Holden Mayhew to kidnap Malachi's mate didn't have any friends as backup," Lawe told her softly. "They're questioning some of the people Mayhew and the team came in contact with and building a profile of their movements as well."

They were being kept busy and out of trouble.

Diane raked her fingers through her hair then shoved her hands into the pockets of her jeans and glanced at the others before asking: "Do we have any intel concerning the whereabouts of the girls or the Bengal Judd?" She hated the fact that part of this mission had been taken from her.

"So far, all we have is the suspicion that Terran Martinez brought them to his ranch. A few hours later they were picked up by a group of warriors wearing war paint and disappeared," Jonas told her.

"Where did you get that information?" Diane asked him, her gaze narrowing in surprise.

"An anonymous call that we haven't been able to trace." His jaw tightened angrily. "Terran isn't confirming or denying the report. He says that if such individuals came into the city looking for safety, then they were now safe, and neither he nor anyone involved at the time would know where they were, who they were with or anyone that could give them that information."

Diane nodded slowly. "When the Navajo first learned of the children who had been rescued whose genetics matched some of their missing, they created a group whose job was to ensure the protection and hidden identities of those children. I haven't been able to find even a hint of anyone who could even guess at who any of them are, but Braden Arness's mated wife, Megan, and her family, confirmed the stories of them."

The Lion Breed Braden had mated a Navajo empath from New Mexico with close ties to Window Rock. The assassin class Breed now worked with his wife whenever his skill set, or her investigative gifts were needed.

"We've informed the chief as well as his father, the medicine man, and Terran, who's currently the Navajo's head legal representative, of the situation regarding Amber. Their refusal to give us the identities of at least the two girls and allow us to debrief them concerning their stay at the labs will be viewed as an act of hostility toward the Breeds. As such, the Navajo Nation will no longer be considered a sanctuary for our people, and they'll be pulled out with all haste."

Diane sighed wearily as she stared at Callan's forbidding expression.

This was simply the wrong way to go about it.

Shifting an accusing look toward Lawe, she clenched her teeth in anger at the fact that Jonas had decided it wasn't prudent to wait for their arrival and allow Diane to do what she did best. Find the people she was looking for.

She didn't like going behind Lawe's back, but that was exactly what she and Thor had agreed to do as they waited for Lawe outside the hotel the morning they'd left.

If he thought giving Thor another assignment had changed that, then he was wrong. It had instead given Thor the chance to work as he and Diane preferred. Under the guise of a completely unrelated mission while Diane remained with Lawe and kept the Breeds off his back.

It was usually the other way around. She investigated while Thor ran interference with whichever parties were deemed the most hazardous to their job. But, she knew how to handle this part. She and Thor had perfected both areas of the mission parameters and understood how each worked.

"The Navajo won't know who they are, where they are or, after all this time, how to reach them," Diane informed them all as she faced them impatiently. "There's not even a number that's called anymore. No one knows how the group becomes aware that a pickup is needed, but they're always there."

"Then they have a Breed working with them," Jonas guessed.

Diane shrugged. "Getting anyone to talk to any of you will not happen," she told them. "I have some ideas, and once I begin investigating—"

"Once *we* begin," Lawe injected.

She glanced up at him, feeling her chest tighten at what she knew she had to do.

"No, once *I* begin," she reiterated softly. "They won't talk to me if you're around or anywhere close enough to identify them. You're a Breed, Lawe. To them, you're the same as a Coyote, a scientist, or a rogue."

She watched his gaze turn to ice as Jonas cursed softly.

"I hate to keep repeating myself, but I know what I'm doing," she stated, knowing that with the exception of her sister, possibly, no one there was willing to believe her at this point because of the fact that she was now a mate.

Her chances of investigating were thin to none, but this was her role to play, and if she simply stepped back, then there was no way Lawe would accept that she and Thor hadn't planned something else.

"Diane, you're the strongest woman I know," Rachel said with an edge of bitterness, a clear indication she'd tried to discuss the matter with Jonas. "But the danger to mates right now won't allow a single Breed in the vicinity to allow you to investigate this on your own."

Despite the grief she heard in her sister's voice, the knowledge it could mean her daughter's life, Diane realized that even her sister couldn't help her here.

"And all of you are willing to lose Amber for this?" She met her sister's gaze and watched the tears that welled in her eyes.

"There's nothing on this earth I wouldn't do to protect my baby." Rachel's voice hitched on a sob. "But nothing is going to change how they'll surround you or their determination and vows to protect you. Nothing will change the fact that not even my child is as important to Lawe or to the animal genetics that are a part of him as his mate is. Even Jonas's orders won't sway him."

Diane refused to accept that.

Her head lifted as she stared back at the males watching her. "Every damned one of you will get over it," she told them coolly before turning to Lawe. "You will get Thor back here if that protection is all important to you. He's not a Breed; he won't be seen as suspiciously as you will be."

"He follows your orders," Lawe growled. "If you told him to back off, then he would do just that. Your safety will always be endangered by the fact that you're his commander."

There was truth to that.

"He would cut off his own arm and tell me to go to hell before he'd allow me to do anything to place myself in a situation that would risk my capture by anything or anyone associated with the Council," she informed them all firmly. It did about as much good to argue with them as it did to attempt to use fuel to put out a fire. And she knew that, to the bottom of her soul.

There wasn't a chance in hell he would ever step back if that were the case.

But she was better at what they were doing than Thor was. She knew how to listen, how to talk to women and how to put men at ease. Thor's size alone intimidated everyone. Emma and Sharone were Breeds, and the fact that the information they had acquired so far had been stolen by listening to conversations, rumors and suspicions before being pieced together, just frustrated her.

She watched Lawe's jaw tighten, saw the denial in his eyes, though he didn't voice it. The muscle in his jaw jerked as he glared back at her for long, silent seconds.

The tension in the room was palpable. His gaze moved to Rachel's, and Diane knew what he saw there, knew the plea that filled her sister's face, while Jonas had moved away, turning his back to the exchange.

Diane stared at him.

He was gripping the back of a chair with claws that

had retracted and pierced the upholstery. Smears of blood from the sharp-tipped protrusions showed against his cuticles as he glared at them.

He was forcibly distancing himself. He could order Lawe to allow it, he could convince him to, but he wouldn't give into the urge to do just that. At least not yet. She knew his devotion to his mate and to the child he called his own. He would do it if he considered it the only option but only if all other options had been extinguished.

Diane closed her eyes for a second, praying for strength. He was going to make her crazy before the night was over, let alone the mission.

This was their last chance. She could feel it.

If he wasn't willing to bend now, when the situation was so desperate, then there would never be a chance that he would allow her to participate in protecting their own child if such a situation ever arose.

"Don't," she whispered despairingly. "Don't make me hate you, Lawe, because you stood in the way of saving my niece. I'll never forgive you."

It was no longer a game. Facing her mate, facing the battle that never seemed to end, she realized she'd had enough.

Thor could do this without her. He had before. But it was *her* niece. She needed to be a part of this.

Lawe's gaze locked with hers as she watched the struggle that waged in his expression as primal fury flashed in his icy gaze and lightened it further.

His eyes were such a flaming blue now that she swore she could see the animal raging inside him, demanding supremacy. Demanding that the man protect, dominate, and use whatever means necessary to ensure his mate's well-being.

"I want to hear your plan first," Lawe growled.

She stared at him in shock. He hadn't just said that. Had he?

"Lawe?" Jonas's head jerked up, his gaze intent, the silver depths suddenly seeming to shimmer, to shift in light and color until they almost seemed reflective.

Lawe's expression was torn, tormented. "You're right, Jonas. It's the wrong time for this battle between me and my mate. She keeps telling me that, and I keep refusing to understand. Until now," he stated heavily. "She's doing nothing I wouldn't do in her place. Hell, I would have shot me long before now if I were my mate, for standing in my way."

Diane's lips parted, hope surging inside her now.

She harbored no illusion that this could be the start of an attempt to compromise, because she knew better. Lawe's devotion to all children, but to Amber in particular, was pulling at him. The fact that he and Jonas were more than fellow soldiers, that they were close friends, played a large part as well.

She watched the claws retract within the tips of Jonas's fingers, barely holding back a shudder when nothing showed but the normal nail now, and the bloody cuticles. He wiped his hand over his face and moved back to his mate, taking her in his arms before turning back to Lawe.

"We all need to hear the plan," Callan stated. "And trust me, Diane, it will be vetoed if it puts you at risk in any way. Are we clear on that? I'm not your mate, and I can't be swayed by your emotion."

Diane glanced at Merinus, wondering if she had an ally there.

Merinus's lips twitched. "Your sister is one of my dearest friends," she said gently. "And I know my soul would shatter if anything happened to either of my babies. But know this, Diane, Callan and I have a trust

I won't break. As cruel, as inhuman and brutal as it sounds, Rachel can have other children. If Lawe loses you, though, then we lose not just you, but Lawe, and any children you may have." She glanced at Rachel as the other woman turned her head into Jonas's chest in grief, and her eyes flashed with sorrow. "Rachel and I have discussed this. If I ever feel there's danger to either of you, then I swear, your mates will know about it."

At that moment, Diane almost hated the other woman.

"Amber can never be replaced," Diane assured the female alpha coldly. "Know this, all of you. If Amber dies because any of you stood in my way, or took this from me, then I swear I'll make damned sure I make all of your lives hell."

Merinus's gentle expression never changed. "We never doubted that for a moment," she breathed out roughly. "But it won't change the fact that your and Rachel's safety is paramount."

"Then I need your assurance," Diane demanded of them. "I want your vow that none of you will take it over and decide you can achieve your ends without me."

She stared at Callan first, then Lawe and Jonas. They stared back at her, and she almost sneered. Oh, how well she knew Breeds. That thought had been uppermost in all their minds. She may be furious at them all, including her sister at the moment for even considering a continued friendship with the prima, but it didn't make her stupid.

"You'll have it." It was Lawe who broke the silence. He turned to Diane. "As long as you're in no immediate danger and as long as I'm confident you have a chance of survival, then the operation won't be taken from you or interfered with in any way."

She lifted her head, debating with herself, knowing

that if any being on earth would keep his word, then it was Lawe. And in turn, Callan and Jonas. But none of them had ever been tested in such a way either.

She swallowed tightly. "There're a few things I'll need, and I'll need your patience."

"Let's hear it first." Callan and Merinus resumed their seats at the table as Diane, Lawe, Jonas and Rachel followed suit.

Diane hadn't expected such easy compliance, she had to admit. She'd expected threats, anger, and when all else failed, she'd expected Jonas to trump all other means of convincing her by using her love for Rachel or, worse for Lawe, against her. Hell, she'd even been prepared to continue to play the silent warrior while Thor, Emma and Sharone tracked down information.

She knew a few things about Breed law. She knew her refusal had broken several statutes, which could result in her and Lawe's imprisonment if it were pushed. And it would have been, if it weren't for the fact that the babe in question belonged to Jonas. If not by blood, then by love.

"The past two days I haven't just been sitting on my ass. Thor, with Emma and Sharone, using the guise of searching for Council Coyotes, has been gathering information. Rumor, suspicion and discussions held behind closed doors but not out of Sharon's ability to hear from a window, a door or other hidden means, has come through. The group responsible for protecting Honor, Fawn and Judd doesn't even have a name," Diane warned them. "At least not one I've been able to learn. What I have learned is that Judd, Fawn and Honor weren't the first or the last children to have disappeared with an anonymous group of men disguised by war paint. There have been others. Children who were brought to them, even before the rescues began, as well as at least one hybrid whose mother was killed, and whose father was fatally wounded."

"Why not come to us?" Callan growled, anger and concern filling his face now.

Diane shook her head. "Not all Breeds trust either Sanctuary or Haven," she reminded him. "The spies found within both bases pose a risk to those Breeds who were created for special purposes or who were already a part of political or private enterprises the Council considered long-term goals. They're Breeds that, for whatever reason, couldn't afford ever to be identified as Breeds. Then"—she breathed in deeply—"there are the missing children. The six that a Breed known as Harmony Lancaster had locations for, but they had disappeared before your teams could get to them. Hybrid babes who were taken from their mothers' bodies then stolen from the labs were smuggled or kidnapped from supposedly secured labs and disappeared almost immediately. There are dozens, Callan, and those are just the ones I know of. I'm certain there are far more actually in existence."

Thor, Emma and Sharone had managed to unearth secrets even Diane hadn't suspected until now.

Both Rachel and Merinus covered their lips in both horror and hope as she spoke. The fates of those children were always on their minds, and the discovery of their whereabouts was considered top priority since the day the First Leo had informed them the girls had disappeared just days before his teams had arrived.

"How long has this group been operating?" Jonas's eyes narrowed, his displeasure that such an operation existed without him clearly outlined in his expression.

She licked her lips, nervous about giving this piece of information.

"If you want me to keep my word, Diane, then we have to know everything," Lawe stated harshly.

"It's not the information itself that's problematic, it's the Breed behind it." She sighed.

Jonas lips tightened. "Should I guess?"

She had a feeling he would be right.

"My intel says Leo Vanderale may have been the force behind the creation of the group," she informed them. "I do know he's put out feelers for information since Brandenmore injected Amber with the serum but to no avail. One of my contacts told me that no one who has come onto Navajo land searching for missing Breed children or adults, has left it to report anything. They've disappeared just as quickly and just as completely as the children do."

Lawe sat back in his chair slowly, his gaze narrowing on her.

"And how do you intend to accomplish your objective without disappearing as well?" He flashed his canines dangerously.

"They won't risk making me disappear." She shook her head, positive it wouldn't happen. "There are too many Breeds here, I'm too well known and by now they're going to be aware I'm your mate. They won't dare touch me."

The Navajo wanted to preserve the Breeds, ensure their survival and make certain that women, especially Breed women and mated wives, were well taken care of. Mates such as Megan Fields Arness and the one married to the New Mexico sheriff, Harmony Jacobs. That one, Diane believed, was the mysterious Harmony Lancaster who had disappeared several years before and at one time suspected to be the Breed assassin known as "Death."

"My original question then." Lawe's brow arched mockingly. "How do you intend to succeed?"

"By discussing the situation with three members of the community who I believe may have information or know someone who has information," she stated. "They may not tell me a damn thing, but I believe they have to know either Fawn or Honor, and they have to know who they are."

They stared back at her silently, and in her sister's eyes, Diane saw hope for the child they all cherished.

"Malachi's mate, Isabelle, her sister Chelsea, and their friend Liza," she stated. "Isabelle was at home and old enough to remember her father bringing those kids in. I'm betting she saw them and perhaps also saw who picked them up. Chelsea Martinez and Liza are her best friends, but even more than that, they're a part of the Martinez family and they work with the Navajo Council, specifically with three of the men I suspect are part of the network. Terran, Ray and Orrin Martinez. I'm certain that at least one of the members of the Navajo Council heads the child rescue team. And if that's true, then at least one of the girls has to know it. Those three work closely with all of them. And I'm betting it's either Chelsea or Liza. If it were Isabelle, her mate would have asked her, and he would have given you that information if she had it."

"She says she doesn't have it." Callan nodded. "We've met with her. But she's hiding something. We can sense it, scent it. Even Malachi is aware that there's something Isabelle is not telling in regard to the information we need."

Surprised, she glanced at Jonas. It wasn't like him to allow anyone to hold information back from him, especially someone he could use Breed Law against.

"I'd prefer to extinguish all options before using Breed Law against her," he said with a weary sigh. "I'd hate like hell to make an enemy of Malachi. But he knows the danger of it is there if she continues to refuse to tell us what she knows."

Diane stared at Jonas thoughtfully for long moments before speaking. "I doubt she knows enough to be of any help," she stated gently, her heart going out to him as well as to the newly mated Isabelle Martinez who must be feeling the brunt of Breed Law beating at her brain.

Malachi understood too well the consequences if those two girls weren't found. They had to know what Amber was facing so they could combat it and hopefully ensure her safety.

Callan rubbed at his jaw before breathing out roughly. "That's my thought as well," he finally stated. "The scent of her deceit isn't strong enough to indicate vital knowledge. But it could be enough to lead us to someone who knows more. The fact that she's hiding it, and refuses to tell even her mate, does concern me though."

"The Navajo team rescuing and hiding these children are here, in Window Rock." Diane knew they were, she could feel it, and Thor was just as certain.

"Diane, I'm going to assume you have more than just gut instinct backing your conclusions." Jonas sighed wearily as he laid his hand on Rachel's shoulder as she fought back her tears.

"Jonas, Amber is my niece and I love her as much as I love my sister. And I would never place all my faith in just my gut if it were my sister's life hanging in the balance in such a way."

She had circumstantial evidence, her belief, her gut instinct and the fact that she knew Terran Martinez had been in the area was enough proof for her.

If Pride Leader Lyons refused to allow her this chance because he didn't like the lack of information, then it was no less than a certainty that Jonas and Lawe would refuse her as well.

That didn't mean it would stop her.

"Do you believe you can draw Fawn or Honor out if they're near?" Jonas finally asked.

This was his child. The child that may not have come from his genetics, but she was definitely a part of his soul, just as her mother was.

"I'm certain if anyone can, then I can," she stated confidently. "This is where I excel, Jonas, you know that."

Callan sighed wearily and spoke when Jonas remained silent. "Very well, we'll go along with it for now," he agreed. "But by the end of the week I want answers. I want some kind of proof I can take before the Navajo Council to ensure their cooperation. Find it, Ms. Broen, before we all end up regretting it."

CHAPTER 16

Find the link to the group of Navajo charged with collecting and hiding Breeds, created or hybrid, as well as the human children and/or adults involved in any experimentation on the Breeds or their genetic profiling, and do it within a week.

What a tall order. And her week was nearly up.

Lawe had kept his word though. He had allowed her to do whatever she needed to do. He even stood back when necessary and without asking; he'd never once questioned the working relationship she had with Thor.

She wasn't fooled though. This battle wasn't over.

And time was running out. She had one day left to produce information. After that, Jonas would threaten the Navajo Nation Council with sanctions if he didn't get the information he wanted on Honor Roberts and Fawn Corrigan.

And she was just tired of wasted time and effort.

It was a damned good thing Diane had excellent contacts. Contacts who wanted the identities of that group to suggest they take the job of hiding more than Council-threatened Breeds and humans.

No matter how they tried, there was no way of finding them, though. If there had been, then the men her uncle collaborated with would have found it.

Moving through the darkened rooms of the suite the Navajo Council had made available for her and Lawe, Diane slipped silently past the balcony doors she had managed to jimmy earlier and keep from locking.

Lawe would have a fit over this, she knew, but she was tired of the shadows and the constant smothering presence of Breeds surrounding her. She needed to run wild and free to clear her brain. Besides, she knew for a fact that Liza Johnson used the running trail that wrapped around the small park for her morning exercise.

If she hurried, she would get there in time to scout out the area, then lie in wait for the friend whom Coyote Breed Ashley Truing cared so much for.

Taking Lawe with her would only serve to intimidate Liza, who seemed to have a sense of fear where Breed males were concerned. Diane knew what a fear of men looked like in wary eyes.

Just as she knew that Liza and Chelsea Martinez had been the reason Isabelle hadn't ended up raped by her ex-boyfriend recently.

Climbing effortlessly from the balcony before grabbing hold of the strong, dense vine that grew along the building, she began silently lowering herself to the ground below.

Lawe had left the room minutes after they had been escorted to it by a team of Breeds. And if she hadn't misunderstood, then she knew those Breeds were outside her door and charged with making certain she was protected while Lawe was busy.

Son of a bitch, she was so tired of protection.

This was becoming ridiculous.

Jumping to the ground, Diane came to a crouch, her gaze adjusting to the darkness outside as she searched for any Breed Enforcers who might have reached this side of the hotel while patrolling.

They hadn't. The soft green grass that met the building was a part of the golf course, which stretched out behind the Navajo Suites. On the other side was a large pool, a park for kids and a variety of other simple amusements.

Straightening up, Diane sprinted quickly across the grass and headed for a stand of trees bordering the golf course before the Breed guards could get a whiff of her scent and stop her.

Liza Johnson was suspected by Diane's contact to have been the go-between in the pickup of several other Breed children, a scientist with Navajo roots who had been forced to work with the Council and a young woman whose mate had been killed.

Liza was highly involved in the Bureau of Breed Affairs as a liaison between the office and the Navajo Council and community, and she was also a close friend to several high-profile Breeds. If anyone in Window Rock knew where Honor Roberts was hiding and the identity she had taken, then it would be Liza.

Using the golf course's heavy boulders, the stand of sheltering trees and the artificial hills for cover, Diane made her way quickly from the hotel to the other side of the course, praying Breed eyes hadn't seen her escape.

Once there, she turned along a narrow path, no longer bothering to stay hidden in the deepest shadows as she pulled the hood of her jacket over her head and hoped any Breed surveillance wouldn't immediately realize who she was.

There were no Breeds assigned to this area, though,

she knew. At least, the plans she'd been privy to hadn't shown any. There was always the chance that Lawe had ensured she not know exactly where the Breeds were patrolling, but she didn't think he had. As he saw it, since she'd been given permission to conduct her investigation, she would have no reason to slip away to do it.

No reason other than the fact that she could no longer bear to be surrounded by big hulking brutes determined to die for her. Lawe had kept his word, but as Rachel had warned her, other Breeds had made a vow, and they didn't care to shadow her and Lawe, and especially her and Thor, whenever they saw her out.

God, could she survive watching another man she knew, possibly Lawe, the man she loved, die for her? She'd seen it once before. She had watched the life drain from Padric's gaze as the bullet he'd taken to his chest to protect her had killed him.

The memory of it flayed her. She had never escaped the nightmares that forced her to relive it and couldn't seem to convince herself that she was older, more experienced, and definitely more merciless than she had been then.

She also wasn't nearly as reckless as Lawe wanted to believe she was. Moving past the small children's playground and entering the city park, Diane stopped at the tall stone monument that marked the missing members of the Navajo Nation as well as other tribes who had been used in Breed research.

There were fifty-seven names total, men and women whose lives had no doubt been lost long before the Navajo had ever learned of their deaths.

Stepping within the long shadow cast by the heavy edifice, Diane stopped, her gaze narrowing against the predawn light as she committed her surroundings to memory. Then, with a soft breath of air, she imitated the happy little chirp of one of the birds singing out so sweetly.

The answering call had her lips tilt up in fondness.

"We're going to get our asses killed." Thor stepped from the shadows of an overgrown pine several feet away and made his way to her.

Dressed in black, a cap covering his white blond hair, his utility belt strapped with a variety of weapons and tools, he looked like the highly efficient warrior he was.

Diane snorted at the prediction. "Are you scared?"

"Pretty much." He sighed, his gaze restless as he canvassed the area.

"Want me to send you home to momma for a diaper and nap, Thor?" she mocked.

"You're a bitch, Di." He sighed again. "A true hard-core bitch."

"Yeah, yeah, so you keep telling me." Her tone conveyed a deliberate lack of concern, but she could feel her heart racing with fear.

The fear that something would happen to him. That if push came to shove, then he too would throw himself in front of a bullet for her.

"I have her schedule," Thor told her before she had a chance to ask if he had managed to get the information she'd assigned him while she and Lawe were at the hospital to check on Ashley.

"Good." Diane nodded. "What is it?" She glanced up at him, wondering if she was going to have to drag every piece of information out of his ass.

"She leaves the house at daylight," he said softly. "She had stopped running after her friend Isabelle was nearly raped by a date. He was stalking Isabelle and the friends were terrified he would strike at them in retaliation. It was the same bastard who nearly kidnapped Isabelle and shot Ashley."

"The same one Gideon killed," she murmured. "Gideon beat us here, Thor."

"But we expected it." Thor shrugged easily. "And what's with this 'us' bullshit? There was no 'us,' boss. You forgot to tell me about this little side trip. I had to guess, remember?"

"Still put out, Thor?" she asked as she leaned back against the memorial to wait for daylight and the woman she was going to track down this morning.

"Still put out," he agreed, though his tone wasn't nearly as relaxed as it had been. "You and I are a team, no matter what. Or so I thought until you ditched me."

She shook her head wearily. "There was too much riding on this, too big a threat to Liza as well as Honor Roberts, if I managed to find her. It wasn't fair to her to add additional danger to her life."

"We both know I'm no fucking traitor," he hissed through the darkness. "Give me a break. And if you believed that crap that just spewed from your lips, then I wouldn't be here now."

Her lips twitched at the angry tone and the descriptive words he used.

"You're right," she agreed. There was really no sense in arguing the point.

She must have surprised him, though, because he didn't say anything for long moments.

"It's because of Padric." He sighed again. "Hell, Di, you can't wallow in guilt forever, you know."

Actually, she could, if she wanted to.

"I'm not trying to wallow in guilt," she told him. "I simply wanted to protect you from Gideon. He has no compunction about killing a man, but he'll allow a woman more leeway. In that respect, he's like any other Breed."

Thor simply grunted, an indication that he still felt his question hadn't been answered.

"So you tracked this Liza girl down," Thor muttered.

"What makes you think she knows where the Roberts girl is, or who she is?"

Diane shrugged. "She's the best bet. She works closest with Terran, Ray and Orrin. She has since she was sixteen. Her family is close friends with the Martinezes and she and Terran meet often with Ray and Orrin Martinez for long discussions. If she's not privy to inner secrets then she's sleeping with all three of them, and I simply can't see that one happening. Just because I agree doesn't mean I like slipping around like this." He sighed. "You and Lawe have an agreement."

"And he refused to listen when I tried to tell him I need to meet with her alone." She sighed.

"He's been damned patient," Thor pointed out. "And he's done his best."

She had to agree, he had done his best. Better than that if she wanted to admit the truth.

"I didn't say I liked it," she murmured. "I said it didn't make sense not to have at least one location, one person who knows where everyone has been hidden or relocated. But she refuses to deal with Breeds. She's not going to talk to me with any of them hovering. Especially Lawe."

That person had to be Liza.

Diane had spent months, more months than she wanted to remember, investigating all the players, scientists, research assistants and techs from Brandenmore Research. In Window Rock, she'd tracked familial lines and all new citizens who had moved into the area within the past twelve years.

She had spent countless hours searching for answers, for the identity of the missing Honor Roberts and Fawn Corrigan along with the Bengal Breed known only as Judd.

Liza Johnson was the closest she had gotten. The daughter of the current chief's best friend and military buddy. She was the granddaughter of the medicine man's best brother. Their families were so entwined as to be all but blood kin.

All but blood kin.

There was no shared blood, only the shared bonds of friendship, battle and loyalty. She glanced at Thor with a sense of overwhelming sadness. They had those bonds, but how satisfying it would have been to have been on this small mission with Lawe. To see how he could handle the woman she truly was.

To have Lawe watching her back, sensing any dangers that would have come, riding the adrenaline high coursing through their bodies. To know, yes, they would die for each other, but that Lawe wouldn't endanger himself for her needlessly or overlook the strengths she had.

As the first light of dawn rose in the sky, both Diane and Thor crouched in the continued shadow of the spear pointing toward heaven.

She tried to pretend it was Lawe at her back, but no amount of pretending, no bit of imagination could place him there when he wasn't.

"Five minutes," Thor said, his voice so soft it was barely a whisper. "She runs alone unless Isabelle and Chelsea Martinez accompany her. Isabelle is currently in residence at the hotel with Malachi Morgan. Chelsea and her father are staying in the Chief's Suite at the Navajo Council chambers. All the members were called in just before you and Lawe arrived, from what I understand. I suspect it's to discuss relocating the two girls and the Breed before they can be found."

Diane shook her head. "They wouldn't risk it."

She glanced around, the ache in her chest intensifying, the regret and feeling of dread pulling her down as the knowledge that she was in this battle without the

warrior whom nature had chosen as her other half tore
at her heart.

She'd never ached like this when she and Padric had
been separated by missions or wounds. She'd never felt
hurt or anger when Padric had disagreed with her or
when he'd refused to accompany her.

She didn't like this.

Blinking rapidly, she fought the emotion that threatened to overwhelm her.

This wasn't mating heat. Mating heat was sexual. It
was a blinding, overwhelming, uncontrolled hunger for
a mate.

This was the pain, the aching loneliness and the
certainty that no matter how she loved, no matter how
miserable she was, Lawe would prefer that to ever seeing her fulfill the other hunger that drove her. The hunger for justice.

"Here she comes, boss."

There she was.

Dressed in gray form-fitting jogging pants and a
matching exercise bra. A gray headband wrapped
around her forehead, while her long, wavy blond hair
was pulled up into a ponytail that trailed past her shoulders. When free, her hair trailed to just above her hips
in thick, silken locks.

Bound high at the back of her head now, the ponytail bounced, the waves of would-be curls dancing and
gyrating like ribbons gone wild.

"Are we clear?"

"Clear," Thor answered.

Holding the crouch, Diane sprinted from the shadow
of the monument and moved in behind the other woman
at a healthy jog to match. Thor, she knew, would stay
hidden in the shadows, watching out for her, protecting
her back.

Lawe should have been protecting her back.

As she came up behind Liza Johnson, she wasn't in the least surprised when the other woman suddenly jumped to the side, twisted lithely and faced her at a crouch.

Diane came to a stop, her brow arching in mock surprise at the obvious training that had gone into the move.

"What do you want?" Gray eyes narrowed, her toned body tense and prepared, she stared back at Diane suspiciously.

"A nice jog?" Diane queried with a small smile as she crossed her arms over her breasts and watched the young woman curiously.

She was damned delicate. For all the grace used to make that move, there was little muscle tone and even less strength in her small frame.

"You're lying." Clipped and clearly distrusting, Liza remained on guard as Diane faced her. "Now what do you want and why are you following me?"

"Who trained you?" she asked rather than answering the girl's question.

"No one you know, I'm certain," Liza sneered back. "Now what the hell do you want?"

Diane tilted her head, curious at the stance and the obvious fear of attack she could sense coming from Liza.

"I'm no threat to you." She gave a small laugh as the other woman straightened slowly, her gaze quickly assessing her surroundings as she searched for hidden threats.

The look was unmistakable. Diane had seen it countless times; she'd had the look herself more than once.

"Then you'll kindly leave the way you came," Liza told her.

Diane grinned ruefully. "Sorry, Liza, but we really need to talk. Just for a bit, you understand. We could return to the hotel for the discussion if you like?" She glanced toward the direction of the Navajo Suites. "I promise it won't take long."

Liza's gaze jerked over her shoulder, her eyes widening as her face slowly paled.

She'd never known Thor to have such an effect at first glance, though she wished he would have remained hidden for a while longer.

"He's harmless," she murmured.

Liza swallowed tightly. "We have to get out of here."

"Thor's not going to hurt you."

"Honey, I've seen that hot-assed Thor of yours, and he makes one. Not four."

Diane swung around, her hand whipping to her back and the weapon holstered there.

Four.

Her heart raged in her chest.

Adrenaline flowed like a racing river through her bloodstream as she faced the four Breeds. And they weren't the good guys.

Unfortunately, severely unfortunately, she watched as the single human male stepped from the shadows of a heavy oak to face her with a triumphant smile.

"Malcolm," she whispered painfully.

For the second time in her life, her heart was breaking. It was shattering inside her, locking her throat tight with the horrifying realization that she shouldn't be surprised. That she shouldn't hurt with such pain or ache with such a feeling of overwhelming betrayal.

"I thought it was Brick," she whispered, the pain searing her rasping in her voice now.

Malcolm chuckled, a cruel, vicious sound. "Good ole Gideon would have gotten me if I hadn't managed to find a way to trip that dumb bastard Brick and throw him in the way. Son of a bitch never figured it out either."

"Where's Thor?" All she could see were the four Coyote Breeds, their lips pulled back to display the curved canines, their eyes filled with malevolent pleasure.

"He's a bit under the weather, boss," he mocked her. "It might have something to do with the knife I shoved in his chest. I do believe I even managed to pierce that bastard's icy little heart."

Pointing the laser pistol at his heart, Diane activated it.

"Liza, run," she said heavily.

She was going to kill him. If she didn't manage to do anything else, she would kill him.

"Where?" Liza's voice was filled with disbelief. "Have you noticed there are four Coyotes here, lady? Does it look like I have a chance?"

One of the Coyotes grinned. A tilt of his lips that covered the curved canines.

"The first one who moves will die," she snapped back at her. "Now get the hell out of here."

"If she runs, one of us will chase," a Coyote murmured. "We can't resist. It's like a dog with a ball. We just have to fetch." He wagged his brows playfully.

As though he were flirting?

"Malcolm, where did you find your Coyotes?" she asked in disgust. "They're fucking crazy."

"They're fucking effective," he snapped back. "They caught your ass, didn't they?"

Well, he had her there, didn't he?

"Where is your mate, little warrior?" another murmured silkily as his dark gray eyes danced in amusement. "I can smell his mark on you and it's fresh. You know, he gets his hands on you, and he's gonna show you exactly how a Breed punishes disobedient little mates."

"Go to hell!" she snapped.

He grimaced back at her. "Aw, come on, it's just hot as hell there and my AC doesn't even make a dent. Let's try for something cooler."

She took a moment to stare at him in complete disbelief.

"Great, a comedian," Liza murmured behind her.

"Yeah, all before breakfast." Diane sighed. "I think I might be nauseous anyway."

"I warned you not to bring him, Malcolm," another Coyote spoke up. "He's going to start playing his incessant games again."

"Loki, stop playing the fucking horndog," Malcolm snapped at the flirting creature. "We're here to kidnap a Breed mate, not see if we can seduce her."

"I'm still maturing." The Coyote shrugged with a cold, far too experienced, far too cruel expression of displeasure.

"He has about as much common sense as his brother Farce had," another drawled. "Remember what happened to him, Loki? The wrong end of a feline weapon I believe."

Diane followed them with her eyes, keeping her position, shielding Liza with her own body. As ignorant as they acted, as playful as they pretended to be, she knew they were now at their most dangerous.

"Liza, go!" she hissed.

"We'll just chase her." The taller, broader Coyote reached into his pocket and pulled a cigar free.

With lazy amusement, he holstered his weapon before lighting the tip, sending the scent of tobacco to fill the early morning air.

She was screwed. She would get one shot off, that was it at the current setting.

She turned back to Malcolm. "I'll kill you first." With a flip of her thumb she placed the weapon on its highest setting.

Malcolm smiled complacently. "No, Diane, you won't," he assured her. "Because if you do, then we're going to take your little friend behind you as well. And I think you know what will happen to her then. You have only one shot. That'll leave three Coyotes for her to deal with. Do you think she'll survive?"

Liza wouldn't survive. What Council Coyotes had been known to do to innocent bystanders was horrifying.

And they were alone with no backup and possibly no hope of backup arriving in time.

The heaviness that settled in her chest was like a crushing weight.

"I'd rather fight," Liza whispered behind her.

Diane nodded slowly. "Do you have a weapon?"

"A knife, that's all I have." Regret filled the other girl's voice.

Diane drew in a hard, deep breath. "Don't let them take you. It would be far better to use that knife on yourself than to be captured by them. Once they come for me, run for the hotel. Breeds will be looking for me. They'll take care of you."

"I'm surprised, Ms. Broen," the sandy-haired mocking Coyote drawled then. "I've heard of your mate. I'm shocked he's not at your side facing us with that prick-assed attitude of his. Or did he do as he always swore he would and run the other way the minute he realized he was mated?"

"He was only delayed a bit," she assured him.

"More like expecting her to be the good girl and stay in their bed rather than heading out to save this little bitch." Malcolm waved his gun in Liza's direction. "How did you know we were coming for her, Diane?"

She hadn't.

Diane stepped back, bringing herself closer to the

other girl in an effort to protect her; she took a deep
breath and prepared herself.

They didn't have a chance. Malcolm had taken out
Thor and that left no one to watch her back. She had one
shot, and not enough time to power the weapon again
for another kill shot.

She didn't have to kill.

With an imperceptible movement of her thumb
against the mechanism Diane lowered the power from
kill to wound and from wound to disable.

She could get off eight shots, and if she aimed at
their kneecaps, she might have a chance.

And so would Liza.

"Poor Malcolm," she drawled with an edge of laughter as she looked back at him, the only plan she could
come up with flashing through her memory.

He scowled as the Coyote with the cigar chuckled
wickedly. "Sounds like a challenge to me, little man."

"Shut the fuck up," Malcolm snapped. "No one
asked you."

Lawe would have missed her by now surely. It had
been over an hour. He knew her and he knew her well.
Just as she knew him. She had been pushing him, challenging him, now all she had to do was stay alive long
enough—

"No one had to ask me." The Coyote gave another
low, amused laugh. "She's cute as hell, Malcolm."

"And she can kick Malcolm's ass to hell and back,"
Diane assured them all. Glancing at the Coyote, clearly
the dominant alpha, she shot him a mocking sneer. "He
knew he would have to face me." She nodded at Malcolm. "He didn't come for the girl, he came for me."

The Coyote turned his head to Malcolm. "That true,
Malcolm?"

Malcolm's lips thinned angrily. "Two birds with one

stone, right? She got her uncle, his second-in-command, killed so she and that bastard Thor could take over the team. I told you I wanted blood."

"That wasn't the mission," he was reminded.

Diane chuckled. "Four coyotes." She sighed. "For little ole me? That scared of me, Malcolm?"

His jaw bunched, his hands clenching the weapon.

"If you want me, come fight me," she suggested with a laugh. "I dare you."

Every Coyote there perked up.

"A thousand on the girl," the leader murmured.

"Shut the fuck up, Dog," Malcolm raged furiously.

"I got your thousand on the prick there. He has muscle where she doesn't." Loki took the bet before turning to the other two. "Mutt, Mongrel? You two in?"

"Thousand on the girl." Gray Eyes took him up on it.

"Thousand on the prick." The last one accepted the bet.

Malcolm was shaking with fury.

Diane smiled in anticipation.

"Knives or fists?" she asked, knowing his strengths as well as his weaknesses.

"You fucking whore," he snarled.

"Take the challenge or walk away," Dog snapped. "We won't take her without the fight."

God love a Coyote's heart and his love of a challenge or a good bet.

"I win, we walk away," she demanded as she kept her eyes on Malcolm.

Dog's smile was clearly anticipatory, but he nodded easily. "Whip his ass and you walk. He whips yours— you run. How's that?"

Diane gave a sharp, firm nod as she smiled at Malcolm. "It's a bet."

CHAPTER 17

He was dying!

Lawe could feel the fury burning inside him like a plague wasting away at his body cell by cell as he watched and listened to the Coyotes flirting with his mate.

The only thing saving him, saving them, was the fact that there was no scent of lust swirling from them. Still, his fists were clenched, his lips curled back from the sharp canines at the sides of his mouth, and the growl that would have rumbled in his chest was only barely held back. It was all he could do to hold back a roar of pure feline rage.

"Hey, Lion-o, would you mind letting up the pressure just a little bit here?"

The hoarse, pain-filled request had him lifting his hand completely from Thor's chest and flicking his fingers to the Breed Enforcer behind them, indicated he should apply pressure to the knife wound Thor had taken.

Lawe moved to rise. He had every intention of rushing to his mate's side, to protect her flank. To share in the triumph he knew she would experience once Malcolm was taken care of.

Then, Lawe decided, he'd make certain the bastard died.

"What did I tell you?" Thor's fingers were suddenly clamped around Lawe's forearm, restraining him before he could surge from their shadowed shelter of heavy pine and rush to the conflict unfolding too far away for him to help his mate if she needed him.

God, how could he survive?

He drew in a deep, hard breath.

"She's hurting," he growled. "I can feel it all the way over here."

Turning, he took a moment to glare at the mercenary before turning back to watch Diane with a surge of pride, and pure terror."

"Of course she's hurting, you dumb fucker," Thor rasped, his voice low and filled with pain of a far different sort. "She's out there alone. She's been hurting since the minute she left the hotel in D.C. without her mate backing her. She's a warrior, Justice, not some pansy-assed wannabe. You're not just her fucking mate—be her partner and you won't smell her soul shredding in half."

Lawe's head jerked around, his teeth snapping dangerously at the Swede before turning to watch his mate once again.

She was incredible.

Standing straight and tall, one hand propped on a cocked hip, her fingers tapping against it lazily as she held that damned laser weapon on the man she had fought with since the day her uncle had brought her into the group.

This was the mercenary Commander Diane—not the Diane her friends and family knew—as the Breeds closest to Jonas, his mate, and Lawe knew her. This was the Huntress. The woman known for her skill at tracking down those she was hired to find, rescuing them and bringing them back safe and sound.

And she had been doing so for more than seven years.

She had only taken official command of the group five years before, but in the two years before her uncle's death, she had been commanding her own missions and making the group more money than they had ever imagined possible.

Confident, self-assured and in her element but for the emotional pain raging through her like flames whipping through her soul.

She needed him.

It wasn't a sexual hunger. It wasn't the mating heat and it wasn't the need to quench the flames of mating heat. It was his mate's need for a partner. For her partner.

He'd promised to stand by her, to give her the space she needed to conduct her mission. Jonas and Callan had given her one week to accomplish her goal. Yet, he'd still hovered near her, going over her plans with a fine-tooth comb. And, he knew, making her feel that he had no faith in her abilities.

What had ever made him believe his mate—the incredibly vital fighting spirit she possessed—would ever accept such management after the years she had put into learning how to do what she was so damned good at doing?

He'd failed her again.

He dropped his head for a moment, pulling in hard, desperate breaths as the animal paced, raged, his genetics clawing at his senses as he fought the need to protect her. The need to stand before her, to snarl in warning at the bastards she believed were a threat.

There was only one threat really facing her.

Dog, Mutt, Mongrel and Loki weren't mercenary Coyotes only recently separated from the Council, as Malcolm believed. They weren't the bloodthirsty, rabid animals willing to help him turn his commander over to the Genetics Council.

They were Jonas's double agents. His eyes and ears into the Council so to speak. They were still soldiers, or so the Council believed, just in a different capacity now than they had been before.

Still, even knowing the danger was minimized, he had to forcibly hold himself back, to throttle the snarls and roars of rage that rose inside him.

Her sense of confusion and disillusionment was driving a spike of bitter rage through his brain and straight into his soul.

"You won't back her," Thor growled, and for a moment, just for the briefest second, it was almost an animal's rasp. "You refuse to allow her to be who she is, what she is. She's a fucking warrior, Lawe. You don't bury that, you encourage it. You train it, sharpen it, you fucking hone it until she fits your hand like the finest steel and slices twice as deep. She's your fucking mate. She's your partner. She's the finest fucking weapon God ever created and gifted to a man. She stands by your side, Lawe. You stand by her side, or you lose the very things you love about her."

His head flipped around as he glared at the mercenary, the anger churning inside him with boiling pain. "Shut the fuck up!"

He moved to rise, only to feel the second hand that clamped on his arm.

His head swung to the other side to see his brother, his grip lighter than Thor's, his expression, though sympathetic, firm.

"I could mate her," Rule said softly, his gaze dark, and for the first time Lawe felt the pain his brother kept locked so deep inside. "We're brothers. I would take the mate who longs to fight and allow her to be the warrior she is as I stand by her side. I'll give you my mate," he whispered. "Gentle. Soft. A woman who doesn't even know how to make a fist, let alone how to hold a gun. Protect mine, Lawe, and I'll protect yours. We'll have what we need without involving our souls as our mother did."

His brother's mate? He stared at Rule in complete disbelief. When had his brother mated and where was the delicate, subtle scent of the woman his animal genetics had claimed?

It was a question he would deal with later. One he would attempt to make sense of once he'd made sense of his own confusion and conflicting needs.

The need to possess the warrior while setting her free. The need to hold the woman, to protect her and shelter her as only her mate could shelter her.

Lawe gave a hard jerk of his head before turning back to the scene before him.

"Let me go." The growl was harsh; the animal was free and it wouldn't be held back any longer. "Now."

Slowly, reluctantly, Thor and Rule released him.

"Rule, on my six," Lawe ordered him. "Take my mate's back. Braden, Megan, you have Liza."

"If she doesn't fight him, Lawe—"

"She'll fight him," the animal swore. "It's her battle unless someone makes the mistake of interfering. Then they die. Malachi, Josiah, move in behind Dog's team. I trust no one, not even Jonas's favorite pets where my mate is concerned. Now move out."

Moving through the shadows, sliding with animal grace and stealth, he made his way with his brother

covering his back, to where his mate ached, where she
wept inside for the man, for the mate she believed could
never see her as a partner. The mate who would never
see the spirit and the fierce, finely honed weapon Thor
knew her to be.

It wasn't the man's decision this time. For the second
time the animal rose inside him and took control. And
what the man learned in that second filled him with
disbelief.

The first time, it had been to mark the woman it had
feared would dare to walk away forever. The woman
the animal had sensed was so very close to denying
the man.

This time, the animal had had enough of the man's
struggle, of his need to protect versus his need for a
partner.

What the hell would he do with a woman who
baked cookies, sewed costumes for the neighborhood
children? A woman whose idea of danger was a drive
through the city?

That wasn't the woman he needed.

Assistant director of the Bureau of Breed Affairs
wasn't the job he needed.

He was a warrior, just as his mate was a warrior.
The warrior would be damned if it would allow anyone,
anything to take that from her, especially the man who
loved her with all his soul. With all the dreams, all the
passion, and all the fear that resided inside him.

As he approached the group silently, his brother
moving in close, sharing his strength and his senses
with him, Lawe found himself reaching out to her.

There were gifts he shared with his twin. The Breed
born less than a minute after he had been. This was why
Rule would make the perfect assistant director. The
same reason Jonas had felt Lawe would. Rule's ability

to focus with his twin, to share the range of his senses, a range that went off the charts. Lawe was suddenly faster, stronger, his hearing more acute, his eyesight sharper, his sense of smell so brilliantly sharp he could detect individuals from miles away.

He knew the Coyote teams were slipping through the desert, silent, moving with stealthy precision to take from Dog's team the prize they sought.

Lawe Justice's mate. Perhaps only one of two mates capable of conceiving twins.

He sensed that. Felt it.

That complete focus identified, marked and memorized each scent that filled a ten-mile radius around him; it detected every sound from the scurry of a mouse to a whisper of passion from countless couples to the soft disturbance of air from the Coyote commander in the desert directing his men to move faster. Every picture his eyes touched, every taste that came in with each breath was suddenly amplified.

The danger was real now. There were two dozen enemy Coyotes and human soldiers determined to take his mate. To take the woman who would one day bear a child, or perhaps twins, to a Breed that shared a psychic bond with his own twin.

"Stay at her back." The order was no more than a breath of sound, but it was one he knew his brother clearly heard. "If she conceives—"

"She conceives a tool that could be used against all of us, just as my mate will," he confirmed.

He knew why they were created. The scientists had been amazingly explicit in detail just hours before they were each given their first woman.

They were the beginning of a unique experiment, one that the scientists believed had failed.

In the equation of mating, they hadn't taken into

account mating heat, which they had believed to be feral fever, and the fact that conception could never be forced where Breeds and their mates were concerned. They had believed Breeds couldn't reproduce, and that even crossbreeding with humans would fail.

Until the first signs of mating heat had begun showing up and the vivisections had revealed the changes both Breed and mate experienced. Internally, both mates experienced a wide range of anomalies.

A heart that beat faster. Adrenaline laced with an unknown hormone capable of throwing their females into ovulation. And in certain cases, by Breeds who were part of a twin set, the animal genetics determined if that ovulation would produce one hybrid, or if the first stage twins would be created.

Moving to the shadows of the edge of the pines, Lawe stepped into the clearing, ignoring Malcolm's shock and wrapping around him his mate's sudden surge of adrenaline-fused excitement, which speared through her.

He and Rule moved to her as Braden and Megan stepped from the opposite direction and surrounded Liza before pulling her back.

"Well, look who's joining the party, boys," Dog drawled. "Looks like the bet's off."

"The hell it is." Lawe moved in, just slightly behind his mate's right shoulder. "You have my thousand. My mate will kick his ass." He laid his palm on the butt of his weapon, a laser-guided, laser-powered bullet-loaded Breed weapon. "And we're going to do it without weapons, aren't we, Malcolm?" He nodded to Dog.

The Coyote stepped forward with a triumphant grin and collected various weapons from a stunned Malcolm.

"Mate," Lawe murmured, the animal still dominant

but now merging with the man fully to create the Breed
he was always meant to be for his mate.

He was aware of Rule flinching, of his animal suddenly surging free of its restraints and doing the same.
He hadn't anticipated that, but perhaps, like him, his
brother needed that push to claim everything that was
meant to belong to him.

"Lawe," Diane whispered, her gaze slicing to him.

"We have a dozen Coyotes and humans moving in.
They're perhaps twenty minutes away and fully armed,"
he told her. "You have seventeen minutes to take care of
this little matter." Turning his gaze down to her he let
a grin tilt his lips. "Show me what you've got, Mate."

Diane felt her lips tremble for the slightest second as
hope rose inside her. Her heart was racing, excitement
and pure anticipation infusing the strength and training
she put a lifetime into.

"What do I get in return?" she murmured as she
released the utility belt, never taking her eyes from
Malcolm.

"More than you've likely bargained for," he assured
her as he felt a rush of sudden joy infuse him. "But you
have to win this little bet for me first."

"No problem," she assured him, her gaze sliding to
him with a hint of sensuality, a subtle little flirt that had
his cock twitching in excitement as she turned back to
the traitor who had failed more than once in his attempt
to kill her.

"You betrayed me, Malcolm." She loosened the belt
and holster at her hips. "What made you think you were
smart enough to get away with it?"

She could feel Lawe's concern, she could feel his
love and the unfamiliar, confusing demands of the primal strength and determination of the animal she could
glimpse in his gaze.

He wasn't comfortable with it.

He would always fear for her, but if he didn't, then the love wouldn't be as strong as she knew it was between them.

"Unfortunately, you survived," he sneered. "You weren't supposed to. You got Padric killed. He was ten times the soldier you were, and then you ran your fucking uncle off before I could kill him. Bitch, how do you like knowing he's hiding from you?"

"He's dead." she said with a sigh. "He never would have hid from me. He wouldn't have deserted me, Malcolm."

"He did worse than desert you." He laughed. "He deserted you for a Council scientist," he screamed. "For a dirty fucking monster maker instead of killing her as he was hired to do."

She would never convince him that her uncle hadn't deserted her, or that he wasn't hiding with the Council scientist he had been hired to find just before he was killed in that warehouse. And she didn't care.

"I'll kick his ass for you if he ever shows himself. How's that?" she promised.

"Kick his ass and let's roll, baby," Lawe murmured. "Dog is friendly and was here to collect intel for Jonas before deserting the Council completely. But the dozen moving in on us are heavily armed and gunning for us. I'd like to be gone before they get much closer."

She paused, her gaze going to Dog and the cigar he was giving her a toothy grin around. Lifting his arm, he tipped two fingers to his forehead in greeting.

"I should have known." Loosening her muscles she stepped closer to Malcolm. "You never did inspire loyalty, Malcolm. I should have known you hadn't done so now."

"Fifteen minutes," Lawe reminded her as his head bent to bestow a kiss to her forehead, a loving tribute of confidence, love and his belief in the self-confidence he could sense surging through her.

"Fifteen minutes." She nodded then turned back to Malcolm.

She rolled her eyes. "Oh look, he's stripped his shirt," she stated mockingly. "God love his heart, does he really think it's going to be that easy?"

He thought the sight of his muscles intimidated. That the flex and ripple beneath his flesh had the power to make mere mortals flinch.

Diane didn't flinch. She didn't leer.

She scratched at the back of her head with a sigh. "So, Malcolm darling, are we gonna rumble?"

He flexed his shoulders. "Come on, whore, let me kick your ass."

Lawe snarled, but Diane was riding a high that held no fear of her mate's interference, and no fear of his inability to allow her to finish the fight.

Fifteen minutes.

"This will only take ten," she promised.

"Just make sure you save enough energy to enjoy your punishment for slipping out on me again, mate," he suggested. "I may understand, but I'll ensure it will never happen again."

Pausing, her gaze raked over him, from head, to the proof of his erection beneath the jeans he wore, to the military ankle boots he wore and up again. "Have no fear, mate." Her smile was cocky, feminine, and assured. "I'll save plenty of energy for all the punishment you can dish out."

"This fucking lovey-dovey bullshit is getting on my nerves, bitch," Malcolm snarled. "Get your ass over here and let me show that unnatural son of a bitch how fucking weak his mate is. Then my friends can collect all your asses and haul you in."

Diane grinned as they began circling each other. She'd kicked Malcolm's ass before. It wasn't easy. He was a dirty gutter fighter, but she knew his weaknesses. She wasn't certain, though, how Lawe was going to react when Malcolm managed to actually pierce one of her weaknesses.

Straight off.

He jumped for her, his fist colliding with a glancing blow across her cheek and knocking her off her feet.

A violent feline snarl echoed around the clearing.

Diane didn't bother to come to her feet. Instead, she caught herself on her shoulders, swept her legs out and knocked Malcolm off his.

Fifteen minutes or less. She didn't have time to play fair. Not that she would have bothered anyway, but she might have drawn it out a bit, just for the humiliation Malcolm would have suffered.

As he went down, she was up. Her steel-toed boot, reinforced to add to her strength buried itself in his side before she jumped back, rounding an openhanded caress to the ground where she swept up a handful of desert sand.

Malcolm came easily to his feet, though blood smeared his side now and he favored it instinctively.

Moving in close enough to direct the sand straight to his eyes, Diane came back, her leg swinging out and up to slam the steel-toed boot straight into his jaw.

She heard it crack as he went down again.

This time when he came up, he caught her short, his fist slamming into the back of her knee and driving her to the ground as she twisted around.

She wasn't fast enough.

Before she could stop him Diane found herself pinned to the ground, blood easing from the deep slice on her lip as she felt the side of her face burning from the blow to it. She could feel the discomfort, the searing rejection of his touch lancing through her body. Rather than weakening it, it pissed her off.

She had to smile despite the slicing pain to her lip.

"Oh, you've been practicing," she sneered. "Too bad you're still a slow fucker with an ego that's going to get you killed. What do you think is going to happen when those buddies of yours show up, and I'm not here. Dog's not here. Just you, all alone without the prize you promised to deliver."

"Then they'll come after you." He swung out in triumph as Diane tried to duck and move in.

Her foot swung out, collided with his balls but not fast enough to avoid the fist that slammed into her cheek.

"Fuck!" she cursed as Lawe roared in rage. "He's going to fucking kill you before I get a chance."

Racing the few steps to where he'd fallen to his knees, Diane threw another hard kick, this time with the flat of her foot to the side of his head.

Hard.

She put all her strength into it. Using the well-toned muscles of her thighs as her uncle had taught her and putting all her power into it, she kicked with the single driving hope that it would take his head off.

It didn't.

Instead, it slammed it back, throwing him to his back and forcing a hard groan from his lips as he lost consciousness.

As she knew he would.

Her uncle had worked with her for months in secrecy to teach her how to take care of Malcolm specifically. He'd been a hardheaded bastard who hadn't wanted to listen to orders on the occasions she'd pulled in contracts for the team.

That was the deal. Her uncle would give command

to the team member who procured the contract if that individual wanted the experience in command.

Diane had.

Thor hadn't, but he was always more than willing to give her his contracts and play second-in-command. As though he had always known what was coming.

Breathing harshly, her body aching painfully, she watched as Dog hurried over to Malcolm and checked his pulse with cool efficiency.

"He's gonna be out for a while," he reported, lifting his gaze to Diane. "Want me to finish this for you?" he asked with a subtle hint of anticipation.

She glared back at him. "If I wanted him dead, I would have killed him myself."

His brows lifted. "Ever killed a man?" he asked softly, gently, as though he believed she were too gentle or perhaps too weak.

She stared back at him in disgust. "Do you want the list?"

"Bullets don't count." He rose to his feet, watching her with that mocking smile of his.

"Do knives?" she asked softly. "Hands? I can break his neck as easily as you can, never doubt it. He simply hasn't suffered enough." Her gaze narrowed in determination. It was the only way to stare a Breed down. "And I want him to suffer."

"He'll suffer." Dog nodded. "Because the commander of the Coyote team moving in is a crazy son of a bitch. He'll make sure he dies for you. And if we don't get the hell out of here, he'll attempt to make certain we join the little bastard."

She shrugged and turned back to her mate.

"You made promises again," she murmured as he stepped to her, the very air around him pulsing with primal hunger and the need to reassert his dominance.

Over her.

She grinned back at him.

A second later he had one hand buried in her hair, the other wrapped around her back and his lips covering hers.

The kiss was wicked, openmouthed, tongues tangling and the taste of the mating hormone spilling to her system.

Ah God, this was what she wanted too. The pain would go away, the need for his touch would never be sated.

Her fingers fisted in the shirt he wore, her hips tilting up to him as he suddenly lifted her, holding her to him as his tongue pumped deliciously into her mouth and within seconds had her pussy burning for him.

"We have trouble rolling in," Rule suddenly announced. "Roll out before we're in a firefight with no backup."

Between one breath and the next, Lawe released her. His hand gripped hers as they began to run for the cover of pines and the safety of the Breed-enforced hotel on the other side.

Megan and Braden had already left with Liza and were headed back across the golf course in one of the fully loaded Desert Dragoons used for military desert operations.

Passing him and heading to where Thor was being helped from the trees by Josiah, two other Dragoons sped toward Lawe, Diane, and the group following them. Jonas drove the vehicle, with a Breed manning the powerful laser-powered weapon mounted to the roll bars. Behind him the second Dragoon bounced over the rolling landscape with Dane Vanderale at the wheel, his partner, Rye Desalvo manning the weapon mounted to that one. The calvary was riding in and if the expressions on their faces were anything to go by, then they were anticipating a hell of a fight.

This was Lawe's area of expertise. He loved the firefights, Diane loved the investigations, the rescues. There was no rescuing needed here. And it wasn't that she didn't get a hell of an adrenaline rush from the firefights. It wasn't as though she wasn't aware she would be involved in far too many where Lawe was concerned.

But in this case, *he* would be in danger if he was forced to worry about her in this instance. He'd given her the investigation, the fight, the chance to prove herself, and she knew it wasn't over yet. Honor Roberts was still out there, and Liza Johnson had yet to be questioned. Gently.

But her part in this particular battle was over; she would wait and see what the war brought.

Turning to him, she threw her arms around his neck and smacked a joyful kiss to his lips.

"Get yourself wounded and there will be hell to pay, Mate," she warned him.

Surprise filled his eyes, but the anticipation that brightened them was something she was familiar with. Something she knew herself. The anticipation of the job he loved.

Justice.

It was what he had taken his name for, and it was a part of him.

She was his mate, but the adrenaline was his mistress just as it was her admirer.

"I love you." He touched her cheek before turning to the Breed Diane hadn't seen until he jumped from the Dragoon that bounced to a stop before them. "Tarek, take care of my mate."

"As though she were my own," Tarek promised.

Tarek Jordan, mated himself and out of active status,

but still part of the support teams when he was available. "Let's move out." He give a quick nod to Diane before they moved out quickly, racing across the golf course to the safety of the hotel.

Worry was a part of leaving him behind, but she knew he'd never be able to do his job if she were at his side during a firefight. A battle with a dozen Coyotes and human soldiers was far different than allowing her to fight Malcolm, and Diane knew it.

She glanced over her shoulder to see the dust of the vehicles racing to meet the oncoming Council soldiers as another Dragoon raced toward them from the hotel.

"Here's our ride," Tarek shouted as Thor was first loaded in.

Reaching the vehicle themselves Diane jumped in the open side, taking one last look at the disappearing dust as Lawe and Dane's Dragoons disappeared over the rise, and four others raced from the trails that cut through the pines to meet them.

Reinforcements. Dane and Jonas hadn't taken chances. There were enough Enforcers joining them, along with Dog's teams, to ensure victory.

And when he returned—

When he returned, it would be to the mate willing to give all of herself to the Breed who had finally set her free.

He was wounded.

Diane stood silently, biting her lip as she watched as the Breed medic worked silently on the gash across his right bicep, and this was after digging the bullet from the shallow wound in his shoulder.

Blood smeared across and down his chest, but he sat silently, almost relaxed but for the edge of concern in his somber gaze as he watched her.

She was frowning at him. Her hands were braced on her hips as she glared at the wounds.

"I told you not to get wounded," she pointed out calmly.

"You did," he agreed with a slow, thoughtful nod. "And I tried very hard to please you, mate, but that Vanderale brat seemed to think his own hide was more important than mine and used me for a shield."

Oh, now this was just wrong. He was blatantly lying

to her. Blatantly, playfully. Almost flirtatiously lying to her. She had already heard the details when he was first brought in, but she turned to Jonas and Dane where they stood behind her anyway.

Both men were glaring at her mate.

Her brow arched inquisitively. "Vanderale brat?" she asked Dane curiously.

He grunted at the insult. "Next time, I'll throw him to the damned Coyotes."

"Looks like he's going to live, anyway," Jonas drawled as he watched Lawe broodingly. "You acted like you actually missed having bullets whine past your head."

Lawe grinned.

The sight of that smile did something to her. It melted her insides. Like butter on a hot summer day she could feel emotion just oozing through her, over-taking her, seeping into all the little hidden, previously locked areas of her soul to fill her with a sense of rich, sudden life.

"And I believe that's our cue to leave," Dane murmured.

"Damned Breed sense of smell." Diane sighed as they both left the suite, the outer doors closing behind them as the medic laid the last skin cement to the degradable staples used to pull the edges of the wound together.

Sealing the exposed raw flesh, the Breed pulled back, packed his instruments into the old-fashioned black case he carried and shook his head at Lawe. "I thought I was done fixing you up."

"This happens often does it?" Diane asked.

The medic grinned. "Just every time he heads out on a mission, finds a Council soldier to fight, or just plain wants to spar with the younger Breeds to prove his experience beats their youth and strength." He chuckled. "Sure you want him back on active status?"

She turned back to her mate. His brow was arched, his expression knowing.

"Hell," she breathed out in exasperation, "it's probably the only way to keep from killing him."

"Yeah, he's pretty tame while he's healing." The medic chuckled as he headed for the door. "Call me if he busts the stitches loose."

Within seconds he too had left the room, leaving them alone.

"In pain?" she asked.

He rose from the bed and quickly shed his jeans. The shirt had been cut from him earlier, his boots eased from his feet the moment they had been lifted to the bed.

He was aroused.

The bronze length of his cock speared out from his body, thick and throbbing, the mushroomed crest gleaming damply with pre-cum as his balls lifted tight to the base of the shaft.

"Pretty sure," she murmured as she tore the loose shirt over her head and quickly shed the yoga pants she had donned.

She was ready for him.

Diane could feel her juices gathering on the lips of her pussy as the inner muscles pulsed and flexed with the need for attention.

Wrapping his fingers around the heavy column, he stroked it lazily as he stared down at her, his gaze becoming intent and brooding.

"Punishment time," he murmured.

Her brow lifted, her gaze flicking to his fingers as they stroked his powerful erection.

"Really?" she murmured.

"Really." Stepping to her, his head lowered, his lips catching hers in a kiss that seemed to sink inside her soul.

The taste of the mating hormone was richer, spicier. It seemed to go to her head faster, the addictive essence a power punch to her arousal as she moaned at the fiery sensations suddenly racing through her.

He'd just been wounded, a bullet had been dug out of the heavy muscle of his shoulder, staples held the gash in his bicep together but the erection pressing into her belly felt stronger, thicker than ever. His arms as they drew her to him sent a surge of heated security—not protectiveness—racing through her.

She was safe here. Emotionally safe. Her heart would always be cherished by him, her happiness always his priority.

Twining her arms around his neck, her fingers sifting through his hair, Diane caught her breath on a moan as the power of the mating hormone continued to build inside her. To rush through her system, and to set fire to feelings, emotions, needs she had no idea how to decipher.

She pulled at his hair and when he nipped at her lips she could have sworn she nearly reached her orgasm.

Her pussy pulsed, her juices spilling from the clenched opening to saturate the swollen folds beyond. Her nipples ached and throbbed as they brushed against his chest, but when his fingers and thumbs found the tender points and began to massage them with erotic roughness she felt her juices dampen her thighs as well.

Heat raced through her blood veins, tore across her nerve endings and left her shaking as she clenched her thighs together and fought for that pinnacle of pleasure.

"Lawe—" Oh God, she needed him.

His hands slid to her rear, his fingers curving over and clenching the rounded flesh as he lifted her to him.

"Lawe." What was that sensation?

The prick of pleasure or impending heat as he pulled at the cheeks of her rear, separating them, the motion tugging at the hidden, forbidden entrance within.

It wasn't the physical sensations that sent that punch of electric flames racing through her womb. It wasn't the echo of increased arousal spilling her juices from her pussy that had her crying out for him.

It was the emotion. That feeling. It was something she had never felt before suddenly tearing through her, weakening her knees, reminding her she was a woman.

She was weaker—her muscles went lax, trembling as though there were no strength within them.

She was feminine—her pussy was melting, spilling the slick essence of that femininity to her thighs.

She was— "Oh God, Lawe." She wanted to say "no." She wanted to deny what she was feeling and yet she was unable to.

When he drew back, turned her and eased her to the bed, her breathing began to accelerate. Her heart raced hard and fast in her chest. Because within seconds he had her on her knees, her shoulders pressed to the bed as his hands ran over the curves of her ass.

"So pretty." He groaned behind her.

His breath feathered the wet curls that shielded the folds of her sex a second before his tongue swiped through the slick juices. Stiffening it, making a point of the tip, he began to probe her clit from beneath, pressing against the sensitive bud before drawing back and rolling it beneath the hood of the tender flesh.

With slow, diabolical movements he began to rub the heated tip against her flesh, searing it with the hormone spilling from his tongue. A second later he sucked the tender bud inside his mouth, closed his lips on it and began to suckle with firm, hungry draws of his mouth.

His fingers parted the flesh, found the snug entrance and before Diane could murmur an assent or denial, she felt the tips of his fingers rubbing against her, slipping inside her, separating the clenched flesh and sending pleasure streaking through her.

"Oh yes." She moaned, her hips writhing against the shallow penetration. "Oh God, Lawe, yes. Please. Take me more."

She was on the verge of crying, tears filling her eyes as the desperation began to burn through her.

His fingers moved in further, rubbing, stroking slowly, working her flesh open, stretching her then pulling back and repeating the process.

A second later, the fingers of his other hand became busy as well.

Slick, cool. Oh God, that was what the small jar beside the bed was for. The lubricant had confused her. It didn't anymore. Not as his fingers rubbed the cooling gel over the tender, unopened entrance.

She couldn't take much more. His tongue flicked at her clit as he sucked at it, the heat of his mouth searing it as sensation built within it. Every nerve ending in her body felt as though it were suddenly filled with electrical currents. They sizzled through her nerve endings, stole her breath and had her fighting for her climax.

When his lips drew back, she wanted to scream in denial. She could barely moan. Then he was kissing a path lower, to where his fingers were easing from her. His tongue rubbed over the entrance, drew her juices to his tongue, then with a hard, quick thrust buried his tongue inside her.

Diane nearly jerked upright. She would have, if there hadn't suddenly been a hand pressing against her shoulder, holding her to the bed.

His tongue was wicked. It speared inside her, stroked

and rubbed and sent her senses spinning. Fucking into the tender, tight entrance he made her feel as though he were relishing each taste of her. As though she were the dessert before the meal.

She was crying, writhing against his mouth, impaled upon his tongue. If he would just thrust it inside her a little harder, a little faster—if he would just lick that one spot just a little more, just a little deeper.

"Ah yes, baby. Sweet Diane." He pulled back despite her cry.

She felt poised, so close.

Just a little more sensation.

His cock pressed at the opening, heated and engorged as Lawe began to move against her, his hips thrusting, working the stiff, poker-hot shaft of his cock inside her by slow degrees, an inch at a time, throwing her into such a maelstrom of sensation that she felt battered by it.

The fingers of one hand massaged, pressed. A tip invaded the untouched entrance of her rear, sending additional pleasure to tear at her senses. Slick from the gel, heated and dominant he pressed one finger inside her, working against the clench of tissue there to stretch the overly tight channel. Just when she thought she could explode in ecstasy from the surge of pleasures, his finger pulled back, his cock pushed inside her pussy with a hard thrust, then his finger returned, this time with another.

Two fingers worked inside her.

His hips moved against her, pressing, plunging his cock inside her as his fingers slowly, easily began to fuck her ass.

"Lawe, please," she cried out hoarsely.

"Please what, Diane?" He groaned behind her. "Please fuck your ass with my fingers? Please stop? Please show you you're fucking mine?"

He pulled back, his cock escaping the grip her pussy
had on him, only to return seconds later, only this time,
to the sensitive entrance tingling from the stretching his
fingers had given it.

"Please," she cried out again. "Oh God, Lawe, anything." Her hips rotated, pressed back against the flared
crest of his cock as fire and ice seemed to consume her
from head to toe.

Pleasure and pain.

Lawe pressed against the entrance, the slick gel he
had worked into her anus and the additional coating
he'd spread over his cock aiding the entrance.

Stretching, burning her.

Agony and ecstasy erupted inside her, blazing up her
spine to tear through her senses as each inward press
buried him deeper inside her rear and unleashed yet
more of that intensity of emotion.

She felt too feminine now.

Her hips worked back. She could feel every shift
of his flesh, every throb through the thickened blood
vessels covering the shaft, every pulse of the engorged
crest. She felt it with such depth, sensations magni-
fied as he retreated, returned, opened her ass further,
stretched her, submitted her.

Her back arched, a cry tore from her throat, and as
his cock surged those last inches inside her rear she felt
his fingers bury into her vagina from below.

She was possessed. She was taken.

She belonged.

She belonged to him so completely, so utterly, that
her body had accepted a possession Diane knew she
would have never allowed another man to take.

A possession that sank inside her soul, outstretched
fingers of emotional bonds sinking past objection and
denial to find a hold she knew he would never release.

He was growling behind her. They were animalistic snarls, groans that were part human and part lion. His head lowered and he hurriedly brushed her hair aside with his chin as his head tilted and his teeth were suddenly locking onto the back of her neck as his hips began moving.

His fingers thrust inside her, fucking her with the same hungry desperation he used as he fucked her ass. In and out, one then the other, shuttling inside her body and tearing aside a veil she hadn't known hid her woman's heart from him.

It wasn't hid any longer.

It was his.

It was her voice crying out for him.

Begging.

"Oh yes," she whimpered as the pad of his palm raked her clit. "Yes, please. Oh God, Lawe, fuck me." She sobbed. "Take me. Please, please take me."

She wanted him to take everything she had to give.

His fingers moved faster, stroked, caressed, roughened tender nerve endings then lit a release inside her that tore a muted scream from her throat and had her jerking against him with a sudden, near violent orgasm that there was no defense against.

His teeth tightened on her neck but she felt no pain.

His cock surged to the hilt, the heated spurt of his semen suddenly exploding in her rear and a second later, she felt the emergence of the barb as she had never felt it before. Thick but not incredibly long. Perhaps half the length of a male thumb and just as thick. It vibrated, jerked with a heated pulse of fluid in between the swift ejaculations of his seed from the blunt head of his cock.

Her pussy milked his fingers as the release tore through it. Her clit swelled suddenly, a bright, sharp pulse of sensation racing as she felt the orgasm burning through it.

She was exploding. Dying in his arms. Melting into him.

He was melting into her. Taking her, overwhelming her.

He was owning her and she didn't even give a damn.

She was his completely. His forever.

Just as he was hers.

Mates.

Created for one another.

Meant to be and meant to belong.

Meant to find that freedom that had always eluded her, the independence she had always been reaching for was right here. In her mate's arms. "I love you." The words tore from her lips. "Oh God, Lawe. I love you."

"You won't run again," he snarled.

"I won't run—"

"You'll fight by my side." Another heavy pulse of his release, a rake of his palm against her clit, prolonging her pleasure.

"By your side," she cried out.

Where she had dreamed of being.

"Love me, baby. Ah God, Diane, I love you past death."

He was shuddering above her, jerking against her as the final waves of release left her trembling beneath him, sweat dampened, sated.

Mated.

Diane was a mate.

And her mate was an alpha: dominant, protective and possessive.

But the animal genetics, primal and powerful, and the human genetics had had enough of the battle they had fought. They had, in those rare cases when it was needed, merged and enhanced the human side, creating a male who would give his mate the best of both worlds. One that would die for her, one that would fight to live for her. A mate who finally saw, who finally understood it wasn't about always being safe.

It was about being together and creating their own safety.

Creating their own world where they could.

She wasn't just a mate, she was a warrior.

She wasn't just a warrior, she was a mate.

And she was loved.

◆　◆　◆

Gideon watched.

He waited.

But still, she wasn't there. Honor wasn't there, and Judd hadn't shown himself.

The deputy chief of police arrived within hours of the successful apprehension of the Council soldiers who had arrived to kidnap both Lawe and his new mate, Diane.

Only three had lived, but that was the way of it.

He watched as the girl, Liza, had been escorted into the hotel and taken to the suite of the director of the Bureau of Breed Affairs, and he waited.

He listened. The electronic device he had placed picking up exceptionally well.

Jonas arrived with his mate.

The alphas arrived.

Lawe, Rule and Diane Broen arrived.

"Ms. Johnson, we need your help," Jonas stated softly.

"You need more than my help, you'll need several good lawyers."

Liza Johnson wasn't happy.

"We just saved your life." Jonas stated.

"Your people endangered it," she snapped. "Let me tell you now—"

And nothing.

He stared at the hotel. Glared at it.

He tapped the headphones. There wasn't even static.

Fuck.

◆　　◆　　◆

Jonas stared at the device Diane handed him, located by another of the altered detectors Thor had tinkered with.

Strong.

The signal had piggybacked on their own wireless devices and betrayed them.

And he had no idea how long it had been in his rooms.

Or if there were more.

Turning to Lawe and using the motions of sign language he indicated a full suite, white noise, as well as jamming technology.

Gideon had just upped the ante.

Jonas stared back at Liza Johnson and in the scent of her fear, learned something more.

He smiled slowly.

The game was just beginning.

From #1 *New York Times*
bestselling author

·LORA LEIGH·

NAVARRO'S PROMISE

Paranormal romance sensation Lora Leigh returns to the world of the Breeds in an all-new novel of animal instinct, carnal cravings, and primal pleasures.

penguin.com

M718T0411